BLOOD OF THE GODS

T0281977

OTHER TITLES BY SAPIR A. ENGLARD

Cloak of the Vampire

The Millennium Wolves

His Haze

Alpha of the Millennium

Ghosted Soul

Painted Scars

One Night

Desperate

CLOAK OF THE VAMPIRE

BOOK 2

BLOOD OF THE GODS

SAPIR A. ENGLARD

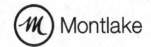

Montlake

This is a work of fiction. Names, characters, organizations, places, events, and incidents are either products of the author's imagination or are used fictitiously. Otherwise, any resemblance to actual persons, living or dead, is purely coincidental.

Text copyright © 2024 by Sapir A. Englard
All rights reserved.

No part of this book may be reproduced, or stored in a retrieval system, or transmitted in any form or by any means, electronic, mechanical, photocopying, recording, or otherwise, without express written permission of the publisher.

Published by Montlake, Seattle

www.apub.com

Amazon, the Amazon logo, and Montlake are trademarks of Amazon.com, Inc., or its affiliates.

ISBN-13: 9781662522277 (paperback)
ISBN-13: 9781662522284 (digital)

Cover design by Faceout Studio, Elisha Zepeda
Cover image: © Amanda Carden, © atk work, © defrocked, © Krasovski Dmitri / Shutterstock

Printed in the United States of America

To Eden.

Your courage will forever be an inspiration.

PROLOGUE

Eight Years Ago
Lewiston, Maine

Darkness spread through the sky when Natalia and her father made their way to the Androscoggin River. They didn't talk, but Natalia wasn't bothered; her father was always silent when the time came for the second rite.

It was better than how loud he was during the first rite.

Though a silent monster was still a monster.

Her father came to a stop near the riverbank. Natalia paused next to him, staring pointedly at the river. Yet not looking at *that* didn't make its presence less prominent. But then her father started speaking, murmuring the words she'd been hearing every month for her entire life, and like every time, she felt the eerie need to gaze at him.

She'd once heard a few of her classmates' mothers calling her father handsome. She shared the sentiment, to a certain extent; at first glance, he seemed like a smart, kind man with warm eyes hiding behind a pair of square glasses. It also helped that he was a scholar, a biochemistry professor at the University of Maine.

What those mothers failed to notice was the fanaticism drawn in the depths of his hazel irises.

"Dear Gods of Faith and Divinity," her father muttered, eyes staring at the river unseeingly, as though he was somewhere far away. "Let us draw from the well of our belief and embrace our true potential as vessels of your blessings."

He looked down at the large glass bowl he cradled in his arms. His eyes were alight with hot anger. "We have failed you," he said, voice louder and more bitter. Natalia jolted, perplexed; her father had never deviated from the speech before. "Last time, we failed to provide you with proof of our faith. Rest assured; this won't ever happen again."

Natalia felt her heart fall as she returned her gaze to the river. She hadn't forgotten about last month's incident. It still haunted her that there was someone out there, other than herself, who knew about her father's true nature. She remembered her father's outburst when he had to forfeit the rite a month ago. It was a sight she didn't want to behold ever again.

And now, her father went to his knees, his body shaking in barely contained rage. "We present you with a worthy tribute to show our unwavering gratitude for all you've given us, O Sublime Ones, for our conviction in your powers is far superior to any other."

He turned his head to Natalia, who realized she, too, was shaking at the utter, zealous devotion in her father's eyes. "Come now, Natalia. Show them your faith."

Natalia nodded jerkily as she stepped forward and pulled out the penknife from the pocket of her jeans. She pressed the blade against her inner arm, feeling a sickening sense of familiarity, welcoming the pain as blood spilled from the wound, shining red under the moonlight.

Then she began to chant.

"Deep in the forest, no bird is safe . . ."

As Natalia recited the old psalm from the Book of Kahil, she pulled her arm over the bowl in her father's hands. It was filled with ashes, which slowly turned a light, distorted shade of red from the blood she spilled over it.

Natalia and her father were immobile, frozen in place, Natalia's soft singing the only sound filling the loaded air.

When the last drop of blood fell onto the ashes, Natalia returned her arm to her side and straightened in her place. "The Morrow Gods have come," she whispered.

Her father climbed to his feet, stepped toward the calm water of the river, and poured the contents of the glass bowl into it, coloring the deep-blue depths a faint shade of red.

Natalia and her father watched until the last drop of blood and ash landed and rippled over the water. They waited for a few more moments before they clasped their hands together, closed their eyes, and murmured, "May the Morrow Gods bestow the Beyond with their eternal inferno."

Natalia was watching the Androscoggin River from the window of the living room as her father rinsed the bowl in the kitchen sink when there was a knock on the entrance door. Both Natalia and her father turned to look at the door, immediately alert.

Neither Natalia nor her father had any friends. Once upon a time, the neighbors had tried to befriend her father, but they realized quickly enough he wasn't interested in trivial things such as friendships. While Natalia had once wished she had friends, being homeschooled with no extracurricular activities didn't allow for such things.

Meaning there was no reason for anyone to visit them, especially when it was close to midnight.

Another knock on the door made Natalia jump. She put the workbook down and leaped to her feet, then tiptoed toward the door. Silently, she checked the peephole.

What she saw made her pale.

She stepped back from the door as yet another knock echoed in the silent house. She then turned to her father, who gave her an inquisitive look and mouthed, *Who's there?*

Natalia parted her lips to speak, but no sound came out. At that very moment, many scenarios went through her head. So many of them, in fact, that she had a hard time breathing.

Her heart raced in her chest as cold sweat dripped down her spine. *This is a chance,* a little, distant voice whispered in her head. *This is the chance you've been waiting for.*

But there was a louder voice, a deeply terrified one, that screamed, *You have nowhere else to go!*

She had no time to choose, though.

The door was thrown open, and five police officers entered the house. They passed Natalia, heading straight to her father before one of them grabbed his hands and shackled his wrists. "Amir Zoheir-Henderson," the officer said in a disgusted, angry voice, "you're under arrest for charges of kidnap and rape. You have the right to remain silent. Anything you say can and will be used against you in a court of law."

Natalia's father did not resist. Quite the opposite, really; he remained calm as they dragged him toward the door. His eyes then turned to Natalia. "She has nothing to do with it," he told the police officers. "Leave her out of it."

She watched as the officers then carried her father out, while one of them, a woman, remained behind, facing her. "It's going to be all right, Natalia," she told her, and Natalia saw the sympathy on her face she didn't bother to hide. "You're going to be okay."

Everything had happened so fast after that, Natalia hardly remembered any of it. She was put in a car, and some people talked to her, saying things she didn't quite understand, and through it all, she uttered not a word and shed no tears.

Until an investigator sat her down and asked, "Were you aware your father imprisoned young girls in the basement of your house?"

That's when she finally snapped out of her dazed stupor. And the first thing she said in many hours was a lie.

"No."

And the investigator believed her. Why wouldn't he, Natalia thought bitterly, when she was merely a thirteen-year-old, supposedly a little girl herself?

In the days after her father's arrest, Natalia didn't sleep. Couldn't, really. She was awake, staring at the ceiling of the motel room the police put her in, wondering what the hell was going to happen to her now.

Because she knew her father's fate was sealed. She was smart enough to know the police wouldn't have arrested him without some sort of evidence.

But what about her fate?

Natalia sat in front of the square glass window, a telephone pressed against her ear. On the other side, her father sat, wearing the orange prison clothes she'd seen many times on TV. It was surreal that her father, the one who always wore those nerdy khaki pants and a buttoned shirt, was now wearing that.

"Natalia," he whispered into the phone. He seemed more tired than she'd ever seen him before; his eyes were bloodshot, with heavy bags under them that reminded her of her own. His dark hair was disheveled, and he had begun growing a scruff, when before he was always so clean shaven. The only thing that seemed normal was his glasses.

"Dad," Natalia mumbled, her emotions all over the place. She didn't know what to feel, didn't know if she could feel again, really, what with the cold numbness that had taken root in her chest since the night of his arrest.

"We don't have much time, so I'll make it short," her father now said, his eyes searching hers. "You must continue applying everything I've taught you."

Something rippled underneath the numbness. Something hot and ugly. "How can you think about that right now?" she hissed, incredulous.

He gave her his disapproving look, the one she used to dread when she was younger. "This is the only thing that matters, Natalia," he said fiercely, a spark returning to his eyes. "We're the last Children of Kahil. With me gone, you have to carry on the legacy. To continue to prove your faith."

It's not my faith, Dad; it's yours, Natalia wanted to respond, but she bit her tongue and looked away. She would break him if she denied him this, she knew. He cared far more about the Morrow Gods than he'd ever cared for her, after all.

Her father had the uncanny ability to read what was going on in her mind, however, because he said, "I'm asking this for your own sake. You know I love you more than anything in the world, Natalia. I would do anything for you."

Lies.

"Look at me, please," he whispered, and reluctantly, she did. His gaze was desperate. "The Book of Kahil is in my office. Take it. Read it. Do what needs to be done."

She wanted nothing but to go back to her childhood home and burn that book. Because that book had brought nothing but misery upon her life—now *and* before her father got arrested. Everything he'd done, all the things she'd witnessed, her part in it all, pretending to be oblivious when she heard screams from the basement . . . It was all because of that damned book.

"Natalia, my love," her father pleaded, and she could look at him no more. "Do not let all of our hard work go to waste."

She pursed her lips and stared at her hands. He tried to speak to her again, but she wasn't listening, unable to listen when all he uttered were pleas for her to commit the same crimes he did in the name of a long-lost faith.

Natalia stared at the milkshake Amy, the social worker, had bought her, wondering whether she should show she was trying, after days upon days of barely nibbling an energy bar per day.

She wasn't hungry, though, and hadn't been for almost a month now. The Augusta orphanage workers tried to feed her relentlessly, and Amy, too, brought her burgers every time she came to visit. On better days, she pretended to eat while actually passing her food to Carter, an exceptionally hungry boy her age in the orphanage, but usually, she just flat-out refused to eat.

If there was one thing she hated, it was adults trying to control her.

Amy now walked back into the room, and a couple in their forties followed her in. "You should drink the milkshake, dear," she said kindly, gesturing toward the vanilla-strawberry mix.

But the milkshake was no longer on her mind now. Instead, she stared suspiciously at the couple, who gave her wobbly smiles and hopeful gazes, as though she was the answer to all their prayers.

That did not make her any thirstier for that stupid milkshake.

Seeing that she wasn't in a cooperative mood, Amy cleared her throat and motioned toward the couple. "Natalia, please meet Ella and Roger Kazar."

The woman, Ella, seemed to be on the verge of tears as she stepped toward Natalia and crouched so they were eye level, what with Natalia sitting down. "Hi there," Ella said softly, smiling tearily.

Natalia did not smile back. "Hi," she said flatly.

"Roger and I have heard so much about you," Ella continued as though Natalia had said nothing, "and we can't wait to introduce you to our son, Logan."

Alarmed, Natalia whipped her head toward Amy, requiring an explanation. Amy smiled widely. "Ella and Roger are your foster parents, starting today," she said excitedly. "Isn't it great, Natalia? You get to have new parents, a new home, and even a brother your age!"

Natalia felt her heart sink. She didn't need a new family. Sure, the orphanage wasn't the best, but she only ever had one family. Her father. And despite everything he'd done, she loved him. She loved him dearly.

But when she turned to Mrs. and Mr. Kazar, she knew she had no choice in the matter. This had all been settled already. They were simply informing her of what was to come, not asking her if she was okay with any of it.

In their eyes, she was a little girl who needed to be taken care of.

In truth, Natalia's maturity was far beyond her years.

And because of that maturity, she knew she had to adapt, and quickly, to what was to come. Frosting her heart, she gave the woman a thin smile and said, "Thank you."

Ella melted. Roger was now crying too. Amy was beside herself.

Natalia was angry.

And that anger made her make an impulsive decision. Something she didn't think through but felt she had to do. If she was going to pretend she was an innocent, clueless girl who went along with everything she was told, she had to do this.

"Also, please address me by a different name," she said, causing everyone's eyes to return to her. She feigned a shy smile in response. "I want to start fresh."

Ella was perplexed, but she softened and smiled widely. "Of course, darling," she said, "and what is your new name?"

Certainly not Natalia Zoheir-Henderson. Not with these people. Not when her father was locked away, perhaps forever, and she, too, was about to move from one prison to another.

She would go by her middle name. The one her father had given her, unlike her first name, so she would always remember where she came from and who she really was.

With conviction far superior to any she'd ever had as to the Morrow Gods' existence, she said, "Aileen Henderson."

CHAPTER 1

AILEEN

I watched as the beautiful view of New England disappeared from the airplane window, and it did nothing to quench my bloodthirst.

Anger, caused by a deep-seated betrayal, reigned over me, so much so I hardly remembered how I got on this plane. Everything that happened after Ragnor Rayne sold me off to the highest bidder was like a blurry haze in my mind.

There was so much I didn't get to do after the Auction concluded. Once Lord Atalon bought everyone he wanted, we had no time to say goodbye or even collect our things. "Your bags will be in your rooms when you arrive" was all he said as he led us out and away from the Rayne League. And while I no longer wanted to stay there, I wished I had been given at least five minutes to tell Ragnor how much I hated him.

Because I did.

I hated him with everything I had.

He'd been like an oasis in a desert I wasn't aware I'd been treading across. Like the light at the end of a long dark tunnel. I foolishly thought that I was like that for him too. That he needed me as much as I needed him. That he couldn't bear the thought of parting with me. That breathing without one another was impossible.

I couldn't have been more wrong.

He'd given me hope for a better future. Made me believe I could become someone better. That I could be less of a monster.

Then he took it all away by willingly handing me over to another.

"Aileen."

I almost jumped as I whipped my head to my right, where the empty seat was now inhabited by Lord Atalon. He looked as immaculate as when we'd left, not one platinum hair out of its sleek place. My eyes met his dark ones, a stark contrast to those of the man I'd just been thinking about, and I forced myself to give him a somewhat cordial smile. "Yes, my Lord?"

"Please, call me Atalon," he said, putting one long leg on top of the other. He was still wearing his classic white tux with a red tie, which clung tightly to his lean figure and also made his skin look paler than its alabaster tone. "Would you like some champagne?"

Before I could reply, an attendant appeared, as if out of thin air, and handed us two glasses of champagne. When she was gone, Atalon raised his glass. "Let's have a toast."

The last thing I wanted was to celebrate, but I played along. We clinked our glasses together, and he then sipped the wine from the plastic fluted glass, a look of elation on his face.

I shifted uncomfortably and looked away, taking a small sip before putting the glass down. I was in no mood to drink, and Atalon's probing gaze would not convince me otherwise.

"I'm looking forward to seeing you flourish in my League, Aileen," Atalon now said, his soft voice drawing my gaze back to him. He gave me a kind smile as he grabbed my hand and squeezed. "I believe you have so much potential. I wouldn't have bought you otherwise."

His words felt sincere, and yet they were not enough to make my anger abate. "Thank you, my Lord," I said, as I was taught to address all vampire Lords.

He sighed as he let my hand go and leaned back. "I told you to call me Atalon," he said, seemingly disheartened.

Chills spread across my skin. "It's all right, my Lord," I said quietly. "I know my place."

And that was the absolute truth. Because unlike before, I knew how things worked in the vampiric society. I understood the hierarchy, especially as a Common vampire. I understood what was expected of me.

My mind went back to the Auction, to my performance. To when, for a few moments, it was as if I was transported to another dimension. There was a naked bird dying in my arms, and I'd felt that loss before I'd returned to the Auction Hall and realized time had stopped.

And that it was me who'd stopped time.

I turned away from Atalon and leaned my forehead against the cool window, closing my eyes. I had no idea what any of that meant, and for a split second, I debated telling Atalon about it.

But even if I trusted him, which I didn't—not yet at least—an instinct told me to keep my mouth shut.

The same instinct that had been telling me Ragnor Rayne was dangerous right from the very beginning, when I'd first seen him at the Hole before knowing who he was or what he was.

And so, for the rest of the flight, I kept silent, stewing in my own rage, grief, and confusion.

Tossing and turning in bed, I tried to put my mind to rest, but I couldn't. It hadn't even been twenty-four hours since I'd prepared for the Auction, believing against all odds that Ragnor Rayne, the cold, aloof vampire Lord, would eventually come around and choose me. Since I'd left the Rayne League.

After being escorted by a Lieutenant, seeing my name on the suite's door and the bags placed neatly inside my new bedroom, I was overcome by exhaustion. That exhaustion took a turn for the worse when I got in the shower and tried to wash the remnants of the Rayne League off my skin to no avail.

And yet Ragnor's face seemed to make camp in my mind, refusing to leave me be.

His midnight blue eyes going neon when he moved inside me.

His lips, which could be either rough or soft on mine.

His bristled jaw caressing the inner skin of my thighs . . .

Too restless to sleep, I shoved the blanket away and got out of bed. I lived in suite 431 along with two other Commons. Each bedroom had its own en suite bathroom, and the common area consisted of a spacious living room with a TV screen and a video streamer. It was similar in design to the newbie suite I'd lived in back at the Rayne League, though a tad bit larger. And red. Because for some unfathomable reason, Lord Atalon insisted the entire underground compound color scheme would include all shades of red, making it look like a mix between a blood cell and a Victorian-era brothel.

When I entered the living room, I saw that I wasn't the only one suffering from insomnia on my first night in the new League. A woman sat on one of the couches, her body shuddering and her sobs stifled.

I debated whether to go back to my room when the woman raised her head from her hands and looked right at me. "Feeling pathetic, too, aren't you?" she said almost aggressively, as if her eyes weren't bloodshot and tears weren't freshly wet on her cheeks. "Feel free to join my pity party. No invitation required."

When she made it sound so appealing, how could I possibly refuse?

Decision made, I took a seat on the couch next to hers. Then, before she could resume her crying, and before I would be tempted to punch the wall to alleviate some of the tension that crept into the room, I said, voice raspy with misuse, "We sat next to each other back at the Auction. You're Isora, right?"

Isora sniffled and nodded. "Yes, that's me," she said bitterly. "The poor second-timer who left one hell for another."

I'd forgotten about that, and now I knew why she was crying. Second-timers were vampires who'd already been through one Auction yet wanted to leave the League they were bought into. Every vampire had one more chance at the Auction, but it wasn't recommended, because in the strict vampiric hierarchy we lived in, second-timers were at the absolute bottom of the food chain. And yet, some vampires were so miserable that they were willing to take that chance. Still, I couldn't imagine why she viewed the Atalon League so poorly. It had to be better than her previous experience.

I did remember Isora used to be a Renaldi League member, and from my own encounters with Lord Renaldi, including that dreadful visit to his League in Las Vegas during the newcomers' field trip a couple of months back, I could understand why she chose to forsake her former station in favor of a lower, possibly worse one.

"I doubt Lord Atalon is as bad as Renaldi," I now said. I didn't think I would've been able to stomach it if I'd been sold to anyone else, to be frank.

Isora gave me a shivery smile. Even with her tear-soaked face, Isora was pretty. Her eyes, red though they were, were a mesmerizing electric blue. Her chocolate brown hair lay smoothly down her back, not a strand out of place. Her small pointy nose and thick lips only added to her doll-like looks. Along with her curvy build, she was an absolute knockout.

I hadn't noticed her like that before at the Auction, but then again, I had been too preoccupied to notice anything or anyone else around me.

It seemed Isora was taking me in for the first time, too, because she gave me a thorough once-over, like the one I'd just given her, and said with half a smile, "I was sure your hair was darker."

"Oh," I murmured absentmindedly.

Isora chuckled, and I raised my eyes back to her. "You look upset," she said, then glanced away. "Though you shouldn't be."

Her words made me pause. "And why is that?"

She gave me a teary smile. “Didn’t you notice?” she asked, and when I frowned, she chuckled again before dropping her gaze. “Our new Lord obviously favors you. He didn’t approach any of us on the plane but you.”

My gut clenched. There was only one man whose favor I wanted, and no one else.

“I wouldn’t count on that,” I told her, unable to contain the anger in my words. “Vampire Lords are extremely fickle.”

And I would do well to remember that.

I was done dancing to the Lords’ tune.

Now, it was time to dance to my own.

CHAPTER 2
AILEEN

The Atalon League cafeteria was vastly different from the one in the Rayne League, and yet I still got a stifling feeling of pained nostalgia. It was large and posh, decorated with twinkling chandeliers and ornamented wall lanterns, arches made of marble holding the ceiling.

It was so early in the morning that when Isora and I walked in, the cafeteria was empty but for the kitchen assistants. Both of us spent the night awake together, though we didn't talk much after our initial chat; we put on a movie and watched in silence, both lost in thought.

Now, the two of us, sporting dark bags under our eyes, made a beeline to the coffee station. We didn't speak as we poured our drinks, but when she mixed her espresso with a quarter of a cup of B-positive blood from the nearby dispenser, I found myself croaking, "That's an odd choice."

Isora turned to me with a frown that accentuated the lack of sleep she'd gotten. "What do you mean?"

"Coffee usually goes better with AB negative," I informed her and yawned, thinking back to my dishwashing team at the Rayne League. Jada, Bowen, and CJ told me all kinds of things during my shifts with them, and one of those things was the secret to a good coffee. While blood tasted like water on its own, when mixed with certain spices, fruits, and, in this case, coffee beans, it took on a variety of different flavors, depending on the blood type.

Isora snorted. “I like my coffee more on the sweeter side, thank you very much.”

When I saw her plopping five packs of sugar into her brew, I stared at her in astonishment. “Would you like some coffee with your sugar?”

She rolled her eyes, but her lips twitched. “So it’s true what they say, then?”

Frowning, I cocked my head. “What’s that?”

“That the Rayne League is full of judgmental snobs?” Isora gave me a smirk.

Arching a brow, I grabbed my mug and raised it to her. “Simple coffee with AB negative, and I’m good to go.”

She made a disgusted face. “That sounds bitter. Yuck.”

“Oh, and I’m the snob,” I murmured.

Chuckling, she motioned toward the nearby buffet. “I smell fresh croissants. Or are you averse to those as well?”

“Don’t be daft,” I replied dryly, and we both headed to the next table. I piled eggs and bacon onto my plate, though I wasn’t feeling particularly hungry, and with a fake dirty look to Isora, I grabbed a small croissant.

We found a table near the back wall and settled there. She made a toast with her coffee mug, and I couldn’t help but be charmed by her antics, especially when she practically chugged her coffee in about three gulps.

A smile teased my lips as we ate our breakfast in a companionable and surprisingly comfortable silence.

It occurred to me then that it was the first time I’d eaten with another vampire voluntarily like this in a League cafeteria. Back at the Rayne League, I’d basically been a social pariah, thanks to my status as a kitchen assistant. But here I was, having a relaxed breakfast with another vampire without any ulterior motives or anything of the sort.

As the Atalon League vampires began slowly trickling into the cafeteria, I felt a sudden sense of melancholy and nostalgia. Would I be assigned to the kitchens here as well and serve this League's vampires? Would I meet a new dishwashing team?

My chest squeezed as I thought of Jada, CJ, and Bowen. The Rayne League dishwashing team was irreplaceable for me. Even the thought of not seeing them again made me queasy with pain. I truly cared for those three. I didn't want to meet another dishwashing team. I didn't want to work in the Atalon League kitchens. It would feel like I was betraying my own precious memories.

Feeling my cheek burning, I glanced at the cafeteria patrons. Many of them glanced at Isora and me, but none of them approached us. Which was just as well; I was in no mood to socialize, Isora notwithstanding.

Despite my earlier difficulties making friends, it felt easy with Isora. We barely knew each other, and yet something about her put me enough at ease to lay to rest the painful memories of my former League.

And because of that, I said, "Can I ask you something?"

She gave me a curious look. "Sure."

Lowering my fork, I studied her face. "What did you mean last night about going from one hell to another?"

I didn't get to hear Isora's response because just then, someone called, "Isora!"

Both Isora and I turned to see a familiar face coming our way. She had long brown hair, large dark eyes, and a pretty, freckled face.

"You left without me?" Eleanor, our third suitemate, said, a pout brewing.

"Good morning, Ellie," Isora said, smiling at her. "We didn't want to wake you. We were both already up, so we just decided to come down. Sorry about that."

Eleanor scowled as she stopped by our table. "Kind of different from the Renaldi League, huh? Geez. Lord Renaldi would die if he saw us eating like this," she said grumpily.

"I was thinking about that too. And how he used to keep us on edge by limiting our blood intake?" Isora responded, her voice full of hope despite what she had alluded to last night about this League. "We wanted to get some coffee in our blood."

Eleanor turned her eyes to me, as if she hadn't realized I was there before. "Oh, good morning, Aileen," she said offhandedly before returning her gaze to Isora. "Let's go all three of us together next time. Remember, there's strength in numbers."

I schooled my face as I nodded, hiding my surprise. I'd been sure she would ask Isora to go with her alone next time. It was nice to feel included, even if it meant I was left out of their bonding over their trauma from Lord Renaldi and his League.

A few minutes later, Eleanor returned with her breakfast and joined us. Unlike when it was just Isora and me, Eleanor didn't seem to be comfortable with silence and spoke the entire time, telling us all about the dreams she had, and who she'd already met from the Atalon League, and all her thoughts and feelings. I listened closely, not that anyone could get a word in edgewise, attempting to discern tidbits of knowledge about Renaldi.

She somewhat reminded me of Zoey, my suitemate from the Rayne League; though, while talkative, Zoey was much less of a chatterbox. My thoughts drifted to her, and I wondered what she was doing now. I wished I knew how she was doing and whether we were feeling similarly.

She had been bought by Lord Renaldi, though, so I had a sinking feeling that she had it far worse.

Normally, I would've been annoyed by Eleanor's ramblings, but it was a welcome distraction from my darkening thoughts. I hadn't even been thinking about him ever since I met Isora in our suite living room, and I wasn't ready to go back there. Not yet.

Breakfast passed in a loud yet peaceful manner. It helped me settle down a bit.

Though that didn't last, because before long, a woman approached us and said, "Isora Elios and Eleanor Simmons?"

My suitemates raised their heads toward the woman. She gave them a businesslike smile. "You are to come with me." She turned to me. "Miss Henderson, Lord Atalon is waiting for you outside."

I tensed, suddenly on alert. Sharing the sentiment, Isora asked, "What's going on?"

"I'm to take you on a bit of a tour," the woman replied. "Now chop-chop!"

Reluctantly, Eleanor and Isora bid me farewell and followed the woman outside the cafeteria. I quickly finished my coffee, no longer feeling so content, and left the table in haste.

I found Lord Atalon right outside the main entrance to the cafeteria, leaning against the wall. Gone was the suit he'd worn to the Auction, and instead he wore beige tailored trousers with an emerald-colored button-down shirt tucked in, the sleeves folded to his elbows, showing the fancy Rolex on his left wrist. His platinum hair shone with gel that slicked it back, and his black eyes found mine before they slid down, giving me a slow perusal.

There was nothing much to see, to be honest. My wavy hair, even if it was somehow lighter than it was a few days ago, was in its usual updo; my hazel eyes were sunken; and my olive skin was pale with exhaustion. I was wearing simple jeans, a V-neck tee, and sneakers. Nothing about me was as posh or expensive as Atalon.

But from the way he looked me up and down, one would've thought I was wearing a nightgown or something.

Shifting from foot to foot, I folded my arms and cleared my throat. His eyes snapped up to meet mine. "Good morning, my Lord," I said, voice taut with tension.

"Good morning, Aileen," he said smoothly, as if he hadn't just blatantly checked me out. "I hope your first night in my League went well. Let us begin our tour, shall we?"

He offered me his arm, but I pretended not to notice and said, "After you, my Lord."

His smile turned into a knowing grin, and we started walking. I trailed behind him, letting him lead, but he suddenly paused and turned around. "Aileen, I'm not Rayne," he said, his voice softly chastising. "You don't have to walk behind me."

For the next hour, Atalon took me through the entirety of the League. We started from the top floor, which was filled with shops that could easily fit in on Manhattan's Fifth Avenue. "Each boutique is managed by some of my Gifteds," Atalon explained as we stopped before the showcase of a luxurious jewelry store. "This one here, for instance, is run by a Gifted jewel crafter with a specific talent for unearthing the purest gold and platinum and the rarest diamonds. The income from these shops accounts for a significant portion of our revenue."

I glanced at Atalon and saw pride shining in his eyes. It made me relax a bit. A Lord who was genuinely proud of his vampires and their accomplishments probably meant me no harm.

Our next stop was the workshop floor. "This is where my artistic Gifteds spend most of their time. They work in leathers, cashmere, wood, silk, and more. We handcraft some of the world's finest goods, from furniture to luggage," Atalon said, motioning toward the few doors spread across the floor. "Behind each door, there is a studio tailored for the artist's needs. Let me show you one."

We headed toward the first door on the right, and I could hear a faint thumping noise. As if someone was hitting something. Atalon knocked, and a feminine voice called from inside, "Come in!"

Atalon opened the door, and we walked in. What I saw made me stop in place and gape.

The studio was large and spacious, with an unexpectedly tall ceiling. Marble sculptures and pieces were scattered around the room, some of them hidden under a simple white cloth, and many tools, like chisels and oddly curved knives, spread across the floor. Despite the mess, the studio was surprisingly clean.

In the middle of the room, a woman sat on the top level of a ladder next to a sculpture of what seemed to be a seven-foot-tall man. She gave us a wide pretty smile as she wiped her hands on the thighs of her faded jeans, which looked as if they had seen better days. "Morning, Atalon," she said, and the friendly, carefree way she said Atalon's name let me in on the fact she must be quite high up the hierarchy. "And morning to you too, newbie. I'm Demetria."

"Aileen," I murmured as she fixed her catlike amber eyes in my direction.

"You've spent the night here again, haven't you?" Atalon said now, sighing as he looked at Demetria, his eyes unapologetically taking in the generous bust she'd failed to conceal under an oversize top.

She laughed. "It's not a crime, you know. And with the gala event around the corner . . ."

Her laughter coaxed a begrudging smile out of Atalon. "Have you at least eaten anything?"

Demetria blushed from the attention and pushed a stray wisp of wine red hair that had fallen across her cheek back into her artfully messy bun. "I'm going to in a few minutes," Demetria promised before turning her eyes back to me. They seemed curious. "Are you a new Gifted joining our floor?"

Confused, I was about to reply when Atalon beat me to it. "No, she's one of the Commons I purchased at yesterday's Auction."

Demetria seemed surprised before her face relaxed into a friendly smile. "Welcome to the Atalon League, then."

Atalon didn't seem to want to dawdle, so we quickly left Demetria's studio after that. Was she surprised Atalon was personally giving a tour to a Common, or was she surprised I wasn't Gifted? Or both?

The next few floors I already knew. One was where the cafeteria was, along with the Atalon League private gallery I'd visited a month ago and the Athenaeum, which was basically a library with a fancy name. The other floor was the Commons residence, and the floor under it was the Gifted residence.

We finished the tour at the first floor, which was home to the many League offices, including Vampire Resources and Lord Atalon's office.

After a quick review of that floor, Atalon led me into his office reception area. I was struck by its sleekness; the walls, marble floor, and ceiling were all painted the same shade of red as the rest of the League. Even the large chandelier was the same color. The color unity had the effect of a padded white room in an asylum.

There were eye-catching paintings on the walls, all of which were abstract with different shades of red, and that, too, added to the suffocating feel of the whole space.

But when we walked into Atalon's actual office, that's when I had to stop and stare.

It was empty but for a desk and a couple of chairs. The wall behind the desk wasn't really a wall but a floor-to-ceiling aquarium with all kinds of fish swimming about. The other walls were filled with so many paintings and framed pictures that there was not even one small spot of the actual wall.

Atalon went to sit behind the desk, and I slowly made my way to one of the two free chairs, trying to tear my eyes away from the aquarium and the walls unsuccessfully.

It seemed Atalon was familiar with this kind of reaction to his office, because he silently let me have my fill for a few minutes until he said, "I'm taking a guess here that you like my office."

Like was an understatement. "It's beautiful," I said, painfully returning my gaze to Atalon. "I've never seen anything like it."

He smiled, pride again gleaming from within. "It took four years to build and another fifty to stock the walls with these rare pieces. And these fish? They come from all over the world. This aquarium looks like it's one piece, but it actually is made up of two hundred pieces and compartments to house lots of different types of fish. Collecting unusual and beautiful things is my passion."

"I thought you were more of an artist," I noted quietly and couldn't help but look back to the walls. I remembered viewing his paintings in the gallery.

"Can't I be both a collector and an artist?" he inquired.

I glanced at him, then back at the walls in amazement. It was as though I'd been transported to another universe, if only for a short period of time. "Apparently, you can."

Atalon chuckled, drawing my eyes back to him. "Now that it's all cleared up, we have some matters to discuss."

And that quickly, I returned to my current life, paintings-filled walls and aquarium forgotten. A foreboding feeling fell upon me, chasing away any lingering feelings of wonder I might've still had. What did he want to talk about?

"As you well know," Atalon began, leaning back into his chair, "every vampire in every League has to work to keep their Leagued status."

Dread crawled into my stomach. I knew that far too well. I'd had to work as a kitchen assistant back in the Rayne League because of this stupid clause in the League System Agreement. Basically, it meant that while I didn't have to pay rent or taxes, I did have to work and contribute in some way to my League.

It had completely escaped my mind that I would have to do this *now* too. Before, I couldn't even imagine life after the Auction, and that did not prepare me whatsoever for what was now coming. That, and the shock of the Auction and its results, made me completely forget about it.

He handed me one of the papers lying on his desk. "Please read this through and let me know if you have any questions."

My eyes dropped to the papers, and my heart stuttered when I saw my name in block letters across the top of the first page. There was a bulleted list consisting of three job titles: museum guide assistant, artist assistant, and vampire resources secretary.

I looked up, baffled. "Can I ask what parameters you are taking into account when you choose which jobs to offer to new members?"

Atalon smiled, but his eyes told me a different story. They were watching me like a hawk, as if he was waiting for a moment to strike to present itself. "Normally, I receive the files the members' former Lords compiled and base the job offers on that."

I froze.

His smile widened as his eyes grew warmer. "Don't worry, Rayne didn't write anything incriminating about you. He simply stated a few facts, including that painting and art in general are your hobbies. Which I could already tell, of course, considering your Auction performance."

My mind exploded with memories that were so sudden, my heartbeat became a drum in my chest. Upon my first meeting with Ragnor, he'd asked me what my hobbies were. I told him I had none. And yet he wrote those anyway—hobbies he knew Atalon would take note of.

Had Ragnor been trying to push me into Atalon's League from the start?

There was only one conclusion to all this.

He never planned to have me.

My gaze lowered to the floor. "I see."

Pain spread across my chest, threatening to suffocate me. I could still remember how Ragnor looked at me right before the Auction began, when I asked him if sex was all he wanted from me.

Then he told me he wanted to change. He'd given me hope. That maybe, just maybe, I was worth more to him.

That I hadn't been the only one of us to develop feelings.

But if there was one thing I should've learned by now, it was to never trust men to stay by my side. They would all abandon me in the end.

It was a pity I had let Ragnor make me forget that important lesson.

I clenched my hands into fists and said, "What do artist assistant and museum guide assistant entail?"

"Artist assistant is pretty straightforward," Atalon replied. "You'll assist the League's Gifted artists, like Demetria. I won't lie," he added, making me raise my eyes to his suddenly serious face. "This isn't an easy job. Artists, as you probably know, have quite the turbulent nature, and it can make them extremely hard to deal with sometimes."

I studied him now. “Are you like that too?”

He smiled again and flippantly said, “Who knows?”

Grimacing, I asked, “What about the museum guide assistant?”

“If you ask for my opinion, this is probably the best job offer of these three,” he said, eyes probing, “and the one I wish you would accept.”

Uneasy, I narrowed my eyes. “Why?”

“The Atalonian Museum is one of a kind, you see,” he replied with his smile still intact. “It is dedicated solely to vampire artists not just from my League, but from others too. It’s full of masterpieces and beautiful exhibits you wouldn’t be able to find anywhere else.”

He rose from his seat and began pacing, hands behind his back. My heart panged as he did so, reminding me of my former Comprehensive Newcomer Three-Month Course teacher, Abe. He used to do that, too, when he was about to launch into one of his long lectures. “Working in the museum is considered a privilege for many,” he said. “Especially for Commons—it’s an opportunity to be closer to the League’s shining stars and make a difference. And a museum guide assistant is possibly the most important role—because you wouldn’t just guide visitors, but would also participate in auctions, special exhibitions, and even deal-making, depending on your performance.”

It sounded like this museum was the heart and pride of the Atalon League, if I read the Lord correctly. It was a good opportunity for a Common—better than, even—and I understood that. But it also sounded like too much.

Why would he offer me, a Common he’d just bought, a job that required so much responsibility?

“Can I think it through?” I asked, feeling a wave of exhaustion hitting me. I was in no state to make such a big decision that could affect my future in irrevocable ways.

“Of course,” Atalon replied, giving me a smile that was supposed to be gentle, I believed, but turned out a bit shark-teeth sharp. “You may have until the end of the day.”

I guessed that was the longest he could give me. "Thank you, my Lord."

"You're most welcome," he replied. "And please, call me Atalon."

I sat in the suite living room, doodling in my small sketchbook absent-mindedly, when the door behind me opened. I turned around to see Isora coming out of her bedroom, rubbing her eyes after a much-needed nap. "Evening," she murmured, going to the fridge to grab a bottle of A positive before plopping on the couch next to me.

"Hey," I said softly, closing my sketchbook and putting it away. "You look well rested."

"I am," she said, giving me a content, sleepy smile. "I need all the rest that I can get before I start my job in the kitchens tomorrow."

Being a second-timer rather than a newcomer, different rules applied to her. "As a former kitchen aide, it's not that bad," I said with a pang in my chest as I thought about how Margarita hazed me every chance she got when I worked in the Rayne League kitchens. Back then, I had been so worried about what had happened to Cassidy. It all seemed so insignificant now. Still, I couldn't help recalling how my stomach twisted and my heart leaped into my chest when I first saw her and Logan stroll into the cafeteria with Ragnor.

"I would've been happy cleaning the bathrooms, too, if they wanted me to," she said, leaning back as she sipped the blood. "I'm just so glad to be here."

Before I could stop myself, I blurted out, "That didn't seem to be the case last night."

I expected her to clamp up at my probing, but to my surprise, she shot me a rueful smile. "I was going through quite the turmoil then," she said, "but after talking to Vampire Resources officials and other League members, I feel so much more optimistic. Don't you?"

Her question might've been rhetorical, but it caught me off guard and forced me to think back on my day. It was almost surreal that it had been only one day in the League, when it felt like three. "I don't know what I think."

Isora took my hand and squeezed, making me return my eyes to her. Her expression turned serious. "You can talk it out with me if you want to," she said quietly. "It might help. I heard Lord Rayne was a hard-ass. Wanted everything his way or no way. Lord Atalon seems much more laid back."

Warmth filled me up at her words, and before I could stop myself, my lips moved on their own accord. "I never considered the option of being sold. I thought . . ." I took a deep breath. "I thought Ra—I mean, Lord Rayne would buy me."

Isora's blue eyes sharpened, but she said nothing, giving me space to talk. And up until now, I didn't realize just how much I needed to talk.

"I was involved with an older, high-status man in the Rayne League," I said, deciding against telling her who it was, exactly. "I believed we felt the same way, but when the Auction happened, he decided to . . . break it off." I paused, grimacing. "And now I don't know what to do. I can't see past the anger."

I fell silent then, staring at Isora's hand holding mine. It was a relief to voice what I felt, but at the same time, it only solidified my pain.

And that made me want to hurt Ragnor as much as he had hurt me.

To avenge myself somehow.

"It sucks," Isora said quietly, and when I looked back at her, I saw my pain reflected in her eyes. "I went through the same thing, back when I was human," she told me, eyes flashing. "I was nineteen at the time, and the man I was involved with was twice my age and a state senator. You can only imagine the kind of things he'd promised me and what I gave him in return, despite him being married with kids."

I didn't expect her to share, and the fact that she did, and that she had gone through something similar, made me feel angry on her behalf. "What a dick," I murmured.

She nodded. "A humongous dick. That's why I put myself on the waiting list. I wanted to become something more, to live a better life than the one I'd led, especially with him in the picture. I decided to become a vampire and start fresh in a different society, as a different creature altogether, to show myself that I was in charge of my own life—and not some man who used me only to discard me once he'd had his fill."

Her eyes glowed a bright cobalt. "You can't change what happened in the Auction, Aileen. You're here to stay, and what better way to show that coward what he missed than to continue living and becoming so much better than he can ever have?"

And just like that, with a few words from this woman whom I'd only just met and whom I'd already felt kinship with, an epiphany knocked me out. Because becoming a second-timer was not an option, there must have been something else I could do.

What better way to take my revenge than to show Ragnor what he and his League missed?

And so later, right after dinner, I went to Atalon's office and gave him my decision.

A large moon set in the midnight blue sky, bright and yet shadowed. I stood and stared at it, mind blissfully empty, when I suddenly felt a pair of arms enveloping me from behind, pulling me closer to a hard chest.

I tensed, but then I heard a familiar voice whispering in my ear, "Aileen."

Shuddering, I huddled closer to the man behind me, feeling warm all over. "You're here," I whispered back, burying my head in his strong, corded arms. "How come you're here?"

He chuckled, a sound I'd never heard from him before. "Of course I'm here," he murmured, brushing his lips against my hair. "Where else would I be?"

His words filled me with warmth, and for one wondrous moment, I let myself sink into him. He was everything to me, after all. He was home.

But I knew this couldn't last. There were too many things left unsaid between us. Too much that we needed to talk about. Things I needed to confront him about before I could ever let myself feel like I belonged with him again.

Reluctantly, I pulled back from him and turned around, opening my mouth to speak. But the moment I did, he was no longer behind me. Instead he was a yard away, barely a silhouette, and I was suddenly cold with his absence.

"Come back," I said, walking toward him.

But the more I walked, the farther away he became. The moonlight above disappeared behind clouds as I started running toward him, heartbeat like a drum in my ears. Fear spread through me when smoke filled the area until I was surrounded by it, unable to tell where he went or where I was.

Frustration and yearning filled me. We needed to talk, and I wished for his warmth . . . his strength . . . the feeling of belonging with someone, to someone—

But the smoke did not let up, and I felt like I was drowning in it. He was nowhere to be found, and he was letting me drown here, all alone, like the bastard he was.

And no matter the need I had for him, the unbending longing and desire, I couldn't help but feel utterly miserable as I sank farther into the smoke . . .

Even in dreams, Ragnor left me for dead.

CHAPTER 3

RAGNOR

A book fell onto the table so loudly that people from nearby tables jolted simultaneously at the sudden noise.

Ragnor stared at the book, then at the person who'd dropped it so carelessly, who now took the seat across from him. "Is that what I think it is?"

Eliza Wains, one of the very few Ragnor called a *friend*, pushed her long hair behind her shoulder and trained her single eye on him. "It took some time, but I found it," she said, grinning cockily.

This was quite the achievement. This book had only three printed editions in existence, and finding—not to mention acquiring—just one copy was quite the significant feat. "That means it's not online," Ragnor deduced as he took hold of the book and pulled it to his lap.

"Nope," Eliza said. "Not even in the darkest of corners of the dark web does this book exist."

Meaning Eliza's skills had been growing. That was the only explanation as to how she managed to lay her fingers on this rare find. "What would you like as payment? Money or information?"

She perked up. "This time, I'll settle for money, Rayne."

He had a feeling her request was related to how she acquired the book, but he didn't ask. "Consider it done."

"Good," she said. "Now look at the last page. That's the only one you can read, anyway."

Right. The book was written in a language Ragnor didn't understand. He flicked through the pages until he reached the last instead of simply opening to the final page. It showed a large family tree and words printed in tiny English letters.

He took a sip of his beer and looked at the bottom. "It has no record beyond the fifteenth century, I see."

"The first-century generations are also missing," Eliza promptly said.

"Not very comprehensive," Ragnor murmured and closed the book, looking back up to Eliza. "But it will definitely be helpful."

Eliza didn't reply, simply studied him. Then, she suddenly asked, "Are you okay?"

That was a good question, Ragnor thought. It'd been over a week since the Auction, and he hadn't done anything out of the ordinary. He worked, started making new Imprinting appointments, signed several trade contracts with other Leagues, and had his usual Friday-night drinks with Magnus, his senior Lieutenant and friend.

And yet he wasn't okay. Not really.

"There are too many loose ends," he now said, staring at the book. "I don't feel comfortable not knowing who I had in my very own League for months."

It wasn't a lie, but Ragnor believed there was more to it. Much more than he was willing to admit even to himself.

Eliza gave him a loaded look before she ordered a beer and said, "I think I know what your actual problem is."

He leaned back. "I didn't ask for your opinion, Wains."

She rolled her eye, and the effect was just as strong as if she hadn't been wearing the eye patch. "You have it regardless," she said and sipped her beer before leaning forward. "You like her far more than you think, and the fact you sold her in the Auction is eating you up inside."

There was no question who *her* was, but he was not having this conversation. "Eliza—"

"Let's recall what happened in the Auction." She cut him off with her eye blazing, the heat of her accusation afire between them. "Aileen Henderson is a descendant of the Children of Kahil. The cult your kind had once upon a time worked hard to wipe off the face of this planet. She's the daughter of a fanatic psychopath who kidnapped, raped, and killed girls so young, it's absolutely sickening. On top of that all, she attempted to summon the Morrow Gods at the Auction." She paused, her face tight with anger. "Do you know what would've happened if the Morrow Gods actually answered her call?"

Ragnor knew. But still he said quietly, coolly, "The Morrow Gods are dead. They've been dead for centuries."

"And what if they aren't?" Eliza pushed. "Are you willing to take that chance?"

Ragnor's anger rose. "But they are, Eliza," he said in a strained, gravelly voice. "I've seen to that myself."

She shook her head, completely unaffected by Ragnor's show of anger. "You refuse to see the point I'm trying to make here," she said, and now she looked exasperated. "The Children of Kahil are your—our—enemies. More so than any other being on this damned earth. They might not have the powers of the Morrow Gods, but their existence is just as dangerous. You yourself taught me about the Massacre of Euphorrey!"

Ragnor's expression refused to soften. Instead, he became even more determined to convince Eliza about how wrong she was concerning his feelings for Aileen. Even if he had managed to successfully compartmentalize his emotions for this long since the Auction, her insistence now brought anger and frustration to the surface in a way that made him uncomfortable.

"But right after that massacre, the Malachi came and wiped them out. That's why Aileen can't possibly be a true Child of Kahil," Ragnor growled, losing his calm. "She might be a distant descendant, but to actually be a Child of Kahil, one needs not just to have the real Kahilian powers, but to follow the Tefat, and even though I can't read the Tefat, I know what's written in there." He felt his eyes glow as he fisted his hands over the ancient book. "There is simply no way she's ever done any of the Three Commandments."

Ragnor could still remember that day, a long time ago, when he spoke to one of the last Children of Kahil. That terrible man had told him about the contents of the Tefat and about the horrible Commandments. "Thou shalt find pleasure in the agony of the feeble. Thou shalt seal thy allegiance with a pact written in the blood of kin. Thou shalt be the harbinger of discord, for the Gods thrive in the turbulence of the suffering."

To execute the Commandments, one had to part with their very soul in exchange for absolute devotion. There was simply no way that Aileen could've done all that in the name of the Morrow Gods to resurrect them and bring absolute chaos to the world.

A little voice whispered in his ear, murmuring, *Though that may explain how she recovered from the Imprint so quickly to begin with . . .*

Eliza slapped the table in loosely contained anger, jerking him out of his disturbing thoughts. "Just how well do you think you know Aileen Henderson, Ragnor?"

"Enough to know that she's not a religious fanatic like her father," he snarled back.

She stared at him for a long moment before she let out a sigh. "You've got it bad, Rayne. Really, really bad." She gave him a pitying look he did not appreciate. "But what does it matter anyway? She's Atalon's now."

He looked away, grinding his teeth.

Silence stretched between them, and Ragnor didn't bother breaking it. Because deep inside him, as much as he hated to admit it, he knew Eliza was right.

If there was one thing he'd learned from that Auction, it's that he hardly knew Aileen Henderson at all.

After Eliza left, the remaining guests exited the pub. The bartender, Moses, came over to him and said, "My Lord, my shift is over . . ."

"You can leave for the night," Ragnor told him, checking the time on his pocket watch. "I'll lock up the place."

Relieved, Moses bid him good night and left. Once the door closed behind him, Ragnor said, "You can come out now."

Out of thin air, a man appeared. He was tall and muscular, with curly jet-black hair and light-brown skin. He wore a pair of faded jeans and a black shirt, and if it weren't for the fact he had a pair of large, feathery, silver wings coming out of his shoulder blades, he would've looked like a regular human.

Though there were his eyes, too, of course. They were like a jungle, full of green, with slivers of red and orange intertwined. No human, or vampire, had eyes like his. Even among his kind, those eyes were unique.

And despite their colorfulness, they were the coldest, most emotionless eyes Ragnor had ever seen.

"Luceras," Ragnor greeted him quietly. "It's been a while."

Luceras turned the chair Eliza had vacated and sat down, leaning his arms against the chair's back. "She was here" were his first words, said in a deceptively melodious baritone voice.

Ragnor couldn't help himself. "She was," he confirmed. "She's also staying in the city for a while. In my town house, in fact."

The jungle-eyed man gave him a look that would've made anyone else shrivel. "I know."

Of course he did. Luceras's sense of smell was better than even a vampire Lord's, and especially when it came to Eliza Wains. "Maybe it's time for you to hash things out with her," Ragnor suggested in a drawl. "Don't you think it's been long enough?"

Unfortunately, Luceras did not rise to the bait. "You called me here for a reason, Deveran."

Ragnor's lips curled down at the derogatory term. "Yes," he said, refusing to acknowledge the insult. "I would like to ask for a favor."

Luceras's eyes narrowed. "My favors do not come cheap."

That much Ragnor knew. "I'm willing to pay in whichever form you'd prefer," he said, knowing the last thing Luceras was after was money.

That seemed to satisfy him. "Then what's the favor?"

Ragnor looked at him. "I need you to go to Vermont," he said slowly, "and find out if there's any abnormal shift in the ether."

The memories of Vegas came rushing into his mind. Those *creatures* that kidnapped Aileen and held her hostage. Their elation at capturing a vampire for their sinister needs. It had been since then that Ragnor had looked for them, for their hideout.

No one laid a finger on what was his and got away with it.

He tensed at that last thought and refocused on the man before him.

If Luceras was surprised at his request, he didn't show it. "Anything specific I need to watch out for?"

"No," Ragnor replied, despite wishing he could request that of him too. But as he'd once told Eliza, Ragnor did not consider Luceras a friend. He hardly considered him an acquaintance. Their relationship, if it could even be called that, was something far too convoluted to be labeled. Still, as long as he paid the right price, Ragnor knew Luceras could be trusted, if only to a certain extent.

And this was worth the price. Because if what he suspected was true, and Vermont was home to a certain type of being, then he had to know. He needed to protect his League, after all.

He was definitely not out to protect *her*.

No matter how much his conscience begged to differ.

CHAPTER 4
AILEEN

Zion was one of Atalon's Lieutenants. He had close-cropped dark hair, deep-brown skin, and a pair of startlingly bright amber eyes. Tall, at six feet, and slender yet with broad, swimmer-like shoulders, he could've easily been a model in a different life, what with how he held himself, all aloof and stoic.

Sitting in front of him in his office, I felt a foreboding sense of danger. Unlike my previous boss, Lon, the kitchen manager at the Rayne League whose combustive emotions were written all over his sweaty face, Zion was a blank slate. I couldn't get a read on him no matter how hard I tried.

And for the past ten minutes, I'd been trying my best, shifting anxiously in my seat as Zion read through my first-ever written compare and contrast essay.

A couple of hours ago, when I'd first walked in the office, Zion had greeted me with a blank face and told me to take a seat. Right after, and without too much preamble, he handed me two printed pictures of different portraits made by the same artist and told me to write an essay about them.

For the first few minutes, I stared at the portraits until I sweated buckets, trying to find what to write about. But the two pictures seemed almost identical in terms of technique and coloring.

In the end, I forced myself to lift the pen and scribbled down nonsense about whatever I could think of, like stating that a paint mark on the first portrait must be a way to show the tears of the artist in contrast to the other or that the second portrait's shades were darker as if to reflect the artist's state of mind.

It took me over an hour to finish, and when Zion took the paper and began reading, I turned into a bundle of nerves. The last time I'd written an essay was back in high school, before I dropped out. To say I wasn't confident about my writing skills was an understatement.

"Who is the artist?"

I whipped my head up and stared at Zion. He stared back, amber eyes swirling, and I gulped. "B. Hightower," I replied quietly, referring to the scribbled signature at the bottom right of each portrait.

Zion's face remained stoic as he asked, "Have you seen other paintings by this artist?"

Was that a trick question? "No," I responded carefully, not taking my eyes off the Lieutenant.

His face didn't change, but his voice sounded a touch colder than before when he said, "Then you shouldn't assume what the artist felt based on two very similar portraits."

After grabbing a chair, Zion took a seat next to me and put my paper on the desk. "When writing a compare and contrast essay about an artist you're not familiar with, do not resort to assuming their emotions, but try to focus on the mechanics of the paintings."

I tensed when he gestured toward the paper with his chin. "For a first attempt, it's not too bad."

Surprised, I turned to look at him. "What?"

"You heard me," he said, and was it my imagination, or did his face soften a bit? "You're perceptive, and it seems like you can capture details well. The only thing you lack is better understanding of terminology."

Then . . . it wasn't bad? I felt my cheeks warming, and I lowered my gaze and turned away from him, not wanting him to see how much his compliment meant to me. It reminded me of that time at the greenhouse back at the Rayne League, when Ragnor saw my sketches and said I had talent . . .

A yawning abyss of pain opened at my chest at the sudden thought, and I curled my hands into fists. "I thought I was supposed to be a museum guide assistant," I said, trying to distract myself from remembering painful things. "How does writing papers come into this?"

"To be a museum guide assistant for the Atalonian, you need to have a depth of understanding that common folk do not have," Zion said quietly, and I focused on his voice to distract myself. "Writing papers is more for you to get familiar with the Atalonian artwork and practice verbalizing the appeal of these works so that when you start working as a full-time guide, you will be professional enough to not just broaden the viewers' horizons but sell certain works to potential buyers. It will take you a few months, but you'll get there. For the time being, focus on these essays." He paused suddenly and gave me a long look. "At least until the annual gala event occurs, that is."

I nodded jerkily, trying not to think of how he said I'd be ready in *a few months*. It was driving home the fact that I was really here, at the Atalon League. That I had a new job now. That I was no longer at the Rayne League, no longer a mere kitchen assistant.

And the pain was so unbearable that focusing on the rest of Zion's lecture became a feat of sheer willpower.

Purple sky greeted me when I opened my eyes.

At first, I simply accepted what I was seeing. But then I remembered that I shouldn't be able to see the sky, since I was in the Atalon League's underground compound. I sat up quickly, and when I saw where I was, my heartbeat quickened, and cold perspiration collected on my skin.

For a moment, I thought I was hallucinating. In the days after I started my job at the Atalonian, I'd been so mentally tired from viewing a bunch of artwork until my eyes bled and writing compare and contrast essays until I wished I could use a thesaurus to find other words for *marvelous* that when I returned to my room in the evening, I would pass out into a dreamless slumber.

But now, I was in a distinctly familiar field. Wilting grass spread across the plain, brushing against my bare hands, and there didn't seem to be an end to this field in sight.

It was the same field from the Auction. The one I'd been transported to, where I'd held the dying bird in my arms.

But why was I here now, in my dream?

I looked around me, and when I turned around, I froze.

It seemed I wasn't alone.

Before me stood a petite woman I'd never seen before. She had curly dark-blonde hair braided down her back and a large scar running from her sealed-shut left eye down to her collarbone. Her other eye was brown and open, trained on me.

With her short build and somewhat smooth face (but for the scar), she could pass as a teenager rather than the adult I suspected she was. The real question here was, Was she a figment of my imagination?

"Aileen Henderson in the flesh," she said suddenly, her voice raspier and lower than I would've expected. "It's nice to finally meet you."

Tense, I folded my arms and asked, "And who might you be?"

She stepped toward me. "I'm Eliza," she said simply, "though who I am doesn't matter. What matters here is who—or rather *what*—you are."

An ominous feeling crawled into the pit of my stomach. "I don't think I follow."

Pausing mere inches away, Eliza raised her hands and pressed her fingers against my temples. "You have some interesting power within you," she said almost casually, as if she was speaking about the weather. "I could feel it the moment you appeared, but this proves it."

I swatted her hands away and stepped back, grimacing. What did she just do? Did she somehow realize I had a time-stopping power? But that wasn't possible . . .

Or was it? I knew nothing about my powers, after all. I had tried using my newfound ability in the past few weeks, but no matter how much I tried wishing time would stop, nothing happened, and I got only a headache for my trouble.

But how could this woman know?

"I can see the wheels turning in your head," she told me with a lopsided grin. "How about we sit and talk for a bit?"

She sat down and patted the spot next to her. Hesitantly and still very much on guard, I took a seat beside her.

"First of all," she said once I sat down, "pray tell, where the hell are we?"

I didn't expect her question, because, to be frank, I hadn't thought about it before. "I have no clue," I replied with a frown. "Isn't this a dream or something?"

Her single eye widened, and she suddenly laughed. "A dream? I highly doubt that." She put her hands behind her and leaned back, smirking. "You might be asleep, but this is no dream, Aileen." She looked ahead, a thoughtful expression taking over her face. "Right now, we're in the space within your mind."

All I could do was stare at her speechlessly.

She glanced at me and smiled when she saw my raised eyebrow. "I see they don't teach you about the changes made to your soul in your newcomer vampire course." She sighed. "Well, I'm not going to get into the whole science of it, but the gist of it is, the moment you received the Imprint, your soul, your very mind, irrevocably changed. This plateau"—she gestured toward the field—"is the shape your soul and mind took after the change."

While what she said was far more outlandish than everything I'd learned about being a vampire, I somehow understood. "So every vampire's mind is depicted like a field?"

She shook her head. "No, it's the first time I've seen a mind like yours. Normally, the mind becomes a chamber of sorts, for all of us—humans, vampires, and other supernatural beings—have a limit to how far and wide our minds and souls can stretch. But here there is this false feeling of limitlessness. Intriguing," she murmured, turning to appraise me once more. "Very intriguing."

I was at a loss now. Other supernatural beings? Limits? What the hell was she talking about?

"Anyway," she said and jumped onto her feet, "show me your powers."

Suspicion crawled into my head. "Why do you think I have powers?"

She gave me an exasperated look. "Lying won't help your case," she said, offering me her hand. "Now get up, and let's see what you've got."

I ignored her hand and stood up on my own. "Why should I trust you?" I asked her directly. Because by now, I fully understood that Eliza was a real person. How she ended up in my mind, so to speak, was a question for another day. Right now, I needed to understand what the hell she wanted with me.

As she turned to me, Eliza's face grew serious. "As things stand, I'm debating whether to kill you or let you live."

How considerate. "That doesn't help your case."

"On the contrary," she said. "I could've lied to you and said I'm here to help you with no ulterior motives, but I'm choosing to give it to you flat out. You are dangerous"—her eyes narrowed—"and I would rather have you be on the right side than falling to the wrong one."

Smiling bitterly, I folded my arms. "You seem very confident about being able to kill me."

She gave me a pitying look that made my hair stand on end. "I hope, for both your sake and mine, that you never find out."

I was about to give her a biting retort when she clapped her hands and said, "Now let's start with homework: take out a book called *A Sacred Past* from the library of the League you're currently in, and start practicing according to the instructions on page five thirty-two. I'll visit you again in a few weeks to check on your progress."

Her words made a different question jump to my mind. "Are you a Sacred vampire, then? Which League do you belong to?"

Eliza smiled, and I realized she was beginning to vanish. In fact, the entire field was growing darker, opaque, as if someone were pulling the shutters down.

But just before the field, the sky, and Eliza disappeared, I heard her whisper, "Study hard, Aileen, and I might feel like keeping your secret."

The clock came to a stop.

With shallow breaths and cool sweat dripping from my face to the cold red-tinted marble floor, I stared at my battered wristwatch, which I'd placed on top of the dresser in my bedroom.

I'd finally done it.

It'd taken two days since Eliza appeared in my dream, or my mind, for me to check out the book she'd told me about. In those two days, I'd been going back and forth between whether to ignore the stranger who appeared in my dreams or to at least test the book out. Eventually, curiosity won, and I went to the Athenaeum, the Atalon League's library, and threw caution to the wind.

And now, after studying this one page incessantly, I'd finally managed to see the results of my hard work.

Time had stopped.

Eliza's words were not empty after all.

My face breaking into a smile, I slowly climbed to my feet and began counting the seconds in my head. I reached only five, though, when the pain began.

Release! I thought determinedly, eyes on the watch, and the moment the clock hands began to move, the pain was gone.

Taking a deep breath, I lay down on my bed and closed my eyes, listening to my rapid heartbeat. I could hold on for only five seconds, but it was better than nothing.

Once I felt my heart returning to its regular pace, I rolled to my side and grabbed the book, *A Sacred Past*. Apparently, it was the first volume in a comprehensive trilogy detailing the accounts of all known Sacred vampires through the ages to date.

It went into quite the minute details too.

For instance, the page I was on read:

> As the second Sacred, Tiglath had the privilege of learning from his maker, Menes. Menes, who had observed his long-gone Lord and the first Sacred practicing the principles of what was then believed to be the "Physics of Light," thus passed his knowledge to Tiglath. In the ancient vampiric texts, it is said that Menes had Tiglath practice the three conditions, which are as follows:
>
> 1. "Šaĝ"—the act of emptying one's mind and launching it into the void.
> 2. "Là-ga"—the act of sharpening the void into pure, undiluted focus.
> 3. "Šu"—the act of pulling one's will to the forefront of their mind.
>
> Once these three conditions are met, as long as the vampire has magic, it will present itself and lead them accordingly. Such was the case with Tiglath; once he perfected the three conditions, he described the experience in his personal journal as follows:

> It was an unintelligible voice in my head. I understood its intentions; it wished me to act. To bring forth the storm inside my heart and conjure it into reality. It is a compulsion that's not meant to be rejected, and I let it enfold me and lead me to my long-craved goal. [p. 1098, "The Fangs of Assyria"]

> When asked about the accuracy of Tiglath's description, my friend, who helped immensely with the creation of this book, advised me that it was a personal experience for each Sacred. Not every Sacred would feel the same way as another when it comes to the conjuration of magic. In Tiglath's case, he heard a voice. In my friend's case, it was close to a physical sensation that guided him. Another Sacred might even smell the intent, or taste the knowledge, or perhaps even visualize what needs to be done.

> So long as the three conditions above are met, in one way or another, the Sacred will know what to do.

This was the page Eliza told me to read, saying that it would help me utilize my powers. While it was definitely helpful—I could finally stop time, even if only for five seconds!—it also made no sense.

I was a Common, and over the course of my few-minutes-long Auction performance, I'd suddenly gained some sort of magic.

But becoming a Sacred only a few months after being given the Imprint was insane. In the end of the book, there was a list of all known Sacreds all over the world to date, Atalon and Ragnor included. All of them gained magic after hundreds of years. Renaldi, too, the youngest Lord in the States (only ten years into his Lordhood), developed his magic after two hundred years, which was considered the fastest out of all known Sacreds.

So how come someone like me gained magic? And to stop time, no less?

Ragnor would've known, a voice whispered in my ear. *If you only put your ego aside, you could ask him.*

I cut that voice off just then, heart racing. I would rather die ten times over than approach Ragnor of my volition after what he did to me.

My chest tightened. Once upon a time, *what he did to me* referred to giving me the Imprint without my consent. Now, it was about throwing me away. How low I had stooped when I had chosen to have an affair with the man who took away my freedom.

Despite it all, it was impossible to stop my mind from betraying me with thoughts about how it had been between us. Ragnor's warm hands caressing the sides of my body, his thumbs softly gliding down my abdomen, then lower . . .

With a jolt at the sudden intrusive thought, I slammed the book shut and went to the bathroom, ready to take a cold shower to give me a good wake-up call, when I caught sight of my reflection in the mirror. At first, I thought my eyes were betraying me, but when I leaned forward, I saw that it was real.

My hair, which I'd dyed only a few days ago, was as fair as sand, when just two hours ago, it was still chestnut brown.

I'd been dyeing my hair regularly once every six months since I was ten years old, and even then, it was always the roots, since they grew in my natural hair color. Never before had the dye worn out of my entire head of hair, and never so quickly that it required I go to the hair salon so frequently.

In one of the vampire-anatomy classes back in the Comprehensive Newcomer Three-Month Course, Abe, my former teacher, taught us about the ways our biology differed from humans'. For instance, we didn't excrete bodily waste through urine or feces. Instead, the food and liquid we consumed was generated into metaphysical energy called Lifeblood. That meant we never had to go to the toilet, but we did need to eat three meals a day and drink blood instead of water—since our blood helped the generating process, it needed to be refilled on a constant basis.

Our hair cells, however, worked exactly the same as humans'. The cortical cells, keratin, and melanin remained the same and could be manipulated by chemical means, meaning that if I wanted to permanently straighten my wavy curls, I could do it just as well as any human, and the same went for the hair pigment—dyeing the hair held steady just as much as with humans, especially since my hair was naturally blonde, meaning it was far easier to darken than if I was a brunette going blonde.

I wasn't stupid. I knew that this was somehow related to me developing the time-stopping magic in the Auction, since this strange phenomenon had been happening since then only. But no matter how much I read about Sacreds, especially in *A Sacred Past*, I read nothing about hair dye wearing off. Perhaps no Sacred had ever dyed their hair before?

Whatever the reason, it was obviously related to my magic. Perhaps I should ask Eliza about it.

Though trusting a mysterious woman who suddenly began to appear in my dreams didn't feel like the best course of action.

I was again in the field under the purple sky, but this time, it seemed different.

Gone was the wilted grass, and instead there was a bed of healthy green grass intertwined with wildflowers of all colors. The vividness of the flowers made me feel a tad bit dizzy, as if it was all surreal.

Was it the space in my mind again, the one Eliza had talked about? But something about it not only looked different but *felt* different too . . .

I began walking, my bare feet brushing against the sleek grass. As I walked, I could see in the distance a silhouette of what I thought was a man. The person was too large to be Eliza.

As if they knew something I didn't, my feet picked up the pace until I was running through the field, watching as the figure became larger, more coherent, and when the man turned around and I found neon-blue eyes looking back at me, desperation I didn't know I still had in me propelled me forward as I tried to reach him—

A hole opened in the ground, and I fell through. Before I even had the time to scream, my vision shifted, and my feet touched solid ground. I looked around and saw a familiar room waiting, one that shared an eerie resemblance to Ragnor's office back at his League. Only, in this office, greenery covered the walls, and wilting flowers, seemingly imported from the dead field, dangled from the ceiling.

My heart booming in my ears, I reached for the office door and pushed it open. Inside the office, the neon-blue-eyed man turned around to stare at me.

And suddenly, I couldn't contain it anymore. "Don't leave me," I breathed out, feeling wetness welling in my eyes. I reached out to him, and to my utter relief, my hands landed on his hard chest. "Please," I murmured, standing on my tiptoes to kiss his neck. "Please stay . . ."

He was immovable as my lips pressed upward, toward his. I curled my arms around his torso and smashed my breasts against him, desperately needing to become one with him.

"Take me," I whispered against his ears. "Take me, Ragnor. I'm yours, after all—"

"Are you?"

His words made me jump, and I dislodged myself from his body as if it was on fire. I stared at his face, confused and hurt. "Yes," I said pleadingly. "Yes, Ragnor, I am—"

"Then why?" He cut me off, eyes blazing, and suddenly it seemed like he was yards away and not just a few steps in front of me. "Why did you never tell me you're a monster?"

I froze, fear climbing up my spine. "That's . . . I . . . Ragnor, I—"

"You're a monster," he said flatly, his voice so cold I jolted as if he'd slapped me. "I don't need monsters."

He turned around and disappeared into smoke that suddenly filled the space. I gasped, tried to grab at the smoke, feeling as if everything I'd built was crumbling under my feet—

My eyes flung open, tears sliding down to my pillow.

I'd been doing everything I could not to think about Ragnor. I'd been busy with my work and secret time-stopping practices. I'd been spending every bit of free time I had with either Eleanor or Isora or both, helping myself to enough social time to not think about unnecessary things.

The days went by so smoothly that I thought I'd succeeded. With every week that passed, I felt like I could make it. That the future wasn't so bleak anymore.

But then night came, and I found myself right back at square one.

I thought it was easier to get used to my new League. I thought I was doing well. More than *well*; I thought I was doing tremendously, wonderfully great.

And yet it seemed it was all for naught.

Ragnor still reigned over a large piece of my heart.

I missed him. Terribly.

But I hated him terribly too.

Ragnor digging his fangs into my throat.

Ragnor kissing me and tearing my clothes off.

Me begging Ragnor not to sell me to another Lord in the Auction.

Him giving me hope that he might still buy me out.

The Auction host exclaiming, "Sold for one hundred and twenty thousand dollars to Lord Atalon!"

Burying my face in my hands, I sucked in a deep shivery breath and told myself, "You're moving on. You'll show him what he lost. None of it is your fault. It's all his."

I repeated this unshakable truth a few more times until the tears dried and my heart stopped breaking.

And yet Ragnor remained lodged in my head, stubborn as ever and refusing to leave.

Would I be able to have a day when I no longer thought of Ragnor Rayne and didn't feel like I was falling into a dark, endless abyss?

CHAPTER 5

AILEEN

In the middle of the wide white wall hung an oil painting on canvas. It depicted a river in the middle of a desert during sunset, with a large silhouette of a bird flying over it, as if it was heading over to the sun. The colors—a mix of reds, oranges, yellow, and light blue—made the painting seem as though it was on fire, vivid and brilliant.

The painting was heartbreakingly beautiful.

I glanced at the bottom of the canvas, where the initials OA were scribbled. I already knew what those initials stood for—Orion Atalon, the vampire Lord of the Atalon League.

All paintings in this aisle were his, and each and every one of them was a masterpiece. Hung on the plain white walls, they needed no special frames or extra ornaments; the paintings told an entire story within the realm of shapes and colors.

And this painting before me, titled *Bird of the Nile*, was probably the best of this collection. It was beyond beautiful; it was undeniably perfect in every sense.

After taking out my notebook, I wrote my findings from the painting. The concept was modern, but it was painted so realistically it was closer to a picture than a painting. It reminded me of Rembrandt's style, especially his piece *The Three Trees* from the seventeenth century. But the colors were far more poignant, meshed in a way unlike anything I'd seen before.

Atalon was beyond a genius. It almost felt like his pieces were the embodiment of art itself.

Since this piece was the last in the aisle, it was about time I went to report to Zion, the Atalon League Lieutenant and also the Atalonian Museum manager and master guide—and my boss. But I didn't feel like I'd had enough of Atalon's works. It felt like I could learn more, be sucked into them, if I just stared at them for a few more minutes.

But I wasn't an artistic genius myself. My knowledge of art and its history was limited. Even if I spent days and nights sitting in this aisle, I would still be unable to scratch the surface of everything these paintings hid within them.

With a heavy sigh, I sneaked one last glance at the *Bird of the Nile* before I reluctantly left.

The Atalonian Museum was a large, seemingly never-ending building that took over the space of four blocks in downtown Rochester. During my first week as an assistant guide, I'd gotten lost more than once, even though I had a map, and I was by no means directionally challenged. Even now, after spending every single day in the museum during the past month since I'd started this job, I still found it hard to navigate, though no longer impossibly so.

The museum's architecture was a collection of crooks and nooks, spiraling aisles, and confusing, intertwined floors—all for the sake of displaying the artwork at their best and according to specific requests by the artists. I was currently in one of those odd, in-between-floors kind of corridors, which I felt was heading down, though it looked as straight as usual, the tilting too gradual to visually notice—especially with the mind-boggling wall paintings that made me realize I was actually going up.

By the time I reached the corridor's end—which was at the ground floor, while I'd come in from Atalon's collection aisle on the fifth floor—I had the already familiar headache. Massaging my temples, I headed toward the elevator and then stopped in my tracks.

Atalon leaned against the wall and gave me a smile and a wave. "Good evening, Aileen," he said, black eyes watching me. "Have you had dinner yet?"

Cautiously, I approached him and replied, "Not yet."

"Then let's have dinner together," he said and pressed the elevator button.

Silence spread through the air as we descended to the underground compound, and I couldn't help but feel nervous. I hadn't seen Atalon since that first day after the Auction—he was a Lord, after all, and quite busy too—so I couldn't help but be confused as to why he sought me out now.

Was it normal for him to have dinner with his bottom-feeder League members from time to time?

Back at the Rayne League, Ragnor had never done so. He'd drawn a clear line between himself and others. He'd made sure that everyone knew who was in charge. That's why he'd wanted his relationship with me to be discreet, so as to not hurt his position or whatever.

Bitterness filled me at the thought. How stupid I'd been, thinking that Ragnor wanted me for more than just being his dirty little secret.

The elevator's ping snapped me out of those dark thoughts as the doors opened, revealing the corridor leading to the cafeteria. "Ladies first," Atalon now said, gesturing for me to go ahead.

After stepping out, we headed to the cafeteria. The moment we walked through the doors, however, I realized something was up.

It was the peak time for dinner, and the cafeteria was crowded and loud with chatter. When Atalon and I walked in, multiple heads turned in our direction as if they had planned it beforehand. Silence spread across the room as Atalon led me to a table for two right smack in the middle of the cafeteria, and when we sat down, murmurs broke out among the diners.

"Who is she?"

"Why is she with our Lord?"

"Has he found a new lover?"

The prickles of their stares made me belatedly realize the table we had settled in was unlike others. It was the only table set for dinner, with a small candle and prepared plates and cutlery on top of a dark-red tablecloth.

It seemed Atalon had prepared it ahead of time. But why make it all romantic?

Clearing my face of the discomfort I felt, I was about to speak when Atalon, staring at me with a wicked grin that made my discomfort grow, suddenly clapped his hands twice. As if he'd teleported, a man wearing kitchen-server clothes appeared. "Good evening, my Lord," he said with a respectful nod. "What would you like to order?"

"For starters, bring us a 1996 cabernet sauvignon," Atalon replied smoothly, "and prepare a menu for me and Miss Henderson here."

The server bowed. "At once, my Lord," he said before he disappeared as though his ass was on fire.

Ignoring the new wave of murmurs from the nearby diners who'd just learned of my identity, I turned to glare at Atalon. "What's all this about, my Lord?"

He leaned forward with his grin still intact and a calculating look in his pitch-black eyes. "It's special treatment," he said smugly.

"I gathered that much," I grated out, "but why?"

He chuckled. "Would you buy it if I said there's no reason behind it?"

"I doubt you do anything without a reason, my Lord," I bit out, feeling more anxious now. I really didn't want his attention. Not in this way.

I wasn't an idiot. I understood Atalon was attracted to me. But I refused to get mixed up with any Lord ever again. I refused to be used and tossed to the side at the first opportunity.

Not when Ragnor kept appearing in my dreams every night.

Before my mood could dampen further, the server returned with two glasses of wine and put them in front of us along with a single piece of paper, which he handed to Atalon.

Once Atalon dismissed the server with a wave, he returned his gaze to me and raised his glass. "To your successful future in my League," he said formally, but a playful smile flirted with his lips.

Swallowing my suspicions, I clinked my glass with his and sipped the wine, trying not to wince at its bitterness. It seemed it was mixed with O negative, which tended to bring a bitter aftertaste to drinks. It wasn't my cup of tea, to say the least.

Afterward, Atalon did a peculiar thing again. He summoned the server again with a clap of his hands and curtly ordered, "Salade Niçoise for starters, duck confit for me, and bouchée à la reine for Miss Henderson."

I was too stunned to speak outright until the server had already disappeared. "Did you just order for me?"

Either he didn't hear the outrage in my voice or he didn't care, because he winked and said, "Worry not, Aileen. I assure you it's extremely delicious."

That wasn't the point! I wanted to argue, but something told me that I shouldn't. Mood officially soured, I grumbled, "Next time, I would like to order for myself." Because I did not need this kind of seventeenth-century chivalry, if it could even be called that.

He perked up. "Does that mean you would like to have dinner with me again?"

After gritting my teeth, I forced my voice to be polite as I said, "It's a figure of speech."

"We'll see about that," he retorted quickly and smiled. "Now, Aileen, please tell me. How have my League and your new job been treating you so far?"

My indignance rose at our former conversation, but I pushed it down. Yelling at Atalon that I had enough agency to decide things for myself—be it food or going out with him again—didn't feel like the right thing to do, so I switched gears and moved on, swallowing my tongue. "It's been good," I replied. "Zion is a good boss, and the League members seem nice."

It was a bit of a stretch, but I didn't feel like getting into it with him.

"I'm very happy to hear that," Atalon said, sounding sincere. "I want you to thrive here, and I believe you'll feel safe under my protection."

I froze. "I wasn't aware there were dangers in the League."

He gave me a knowing grin that made my stomach somersault. "I've heard of what happened to you in Vegas during your field trip a couple months back," he said, practically dropping a verbal bomb. "I heard you were kidnapped."

Shock rooted me to the seat, so much so that I barely noticed when the server returned with our orders. If I'd had an appetite, it was now completely gone. "How do you know about that?" I asked, voice demanding. Because other than those kidnappers and Ragnor, no one should've known.

Or maybe Ragnor told someone? Told him?

But why would he do this? Ragnor wasn't the sharing type, especially when a noob under his watch tried to escape.

"I have my ways," Atalon replied mysteriously. "But that's not the point. I can assure you that in my care, nothing of the like would ever come to pass."

He dug into his food then while I just stared into space, trying to make sense of things.

Could he have been in league with my kidnappers?

I remembered my kidnapping like it was yesterday. The men who took me seemed to be extremely antivampire. After Ragnor rescued me, he informed me that he knew who they were but told me nothing beyond that.

If Ragnor knew who they were, then Atalon could possibly know too.

"Please eat," Atalon said, snapping me out of my thoughts. "I assure you it doesn't bite."

I looked down at my dish for the first time and tried my hardest not to scrunch my nose. It was some sort of puffy pastry filled with a creamy mixture of chicken, mushrooms, and béchamel sauce. It did not look appetizing to me, mainly because I couldn't stand béchamel sauce.

But since I didn't want to cause a fuss under Atalon's expectant eyes, I forced myself to bite into it and murmured dryly, "So good."

As if he didn't hear the sarcasm, Atalon gave me a grin and continued eating his much more appetizing meal.

For the rest of the meal, neither of us spoke. When Atalon suggested we order a dessert, I said I was stuffed, when the truth was I had simply lost my appetite altogether.

Once we were done, Atalon insisted on accompanying me on the walk back to my room. I was reluctant since I didn't want any more rumors going around about us, but eventually I just let it go. I was tired from a full day of work and dinner with him.

When we reached the door of my suite, Atalon paused in front of me and said, "You make a good dinner companion, Aileen. I enjoyed our time together."

The smile I offered him was strained, fake even. I didn't want him to ask me out again, and I most certainly didn't want him to think he was getting a good night kiss. "Glad to be of service. Good night, my Lord—"

He was suddenly right in front of me, his face mere inches away, his hands grabbing mine. "I've waited until you've acclimated to the League before making my move," he said quietly, eyes on mine. "But the truth is, Aileen, I've had my eyes on you ever since we met during your field trip."

My muscles tensed. "I . . ."

"Shush," he said, putting his finger over my lips. "I don't expect a response from you right away. I'm well aware that your heart lies elsewhere. But I have every intention of changing that; so be ready, Aileen."

He moved forward, pressing his lips against my cheek. "I'm going to do everything in my power to make you mine."

Before I could think of a response other than to simply gawk at him, Atalon turned around and left.

Neon-blue eyes stared straight into my soul as a hard chest pasted itself against mine. Hands slid down the backs of my thighs, spreading my legs wide. Lips pressed against my own, making my heartbeat quicken and my legs automatically wrap around his torso.

Just when I was about to kiss him back, trying to wriggle closer to him, to have his cock rub against my aching pussy, he suddenly leaned back and rose to his feet, leaving my skin burning with desire and need, yearning for his touch.

He stared down at me, grimaced, and then turned around as if to leave.

But he couldn't leave me like that! "No," I whispered, climbing clumsily to my feet and trying to go after him, but it seemed like he was getting farther and farther away. "No, don't leave me—"

I woke up with a start. Perspiration covered my skin, wetting my pajamas, and my thighs were squeezing together, as if to try to stop the overflow of moisture in my pussy.

Release. I need release.

But the release I needed, the release I longed for, would not be able to be reached with my own fingers. I needed *him*. I needed *Ragnor*.

And yet he wasn't here.

So all I could do was bite my lip and grab the sheets, trying to ride the wave of need and desire that made me feel more alone than ever.

CHAPTER 6

AILEEN

Purple sky greeted me again, and this time, I knew where I was and what to expect.

Climbing to my feet, I saw the one-eyed woman, Eliza, walking toward me with a satisfied smile on her face. "I can feel you've been practicing," she told me as a way of greeting.

"I have," I responded, which was the truth. I'd been reading more than just that single page of *A Sacred Past* to make more sense of my newfound powers, and reading about how other Sacreds throughout the centuries cultivated their magic was quite helpful. However—"I can only use my magic for about five seconds, tops."

Eliza cocked her head. "And what is the nature of your magic, again?"

I gave her a Cheshire cat smile. "The book said Sacreds never reveal these things as a self-preservation method."

She did not seem impressed with my response. "If you tell me, I can better help you, you know," she said dryly.

Feeling a sense of tart viciousness after my dinner with Atalon, I folded my arms and countered, "Would you tell me why you're helping me, then?"

Her single eye packed quite the glare. "Touché," she murmured almost ominously.

The truth was, I had no idea who Eliza actually was or why she was helping me, and it seemed she wasn't about to reveal any of this. The same went for my magic; I refused to tell her that I could stop time. Everything in me rebelled against revealing it to her—or anyone else, for that matter.

Which was fine by me. She could have her secrets, and I would be keeping mine too.

"All right, then," she said, putting her hands together. "Let's discuss meditation."

The word made me feel put out at once. "I'm really not into this type of thing, Eliza."

She shrugged. "Then start getting into it if you want to use your magic for more than five seconds."

Pacing across the wilted grass, she gave me a meaningful look. "Mental fortitude is the key to mastering your Sacred ability," she explained, "and meditation is the best way to achieve it."

I grimaced and asked, "Isn't there another way?" I was not the spiritual type. I'd never been, despite what I'd done in my childhood. Meditation was more than simply an alien concept to me; it was inconceivable.

Eliza smirked. "Sit down and close your eyes."

Glaring at her, I debated whether I should do as she said. I never did well with authority, and Eliza's commanding voice made my ire rise.

Seeming to realize that, she sighed. "Please sit down and close your eyes, Aileen."

Scowling, I forced myself to do as told.

"Good," she said, and I heard her moving closer. "Now empty your mind—"

"Don't feed me this bullshit." I cut her off, annoyed. "What does it even mean to empty your mind? It's not like I can just turn off my thoughts."

"Let your mind roam, then," she said. "Think about everything and nothing, for all I care. You just need to make sure you are calm and relaxed, so refrain from any intrusive thoughts."

Pursing my lips, I attempted to "let my mind roam." What it meant was that, in the silence that followed Eliza's latest statement, my mind seemed to make a beeline to one topic only.

Ragnor looking at me with midnight blue eyes filled with heat as he pressed me against the wall, lips crashing against mine.

Ragnor licking my throat before penetrating my skin with his sharpened fangs.

Ragnor's cock pushing into me with force, making me see stars.

I snapped my eyes open and glared at Eliza. "It's not working," I growled.

She stared at me silently. "What did you think about?"

Having no urge to tell her, I folded my arms and replied, "That this whole thing is useless."

"No, it is not," she said in a clipped tone. "This is your homework for next time; work on clearing your mind."

My jaw ticked. I really hated the idea of taking orders from anyone, especially from someone I couldn't trust, and yet my intuition told me it was for my own good, and not just for the sake of developing my powers.

It seemed that no amount of distraction could get Ragnor Rayne out of my head, and I needed to stop thinking about him.

"Have you written me a compare and contrast essay?" Zion, my boss, said curtly as a way of greeting when I stepped into the Atalonian Museum manager's office the next morning.

I gave him a short nod. "I did. Here." I handed him a sheet of paper.

As Zion read through what was on the sheet, leaning against his office chair, I took a seat in the chair on the other side of his large mahogany desk. Waiting nervously for him to finish reading—I was not confident in my writing skills—I studied the office as I'd done many times before.

Unlike Atalon's office, which was full of art, Zion's was entirely lacking. The walls were a shade of maple with nothing on them but for a stuffed reindeer head that gave me the willies.

"Good job." Zion's voice brought my eyes back to him. He stared at me and nodded. "I think you're ready for the next step."

Relieved, I said, "Thank you, Lieutenant."

"There is something else I would like to talk about before we start the second phase of your training," he said, folding his arms. "The annual Atalonian gala event is set to happen next month."

Vaguely, I remembered him mentioning something about it before.

"Guests from all over the States will be in attendance," he continued. "Humans and vampires alike. There will be an official briefing about it later on, but I just wanted to let you know so you work extra hard until then." His face grew even more serious, which I hadn't thought was possible. "It's your chance to prove yourself not just to our Lord but to the rest of the Atalon League members."

Even if he hadn't said it, I knew it to be an opportunity. It was a chance to raise my status in the League.

But my mind was not on that. "When you say vampires will be in attendance, do you know from which Leagues?"

If he found my question odd, Zion didn't show it. "The guest list hasn't been finalized yet," he said curtly. "But a few Lords have already confirmed their attendance."

My heart sank as I reluctantly asked, "Is Lord Rayne one of them?"

Zion's eyes landed on mine, and I had the odd feeling that he could see right through me. "Yes."

Fan-fucking-tastic.

When I unlocked the suite's door after a long, tedious day at work, I saw my two suitemates were sitting in front of the TV screen, watching what looked like a romantic comedy movie.

After Zion put me through mental drills just to become a freaking museum guide assistant, my head was going in circles about the fact I was going to see Ragnor sooner rather than later.

And watching a romantic comedy would not help my foul mood.

Isora paused the movie and waved at me. "Aileen! Come join us!"

"It's a really good movie," Eleanor chimed in. "Promise."

The last thing I wanted was to watch a movie, let alone a rom-com, so I gave both of them a smile I hoped wasn't too strained and said, "Thanks, but I'm gonna hit the hay."

Their faces comically fell together. "You always refuse to join us for movie nights," Isora grumbled.

I untied my sneakers. "I can't help that I'm busy."

Eleanor rolled her pretty brown eyes. "We're all busy, Aileen, but you need to let loose a bit, you nerd."

High strung as I was, I doubted I was good company. But Eleanor and Isora looked at me with such pleading eyes I felt it was beyond me to refuse again. "Fine," I grumbled and stomped toward them, then plopped myself on the sofa between the two. "Just no romance, okay?"

"No problem," Isora said perkily while Eleanor murmured something that sounded suspiciously like *party pooper*.

I shot the latter a look. "That's my one condition. Deal with it."

Eleanor stuck her tongue out before we settled on an action-comedy movie that had no romance in it.

Or so I'd thought. Apparently, even an insignificant subplot of the hero's flirting with the pretty and shallow damsel in distress was enough to put me in distress.

When an abrupt sex scene came on screen—a far too revealing scene, too, for a supposedly R-rated movie—I found myself looking away. Isora and Eleanor, however, provided commentary that didn't let me ignore the scene in peace.

"Damn! Why did they censor his dick?" Eleanor protested. "His ass is fine, but it's not enough!"

Isora snorted. "Yeah, that's one hell of a double standard, considering you could almost see her crotch."

Eleanor murmured in agreement before she suddenly asked, "Do you think they have sex for real when filming these scenes?"

"I highly doubt it," Isora replied. "But some part of me wishes they did. It would make all the moaning sound less fake."

A chuckle escaped me at that last remark. Isora and I locked eyes right after, and we both grinned and looked away when Eleanor began defending the movie for doing a good enough job to make her think the moans were real.

It was such a mundane thing to do, chatter about a B movie with friends, that for a moment, I almost felt like I was in a different universe. Surely we weren't vampires finding our feet in a new League. How could we be so normal, then?

That feeling didn't last long, however, and when the movie ended and Eleanor went to sleep first, telling us she was going to open our Lord's secretarial office for the first time since she was appointed there, reality came back with a vengeance.

Right. I wasn't with Skye and Cassidy, back in my tiny apartment. I wasn't working in a grocery store and barely scraping by. I was no longer free.

And if Ragnor had agreed to keep me with him, perhaps I wouldn't have minded losing my freedom, if I got him in return.

But that was not the case.

"Aileen?"

I jumped and turned around to look at Isora. I realized then that I was standing in the living room, too lost in thought to move.

Isora stepped toward me hesitantly. "Are you all right?"

She must've been worried about how I'd stared into space like that. "Yeah, I was just thinking about the movie," I said airily, giving her a breezy smile I hoped didn't look as fake as it felt. "Don't worry about it."

"I saw you looking away, you know," she said quietly, ignoring what I'd just said. "At the sex scene. You seemed in pain."

My first instinct was to fold my arms, as if it would defend me against whatever this was, but when I looked at her pretty face and saw she was genuinely concerned, I voted against it. "It's nothing much," I said quietly. "Just . . . it reminded me of what we talked about before."

She gave me a long silent look before she grabbed my shoulders, a wicked grin spreading over her face. "I have the perfect idea for how to take your mind off everything."

I frowned at her. "What are you talking about?"

She smiled like the cat that got the cream. "What do you think about breathing some fresh air?"

My eyes widened. "You don't mean . . ."

"Oh, but I do." She chuckled almost evilly. "Put on your shoes, Aileen. We're going out."

CHAPTER 7
RAGNOR

Two grown men sat in front of him, looking like shameful three-year-olds. And that made Ragnor feel like he was getting far too old for this job.

"When I gave you the Imprint," he said now, pacing around the two crestfallen newbies, "I did so knowing that, at twenty-five years of age, you should be mature enough to acclimate to this new life."

The two did not raise their heads. Good. "The waiting list is long and full of potentially special individuals. Not everyone gets to be on it, and not everyone gets to be given the Imprint."

He paused before one of the two. "Both of you have been on the list for five years, during which my team and I conducted a thorough background check and extensive interviews to make sure you two are fit to become vampires." He couldn't help the disgust dripping from his voice. "You two have an impeccable record. Both of you went to Ivy League schools and graduated summa cum laude. Both of you come from good families. Your records are clean, your peers and family had nothing bad to say about either of you, and your personalities showed good-naturedness that is rare with young men in this day and age." He paused. "Allegedly."

The man he stood before, Jerome Foster, started trembling. His friend and accomplice, Denny Kurtz, was perspiring so much Ragnor's nose itched at the stench. He never liked the smell of fear; it was acerbic and foul. And yet, in cases such as this, when fear was not just required but necessary, it could smell absolutely euphoric.

Jerome and Denny needed to be scared. They needed to feel like they had no way out of this. Because they didn't. He refused to let criminals stay in his League.

"There are certain options for trash like you two," he said now. "None of them are good. Disciplinary actions won't cut it for the likes of you. Even the League System Agreement can't protect you in this case. Thus, your options are limited."

He crouched before Jerome, whose trembling increased until the chair he was sitting on started to crack. "This is the first and last opportunity for you to speak, Foster. So tell me, in your own words, what you think happened last night."

Jerome dared raise his eyes, but when he saw the glow in Ragnor's, he immediately looked away. "It–it was c-c-c-consensual," he stuttered. "I–I s-s-swear."

Ragnor grabbed his hair and pulled his head back harshly. Jerome squeaked. "Lying won't do you any good, Foster."

This time, the one who responded was Denny. "She was flirting with us!" he yelled. "She kept on making moves on both of us, and then she invited us to her room and . . . and—"

"And she told you loud and clear to stop." Ragnor cut him off, his disgust for the two making him release Jerome's hair so hard his neck made a satisfying popping sound. "She could've begged you for sex for all I care, but the moment she told you to stop, you should have fucking stopped."

Neither of them replied. Which was what Ragnor wanted. Because there was no good answer they could give him now. "I can be pretty lenient when it comes to newbies," he said, "but rape, among other things, is where I draw the line."

He straightened and walked to his desk phone. Pressing the intercom, he told his secretary, "Bring him in."

"At once, my Lord," his secretary replied, and a moment later, his office door opened, and Magnus, his senior Lieutenant, entered. His face was contorted in rage, his eyes full of wrath he couldn't wait to unleash.

"Take them to the cellars," Ragnor told his Lieutenant.

With a vicious glint in his eyes, Magnus grabbed the two men and dragged them out of the office.

Now that this was dealt with, Ragnor left his office and took the escalator to the infirmary. Usually, the infirmary didn't see a lot of action—vampires healed much quicker than humans, after all. But some wounds ran deeper than skin, and for that reason, the infirmary was still in place.

There was only one occupied bed in the infirmary when he entered, and it was closed with a veil for privacy. The nurse in charge, Eva, approached him before he could go there. "She needs more time, my Lord," Eva now said, her eyes full of pain. "She's not in her right mind—"

"I would've given her all the time in the world if I could," Ragnor replied, meaning every word, "but given the nature of things, I'm afraid I have to speak to her before this gets out."

Eva grimaced. "Then I'm sitting in," she said, folding her arms. "I'll sign an NDA if that's what it takes. She can't be alone with a man right now, my Lord."

He understood Eva's worry—and accepted it too. "No need for an NDA," he said as he started walking toward the veiled bed. "Just give me your word you'll keep everything you hear to yourself."

She gave him a sharp nod. Ragnor, of course, didn't trust Eva—he hardly trusted anyone nowadays. So it was a good test to see if Eva could earn some of his trust, after almost five years in his League.

Eva now pulled the veil, revealing the bed with the tiny woman lying in it. The woman, one of the youngest he'd ever given the Imprint to, looked so pale and fragile, as if one blow of the wind could snap her bones in half. She was thinner than when he last saw her, and with her absurdly long strawberry blonde hair and large baseball-size blue eyes, she looked closer to a corpse than a living being.

"Hello, Tansy," Ragnor said quietly, taking a seat near her bed. Her eyes were open, staring at the ceiling almost unseeingly. "How are you feeling?"

For a few long moments, Tansy didn't respond. He was willing to wait, though, and minutes later, as if only then the words computed, Tansy finally spoke. "Déjà vu."

Ragnor tensed and glanced at Eva. She seemed just as perplexed as he was. Curling his hands into fists, he returned his gaze to Tansy. "I truly hope that is not the case," he said as gently as he could, but it was hard, what with his emotions riding him at the moment.

She rolled her head toward him slowly and stared at him unblinkingly, her face sealed. "Lord Rayne," she suddenly said, in a voice so airy and dreamlike he started to think that perhaps she thought she was asleep. "It's not the first time, and certainly not the last, when people see me as a tribute."

"My Lord," Eva whispered, "I think it's enough—"

"What do you mean by *tribute*?" he asked, ignoring Eva for now. He recognized the same thing Eva did, but he couldn't just let it be. Because a dark feeling crawled into the pit of his stomach, trying to tell him something he still wasn't sure of.

Tansy smiled eerily. "Doesn't matter now," she murmured, "because I was chosen. They were with me."

Ragnor stilled. "Who was with you?"

Her lids dropped over her eyes as she whispered in a barely audible voice, "The Morrow Gods."

Ragnor had gone over the family tree in the Tefat repeatedly. There were all kinds of names in there but none that could help him.

The only way to solve the mystery was for Aileen Henderson to talk to Tansy Contos herself.

And for the first time since who knew how long, Ragnor admitted that he'd made a mistake.

He should never have let her go. And it wasn't simply about his incessant need to know about her origin, past, and everything in between.

It was because he couldn't rest even for a second not knowing what she was doing at any given moment.

"She's a threat," he now told Eliza as they had their weekly meeting at his League-owned pub.

Eliza stared at him, evidently impatient. "That's what I've been trying to get into this thick skull of yours," she bit out. "So. Are you going to eliminate her?"

His eyes glowed as his entire body tensed with rejection. "No," he gritted out. "She can be an asset, if I have her. But as long as she belongs to another League—to Atalon, of all people—she'll never cease to be a threat."

"So it all comes down to the fact you want her," Eliza said, looking at him with something akin to disgust. "Fucking men and their dangling dicks."

He glared at her. "My personal feelings have nothing to do with it."

"Liar." She shook her head. "Your personal feelings have everything to do with it, but sure, keep telling yourself otherwise, you fool."

"Eliza," he growled warningly.

She threw up her hands in frustration. "Don't use that tone with me!" she snapped. "You know I'm right, so why are you trying so hard to deny it?"

Ragnor's fury rose so quickly and hot, a red haze fell over his eyes. "I'm not denying shit," he grated out. "You're just romanticizing something you shouldn't—"

"You're so fucking full of it." She cut him off angrily, her eye flaring. "You can use all the words in the entire world, but the truth is, you like her. Hell, you more than like her. You have serious feelings toward this woman. Maybe you even love—"

"Shut. Your. Mouth." His growl this time was so loud, the humming buzz of chatter in the entire pub came to an abrupt stop.

The silence was so heavy, a few customers hurried to escape the aftermath of his outburst. But when the chatter resumed, Ragnor's anger transformed to a self-directed rage at losing his cool. Eliza, too, looked at him as if she had never seen him before. And this Ragnor, the one who would dare lose his cool in front of anyone, was indeed someone she had never before seen.

She was the first to break the silence, and when she did, her voice was awfully gentle. "Does it always have to be Yulia?"

An old pain bloomed in his chest at the sound of that name, and he didn't respond. But Eliza, who'd never cowered from him, pushed on. "It's been almost six centuries, Ragnor. Don't you think it's . . . well, that it's time you move on?"

It was never a question of moving on, but Eliza knew too much as it was. She didn't need to know *that* too.

A plain full of beautiful grass spread around him. Flowers of all types and colors bloomed within the grass strands, glinting in the soft light of the setting sun. A cool breeze swept his hair away, blowing at his sweatpants and his naked chest.

Distantly, he wondered where he was, but before he could dwell on that, he saw a figure coming from the other direction. That figure grew closer and closer, until he could finally see her face.

Her beautiful hazel eyes looked at him with so much affection, he was caught off guard. A smile he'd never seen on her face before stretched her pretty lips. Her gray summer dress clung to her curvy, gorgeous figure, contrasting against her smooth olive skin.

But most curious was her hair. It was in its usual high ponytail, sliding in soft waves to the middle of her back, but it wasn't brown, as he knew it to be. Instead, it was the color of pure gold.

"Ragnor!" She called his name and started running toward him. Instinctively, he held out his arms, and she laughed in delight, a sound he'd never heard her utter, and fell into his arms, wrapping her own around his neck. He sucked in a breath, and her sweet cider smell hit him in full, making him bury his head in her neck, needing to take a deep breath, to brand this smell into his skin.

When he wrapped his arms around her, he could feel all his worries melt away. It was as though he'd been parched in the desert for so long, and she was the oasis he didn't know he was looking for. It felt like he'd been roaming around endlessly, and she was his home.

"God, Aileen," he whispered, unable to help himself as his arms tightened around her, needing to meld her body to his. "I need you. I need you so much."

That beautiful laughter left her again, a sound he wished he could hear forever. "I need you too," she whispered before leaning back and facing him. Then her smile slowly disappeared. "But you left me, Ragnor."

He felt as if his chest was split open. "I didn't mean to," he said, cupping her head in his hands. She leaned against them, her eyes closing. "I wanted to take you back. But I was a fool." He leaned his forehead against hers. "I waited too long, and I let you get snatched away before I could do what I really wanted to do. Please," he said, almost shocked that he uttered that word. "Please believe me."

She let out a sad sigh he could feel breaking his heart. "I want to believe you," she whispered, opening those beautiful eyes of hers and staring at him, "but how can I, when you're not here?"

Her words cut him deep. "I . . . ," he started but then stopped. What could he say, when she was absolutely right? He didn't come to her. He kept on stewing on everything by himself, stubbornly indecisive.

She retreated her arms from him and stepped back, but he didn't want to let her go. "Wait," he said, reaching out to her, but she was somehow out of reach now, so far away from him. "Please, Aileen—"

She gave him a smile so sad, Ragnor fell to his knees. "I can't wait, Ragnor," she whispered. "You've made your choice, and I will now make mine."

"No," he growled now, climbing to his feet. "I won't let you—"

But she was gone now, out of his reach, leaving him alone in the beautiful field of grass.

Ragnor woke up with a gasp.

His breaths came out shallow and short. His heart was beating hysterically in his chest. Perspiration covered his face, mixed with something salty that came out of his eyes.

He was crying.

"No," he whispered, pushing away the blanket. He strode to the bathroom and stared at the mirror. He saw the fresh tears sliding over his cheeks, a sight he did not know what to do about.

Because it hadn't happened in more years than he could remember.

And that's when he knew.

He couldn't keep doing this to himself. Pride? Ego? Since when had these things prevented him from going after what he wanted?

Eliza had been right all along. That dream proved it like nothing else ever could.

Because he recognized that field from the dream. He recognized its meaning, which was far deeper than simple dreamscapes could ever be.

And unlike in his dream, he refused to leave Aileen again.

No matter what.

CHAPTER 8
RAGNOR

The cool wind welcomed him when Ragnor threw the terrace doors open and walked out. He came to a stop before the balustrade and leaned his forearm on it, closing his eyes as he breathed in deeply, trying to put his raging mind to rest.

He'd just returned from a meeting with both his Lieutenants—a rare occasion nowadays, what with Ragnor being constantly busy—and he was reminded of his past inadequacy.

Margarita Wallen, his second Lieutenant, was a pain in his ass. Once upon a time, she'd been useful, what with her extremely unique Gift and sharp mind, but in the past decade or so, she had started testing the boundaries he'd set. So far, he'd let it go, if only because she'd earned his trust a long time ago, but the meeting two hours prior told him that the time of letting go was reaching an end.

For the first time since her appointment forty years ago, Margarita had questioned his decisions.

Ragnor allowed only a select few to question him, and Margarita wasn't one of them.

Thus, he left the underground compound of his League and visited his town house to take a breather.

Now, as the silence surrounded him, thoughts he was fighting day and night came rushing in.

Hazel eyes, framed by thick, dark lashes, crashed into his mind. He used to love looking into those expressive eyes as he moved inside her, seeing the pleasure spreading across her as he brought her to climax after climax.

His knuckles turned white as he clutched the balustrade with the aching, unbearable need to hold her again in his arms. To caress her beautiful body, her soft olive skin, and feel her shattering under him.

He yearned to hear her pretty lips taunting him again. Unwilling to bend even an inch for him. He longed to hear her husky voice throwing curses at him as her eyes flared with heat.

He missed her so much, it was as though a limb had been torn off, and he was incapacitated, unable to do a thing as long as she wasn't by his side.

A distant flapping sound made Ragnor's eyes snap open and his muscles tense. He did not expect any company, and yet the flapping noise grew closer until a winged man appeared out of thin air, floating right above the balustrade.

Ragnor straightened himself and stepped back. "Luceras."

The Malachi's jungle eyes were alert as he landed on the terrace floor. "I have news," he said, and there was a sense of urgency in the Malachi's voice that made Ragnor extremely alarmed. There were very few things that could ruffle a Malachi's feathers, and none of them were good.

By nature, they weren't emotional beings. Rather, they were able to remain levelheaded. Stoic. The Malachi doled out justice when needed. They waged war upon the unjust and made sure to win. And when the time came for the Malachi to ask something of Ragnor, he would not be able to refuse them.

"Is it about Vermont?" Ragnor now asked, eyes trained on the Malachi. It had been about a month since he'd asked him for this particular favor.

Luceras's eyes seemed to penetrate Ragnor's. "When was the last time you encountered the Jinn?"

Ragnor grimaced. "You sensed them there, then."

"Answer the question, Deveran." Luceras's voice grew low and threatening as he said the derogatory nickname.

Unfortunately for the Malachi, Ragnor wasn't one to be cowed. "Tell me what you found first. Quid pro quo."

While Luceras's face remained blank, a spark of annoyance appeared in his eyes. "I found strange shifts in the ether south of Montpelier, near a large farmhouse that seemed to have been built in recent years."

It was just as Ragnor suspected. As the Lord of a League that functioned as an information guild for all intents and purposes, Ragnor was mostly in the know when it came to what happened in his part of the world and some other parts too. When he received tips that several vampires—both members of different Leagues and Leagueless—disappeared in the northeastern area of the States, he knew something had to be up with the Jinn. No one but the Jinn would mess with vampires.

He'd asked Luceras to scout Vermont using the Malachi's special capabilities. Ragnor had a few affiliates in other nearby states who didn't report anything was amiss, and he knew for a fact that Maine, the home state of his League, was clear. Vermont was all that was left, and it appeared he was right.

"It's your turn, Deveran," Luceras said now as he gracefully jumped into the air and swiftly sat down on the balustrade.

Ragnor let out a rough sigh. "The last time I encountered the Jinn was a few months ago, in Las Vegas." He could still remember what happened there. Aileen had attempted to run away and was caught by three lesser Jinn, two of whom he'd killed. Thinking about that incident made his chest clench. If he hadn't been there in time . . .

Shaking himself out of these unpleasant thoughts, Ragnor folded his arms. "According to extensive research I'd done after, I found that there weren't any Jinni branches in the Nevada-California area. Those Jinn must've been sent there to snoop around and stumbled upon a golden opportunity when they caught a . . . League member of mine."

Luceras stared at him silently for a few moments before he spoke again. "You can't let the Jinn run rampant, Deveran."

"I know," Ragnor said, irritated. "Send me the exact coordinates. I'll take care of it."

Giving him a curt nod, Luceras jumped again and landed on his feet on the balustrade. "She's here," he suddenly commented.

Ragnor gave him a curious look. "I told you she's staying here."

Luceras's jaw ticked. It was a rare show of emotion from the Malachi that put Ragnor immediately on guard. "How is she doing?" he asked, his voice like gravel.

Cautiously, Ragnor responded, "She's doing well, for a woman on the run."

If he was feeling any sense of guilt, Luceras didn't show it. "Take care of her," he said quietly, and it sounded like an order.

Ragnor gave him a humorless smile. "Eliza can take care of herself."

Without any farewell, Luceras disappeared into thin air, and Ragnor could hear his invisible wings flapping away as the Malachi left.

Once he was gone, Ragnor returned to leaning against the balustrade and pinched the bridge of his nose. He told Luceras he would take care of the Jinn, which he absolutely intended to do, but he had to be careful.

The Jinn weren't creatures to be messed with. Ragnor himself, who was powerful even by Sacred standards, couldn't exactly march into a farmhouse full of Jinn and expect to come out of it without a scratch.

Ragnor thought of Aileen then. The bane of his existence and the light of his darkness alike. He wondered if she was all right. Was she thinking about him? Did she have any lingering feelings for him, despite what he'd done?

He doubted it was the case, but that didn't matter. He would snatch her back from Atalon's clutches whether she wanted him to or not. He'd won her over before, after all, and so he was confident he could win her over again.

And once that was done, he would deal with the Jinn.

Because right now, Aileen was his top priority.

CHAPTER 9
AILEEN

After leaving our suite, Isora and I walked toward the elevator leading to the exit. So far, we hadn't encountered anyone patrolling—security was quite lax in this League—but when we reached the elevator, we realized we needed a handprint.

"Aren't you registered in the system?" Isora asked me in a whisper.

"Only for the elevator leading to the Atalonian," I replied in the same manner. "Though perhaps it can work here too?"

Isora bounced in excitement. "Do it!"

Swallowing hard, I gave the system my handprint. To my surprise and relief, the plate blinked green, and the elevator doors opened. "Our Lord is surprisingly careless," I murmured as we hopped on the car and the doors closed.

"Who cares?" Isora said, grinning from ear to ear. "What's important is, we're on our way out, baby!"

I couldn't help but smile at her enthusiasm.

We reached the empty lobby of the skyscraper that led to the League and walked toward the exit. Once the cold air hit my lungs, I immediately felt better.

"Let's go!" Isora said, grabbing my hand and leading me away from the skyscraper, away from the League, and right into the downtown of Rochester.

We jogged through the streets, and a thrill climbed up my spine. It was exhilarating, doing something I shouldn't and having an accomplice. It was even more exhilarating when we stopped before a fast-food diner, because I couldn't remember the last time I ate a cheeseburger.

Isora and I both inhaled the smell of greasy goods, and our stomachs simultaneously roared. "Let's grab a quick bite," she said, drool dripping from her mouth.

"Agreed," I murmured, and we entered the diner.

Since it was late in the night, maybe even early morning, the place was pretty much empty but for a few odd people who seemed to only be able to afford the food of this humble abode. Isora and I instinctively kept a low profile as we talked between ourselves.

Once we settled at a booth and ordered food, something suddenly occurred to me. "Isora," I whispered once the tired waitress went away, "we don't have any money."

She blanched. "Shit."

The waitress returned with our double cheeseburgers and large fries, gave us a strange look, and left again.

"Well," I said, staring at the food, "eat first, think later."

There were no other words for it. We quite literally devoured the meal. In less than a minute, the entire thing was gone, and both Isora and I had to lean back and force ourselves to keep the food in.

Apparently, eating too much fast food after not eating it for such a long time was bound to upset your stomach.

"I'm going to be sick," Isora said, burping.

"Same," I ground out.

As if we were completely synchronized, we went to the toilet together, occupied the two stalls, and filled the air with the lovely sounds and smell of puke.

In the end, Isora and I did something neither of us was proud of.

We dined and dashed.

After the fiasco in the toilet, instead of going back, we escaped through the rear door. We were both still feeling sick, so we took it easy, knowing that the tired waitress would take some time until she noticed we were gone.

"What do we do now?" Isora asked as we lumbered through the street.

That was a good question. So, thinking out loud, I asked, "Wanna go drinking?"

"And dine and dash again?" Isora laughed. "No thank you. But I do have an idea."

At the guilty look that crawled onto her face, I found myself immediately on guard. "What is it?"

She nibbled her lip. "Well . . . I was thinking we can go on a drive . . . It's been a while since I drove a car, and I kinda miss it."

I looked at her. "But we don't have a car."

She avoided my gaze. "I can get us one . . ."

A smile stretched over my lips. "Damn, Isora," I murmured mirthfully. "I didn't think you had it in you."

She shifted uneasily. "I'm not gonna lie—I wasn't exactly a law-abiding citizen back when I was human." She raised her electric-blue eyes to me. "But I want you to know the truth about me. I'm not the type of woman who hides who she is."

I gave her a reassuring smile. "Isora, my father is a convicted criminal, and yet I still . . ." *care for him. Hate him. Love him.* Unable to finish that sentence, I swallowed hard and hastily continued, "And it's not like my hands are clean either. I'm hardly one to judge."

Her eyes widened. "Really?"

"Really," I grinned. "Now, let's go steal a car."

The next thing we did was find a parking lot. Once there, we found a beautiful Corvette that made Isora drool. "If its owner has enough money to buy this, they'll be able to buy another one," she said as she pulled out a pocketknife.

Silently, I watched as Isora worked. I had no idea how she did it, but she managed to open the driver's side door and disable the alarm before connecting several wires and making the Corvette roar to life.

She looked like she'd done this type of thing many times in the past. But as I told her before, I wasn't the judging type.

For me, this whole thing was thrilling.

Once we were inside the car, Isora revved the engine and drove us out of the parking lot. "I've always wanted to drive a Corvette," she said dreamily as she patted the steering wheel. "It drives so dang smooth . . ."

For the first time, I heard a soft southern twang to her voice. "Where are you from?" I asked her, curious about my new friend.

She smiled widely. "Houston, the Space City," she said wistfully before glancing at me. "What about you?"

"Lewiston in Maine," I replied dryly. "A very boring city in a very boring state."

Isora was quiet for a while as she drove us through the roads of Rochester before she suddenly asked, "What is your dad doing time for?"

I froze. For a split second, I thought, *How the fuck does she know this?* when I suddenly remembered I had blurted it out before. Had I actually told another living being about my father being a criminal of my own volition? What the hell was wrong with me?

Glancing at Isora, whose face was clear of judgment, I realized what was wrong. I'd made a friend. A real friend.

I had known Cassidy, my former friend, for three years, and yet I'd never thought of us as true friends. Our friendship had been quite superficial, even though I'd felt a sense of responsibility for Cassidy, believing her to be too vulnerable for this big, cruel world.

And yet I'd known Isora for just a bit over a month, and I felt the kind of kinship and trust with her I hadn't felt with Cassidy or Logan, my ex, or even Ragnor—though in Ragnor's case, it was for different reasons altogether.

So I found myself talking. Telling her about the atrocities my father committed, leaving out my part because I wasn't ready to talk about it, not now and not ever. But I did talk about the rest. I didn't hide. I told her everything.

Isora listened in silence, and when I was done, she stopped the car on the side of the road and pulled out of her seat to give me a hug.

"Thank you, Aileen," she said quietly, "for trusting me enough to tell me. And I'm sorry you had to go through that."

I hugged her back, feeling a warm and fuzzy feeling I wasn't familiar with spreading inside me. "Thank you for listening, Isora."

She returned to her seat and resumed the drive. "Now I know why I liked you from the moment we met," she suddenly said. "You see, my parents were shit as well."

I knew it was my time to stay silent now, and Isora continued. "It's the classic story of a drunk man beating his wife and daughter. When I was ten, my father was killed in an armed manslaughter, and when my mother learned of our huge pile of debts, she hung herself."

Her voice was nonchalant, but I couldn't help but wince.

"As an orphan, I was supposed to go into the foster system, but my father's friend adopted me instead," she said dryly. "He was just as much of a piece of shit as my dad, but unlike my dad, he didn't beat me. Instead, he had me help him commit certain crimes—stealing cars being one of them."

She sighed. "When I turned eighteen, he started giving me uncomfortable looks, and I knew it was time for me to leave. So I ran away, hooked up with a gang-like group, and used my skills to earn my place as more than simply an available pussy. Long story short, I ended up trying to hustle Renaldi, and he took a liking to me and offered to give me the Imprint."

When she fell silent, I took her free hand and squeezed. "Thank you for confiding in me too."

She grinned. "We are both pretty messed up, aren't we?"

I snorted. "You can say that again."

"Anyway," Isora said conversationally, "I think we are being followed."

Tensing at the sudden change of subject, I turned around to see a black Jeep driving right behind us. "How long?"

"The last few minutes," she replied. "I intentionally made a few turns, but the Jeep hasn't laid off us."

I squinted, trying to see through the windows, but it seemed that, in addition to the lights blinding me, the glass was tinted, and I couldn't see who was inside. "Head toward the highway," I told her, heart quickening in my chest. "We can try and lose them there."

Isora nodded, and soon enough, we got on the highway leading to the surrounding suburbs. The Jeep stuck to us like glue, and unfortunately, there weren't enough cars around us to mask our escape. "Shit," Isora murmured. "What should we do?"

Trying to think, I asked, "Will the Jeep be able to catch up to us if you drive at full speed?" It was a Corvette, after all, and the Jeep was simply a Jeep.

Isora grinned. "Let's check it out, shall we?"

As she pushed the gas, the Corvette was thrown forward at such speed, my heart almost lurched out of my chest. Turning around, I looked for the Jeep and saw it slowly fading away.

"Is it working?" Isora asked, grinning madly, with exhilaration burning in her eyes.

"Yes," I said, giggling uncontrollably. "Keep on going!"

She laughed as she somehow made the car drive even faster. "It drives like a fucking dream!" she yelled in excitement. "I'm so fucking happy, Aileen!"

Her laughter was contagious, and I found myself laughing as well. "It's—" I started, when my gaze landed on the road, and I realized we were heading full speed toward a curve, which Isora didn't seem aware of. She kept on going straight instead of pulling the wheel to the left.

"Isora!" I screamed. "There's a curve—"

"Fuck!" Isora screamed back as she kicked the brakes violently, and for a moment, I thought it was too late. We were on a highway bridge with nothing but trees underneath, and if we weren't going to make it, our car would fly right off the bridge and straight into the forest—

With a jolt, the Corvette screeched to a stop right before the railing.

We were silent for a few minutes as both of us tried to catch our breath and calm ourselves. Then, I growled, "You almost Thelma and Louised us!"

"Not true," she argued, leaning her head against the back of the seat. "In the movie, the car flew over a canyon, not a forest."

"Same fucking thing." I snorted. "Anyway, we need to get moving—"

The Jeep that had been following us came to a stop right before us, blocking our path. Isora and I froze as we saw three men leaving the Jeep, one of them especially familiar.

Atalon stood right in front of us with his arms folded and black eyes glowering at our car.

Isora and I looked at each other, and she said, "We're screwed, aren't we?"

CHAPTER 10

AILEEN

Atalon was absolutely furious as he paced back and forth in his office while Isora and I sat like scolded schoolkids before him. Zion and Malik, the twin Lieutenants, stood at the door, keeping guard, as if we would attempt running away again. Zion seemed to think so, though, judging by the look of utter suspicion he had when he stared at Isora and me, but Malik, who might've been Zion's identical twin, seemed far more empathetic to our situation. I'd never interacted with Malik before, but after he gave me an encouraging smile earlier when we were ushered into Atalon's office, I thought him to be far more approachable and amicable than his stern-faced brother.

"Foolish," Atalon said now, eyes glowing in a way that made them look like shadows. "Reckless. Insolent. What were you two thinking?"

Isora and I said nothing, since it was obviously a rhetorical question.

"I'm extremely disappointed in both of you," Atalon hissed, coming to a stop in front of us, staring down at our frightened faces with rage in his eyes. "You broke at least ten rules with the stunt you just pulled. I could expel you from my League if I wanted to, rendering you two Leagueless."

Neither Isora nor I liked the sound of that, I knew, and we exchanged fearful glances.

"Zion, Malik," Atalon said curtly, "escort Isora back to her room. I'll deal with her tomorrow."

"Yes, my Lord," Zion and Malik said as they came toward Isora, who sent me a worried look.

I mouthed to her, *Don't worry*, before she was escorted out of the office, leaving me alone with Atalon.

With a deep sigh, Atalon took a seat on the chair Isora had just vacated and looked at me with eyes no longer emulating eerie shadows. "You've done a really foolish thing, Aileen," he said now, voice no longer curt but rather gentle, almost. "Do you know what kind of dangers are out there?"

I looked at him while remaining quiet. What could I say, really? That I felt suffocated and on edge and needed to breathe in fresh air? Despite my distrust of him, Atalon had been treating me extremely well. Sure, it could have been because he was interested in me, but still. From his perspective, I believed that what I'd done was like poking him in the eye.

So all I could say was "I'm sorry, my Lord."

He gave me a look that was surprisingly sad. "I don't know what I would've done if something had happened to you," he told me, grabbing my hands. "You're important to me, Aileen, and the fact you recklessly put yourself in danger is driving me mad."

I studied his face. He seemed sincere. "What kind of danger do you think would've waited for me out there?" I asked, thinking back to Las Vegas, when I'd been taken by those men when I'd attempted to run away. But back then, I'd acted rashly. This time, I was careful, and besides, I'd been with Isora.

Atalon gave me a serious look. "Have you heard of the Jinn?"

I frowned. "No. What is that?"

He leaned back and looked away, grimacing. "In nature, there is a food chain. Zebras eat grass, and lions eat the zebras. This is the way of this world—and the same goes for the anthropomorphic races." He paused and leveled his gaze on me. "If humans eat animals, and vampires consume humans—albeit only their blood—then who, or rather *what*, eats vampires?"

Since I didn't expect this almost philosophical conversation, I said, "Aren't vampires supposed to be at the top of the food chain?"

Atalon shook his head. "There is no such thing. The food chain is never ending. Infinite. Thus, something must always consume something else, and those who consume us vampires are the Jinn."

A chill trickled down my spine at his foreboding words. "In what manner do these Jinn eat us, then?" I inquired, not really wanting to hear the answer if it was something along the lines of how humans ate animals.

As if he'd read my mind, Atalon gave me a humorless smile. "They feed on our Lifeblood."

I was at a loss. "Isn't Lifeblood the essence that makes us what we are?" I asked, confused. "Then how can they eat it?"

"They don't exactly *eat* the Lifeblood but rather suck it," Atalon replied with a dark look before locking his gaze on mine. "What are the two ways we can be killed?"

An ominous feeling crawled into my gut, and I answered, "Beheading or having our hearts carved out."

"You're only half-correct," Atalon said. "There is a third way, though it's far slower." He paused and gave me a pointed look. "Having our Lifeblood utterly depleted."

His answer irritated me. "They didn't teach us that in the Comprehensive Newcomer Course," I said accusingly.

"Despite its name, the course doesn't cover everything," Atalon said evenly. "And all of us Lords have decided not to teach about this method of killing, if only because it's very easy to find out that vampires can do so to other vampires, not just the Jinn. However," he added when I opened my mouth to speak, "the difference between how vampires and the Jinn empty one's Lifeblood is what matters. You see, vampires can deplete other vampires of their Lifeblood, but if given enough rest, that Lifeblood can be easily replenished with time. If a vampire's Lifeblood is sucked by the Jinn, however, the damage can be far more severe. Meaning, unless the vampire gets fed with another vampire's blood—preferably a Gifted's or a Sacred's blood, for they have a large amount of Lifeblood—they won't be able to recover and eventually will perish."

I looked at him in silence as I processed this information. Many questions ran through my head, but the main one was "Why are you telling me about all this?"

Atalon put his hand on my shoulder, and I tensed. "The Jinn are lurking everywhere," he said quietly. "They can sense us, which is why all vampire Leagues make their bases underground and difficult to find through regular means. But the moment we go aboveground, the Jinn can find us from miles away."

I understood what he was saying. He'd basically said that Isora and I put ourselves in danger when we went out. That the Jinn could've found us. But one thing I wondered—"The Atalonian Museum is aboveground, though," I said, scanning his face. Something about his words struck me as odd. His pitiless black eyes were too careful when he looked at me. Too cold and calculated.

"The Atalonian is full of trained guards," Atalon replied. "Unless they come in a horde—which the Jinn would never do due to certain circumstances—the guards can take care of a few who try to get in."

While what he said sounded logical enough, there was still something amiss about Atalon's words, though I couldn't put my finger on exactly what. And yet, when he spoke about the Jinn and the danger they posed for us, his repulsion was genuine. They were real, and they were a true danger, and perhaps that's all that mattered.

I deflated and looked away. "We won't do it again, my Lord."

He took his hand off my shoulder and leaned back. "I'm glad you understand, Aileen," he said quietly, and when I returned my gaze to him, I saw him give me an almost exasperated smile. "And please, call me Atalon."

Whether it was due to luck or not, Atalon decided not to punish me for my transgression. Isora was a different story, though; she had to not only work in the kitchen but clean the cafeteria as well. For the next week, she left right before sunset and returned well after dawn. I hadn't been able to see her at all.

Guilt gnawed at me in my mind. As a second-timer, Isora was in a grace period, meaning she had three months to prove her worth to her new League and get reevaluated. If she was found to be worthy of becoming a proper member, she could elevate her status to a bottom-ranking Common. But if she was found disposable . . .

Needless to say, our little outing must've put her already precarious hierarchical standing in even more danger. And while we'd both made that choice, I still felt I should've said no when she'd offered to sneak out.

And not just for Isora's sake, but for mine too. What if Isora resented me for Atalon's blatant favoritism? What if she hated me and wanted nothing to do with me?

Those thoughts refused to leave me alone.

"I feel sorry for her," Eleanor told me as we headed toward the League's hair salon at the top floor, right near the boutiques. "And I'm also angry. You should've taken me with you!"

While the story of Isora's and my escapade thankfully didn't spread beyond Atalon's office, I did tell Eleanor, who was our suitemate, about the little adventure. "You would've been in extra trouble," I told her. "You work at our Lord's secretarial office."

She shot me a dirty look. "So what? I'd rather be punished than feel left out."

While Eleanor and I weren't as close as I was with Isora, it wasn't as if I had an abundance of friends. So I felt somewhat bad about not including her. "This is why we're spending our free day together," I said, trying to lighten the mood as we entered the hair salon.

"Which is great and all, but why here of all places?" Eleanor said, glancing at my hair. "Are you planning to cut your hair?"

Before I could respond, the hair-salon manager, Torrence, approached me with a big smile. "Ah, Aileen! Long time no see."

I rolled my eyes at his joke. "I need to dye my hair." I grimaced. "Again."

Torrence's smile turned into a frown as he studied my hair. "I've never seen such a phenomenon before," he informed me. "I mean, we just dyed your hair two weeks ago, and it's already such a light brown? Insanity."

"Just take care of it, please," I said with a sigh.

For the next two hours, Eleanor and I chatted with Torrence while he dyed my hair back to its normal dark-brown hue. I hoped that this time it would hold, because I was sick and tired of visiting the hair salon every other week.

I really had no time or energy to deal with this, and yet I had to.

Once we were done at the hair salon, Eleanor and I went window-shopping at the boutiques before we headed to the cafeteria for lunch.

Because Isora had been working so much, Eleanor and I had settled in with new dining companions for the time being. Our new companions were Fareez and Oz, the other two newcomers Atalon had purchased at the Auction.

Fareez Goshenan was a sexy, scruffy man. He was tall and muscular, with a mop of dark curls on his head, and he had this air of authority about him that immediately drew the eye.

Then there was Oz. He was the oldest-looking vampire I'd met so far, with him being in his thirties when he was given the Imprint by Lady Kalama of the Kaḷama League. Oz was a handsome man, with waist-long ashen hair and quicksilver eyes. He had a tall body that was built like a tank, with tree-trunk-thick, corded arms and long athletic legs.

"Hello there, Fareez," Eleanor now said when the two joined us at the table. "I heard a particular rumor earlier today." He raised a bushy eyebrow in her direction and nodded, his dark eyes quickly running over her outfit.

I frowned. That was news to me. "What rumor?"

"Haven't you heard?" Eleanor looked at me with wide eyes. "Fareez is allegedly dating Demetria, the Gifted!" She whipped her head to Fareez. "Aren't you?"

Fareez leaned back with a smirk. "No comment."

I gave him a long look, but before I could speak, Eleanor jumped in again. "You've got to teach me your ways, master," she grumbled teasingly. "I've had my eyes on this Gifted guy since we arrived here, and he won't even look my way!"

Yet again, this was news to me. "Why didn't you say anything about it?" I asked her, surprised.

Eleanor flushed and looked away, folding her arms. "It's embarrassing," she murmured. "I mean, before I learned you, Fareez, got with Demetria, I didn't think someone like me had a chance. Especially not with a Gifted."

Fareez's cocky posture changed, and he gave Eleanor a seemingly genuine sympathetic look. "I don't think I'm a good example, though," he said quietly, smirk gone.

I glanced at him, frowning. "Why?"

Fareez opened his mouth to say something before he shut it and looked away, his face clear of any expression. After a few moments, he spoke. "I suggest you stay away from the Gifteds, Eleanor."

Eleanor seemed puzzled and fell quiet.

Since I refused to let the conversation turn awkward, I focused on Oz, who was sitting next to me, and asked, "How's work been for you?"

Much like me, Oz got a job at the Atalonian Museum—only unlike me, he worked behind the scenes, at the museum's bookkeeping office. His response, unsurprisingly, was monosyllabic. "Good."

So far, I got the impression Oz wasn't much of a talker.

But I was desperate for conversation that wasn't about gossip and rumors. Something that would take my wandering mind off all my ailments. "I heard there has been a rise of donations in the past few months because of our Lord's decision to showcase new art rather than curating classical pieces."

Oz glanced at me. He didn't respond verbally but nodded to agree with what I'd said before he stared at me for a few long moments. Feeling discomforted, I glanced away and focused on breakfast, my irritation rising. Why did he make every conversation awkward?

For the rest of breakfast, Eleanor managed to change subjects and get a conversation going. But I wasn't entirely into it, since I began hearing murmurs around us from the nearby tables, and it took everything in me to keep a blank face.

"I heard our Lord is utterly infatuated with her."

"He must be, considering she's the first noob he bought from Lord Rayne in decades . . ."

"Someone said she also had a thing going with Lord Rayne . . ."

"Is her pussy made of gold or something?"

"She's not even that pretty . . ."

After my dinner with Atalon, these kinds of rumors began running around the League. I knew Eleanor, Isora, Fareez, and Oz had also heard about these rumors, but they pretended they hadn't and never asked me any questions about the gossip, which I appreciated.

It made me wonder if part of the reason why Ragnor had insisted on keeping our little affair under wraps was because he knew this would be the reaction and he wanted to protect me.

Internally, I snorted, even as an ache made my stomach clench. Right. If he cared about me that much, then he wouldn't have sold me off to begin with.

Deluding myself into thinking he might've cared for me would do me no good.

I suddenly remembered that one moment, back in the Rayne League greenhouse, when Ragnor had shown me, perhaps for the first and only time, his vulnerable side. For that one instance, he'd let his walls down and let me see his devastatingly gorgeous grin.

It had given me butterflies all over. Especially since that was one of the very few moments when Ragnor and I didn't fight.

He threw you away, I reminded myself weakly.

But then why was it so hard to do the same?

CHAPTER 11
RAGNOR

They said trouble sired three.

For Ragnor, the first was when his Ram truck broke down. Not an existence-ending event but enough of a hindrance, considering he'd had an Imprinting appointment to catch earlier today.

Second, Magnus, whom he'd sent on a spy mission in Vermont, wasn't answering his calls. Ragnor had faith in his Lieutenant, knowing full well what he was capable of, but never before had Magnus gone off the radar so completely.

And three, the worst one yet, was his subordinate standing before him, in perfect military resting position, telling him, "No."

"I'm afraid I didn't hear you correctly," Ragnor now said, his eyes boring holes into Maika, the deputy director of the Rayne League Vampire Resources office.

Maika blanched but stood her ground, something Ragnor would've found admirable in any other circumstance, considering Maika rarely had a backbone when it came to him. But this was not one of those circumstances. "It's exactly as you heard, my Lord," she said, and while her voice trembled, she held her chin high. "You cannot join the CNC's field trip this time."

The Comprehensive Newcomer Three-Month Course's field trip was a quarterly occasion, during which each League's newcomers visited other Leagues all across the country at the same time to get to know the Lords and specialization of each League. Normally, the Lords themselves didn't accompany the newbies and their teachers; they were supposed to stay in their respective Leagues and introduce themselves to the visiting newbies.

Be that as it may, Ragnor had already decided to ignore that rule once, and he planned to ignore it yet again. Maika growing a spine overnight wouldn't change that.

"I wasn't asking for permission, Russo." Ragnor's voice was cool, and he gave her the kind of hard stare he usually refrained from where she was concerned, considering their history. "I was merely stating a fact: I am going on this field trip."

"But you can't." Maika shook her head frantically, almost as if she was in a panic. Ragnor narrowed his eyes in suspicion. "Your secretaries cannot adjust your schedule, and with Magnus gone and with Margarita busy with the new Commons' job reassignments, there is no one to fill in!"

Under normal circumstances, he would think Maika was absolutely right. He couldn't trust anyone but his Lieutenants to fill in while he was gone, and even that extended only to Magnus, considering Margarita's erratic personality that made him regret more than once that he'd even appointed her a Lieutenant to begin with.

But now that he'd made up his mind, he refused to wait until a more manageable time could present itself.

Yet Maika needed a logical response. Something that would convince her it was okay for him to leave for a couple of weeks. Normally, he wouldn't bother explaining himself to anyone other than his Lieutenants, but Maika was so fragile that he refused to push her to that brink for her own good.

So he said, "In order to be a good Lord, what does a Lord need to have?"

Maika seemed baffled but replied nonetheless. “Authority, power, and control.”

“Right.” Ragnor nodded. “Now, what would happen if a Lord had only two of the three?”

She frowned. “It depends on which one they lack, I believe.”

“Right again.” Ragnor leaned back and folded his arms. “Now, here are a few examples of certain Lords who lack one of these crucial three. Take Lord Daugherty, for instance. Do you know what he lacks?”

Maika, who’d met all the Lords on different occasions, thought it through. “I believe he lacks authority, my Lord.”

“Correct.” Ragnor gave her a somber gaze. “Daugherty has no authority over his people. He has an inherent inability to rule as a Lord over the vampires in his care who are in need of tight community and guidance. Thus, his many falters throughout the years.”

“That can also be attributed to a lack of control, though,” Maika murmured, frowning.

Ragnor’s eyes sharpened. “You’re starting to understand what I’m getting at. Now, let’s take Lord Bowman. What does he lack, in your opinion?”

“Power,” Maika said at once. “On the Lords’ scale of both magical prowess and charisma, he’s dead last.”

“And what does that say about his authority and control?”

Maika was now fully at attention as she realized what he was trying to tell her. “His authority is still undeniable because he has other attributes supporting that,” she said quietly, “but his control suffers because of that.”

“So,” Ragnor prompted, “what can we conclude?”

“That while authority and power are important,” Maika said, conviction bright in her eyes, “in the end, control is everything.”

Ragnor let those words sink in for a few moments before he spoke again. “What happens to a League if its Lord lacks control?”

"It perishes," Maika answered without pause, her eyes filling with sadness. "I can still remember the Al-Biran League's disaster in Dubai back in the seventies."

Ragnor remembered that too. He'd been fond of Hakim Al-Biran. But the man knew no bounds, and in the end, he'd asked Ragnor to do the one thing for him to save his lost pride, as both a friend and a fellow Lord, and Ragnor obliged and gave him a clean, painless death.

"So you see how it all goes back to one thing," Ragnor said. "Control. Now, Maika." He saw her eyes widen at him using her first name rather than her last. "Do you believe I lack one of the three?"

Maika immediately shook her head. "No, my Lord. Never!"

Ragnor pushed. "You can agree with me that if I lose one of those, especially control, the League would be in danger?"

She gasped, horror in her eyes as she probably imagined such a scenario. She didn't need to reply; Ragnor knew she agreed. And it wasn't because his ego was large; the Rayne League wasn't simply the oldest in the United States, but it was also extremely important to the North American vampiric ecosystem. Ragnor had made sure of that throughout the many years he'd been in charge.

But Maika needed to understand that for the next part to make its necessary impact. "In my current state," Ragnor said quietly, trying to hide his self-directed anger, "I'm a hairbreadth away from losing control."

Maika took a step back. "That's not possible, my Lord," she said, staring at him as if she'd never seen him before. "How can that be possible?"

Her surprise was warranted. Ragnor wasn't the type to air his dirty laundry in public. He kept his private affairs private, for everyone's sake. He hardly ever confided in his Lieutenants—not even Magnus, his oldest friend—and while it suited him just fine, it was also a double-edged sword, because when things went awry in his private life to the extent it affected his job, none would be the wiser if he flipped a switch.

Which was why he'd always made sure to be in control. It was the price he had to pay for keeping his private life off the radar.

But now, for the first time in his existence, he couldn't manifest that control he was so proud of.

Because, ironically, that control had led to his current lack thereof.

And so, he looked at Maika and admitted out loud, perhaps for the first time, "I made a mistake."

Maika didn't know what to do with this information, he knew, seeing as she started to shift from foot to foot uncomfortably. "W-what kind of mistake, my Lord?" she asked hesitantly, shock on her face.

His self-directed anger rose, and he glanced down at the canvas painting he was hiding under his office desk. While he could admit he'd made a mistake, he couldn't tell her the nature of that mistake. He could still hardly believe it himself.

"Let's just say that by going on this trip, I'll be able to rectify that mistake," he said. *Or try to,* he added silently in his head.

Because he knew it wouldn't be simple. It might even be impossible.

But he had to try.

And he had to succeed against all odds.

CHAPTER 12
AILEEN

The moment I set foot inside my bedroom, exhaustion washed over me. The bed looked so tempting, it took everything in me to drag my feet to the washroom for a much-needed shower.

After a quick shower, I sat down on the bed and ignored my moaning muscles willing me to lie down and get a good, deep sleep. I had something to do before that.

Staring at the clock hung on the wall, I let my mind roam.

Like every time I tried to calm or empty my mind, the first thing I thought about was the one thing I always pushed away.

Ragnor.

Despite my aversion to thinking about him at all, I let myself sink into those thoughts. I let myself remember his face, his eyes, his lips. In my head, I could vividly see his beautiful body standing right before me, accompanied by a low growly voice murmuring, "Henderson."

Slowly, I nudged at my mind to pry away from him, gently led it to think about the large plain of wilted grass I'd been seeing often nowadays, and thought of the dream I had of Ragnor before, when I saw him at a distance in this field, calling to me.

If I dreamed of this again, I wondered, what would I do?

I shook my head and grunted. "That went well," I muttered grumpily. It seemed that no matter what I did, I couldn't calm my mind, since it always went back to Ragnor.

Meditation was definitely not for me.

I fell on my back, looking at the ceiling. Now what? If I couldn't empty my mind or focus on anything but Ragnor when I was alone, how would I be able to control my powers?

"Maybe I don't need meditation," I thought out loud. Considering I'd managed to stop time before without using meditation, was it really necessary?

Sitting back up, I determinedly looked at the clock and willed everything to stop.

The clock hands froze.

Heart quickening as pain crawled into my head, I focused on the need to keep the frozen moment intact. In my head I counted out how long I could keep this concentration. But once I reached five seconds, the pain in my head became unbearable.

I could feel the blood trickling from my nostrils but ignored it, forcing myself to hold on, to not let the time get away from my grasp. *You can do it, Aileen. Come on . . .*

A spasm took over my body, shaking me out of my focus, and I crumbled down on the bed, shuddering and sweaty, with an insistent pounding in my temples and a terrible nosebleed.

Time resumed, and as it did, the pain slowly subsided.

And I knew that I couldn't do it like this anymore. Headaches and nosebleeds might not be life threatening, but I had a bad feeling every time they occurred when I tried using my powers.

I had to find an alternative way.

And since the book, *A Sacred Past*, did not cover anything remotely similar to these side effects of using one's powers, there was only one solution.

As if she'd read my mind, Eliza appeared in the field under the purple sky the moment I fell asleep. She was standing only an inch away from me in the wilted grass, peering down at me.

"Let me guess," she said as I was about to speak. "You couldn't meditate to save your life."

Irritated, I glared at her. "If you guessed this would be the case, then why did we go that route?"

Eliza sighed. "Because it's the easiest path to controlling your powers," she said quietly. "But since it's not working, we'll have to do it the hard way."

"Which is?" I prompted.

"Disruption." Eliza gave me a somewhat twisted grin. "Magical powers are all related to one's mental state. When you meditate, you gain easy access to your magical powers, which results in better control but a decreased output. Disruption, on the other hand, is all about intentionally interrupting your mental stability, pulling yourself into chaos, from which you can access your powers. The downside of this method is both its volatility and lack of control."

"So basically, it's about causing myself distress," I surmised darkly. "Sounds healthy."

"I told you meditation was the easier way." Eliza shrugged. "But since you're incapable of that, you'll have to take this path."

I made a face. "The whole point is controlling my powers, right?" I said, folding my arms. "If we go the disruption route, doesn't it mean I won't be able to control my powers at all?"

Eliza gave me a strange look. "You'll be able to control your powers if you learn to harness the chaos."

I snorted. "You make it sound like I'm in *Mortal Kombat*."

She seemed confused. "What's that?"

"Never mind," I murmured, scowling. "So. What should I do?"

"Let's begin practice," she said with a barely discernible smirk. "I hope you don't have any plans for tomorrow, 'cause you're going to be dog tired."

I lay in bed for a while after waking up from my session with Eliza. I was as dog tired as Eliza said I would be, but while I had a couple of more hours to sleep, I chose not to.

Because now that I was getting better at controlling my powers, I couldn't help but think of the new possibilities that opened up for me. Since everything pointed to me being a Sacred, didn't it mean I could choose a new path for myself?

When I was first given the Imprint by Ragnor, I felt like I had no choice but to sign the League System Agreement to become a Leagued vampire because otherwise, I wouldn't have been told anything about what being a vampire entailed in terms of dangers and physical capabilities. But what if I chose to breach the contract and become Leagueless? With my powers and current knowledge, I could, hypothetically, live as a roaming vampire and do whatever I wanted . . .

But that would mean starting from scratch.

Again.

And someone like me, living without a carefully cultivated routine was a no-go. I needed stability. A monster in a cage was better than a rampant one.

What was my other option, then? Telling anyone else about my powers made me feel queasy. I had a disturbing feeling that disclosing my newfound magic to anyone, be it my new Lord or friends, was a recipe for disaster. It was already enough that Eliza knew about it. What would I achieve by having someone else know?

Maybe it will raise your social standing, a voice murmured in my head. But was that what I wanted? What the hell did I want, anyway?

I'd been aimlessly going along with everything thrown my way ever since Atalon bought me, or even before—since the moment I became a vampire. I'd been too busy trying to survive this new world I was thrust into, both mentally and physically, to think about what it was that I wanted to do now.

When I was human, all I wanted was to live an unassuming, simple life of freedom. I wanted my only worries to be about whether I would ever get a raise or if my apartment was clean enough.

Now? The future felt shrouded in mist, making me feel more lost than I'd ever felt.

Ragnor gave you purpose, that annoying voice from before whispered in my mind. *Ragnor made you feel like you're home. Like you have a place to belong. Like you could find yourself, find your purpose in life, if you just stuck close enough . . .*

My bedroom ceiling turned blurry as tears filled my eyes. I hated that voice. I hated that it was most likely right.

Even if I wished with everything in me that it wasn't.

The suite was dark when I walked into the living room in the morning.

Putting on my sneakers, I was about to leave the suite for work—wishing I could've called in sick, I was that tired, but I was unable to do so since vampires didn't get sick—when I heard something breaking. Whipping around, I scanned the living room, trying to decipher where the sound came from, when it echoed again.

It came directly from Isora's room.

Heart drumming in my chest, I strode toward her room and flung the door open. Then I froze.

Isora was sitting on the floor, her long hair a mess, spilling down to the floor. Her eyes were open but unseeing as she stared at a letter she was holding. A glass was shattered on the floor, its contents—blood, it seemed—spilled over the marble.

Alarmed, I stepped into the room. "Isora?"

She raised her eyes to me, and I realized tears were streaming down her face silently. "It's over," she said, voice raspy. "The grace period is over."

"No," I blurted out, shaking my head. My heart was speeding now as my mind struggled to wrap itself around what she just said. "It can't be."

She raised the letter for me to take, which I did. Then I had to read it twice to fully comprehend its contents.

Because it couldn't be.

She still had a month left.

And yet the letter said, "Due to recent circumstances, you're hereby discharged from your position as a kitchen assistant and expelled from the Common suite. You are to report to Genevieve Danvier of the Vampire Resources offices by the end of breakfast for your new position."

I knew what this "new position" was. So did Isora.

Because she'd been an Auction second-timer.

And second-timers' fates were similar to those who weren't bought in the Auction at all—to become slaves.

Every League treated slaves differently. In the Atalon League, second-timers received a three-month grace period, meaning they could try and prove their worth to their new Lord and the other higher-ups and perhaps avoid this fate.

But Isora's grace period was cut short.

She did not convince Atalon or anyone else of her worth, apparently.

And now . . .

Panic made it hard to breathe. "I'll talk to Lord Atalon," I said quietly, falling to my knees next to Isora's shuddering body and wrapping my arms around her. "I won't let them make you a blood slave."

She didn't hug me back, but she leaned her head against my shoulder. "It's no use, Aileen," she whispered. "This is what happens to all second-timers. I knew that when I participated in the Auction again. I was prepared."

It didn't look like she was prepared. "I'm going to make this right," I said, letting her go and rising back up to my feet. "You're not going anywhere."

She gave me a look full of despair that cut through my chest like a knife. "Aileen—"

But I refused to wait to hear her response. I stormed out of the suite and took the escalator leading to the first floor—and to Atalon's office.

Isora was my friend. I didn't have many of those, and once I decided someone was a friend, I would do absolutely everything within my power for them.

I refused to let her be taken away.

CHAPTER 13
AILEEN

Neither Atalon nor his secretaries were in the office. As I took the escalator leading to the cafeteria level, my work phone went off. After pulling it out of the pocket of my black work trousers, I saw it was Zion.

"Briefing for the gala event starts in an hour. Make sure to be there," he said once I answered.

Right. There was a gala event soon. But that didn't matter right now. So I said, "I might not be able to make it because I need to speak to our Lord first. It's urgent."

Zion paused for a short moment before he said, "Our Lord is a busy man, Henderson. He won't be available until late evening. Just like you. You won't get another extensive briefing like this—it's a full-day briefing meant to prepare you for the biggest annual event in the Atalon League—"

"Then how can I reach him?" I cut him off, my panic growing. "It's really urgent, Zion. Please."

He didn't pause this time. "And what can be more urgent than your job?"

My friend. But I couldn't say that. So instead, I said, "Can you at least tell me where our Lord is?"

"As I said, he's busy," Zion responded, sounding impatient now. "So just come over here and—"

Seeing a familiar face in the cafeteria, near the blood dispensers, made me hang up on my boss. "Malik!" I called, running toward Zion's identical twin and Atalon's other Lieutenant.

He turned to me, surprised. "Henderson," he said cautiously, showing far more emotion than his cold brother ever would. "What can I help you with?"

"Please tell me where our Lord is or how I can get in touch with him," I said, trying not to sound too desperate and failing.

Malik frowned. "He's busy right now—"

My fuse snapped. "I understand that he's busy, but I have to talk to him!" I almost yelled. Almost.

Atalon had always made himself available to me. Hell, he even told me to come to him if I had any questions, not to mention he obviously favored me and was interested in me. So why was he suddenly off the grid when, for the first time, I urgently needed him?

Malik stared at me for a few long moments before his face filled with concern. "I can't tell you where our Lord is right now," he said quietly, "but if it's something I can help you with, then by all means, please tell me."

I shook my head and stepped back. "Just tell me this—is he here, in the League?"

Malik sipped his glass of blood as he looked from right to left. Then he gave me a jerky nod and turned his back to me, as if he didn't want to be caught doing something he shouldn't. "Gallery," he murmured so quietly I almost didn't hear him before he walked away.

The Atalon League private gallery was meant for the eyes and appreciation of the League's vampires only. It was a haphazard collection of art pieces that were no longer relevant to the Atalonian's exhibitions and consisted of Atalon League artists only.

I made my way to the sixth floor, where the large doors of the gallery greeted me. Usually, they stayed closed, since visitation times varied, and it seemed like Atalon wasn't fond of having the place be open constantly.

Now, however, the doors were wide open, showing me a glimpse of what was going on inside.

About a dozen vampires roamed around the space, none of them familiar, and all wearing an expression of awe. Distantly, I could relate; the gallery was a magnificent place that didn't cease to amaze me, no matter how many times I visited. The collection remained mostly unchanged, but its impact gave a punch to the gut every time you wandered in.

The most interesting piece in the gallery, the one that always drew me, was the painting of a beautiful redheaded woman running toward what looked like a landscape of paradise incarnate. Even now, the painting, from as far away as I was, still had this distinct feeling of aliveness that made me shudder with its eeriness.

But I couldn't bring myself to care about the painting. Instead, I watched vampires roaming around the room and couldn't help but feel a chill run down my spine. They were far too bright eyed to be veteran vampires.

Slowly, as though I was in a sort of dream or an alternate reality, I stepped into the gallery.

None of the vampires paid me any notice; they were too invested in the artistic exhibits. One of them spoke to a familiar tanned-skinned man with a crooked nose who made me freeze in place as the pieces came together in my head, completing the whole dreadful puzzle.

The man must've felt my gaze, because his eyes slowly turned to me and froze on my face. Shock like I'd never seen on his face before etched in the tight lines near his dark eyes. He then murmured something to the man he was talking to before he turned his back to me and started striding in the opposite direction, as if he was trying to get away from me.

And that snapped me out of my temporary stupor. Abe, my former teacher, was here and actively ignoring me.

What the actual fuck?

My dreamlike feeling was replaced with indignant fury. My mind a jumbled, incoherent mess, I didn't think twice before I strode toward Abe's retreating back, angrily determined to reach him and demand to know why he was ignoring me.

But before I could, a hand grabbed my wrist, wrenching me to a stop. I whipped around and froze once again, my anger coming to a temporary halt.

Atalon was looking at me with an inscrutable expression, neither happy nor angry, and said simply, "Come with me."

Unfreezing, I shook my wrist out of his grip and gritted my teeth. Right. Abe being here and ignoring me made me forget the real reason I was here. But I couldn't shake the feeling that if I went with Atalon now, I would miss my chance to corner Abe, and I refused to let that happen.

But Atalon was my Lord. Defying his orders wasn't recommended.

Taking a deep, slow breath, I looked at him and said carefully, "May I please speak to my friend first?"

Atalon's pitiless eyes didn't leave mine. "I'm afraid that's not possible," he said, and while his tone was somewhat gentle, his eyes were hard. "Now, let me escort you outside."

Before I could argue, he grabbed my wrist again and practically dragged me out of the gallery. Then he closed the gallery doors, which made me raise a brow—why did he bother, when the vampires would soon leave anyway?—and turned to me. "Why aren't you at work?" he asked at once, eyes searching mine.

Renewed anger overcame me. "I was looking for you, actually," I said, trying to calm myself and failing. "Give Isora another month like she deserves." I paused, then added tightly, "Please."

Atalon sighed. "And I suppose that couldn't wait until I was free to talk and you finished work for the day?"

He tried to sound calm, I could tell, but as always, his eyes betrayed him. They looked at me with an almost reddish glint in their pupils, as though he was trying to contain his irritation with me.

"No, it can't," I responded obstinately. I refused to be denied. Not on this.

Obviously, that's not what Atalon wanted to hear, but to my shock, he sighed and gave me an almost defeated smile. "What are you doing to me?" he murmured, stepping closer to me as he raised his hand to tuck a few rogue strands of hair behind my ear. "Why do you make it so difficult for me to tell you no?"

I was not prepared for the conversation's sudden change of direction, but before I could respond, another voice spoke from behind me.

"Aileen."

For the third time, I froze. But this time, unlike the former two, was completely different.

Because this time, the sharp shards of my broken heart rose from the ashes, jagged and bleeding.

This time, all thoughts of Isora or Atalon or Abe fled from me, replaced by such raw emotions, I felt so full and yet so empty at the same time.

Because I recognized that voice.

A voice I hadn't heard in two months.

A voice that didn't speak up when I needed it the most.

A voice I wished with all my heart, mind, and soul I could erase from my memories.

Slowly, I turned around, until my eyes landed on the man who'd built me up only to knock me down and destroy me completely.

And who was looking at me with his torn midnight blues as if no time had passed at all.

Ragnor Rayne.

CHAPTER 14
AILEEN

I stared at Ragnor as he walked toward me, his eyes not leaving my face. I found it hard to look away, too, as though if I did, he would disappear.

It felt as if no time had passed at all, and yet it had. His dark-brown hair was just as wavy as always, curtaining his captivating face full of hard jaw, pretty midnight blue eyes, and faint bristles that hadn't been there before. He wore simple faded jeans, his trademark black combat boots, and a tee, accompanied by his ever-present trench coat. He was just as tall, just as muscular, and just as overwhelmingly charismatic, his entire presence felt oppressive, thickening the air.

My instincts stood at attention, screaming *Danger!* As if I didn't know that already. Only this time, the danger wasn't just physical; it was emotional. Ragnor Rayne was dangerous to me on so many levels, it should've been a fucking crime.

He stopped only a footstep away, his eyes looking into mine as if he could see straight to my soul. And when he spoke, his deep unyielding voice made me involuntarily shudder. "Hello, Aileen."

My heart raced, and I was inwardly hyperventilating. I opened my mouth, as if on instinct, when it suddenly occurred to me, he was casting his invisible spell on me again. He was drawing me in against my better judgment. He could almost make me forget, so fucking easily, everything he'd done to me.

With just two words, he could make me abandon all reason and jump into his arms.

And that didn't just anger me. It infuriated me.

The anger was so palpable, uncontainable, that I had to take a step back. "Don't," I growled, glaring at his heartbreakingly, stupidly gorgeous face.

Before he could speak, I felt heat at my back. A different kind of heat that made me grow still. "Rayne." Atalon's voice came from behind me, where he pressed his chest against my back. "I suggest you return to your newbies. Aileen and I are in the middle of an important, private discussion."

Ragnor's eyes left mine for the first time, and he looked above my head, at Atalon, I assumed. As he did, I took the opportunity to step away from Atalon's uncomfortable closeness, but to my shock—and anger—my current Lord wrapped his arm around my waist and drew me back to him.

I pushed at Atalon's arm, but he refused to move. "Let me go, my Lord," I said through gritted teeth. I didn't want to aggravate him, but at the same time, it wasn't like we were a thing. He shouldn't feel like he had permission to touch me whenever and however he liked.

"As you can see, Rayne," Atalon said quietly but resolutely, "we're quite busy here."

To my surprise, Ragnor's lips twitched. But it wasn't in humor; it was in complete arrogance that I did not expect. "No worries," he said, eyes flicking to me. "Aileen and I can always speak later, considering I'm staying for a few days."

The news made me jolt. Staying for a few days? Why? What the hell was he doing?

It seemed I wasn't the only one surprised. "Rayne, you didn't clear that with me," Atalon said, his voice tight.

Ragnor now grinned, his eyes gleaming as if to say *Gotcha.* I stared at him, mouth agape. Who was this expressive man, and what the fuck did he do to Ragnor? "Keep your calendar open, Orion," he said now, and I felt Atalon tense. "We have a lot to discuss."

Atalon's arm tightened around my waist, making me grind my teeth, as he almost growled, "Rayne—"

"I'll see you soon," Ragnor said, turning around. "Both of you."

When I saw him walking away like he hadn't a care in the world, something inside me snapped.

The fury I felt consumed my mind, and in the mental chaos, I found what I'd been looking for.

STOP!

Everything came to a chilly standstill. Particles of dust froze in the air as the faint noise of chatter from the gallery came to an abrupt stop, replaced by an eerie silence.

After removing Atalon's frozen-in-time arm from around me, I walked toward Ragnor and came around him to see his face.

What I saw made my rage multiply.

He looked pissed off.

How dare he look so pissed off?

Before I could stop myself, I grabbed his face and felt a spark tingling at my fingers. "Why?" I hissed at him, my nails digging into his cheeks. "Why did you throw me away?"

Frozen in time, Ragnor did not respond. But I didn't need him to. It was a rhetorical question, after all.

He simply didn't want me as much as I had wanted him.

But that was all over now.

"I will never throw myself at your feet again," I said against his lips, feeling a headache looming over me. I'd passed the limit I'd had when stopping time, meaning I had to wrap it up now.

I stared at his midnight blue eyes, full of angry determination. "I hate you," I told him. "I really, really hate you."

After taking my hands off him, I walked back to Atalon and, though I really didn't want to, put his arm around my waist again, if only to make it appear as if nothing happened.

Then I released my hold on time, and the wheels of time resumed turning.

Ragnor returned to the gallery, promptly shutting the doors behind him. But even though he was gone, the air was still tense and oppressive, as if his presence lingered behind.

I forcefully pushed Atalon's arm away and stepped out of his hold, then turned to face him. "What the hell was that?" I asked, glaring at his face.

Atalon's pitch-black eyes were on the doors of the gallery. "I was willing to wait," he said, but his voice sounded somewhat strained. "But I refuse to wait a second longer."

He returned his eyes to me, and his determination was clear. "I want you, Aileen," he told me, voice stark with sincerity. His eyes usually betrayed his true feelings, but they seemed genuine as well, making me reel back in shock. "I've liked you since the first time we met, all those months ago, and I still like you now."

His confession, much like everything that happened in the past few minutes, set me on edge. "I . . . ," I started but paused, realizing I was speechless. My emotions were a mess. My head was disheveled. What the hell was happening?

Atalon let out a rough sigh and looked away. "This is not how I wanted this to go," he said quietly. He straightened, his eyes locking with mine in an unbreakable gaze. "Go out with me, Aileen."

I tried not to look so gobsmacked and probably failed. "I . . . I don't know what to say, my Lord—"

"I told you to call me Atalon," he interjected softly, giving me a half smile that made my lips purse. "Just . . . think about it, will you?"

Before I could even give him a reply, he threw the gallery doors open and disappeared inside. But much like with Ragnor, he didn't disappear, and his words kept echoing in my head.

Since vampires couldn't get sick, calling in sick for work wasn't something we could do. But since I felt mentally unwell, I decided to hell with it and texted Zion, I don't feel good, so I won't be coming to work. Please fill me in on the gala briefing at a later date.

Zion's response was a simple Fine.

He was not happy with me—that much was obvious. But I couldn't bring myself to care. I had enough on my plate to bother giving a shit.

I returned to the suite in quite a daze. It felt as though I had just woken up from a vivid fever dream, in which Ragnor appeared out of nowhere, back in my life, and Atalon told me he wanted me and asked me out. None of that seemed real. None of that seemed plausible. It made me wish it was April 1, because this seemed like one cruel joke.

But the moment I was back in my suite and saw Isora's room open, the inside empty, I snapped out of my daze and felt my heart sinking. In all the turmoil of the past hour, I had forgotten about the most important thing.

And now, Isora was gone.

Eleanor, who always had Fridays off, came out of her room when she heard me enter. Her eyes were bloodshot, and she seemed just as defeated as I felt. We might not have been best friends, but both of us liked Isora just the same. "She left earlier to God knows where," Eleanor now said, voice breaking and lips trembling. "I can't believe this is happening."

Neither could I. After two months of being lulled into a false sense of normality, it was as though today had just burst this little bubble I'd built for myself.

I sat down on the sofa and put my head in my hands. I'd promised Isora I would take care of this. That I would try and make sure she would at least have the extra month she deserved to prove herself worthy. And yet instead, I was caught in an uncomfortable power struggle between my former Lord and current one, and I'd let myself be carried away.

Eleanor sat down next to me. "Did I ever tell you the story of Isora and me?" she asked all of a sudden.

Turning to look at her, I saw fresh tears staining her cheeks. "No," I said weakly, defeatedly.

Eleanor gave me a wobbly smile. "Isora was given the Imprint by Renaldi two years ago," she said, "and was bought out by him despite wishing to be anywhere else, like most of Renaldi's female members, me included. But Isora was a special case; she'd known Renaldi from way before she got put on the waiting list. Before Renaldi had even become a vampire Lord."

She looked down, her body shaking. "Renaldi gave Isora preferential treatment most of the time, even more so than he did his Gifted members or Lieutenants. He never added Isora to his harem, never laid a hand on her, and treated her like a queen." She grimaced. "Much to the League members' chagrin."

I could see where this was going, and when Eleanor said, "She was bullied by the harem women in ways you can't even imagine." My suspicions were confirmed.

"When I arrived at the Renaldi League, Isora was appointed as my tutor," Eleanor continued. "She was working as the Renaldi casino hostess, and I was primed to be her assistant. She was guarded with me at first, distrustful of practically everyone, but I beat down her guard and managed to befriend her."

Regret flashed in her eyes. "The other members didn't like that we'd become friends and started ostracizing me as well, even started their bullying tactics on me, too, but I refused to take it." She shook her head, lips trembling. "Since it was my first month at the Renaldi League, I didn't understand the dynamics quite well and made the mistake of informing Renaldi himself about the bullying."

She gave me a pleading look. "I wanted only what was best for Isora and me. I never for the life of me thought that Renaldi would add us both to his harem as a way to stop the bullying."

I still vividly remembered that harem. I remembered how Renaldi treated the women in that harem. It couldn't have been good.

"It might look like Renaldi has the harem for himself, but that's not quite the case. It's a cunning front to what the harem of women are really required to do." She paused, face darkening, before she whispered, "Torture and murder. We may have appeared to be prostitutes to unkeen eyes, while in truth, we were forced to dole out punishments and kill, if need be. Renaldi's smart. Sure, he's a selfish piece of shit, but he leverages his sullied reputation to get ahead. No one would ever suspect him of building an army of killer women right under their noses."

Eleanor was sobbing now. "None of us are killers, Aileen. Not Isora or me, or the others. Do you know what it's like to be told to not just torture both men and women until they're driven to insanity but actually put an end to their life—or, if they were vampires, to their existence—with your own bare hands?"

Unfortunately, I knew. I knew so well what it felt like to be at the mercy of a monster who would do anything to get what he wanted. To be forced to become a monster too. To have to go so far outside myself and become so numb that I could even consider following the order to kill and maim and torture, let alone not even question it.

"Isora couldn't deal with that," Eleanor whispered. "She couldn't deal with having so much blood on her hands, so much so that she begged Renaldi to release her. To become Leagueless. She'd rather die or starve to death and take her chances on the outside than do what he was asking of her."

Isora had once told me anything was better than staying in the Renaldi League, and while I agreed back then, too, I hadn't understood the extent of it until now. Now I fully understood why.

"She's finally free of that hellhole." Eleanor's face was pained. "And now she's going to be a slave. That's just far too cruel, Aileen. So fucking cruel."

Yes, it was cruel. The vampiric society in the first place was cruel. That's why I would never for the life of me understand why people put themselves on the waiting list to begin with. Why did anyone want to be a part of this? Immortality was worth nothing if it meant your existence was shit.

"I'll get her out of this," I said quietly, hands clenched into fists. "I'll find a way, Eleanor."

She laughed bitterly. "As if you can."

But I could try my hardest. Atalon claimed to want me, after all. Perhaps I could use that to my advantage. Perhaps there was a way.

Isora didn't deserve any of that.

And Ragnor's sudden reappearance in my life was not going to deter me from what was truly important.

He'd already thrown me away, after all. He had no right to approach me, speak to me, or even look my way.

I was no longer his. Perhaps I never was.

So, for all I cared, he could go to the hell I would get Isora out of.

CHAPTER 15

AILEEN

I stared at the ceiling of my bedroom, abandoning all hope of sleep. Insomnia, my old friend, had returned with a vengeance after the events of the past day.

After the hellish day I'd just had, it seemed I was bound to be slumberless.

Which wasn't good, considering just before I went to bed, Zion had texted me, telling me to be at the Atalonian early tomorrow morning for a makeup briefing session, the one I missed today because I'd attempted to be a good friend and failed miserably due to my stupid self-centeredness.

Angry with myself, Atalon, Ragnor, and the entire world, really, I pushed back the blanket and went to the living room. I took a bottle of corked AB positive from the mini fridge and was about to indulge myself in some mind-numbing movie when there was a knock on the door.

Frowning, I headed toward the door, feeling confused and on guard. Who the hell could it be in the middle of the night? I doubted Eleanor, who was probably asleep, was expecting anyone, and of course I wasn't either.

Since there was no peephole, I cautiously opened the door and stared.

Ragnor, looking fresh as fucking daisies, gave me a wicked grin that made me blink twice to make sure I wasn't seeing things. "Hello, Aileen. I had a feeling you'd be awake."

The urge to punch something—preferably his face—consumed me, and it took me a few moments to get rid of the red haze. "I'm asleep," I said, glaring at his stupidly pretty eyes. "Go fuck yourself."

I was about to slam the door, but he put his foot inside. "You know I'd rather fuck someone else," he said, and his gaze turned smoldering, his grin widening. "But I'm willing to start with a chat."

Despite my better judgment, long-forgotten heat flared inside me, pooling in my loins. And that just made me madder. "What part of *go fuck yourself* did you not understand, Ragnor?"

He seemed far too amused for my liking. "The part where you think I'm going to go away just like this."

Following that statement, his eyes suddenly dropped to my body and grew even hotter. So hot, in fact, that they glowed neon blue. I realized then that I was in shorts and a tank top with no bra underneath. My legs were exposed. My breasts were as good as.

His eyes flickered back to mine after he so blatantly checked me out, making my skin burn. "Let me in, Aileen," he murmured in a low voice, and I hated that I found it so fucking sexy. "We need to talk."

I folded my arms and used my knee to keep the door as closed as possible with his foot stuck in between. "No, Ragnor, you need to talk," I said quietly through gritted teeth. "I have nothing left to say to you." *Not after everything you put me through.*

His grin disappeared, and Ragnor's face turned serious. Finally, an expression with which I was familiar. His next words, however, could've belonged to a stranger.

"I made a mistake."

I froze. "Say what now?"

Ragnor grimaced. "Let me in, Aileen," he said quietly. "I'll just say my piece, and if you still want me gone, I'll leave."

Narrowing my eyes, I thought it through. Letting him in wasn't an option. I didn't need him in the living room or, worse, my bedroom.

Thoughts of him lying on my bed, giving me a hazy look with his stunning eyes as he pulled me under him, naked and beautiful and so fucking sexy, while he whispered my name against my lips made me shudder in half-fear, half-arousal.

Letting him talk wasn't an option either.

Because I was done talking where Ragnor Rayne was concerned.

"I think it's time you learn a valuable lesson, Ragnor," I said, opening the door. "And that's hearing and understanding the meaning of the word *no*."

Before he could react, I kicked his shin, catching him by surprise as he retreated his foot, and slammed the door shut on his stupidly handsome face.

I turned my back to the door, feeling viciously victorious, if a little out of breath. Ragnor Rayne had no hold on me anymore. Once he threw me away, he lost the legal and personal right to tell me what to do.

He could smolder and grin and act all sexy as much as he wanted, but I wouldn't cave. Because what he'd made me go through would forever be a barrier between us.

Even if my hands tingled, aching to touch him.

Even if my thighs clenched and slick wetness dripped down my crotch.

But none of that mattered. He'd already broken me once.

Breakfast was a dreary affair.

Eleanor, Fareez, Oz, and I ate breakfast together, which had been a common enough occasion ever since Isora had been overworked as punishment for our little outing, but today was different.

Because Isora wasn't just working overtime.

She had completely disappeared.

"She's not in the kitchens," Eleanor said, looking as miserable as I felt.

"I didn't see her anywhere else either," Fareez murmured. "I tried asking if there's a slaves wing somewhere around here, but our League members seem to be tight lipped about the matter."

Eleanor's eyes filled with tears. "I'll talk to our Lord," she whispered. "I have a shift later at his office. I'll catch him and ask him where he sent her. I need to make sure she's all right."

I shared that sentiment and had already cooked a plan last night. I just had to survive the private briefing with Zion first before I went hunting for Atalon myself. The plan was a good one. It would serve more than simply knowing where Isora had gone to.

We were somber for a while, each of us barely touching our food but for Oz, who seemed to act as if nothing had happened. But Oz wasn't the expressive type, so who knew what he really felt.

As if he couldn't take either Eleanor's tears or the loaded silence, Fareez switched subjects. Only the new subject wasn't going to alleviate my mood. "I saw Lord Rayne earlier, eating breakfast with our Lord and the Lieutenants. You know what it's about?"

Wiping her tears, Eleanor smiled gratefully at Fareez. "Yeah, I got a call from our Lord's head secretary—my boss, Gina. She said Lord Rayne would stay here for a week due to urgent business with our Lord."

"Interesting," Oz murmured, surprising us all that he even spoke.

"Yeah, it is," Fareez said contemplatively. "What's even more curious is that our Lord didn't seem too happy about Lord Rayne's presence."

Eleanor sighed. "Well, our Lord is on somewhat amicable terms with Lord Rayne, but only to a certain extent. I doubt he feels comfortable with another Lord roaming around his League for a whole week."

"True," Fareez said. "I'll ask Demetria about it. Maybe she knows something we don't . . ."

The conversation died down after that, and all of us quickly made ourselves scarce to escape the heavy silence and the words none of us wanted to say.

I wasn't in the greatest mood when I reached the Atalonian's study room, and said mood plummeted further when I saw who was present. There was Zion, of course, wearing the same clothes as I did—the guides' attire of black trousers, buttoned white shirt, and black blazer—but he wasn't alone.

Next to him sat Ragnor fucking Rayne.

As if to mimic us, Ragnor wore black jeans and a white tee, along with his go-to combat boots and black trench coat. His hair was pulled into a small ponytail, and he gave me a nod, face serious but eyes glinting triumphantly.

Fury rising inside me, I turned to Zion, whose face was as sour as I felt. "What the hell is he doing here?" I demanded to know.

Zion gave me a warning gaze. "He's a Lord, Henderson," he said quietly, "so mind your manners."

"That's all right, Zion," Ragnor said, eyes not leaving me. "She can speak however she likes."

Zion seemed distraught at that news but pursed his lips and grated out, "Sit down, Henderson, and let's start."

"You haven't answered my question," I insisted, scowling.

This time, Zion's eyes flickered from me to Ragnor and back. They then widened as he seemed to reach some sort of conclusion. "Meaningless matters should be saved for after the briefing. For now, let's get to it. There is a lot to fill you in on."

Unfortunately, I couldn't quite concentrate. Not with Ragnor sitting there, staring at me with those eyes of his, his presence suffocating me as he took all the air in the room.

To his credit, Zion did his best to ignore Ragnor, but even he couldn't quite refrain from glancing in the Lord's direction from time to time, as though, like me, he was trying to understand what Ragnor had to gain from sitting in on this boring briefing session.

Two uncomfortable hours later, Zion was finally done. "The gala is in two weeks," he said. "If you feel like you're not sure about something, do not hesitate to ask." He paused and glanced at Ragnor momentarily before he added tautly, "The gala has no room for mistakes. And since it's going to be your first guidance job, the expectations are much higher for you."

"Understood, sir," I said, feeling Ragnor's eyes boring holes in my face, as they'd been doing the entirety of the session.

Zion gave me a jerky nod and shot one last dirty look to Ragnor before he said, "Dismissed," and practically fled the room.

Now I could openly glare at Ragnor without inhibitions. "Was I not clear last night?" I asked in a barely contained snarl.

He rose to his feet, putting his hands in the pockets of his trench coat. "You were," he said conversationally, "but I don't think I was clear."

I jumped to my feet when he walked toward me, and when he invaded my personal space, stopping only an inch away from me, I refused to step back. I stood my ground. That, of course, made electricity burn through my veins. Folding my arms, I held my chin high and did not avert my gaze from his. "You're here to hound me for whatever fucked-up reason you have," I said darkly. "I think that's clear enough."

He gave me a hard look. "I made a mistake," he said, and hearing him admitting to making a mistake for the second time in less than twelve hours made me freeze. "I was too slow to make another bid, too indecisive, and I lost you."

Talking about the damned Auction was not an option. "What's done is done," I said, trying to ignore the pain filling my chest. "I belong to the Atalon League now, and that's on you. You're just an ex-fling for all I care."

His eye twitched. Good. I didn't want him all composed like this. I wanted him to be angry. Just as angry as I was. I wanted to hurt him. To make him feel some of the pain I did. I wanted to make him regret forcing this talk on me.

"I'm more than that to you," he said in a low voice on the verge of a growl. "You know it, and so do I."

I snorted. "Someone thinks highly of himself."

"This bravado doesn't work on me, Aileen," he said tightly, making me feel a menacing kind of glee. "You should know me better than that."

I did know him, and I knew that this "bravado" was working exactly as it should. "Then get this into that thick head of yours," I said, giving him a humorless smile. "I'm so over you, it's not even funny. I couldn't give a fuck if you feel like you made a mistake." I laughed bitterly as the hole in my chest grew, the pain spreading down to my stomach, making me want to hurl right then and there. "You're out of your mind if you think I'm going to take you back in any way."

I turned around and strode toward the exit. He didn't follow me.

And I wished my relief would've been greater than the agonizing disappointment that threatened to drown me whole.

Atalon's waiting area was empty when I walked inside later that day. The secretaries were nowhere to be found, but I could hear voices from inside his office.

I knocked on the door and waited. The voices inside paused, and then Atalon's voice, curter than usual, snapped, "Come in."

Once I opened the door, I felt like crying. Because Ragnor was there, of fucking course, and he was looking at me with a determined expression that made my pain and anger rise so quickly, I got internal whiplash and my mind short-circuited.

Atalon looked at Ragnor coldly before turning his gaze to me. "What is it, Aileen?"

Feeling just as cold myself, I folded my arms and tried not to shiver. "I need to talk to you." I paused and stared pointedly at Ragnor. "About a private matter, that is."

Ragnor walked toward the door, and while he looked at me, he spoke to Atalon. "I'll see you tomorrow to finalize our discussion, then."

"Sure," Atalon drawled, irritated. "Do that."

Ragnor gave me one last soul-searching look that made me almost wince before he left, closing the door behind him.

Once he was gone, I let out a deep sigh and took a seat before Atalon, whose entire focus was now on me. "What is it?" he asked, eyes searching mine.

Seeing Ragnor again made my resolution even stronger than before. "I was wondering if you could tell me where Isora is, my Lord," I said without preamble.

He leaned back and pinched the bridge of his nose. "I told you to call me Atalon," he repeated like a broken record. He then sighed again. "Isora has been reassigned, as you must know by now."

Clenching my teeth, I gave him a sharp nod. "I know that," I said tightly. "I just didn't know it meant I could no longer see her."

Atalon gave me a long look before he gave me a smile that didn't reach his eyes. "Rest assured, Aileen. She's being taken care of. And no, you cannot see her. No one can."

I couldn't discern any lies from his voice, but that didn't mean it was the entire truth either. "I'll tell you what," I said, catching his gaze in mine. "If you let me see her, I'll go on that date with you."

That brought him to attention. "Are you sure?" he asked, straightening in his chair. "I'm a selfish man, Aileen. If you give me a chance, even with conditions, I'll take it."

That's what I counted on. "I am sure," I said, giving him a serious nod.

He cocked his head, frowning. "Perhaps I was mistaken, then."

What was it with these Lords nowadays who admitted to making mistakes left and right? "What about, my Lord?"

His eyes flashed at the way I addressed him, but this time, he didn't comment on it. "I thought there was still something going on between you and Rayne."

I almost laughed. "There's nothing left between us." I grimaced. "If there ever was anything, that is."

Atalon stared at me for a long moment before his face broke into a grin and he said, "Then I accept your terms. Be ready tomorrow at seven. I'll pick you up."

That wasn't enough, obviously. "What about Isora?"

He maintained his grin. "I'll let you see her after the date."

Seeing how resolute his eyes were, I knew I wouldn't get a better deal than that. "It's a date, then."

His eyes dropped to my lips momentarily before rising to meet mine. "It definitely is."

CHAPTER 16

AILEEN

Soft hands caressed the sides of my body, and I arched into the touch, sighing when a heavy, hard weight came down on top of me, caging me between him and the bed.

I stared at the chiseled chest of the man whose hands now rested against my ribs, just below my breasts. Arching again, I muttered, "Please . . ."

The hands cupped my mounds from below, making me gasp as he began kneading them, his hot breath hovering over my mouth. Refusing to have even an inch of distance between us, I grabbed his face and kissed him.

Growling into my mouth, he pushed my legs apart and settled between them, his erection nudging at my entrance. Excitement caused wetness to leak out of my pussy, and I wrapped my legs around his hard, sexy body and wriggled my thighs, wishing he would enter me.

He grabbed my wrists and shoved them down on the mattress as he stared at me with midnight blue eyes gone neon. He then teased at my entrance with his cock, and I whimpered, needing him closer. Deeper.

"Admit that you are a monster," he murmured then, "and I'll give you what you want."

I couldn't speak. I was lost to the sensation of having him on top of me, so hot and sexy and unbearably gorgeous, I was drowning in endless need.

"Say it, Aileen," he whispered against my lips. "Say that you're a monster, undeserving of love."

I froze as I suddenly took him in again. I realized then just who exactly I was having on top of me, willing to enter me, and my desire quadrupled along with my horror, now that his harsh, cold words penetrated my desire.

"No . . . ," I said, taking hold of his face as despair rose from deep within, mixed with blinding lust. "Ragnor—"

His hands curled around my neck all of a sudden, his face full of terrifying apathy. "Say it."

I thrashed under him, and lust burned in his eyes again. He let my neck go and grabbed my ass, angling me higher so his hard length grated against my wet entrance. "Fuck, Aileen," he murmured. "Fuck—"

"Ragnor," I exhaled his name as I tried to reach release. "Ragnor, please—"

My eyes blinked open as I woke up, short of breath and sweaty and so fucking horny, it was unbearable.

Before I could think twice about the fact I'd had a sex dream about Ragnor, I slid my hand under my shorts and found my pussy slick with need. Gritting my teeth and feeling both ashamed and needy, I flicked my bundle of nerves and cried out as those midnight blue eyes penetrated my mind, memories of his touch rising to the forefront.

I rubbed at my clit quickly and roughly, needing to find release more than anything else, and thoughts of Ragnor's mouth on mine, his teeth grazing the skin of my neck, his magnificent cock pushing in and out of my pussy with power that had always left me wanting more—

"Fuck!" I cried as the orgasm tore through me, causing spasms to take over my body. I rode it until I finished, feeling dissatisfied despite the release.

Because it wasn't enough.

I might have hated him, but my body remembered Ragnor's touch and craved it. Seeing him again had caused that need to come to life once more.

But I knew that the only way to satisfy that need was in the darkness of my bedroom and nowhere else.

And that made me want to cry in frustration and anger.

Yet I still had my pride. Even if my lust for him was intact, I refused to give in.

He'd hurt me so badly I was still picking up the pieces.

There was no way in hell I was letting him have me again.

The next day, I didn't see Ragnor at all, which both relieved and irritated me. Because for the entire night after my wet dream and little masturbation session, I tossed and turned for hours, thoughts of him filling my head, until I could barely have an hour of sleep.

He was so eager to talk to me yesterday, and now, it was as if he decided I wasn't worth his time. Typical Ragnor, thinking of me as disposable. What an asshole.

Thankfully, I had work to keep me occupied, and even though it was hard, what with Ragnor refusing to let me be even in his absence, I managed to scrape an essay together to hand over to Zion at the end of the workday. This essay was about the works of Demetria, the sculpturer Atalon had introduced me to back on my first day. Since she was going to be a key figure in the upcoming gala event, what with her artwork being famous in both vampire and human art-curation circles. It was also one of the last essays I was going to write, since Zion would soon start teaching me how to be a guide. Finally.

When I returned to my suite, I took a long cleansing shower before I started getting ready. I had a date tonight, after all. My first date ever, actually, now that I thought about it.

Logan, my ex, had never taken me out on dates—and for a good reason too. Our relationship had to be discreet due to certain circumstances, so dates were a no-go.

Ragnor's and my relationship hadn't been much better in that regard. We fucked in secret, and when we didn't fuck, we were constantly at odds, what with him not wanting to get serious and me begging him not to sell me to anyone else in the Auction.

Needless to say, we'd never gone on a date either.

But it seemed third time was the charm, because Atalon wanted to take me on a date first. It was actually quite flattering; he didn't seem to be after my body like Ragnor had been. Though there were a few questions that still lingered in my head, the main one being, Why did he want to date me in the first place?

I knew he was interested since he bought me in the Auction. He hadn't tried to hide it either; we had dinner together in the cafeteria with half the League present, and he'd made his intentions very clear, both with his actions and his words.

Atalon was a courteous man, but as proven to me yesterday, he wasn't above using all means at his disposal to get what he wanted. But the question remaining was why.

Whatever his reasons were, I nevertheless had agreed to this date, and so I had to put in my best effort. I might not be interested in Atalon that way—he was handsome, sure, but unfortunately wasn't my type—but I could at least give it a go. Perhaps he would charm me tonight.

Perhaps he would make me forget all other Lords.

Or perhaps I should simply consider this date as an opportunity to learn more about my current Lord.

I put on the fanciest dress I owned—the simple black dress Zoey, my former suitemate in the Rayne League, had lent me what felt like ages ago. It didn't look special when hung in my closet, but when I put it on, it fit like a glove, molding itself to the shape of my body. *It looks better on me now than it did the last time I wore it,* I couldn't help but think as I studied myself in my bedroom mirror.

Once I had makeup on and my hair pulled into its usual tall ponytail, I slid my feet into short black heels, grabbed my checkered black-and-white purse, and walked to the living room.

When she saw me, Eleanor paused the movie she was watching, stood up, and walked toward me. "Take this," she said and handed me an envelope. "Give it to Isora when you see her."

I didn't tell Eleanor the details of how and why I managed to secure a visit with Isora, but all she cared about was that at least I would get to see her. "I will," I replied somberly and put the letter in my purse.

Eleanor let out a breath. "Tell me everything when you come back," she said, and just then, there was a knock on the door. Giving me a strained smile, she said "Good luck" before she returned to the couch and resumed her movie.

After taking a deep breath myself, I murmured, "Thanks" and opened the door, sliding outside to the corridor so Eleanor wouldn't see who was waiting for me.

Atalon was dressed impeccably in a crimson three-piece suit with a black shirt, a silver tie, and a pair of shiny black leather moccasins. His platinum hair, too, received a special treatment, with it being meticulously slicked back and probably gelled to the max, because not one hair, not even the tiniest one, was out of place.

His alabaster skin seemed especially pale in contrast to his clothes, especially with how clean shaven his jaw was. It suddenly made me wonder what age Atalon was when he was given the Imprint, because unlike others, he could've easily been in either his twenties, thirties, or forties at the time. He looked that ageless.

This agelessness fit him, though, because he looked good. Very good.

It was a shame, really, that clean-cut men weren't my type.

"Good evening," he said, pitch-black eyes raking me down and back up with heat that made me shift a bit uncomfortably. "You look gorgeous."

Refusing to fuck this up, I forced on a grin and said, "Thank you. You look quite dashing yourself."

He chuckled. "Thank you too. Now, shall we?"

He offered me his arm, and I put mine in his, letting him lead us away from my suite and toward an express escalator leading to the top floor of the underground compound. It was where the Atalon League's reservation-only two-Michelin-star restaurant, Le Beau, was, among other forms of entertainment for the League members. But something told me Atalon wasn't taking me bowling.

My thoughts were confirmed when he said, "I hope you're hungry."

"I am," I said, though appetite and hunger were two different things. "I hope Le Beau is as good as everyone says."

Atalon gave me a grin. "Put your worries to rest, *tesoro*, and have a little faith."

I raised my brow. "Tesoro?"

His grin widened, and he leaned toward me so his breath tingled my ear. "It means *darling* in Italian. I would've preferred to call you *mi amore*, but we're not there yet."

That made me shudder, though for all the wrong reasons. First, he was far too close for my liking. Second, receiving a pet name before the date even started felt far too intense. And third, assuming that we would get to the *mi amore* part at some point in the future made me want to bark out that taking that for granted was in very bad form.

But I was here to give this date my utmost sincerest chance. So I forced a chuckle and ground out, "How nice."

He seemed to like my response, because he straightened with a triumphant glint in his eyes. That did not make me feel very optimistic about our date to come.

We arrived at Le Beau, and the host showed us to our special reserved table meant for two. It also had the best view out of everything else; it was at the end of the terrace that the restaurant was built on, and it overlooked a pretty inner courtyard with a fountain and everything.

The other guests wore clothes as posh as Atalon's, to the point that I started to feel underdressed. But Atalon didn't seem to share my sentiment, because he sat with pride, as if he wanted to show me off or something absurd like that. He didn't need to try so hard, though; the other guests were openly staring at us, probably wondering what the hell their Lord was doing with a mere Common like me.

Which was a very good question.

Once we put in our order, Atalon turned to me and smiled. "I'm so glad to have you for myself tonight," he said, his eyes roaming my body from head to toe. "I've been wanting to ask you out for far longer than you think." The appreciation in his eyes told me he meant every word. And, as much as it had been a while since a man had looked at me like that, I was creeped out more than excited.

To be frank, I wasn't interested in learning that. But he was waiting for the obvious question, so, pretending to be intrigued, I asked, "Since when?"

Satisfied that I was playing along, he promptly replied, "Since the first time I laid eyes on you." His mouth turned up in a smile, and his eyes glossed over as if he was remembering our first encounter. "I hope you know how enchanting you are, Aileen. Surely I'm not the first man to plead for the pleasure of your company." Atalon raised an inquisitive eyebrow and then ran his tongue over his thin bottom lip.

I didn't respond to that, and not because his words caught me off guard; such clichés didn't work on me. What made me far more alarmed was the fact that his eyes conveyed the same truth. He was being absolutely honest.

But I wasn't dumb. I knew when I was being played, and Atalon was doing his best to play me by flirting his ass off. Had I been less perceptive, it would've worked like a charm. He did say all the right things, after all. But instead, I couldn't help but wonder why he was trying so hard.

Since he was still waiting for any kind of response to his declaration, I gave him a tight smile and said, "Then I guess your wish came true."

His shoulders relaxed. I didn't even realize he was so tense. He was about to speak when a voice from right behind me suddenly said, "Ah, Orion, Aileen. What a coincidence."

And just like that, I was fuming. I whipped around to see Ragnor—a sight that already made my blood boil, but seeing him dressed in a black three-piece suit with his hair down and a daylong scruff covering his hard jaw made it even more unbearable.

That, and the fact he wasn't alone.

A woman stood next to him, a woman I very well recognized.

The woman who'd appeared in my dreams.

The one who was helping me sort out my newfound abilities.

The strange woman who seemed so out of place here, wearing a pair of faded jeans, a simple tee, and worn-out sneakers. The scarred left eye I'd seen in my dreams was hidden under an eye patch, and her unruly dark-blond hair rested on her shoulders, as though she'd just rolled out of bed.

I openly stared at her, refusing to believe my eyes. What the hell was she doing here? Why was she with Ragnor?

Eliza caught my gaze and gave me a somewhat smug smile.

I returned my attention to Ragnor, whose eyes were on me. His face was blank, but his midnight blues were twinkling with amusement. He said it was a coincidence. Coincidence, my ass.

"Evening, Rayne," Atalon said, making me look at him. His gaze was as cold as ice, fixed on Ragnor.

Casually, as though it was obvious, Ragnor called a waiter, and once one arrived, he said, "Please join our tables."

"Yes, Lord Rayne," the waiter said in a trembling voice and got to it.

Atalon's eyes narrowed. "I don't think I invited you to join us."

To my shock, it was Eliza who responded. "Don't fret, Lord Atalon," she said, smirking. "You can have her all to yourself later."

Atalon would've responded, but the waiter was quick, and soon Ragnor was sitting next to Atalon, and Eliza was right next to me.

To say it didn't bode well—not just for Atalon but for me too—was an under-fucking-statement.

"And who might you be?" Atalon now asked Eliza. He managed to school his face into a blank expression, but his eyes were frosty.

"Eliza Wains," she said, giving him a big friendly smile I didn't trust an inch. "I'm an acquaintance of Lord Rayne."

I glared at her. "What the hell are you doing here, Eliza?" I asked, barely able to contain my anger. I hated being blindsided. I especially hated it since Eliza never mentioned she had any sort of connection to Ragnor.

From the corner of my eye, I could see Ragnor's gaze shifting from Eliza to me and back. There was surprise in his eyes he couldn't quite hide. If my guess was correct, Eliza hadn't told him about her mental visits to my dreams.

Bitch.

Before Eliza could give me some sort of response, the waiter returned and asked for their orders. As Ragnor and Eliza rattled off their orders, I stared at Atalon. If I didn't know what was going on, I would've thought Atalon was on a date with Ragnor, since he was looking at him with so much heat, I felt scorched. But this heat wasn't a sexual one, obviously. Atalon was furious, and somehow not a muscle moved in his blank face.

I turned to look at Eliza, who stared at me with a Cheshire cat smile that put me on high alert. "To answer your question, I'm just having a night out with my . . . friend."

I had no clue what she was playing at, and honestly, I wasn't sure I wanted to know. Just hearing the hesitation in her voice before she said *friend* was enough to make me lose all sense. Gritting my teeth, I turned away from her to look at Ragnor and saw he was murmuring something to Atalon, which made Atalon's calm facade crack and his eyes grow impossibly colder. Then, Ragnor must've felt my gaze on him, because his eyes flickered to me, and a grimace appeared on his face.

Angry beyond reason, I turned back toward Eliza, who'd been studying my face for a few long minutes by now. "You should've told me," I murmured, clenching my hands into fists. "That you knew him. That you were friends."

Eliza's smile fell, and her face turned serious as she leaned closer. "It's because we're friends that I didn't tell you," she said so softly, I almost didn't hear her. "I wanted to make sure that you deserved him first."

I felt as if she'd just slapped me. "What?"

She shrugged and leaned back. "Don't worry, though," she said, her gaze turning pointed. "I still haven't made up my mind yet, so you still have a chance. As long as you keep practicing what we talked about, that is."

Since I had no idea what she was talking about, I looked away and glowered at the table.

A terse silence spread across the table, broken only when the waiter, returned with the aperitifs. My appetite was gone, though, and it seemed I wasn't the only one. Eliza ate as if she hadn't a care in the world. Ragnor and Atalon were too busy being locked in a battle of wills with their stares.

I couldn't take this anymore. I rose to my feet, said offhandedly, "I'll be right back," and walked away from the table, my emotions so haywire, I was a moment away from having a complete meltdown. I needed to get away before I humiliated myself.

Why the fuck was Eliza here? What the hell did she want from me?

But more importantly, why couldn't Ragnor leave me alone? Why did he have to interrupt this date, which he obviously knew about in advance? Why was he trying to stir everything I'd worked so hard to turn off inside me?

I never took him to be a sadist, but it seemed that's who he really was. Because there was no other reason for this torture.

I reached the washroom and was grateful it was empty. Then I washed my face, hoping the freezing water would calm some of my fried nerves.

"Are you all right?"

I whirled around and pushed Ragnor's too-close-for-comfort chest. "Get out," I snarled, glowering at him.

When I attempted to shove him again, he caught my wrists, and after last night's dream and him messing with my emotions, his touch sent sparks all over my skin. "You're not over this, Aileen," he said quietly, eyes searching mine. "Just as much as I'm not."

I shook my head and struggled against his hold, but his grip was like a vise. "I hate you," I growled. "I hate you so much—"

"I'm sorry." He cut me off in a somber voice, his gaze burning a bright luminous blue with an emotion I refused to acknowledge. "I'm sorry for the Auction. I'm sorry it took me so long to come back for you. I'm sorry, Aileen."

Shaking my head, I pulled at my wrists, and this time he let go. My body moaned about the loss of his touch, but I ignored it. "I don't care," I said, my anger turning frosty cold. "Your *sorry* doesn't mean shit. Not now, not ever."

"Aileen—"

"I meant it when I said I was done talking," I interjected before he said anything else to drive me mad. "So if you're really sorry, go back to your League and stay out of my life—hell, my existence—forever."

He stared at me silently, his face tight with barely contained anger. His eyes, too, were burning. Then he said, "I'm afraid I can't do that."

"Excuse me?" I exclaimed, outraged.

"I said I can't do that, Aileen," he growled, closing the inches between us until his chest pressed against mine and his hands caged me to the sink. The way his voice whispered my name, my actual name, the one he'd refused to call me before the Auction, made me shiver. "We can play stupid games like feigning interest in other people if that's what you want. I can keep following you everywhere if that's what it takes for you to listen. But the one thing I can't do is let you go again." He paused, his eyes boring into mine. "That's beyond me, Aileen."

What he was saying was beyond me. "Don't you get it, Ragnor?" I hissed, staring at him in half-shock, half-fury. "Nothing can make up for what you've done to me."

His face contorted in pain, and that made my own pain rise too. "One month," he said quietly. "Give me one month."

I parted my lips to respond with the obvious answer, but he leaned his forehead against mine and closed his eyes. "Just one month," he insisted quietly. "If after that month you tell me you're done, I promise to take it at face value."

Against my better judgment, I was torn. Because here was Ragnor, the man I'd been wanting all those months back at the Rayne League, the man I'd been craving, and he was telling me all the things pre-Auction Aileen would've given her right arm to hear.

But I was no longer that lovesick fool. Ragnor had made sure of it.

Yet now the very same Ragnor was the closest to begging as I'd ever seen him. And that made something inside me break. Because looking at him like this, I was reminded of when I pleaded with him to buy me out.

Did Ragnor listen?

No.

He did not.

And perhaps I shouldn't either.

But as I opened my mouth to give him my response, the words got lodged in my throat, refusing to leave. As if some divine being was controlling my vocal cords.

So instead, I blurted the one question I'd been refraining from thinking about. The one question that really mattered. "What the hell happened to you, Ragnor?"

He leaned back and gave me a stare full of thousands of things he didn't and probably would never say. "You happened, Aileen Henderson."

CHAPTER 17
AILEEN

I couldn't get Ragnor's words out of my head. So much so that I could hardly speak for the rest of the date.

After our little altercation in the washroom, I left without another word, far too confused to form any coherent sentence. Ragnor followed me out, and we returned to our table silently.

To say the rest of the supposed double date was awkward would be an understatement. Since I was stuck in my own head, and it seemed that Ragnor was, too, Eliza had taken it upon herself to carry the conversation with Atalon, who seemed to be quite dissatisfied with the recent development. For some reason, Eliza seemed positively chirpy.

I was unable to follow the conversation for the life of me. All I could hear was Ragnor's voice, practically begging me to give him a chance, and all I could think of was his torn, desperate face.

In a different life, when I was still human and Cassidy and Skye were my friends, I remembered that one incident in which Skye's boyfriend, Tyler, was caught cheating. I remembered that Cassidy and I had taken Skye to the nearest bar and gotten her drunk to forget about the event, which she deemed to be relationship ending.

"I would never forgive that piece of shit!" Skye had said drunkenly, almost falling on her ass.

I'd caught her. "Then break up with him," I said gently, keeping up the pretense I was actually her friend, just like she pretended to be mine.

She glared at me and pushed me off. "You don't understand!" she yelled. "I can't!"

Cassidy looked at Skye with disgust. "Of course you can, and you should, Skye. He obviously can't give two shits about you—"

"But I love him." She broke down, tears escaping her eyes. "I love him so much, and I know he loves me! It's just . . . It's my fault . . ."

I remembered thinking how pitiful yet stupid she was being. Because if Tyler had loved her, why did he cheat? That couldn't possibly be love. Didn't it mean she was utterly worthless to him?

Later that night, when we took Skye home, Tyler was waiting for her near the large gates to her parents' mansion. Skye had launched herself at him and hugged him, and I'd seen him hugging her back and crying, telling her how sorry he was, how he'd made a mistake, and he promised he would never, ever do it again.

And Skye, so blind with love, believed him.

He did end up cheating on her again, of course. But Skye started to care less and less about that. Her reasoning had been, "He can visit as many beds as he wants, but what matters is that at the end of the day, it's my bed he wants the most, and my finger he'll eventually put a ring on."

Cassidy had given up trying to shake some sense into her. I had never even tried. All I could do was judge her in the privacy of my mind, thinking how low one needed to stoop to cheat.

Now, I was horrified to find out I was actually relating to Skye.

Ragnor might not have cheated on me, but he'd betrayed me nonetheless.

While Tyler simply wanted to have other options while keeping Skye close, Ragnor had thrown me away, not giving us any sort of option at all.

In a way, it was worse than cheating. At least cheating meant that person still wanted to be with you, even if they were with other people—otherwise they could've just broken up with you.

Ragnor had acted as if I was worth absolutely nothing to him.

And now he wanted me back.

Was it a case of FOMO? Had his interest in me suddenly multiplied because I was no longer begging for his affection? Was that what it was? He liked them hard to get?

But even if that was the case, would Ragnor plead to be given another chance just to win someone, anyone, over?

"You're quiet."

I snapped out of my thoughts and turned to Atalon. We had left the restaurant a few minutes ago, bidding Ragnor and Eliza farewell, though I wasn't fully there and managed to give the two of them only a nod before I followed Atalon out.

Now, we were on our way to finally meet Isora, the reason this whole fiasco happened to begin with.

"Yeah," I murmured, giving him an apologetic smile I knew looked fake. "I'm sorry about that. Ra . . . Lord Rayne and Eliza's presence was kind of, you know . . ."

He gave me a reassuring smile that seemed just as fake. "You and Rayne were gone for a while," he said, basically telling me I couldn't fool him.

I looked away and didn't respond. He didn't take the hint and pushed. "It seems like you two have some unfinished business. Did you agreeing to this date have to do with something other than bargaining to see your friend? Because I don't like being played for a fool, Aileen."

Shit. He was spot on. But telling him that would make me feel like an even bigger asshole, so instead, I decided to redirect the questioning. "What about you, my Lord?" I asked, glancing at him to see his lips curl unhappily at the formal way I refused to stop addressing him. "Wasn't there an ulterior motive to you asking me out to begin with?"

His jaw locked. "And if I say there wasn't?"

I would definitely call bullshit. "Then I won't probe," I said quietly. "But I'll let you in on a secret, my Lord; I know what romantic interest looks like. When you look at me, I can tell you're attracted to me to some extent, but I also get the feeling there's something more you want. Something that has little to do with me. Like maybe you want to stick it to Ragnor?"

He chuckled, but it was a twisted, nerve-jerking sound. "I didn't know you think me to be such a cold, calculating person," he said, getting the gist of my words without me needing to spell it out to him.

I turned to face him and gave him a serious look. "No matter how hard you try," I said, "your eyes will always tell the actual truth. I prefer not to be a pawn in your vendetta against Ragnor, or whatever this is about."

Those black eyes caught mine, and this time, when he smiled, it finally fit what I'd always seen in his eyes: cruelty and coldness. "You're a dangerous woman, Aileen," he said in a smooth voice that made the tiny hairs on the nape of my neck stand on end. "Thankfully, you're in my League."

He came to a stop, and I realized we'd arrived at the inner courtyard I'd seen before from the restaurant. "I told you I would take you to see your friend. But, before I take you to Isora, I would like to make something clear," he said, motioning toward an empty bench.

I was extremely impatient to see Isora, but since I didn't want to get on his bad side, I followed Atalon and sat down on the bench next to him.

"When I was a young Lord in the process of building this League," he said without preamble, "I gave the Imprint to a beautiful, young, and talented opera singer, believing she would become the first Gifted member of my brand-new League. Unfortunately, she turned out to be a Common."

I didn't realize it was story time, but I kept silent and let him speak, knowing there must be a reason why he was telling me that.

His eyes glossed over as he seemed to sink into the memory. "One day, Rayne came for a visit."

I tensed, realizing where it was going now.

"He wanted to make a trade deal with me, which was far more beneficial to me than to him," Atalon continued. "I should have suspected, for nothing in life comes free, but I was young and ambitious and saw this as a once-in-a-lifetime opportunity." He paused dramatically before he said, "He offered me one of his Gifted vampires in exchange for the Common opera singer."

Atalon's eyes were watching me closely, intently, as if he were waiting for some sort of a reaction. But all I could do was look at him and listen.

His shoulders sagged with his disappointment at my lack of response. He nonetheless resumed his story. "This trade happened before the Auction was established, you see. Back then, if a Lord wanted to acquire a vampire from a different League, he needed to make a fair offer in return. In this case, I was giving away a Common in exchange for a Gifted. A trade that didn't seem beneficial for Rayne. But as long as both Lords agreed, that's all that mattered."

His hands clenched into fists. "Little did I know Rayne and the wench had plotted behind my back."

For the first time, true anger flashed in his eyes. "A few months after the trade was made, it came to my attention Rayne had gotten a mysterious Gifted vampire whose Gift was her bewitching voice." His eyes glowed with that shadowy sheen of theirs. "Imagine my surprise when I came to an event at the Rayne League and learned that that Gifted individual was none other than the supposedly Common vampire I had trustfully given away."

He took a deep breath, and the shadowy glow in his eyes dimmed. "Rayne tried to save face by telling me she became Gifted only after the trade had happened. And while such cases can happen, it is rare. Extremely rare. I didn't buy his lies." His face contorted in fury. "So I investigated what really happened."

Suddenly, his face cleared, and he shot me an almost eager look that gave me pause. "Rayne and the wench had been seeing each other since her days as a human," he told me in a distasteful tone. "After I gave her the Imprint, she and Rayne exchanged secret love letters that also detailed their plan: she pretended to be a Common, and he promised her he would get her to his League by baiting me with a Gifted of his own in exchange. Thus, the two of them defrauded me."

He breathed heavily, looking at me expectantly.

Outwardly, I gave him a blank gaze, showing him I couldn't care less about how Ragnor wronged him. To be fair, I didn't even think it was that big of a deal to begin with—I mean, he still got a Gifted in the end, didn't he?

But on the inside, I was seething. Anger and pain encompassed my mind, making it almost too hard to breathe.

Ragnor had been dating a human. Human. And he'd gone the extra fucking mile to get her back when she became a vampire.

He cared for a human far more than he ever did for me, a vampire of his own creation.

I couldn't give Atalon the satisfaction of knowing that his words hit home. That it was like a kick to the fucking gut.

I knew Ragnor had dated women before, thanks to the dishwashing team in the Rayne League kitchens, who loved sharing such gossip. But they'd never told me about this. About him having a wild affair with a human and taking extreme measures to bring her to his League.

Was she even at his League still? What had happened between them?

And why did it hurt so much?

I looked at Atalon vacantly and cocked my head, feigning indifference as I asked, "What am I supposed to learn from this?"

Atalon seemed taken aback. "He's a lying, conniving son of a bitch," he said as his pale cheeks reddened in anger. "That's just one example of his rotten character." He paused and took a deep breath, and his flush disappeared as he gave me an almost pitying look. "You have experienced that yourself, too, haven't you?"

It felt like he'd put a knife to my heart before, and now he was viciously twisting it. "I thought you were on good terms, you and Ragnor," I said quietly, doing everything in my power to keep my voice even. I wasn't going to break. Not here, not now.

His eyes gleamed ominously. "It's a farce I'm willing to keep up," he said darkly, "until I achieve what I want."

"And what is it that you want?"

He gave me a smile that made chills run down my spine. "To make him feel what it's like having something he wants taken away."

And just like that, everything suddenly made sense.

Stunned, the pain coming to an abrupt halt, I stared at Atalon, taking in the vengeful glint in his gaze, the smug smirk on his face, and said, "So just because he bruised your pride hundreds of years ago, you want to date me to get back at him?"

His smirk disappeared, and he leaned forward. "You make it sound as if it's about pride, but it's not, Aileen," he snarled, rage in his eyes. "He sold you out! He cast you aside in his typical, enraging fashion!" He huffed and puffed, so riled up his eyes were glowing in their shadowy way the strongest I'd seen them so far. His lips unfurled, and he held on to the bench's back, knuckles white. "You should want to break him far more than I do!"

I never saw Atalon losing his calm like this, and the direction in which this conversation was going made my own anger rise.

Atalon's interest in me was clear now. He was interested in using me as a pawn in some long, stupid feud he had with Ragnor. He wanted to get revenge on Ragnor like a petulant little boy whose toy had been taken away.

I rose to my feet. "I understand," I said evenly, keeping my anger locked inside. "Are you done? I would like to go to Isora now."

He stood up as well and grabbed my arm. "Think about this, Aileen," he said quietly, searching my gaze. "Think about what I said.

What I'm offering you here. It's not just a chance at getting back at him for ruining both of us—if you choose me, I vow to give you everything he didn't."

Pursing my lips, I tugged at my arm, and he let go. "I need to think about it," I said, though I didn't really mean it. In all honesty, I just wanted this conversation to end. I didn't know what to think or what I even wanted.

Because what Atalon had said wasn't wrong. Ragnor had done me dirty, and sure, I had wanted to get revenge by showing him how great I was doing without him. But I wasn't sure I wanted Atalon to be part of the equation.

"All right," Atalon said with a rough sigh. "But do know this, Aileen." He gave me a profound look. "I have never, and will never, treat you the same way he did. I will continue being fair and protect you from all dangers. I won't toss you away. I will cherish you the way you're meant to be cherished."

His sincerity was clear, but it did the opposite from what he probably intended.

Sorrow filled the pit of my stomach like lead. Those were the words I wished I could have heard from Ragnor.

CHAPTER 18
AILEEN

Atalon led me toward a large metal door at the far end of the kitchens, where Isora was probably. "Before we go in, a word of advice," he said, voice serious suddenly. "Whatever you're about to see is not as bad as it seems."

Immediately alert, I waited as he opened the door and led me through, toward manual stairs leading down to yet another metal door, this one requiring a code or a handprint. Using his hand, he opened the door, revealing a sight I never thought I would see deep within the Atalon League, of all places.

At first glance, it looked like some sort of underground techno club, eerily similar to the last nightclub I'd been to back in my human life, the Hole. But then I realized that, aside from the fact the lights were awfully dim, nothing about this place resembled a dance club.

Across the circular room, dozens of cushions were spread out, creating a few cozy stations like in traditional Japanese restaurants. At each station was a person whose gender I wasn't quite sure of—wearing the oddest piece of clothing I'd ever seen. It was black, for starters, and it covered the entire body, leaving only the wrists, neck, and a bit of the shoulders naked. There was nothing sexy about this clothing; in fact, it seemed suffocating, considering the cloth also covered their heads, eyes included.

All seven stations were occupied by vampires I'd seen in passing. There was only one common thing about them all.

They were Gifteds.

And they were all sucking the covered people's blood, using the small patches of skin that were offered.

Sick to my stomach, I slowly turned to look at Atalon. He trained his eyes on me, seemingly waiting to hear my thoughts.

But I couldn't. There were no words that could describe what I was thinking right now. Because only one thing mattered—"Where is Isora?"

Without a word, Atalon led me across the room, to a station that had only one person. That person, I realized with a jolt, was Oz, my fellow new purchase and breakfast company. What the . . .

Raising his head from the covered person's neck, Oz turned to look at Atalon and me. His silver eyes showed no emotion. He seemed as completely apathetic as always, like I hadn't just caught him doing something that, aside from him, only Gifteds were doing.

Did it mean . . . ? But Oz had been Auctioned, just like I was. Only Common vampires could be Auctioned. So what the hell did that mean?

"Oz," Atalon said quietly, "please pause for now and resume after Aileen and I are done here."

Oz wiped his mouth and rose to his feet. "No need, my Lord," he said flatly. "I'm done."

He gave me an acknowledging nod before he left, leaving the covered person—a woman, I could tell by the elegant slope of her neck—slumped across the cushions.

Atalon now took a seat to the right of the woman, whom I realized must be Isora, and hesitantly, reluctantly, I took the left one. Then with a tap on her wrist, Atalon murmured, "You have a guest."

Weakly, the woman raised her hand to the cloth hiding her face, but just before she reached it, her arm fell, as if she lost all power in her body. The sickly feeling in my gut grew when Atalon gently took the cloth off for her, revealing a face that was familiar yet belonged to a stranger.

Isora looked as though she'd aged ten years in the two days since she'd been gone. Her blue eyes, normally so alight with mischievousness, were now sunken and empty, no spark to be seen in their depths. Her hair, which had been healthy and pretty, was lying down her shoulders like a muted rag. Her cheekbones were jutting out, her lips wore a blueish tint, and her skin was ghastly gray and full of spots.

Her eyes were now staring ahead, as if she didn't see us. Didn't see me. I turned to Atalon, feeling a surge of brilliant rage consuming me whole. "What the hell is going on here, Atalon?" I asked in a barely contained growl.

Atalon gave me an almost haughty look that made a chill run down my spine. "What you see here is necessary for the existence of vampires."

I was shaking now. "Explain," I bit out.

His black eyes gleamed warningly at my order. "I'm going to give you a pass now because you're highly emotional," he said coolly, "but if you try to order me again, prepare to suffer the consequences."

Finally, Atalon was showing his true colors. Gone was his little act of the friendly, flirty man. Now he was acting like the asshole vampire Lord I knew he was.

He turned to look at Isora, and when he ran his knuckles against her sunken cheek, I felt the urge to slap them away. "All vampires require blood to survive," he said quietly, eyes on Isora's face. "For Commons, you can simply be satisfied with human blood, and, to a certain extent, animal blood. But this is not the case for the Gifteds and, of course, the Sacred."

His eyes turned to me as he let his hand fall. "The Gifteds, and especially the Sacred, have far more Lifeblood to maintain than Commons. I assume you know that."

Ragnor's fangs grazed the skin of my neck before sinking into me, sucking my blood in the small cupboard closet with no room to move . . .

The memory flashed through my mind, making me grow cold. Was that why Ragnor drank from me?

Lifeblood was basically the metaphysical energy that made one a vampire. Commons had a speck of it, while the Gifteds had more, and the Sacred had about five times what the Gifteds had. I knew that blood intake was related in one way or another to Lifeblood, but I didn't know that it was to this extent.

Atalon gave me a smile that made me feel cold all over. "This is why the Gifteds and Sacred require not just human blood—they need additional Lifeblood in their blood diet. Thus, we also drink from the Commons."

He motioned toward Isora. "Blood slaves are necessary for our survival. It's a monitored way to ensure us Sacred and Gifted, of course, get the supplements we need and also give the slaves a safe environment removed from any form of abuse."

There were so many wrong things in what he'd just said, I didn't know where to start. "Blood slaves." I repeated the term, feeling so sick, I was sure it showed on my face.

Atalon cocked his head. "Is there a problem?"

So fucking many, I wanted to snap but swallowed my tongue instead. I turned to look at Isora, feeling bile rising up my throat. "Why Isora?" I gritted out.

"Slaves are used for many things, depending on the League," he said quietly. "Here, I use slaves to do the menial tasks no one else wants to, such as housekeeping. But before I appoint slaves to such tasks, I first check their Lifeblood."

What?

He smiled eerily again. "As a Lord, just one taste of someone's blood allows me to determine how much Lifeblood a vampire has—Common, Gifted, and even Sacred alike. Some rare Commons"—he jutted his chin toward Isora—"have just a tad bit more than others.

Those of them who were unlucky enough to become slaves, like Isora here, I make into blood slaves. Their blood is more decadent and nutritious for the Gifted and Sacred, you see."

I didn't see. I didn't see anything at all. This was madness. This was sick. I didn't know where to even start with how fucked up this whole thing was.

"Aileen."

My eyes snapped to Atalon. "What?" I barked, unable to control myself right now.

His eyes narrowed. "Isora knew what she was signing up for when she chose to become a second-timer," he said coldly. "The three-month grace period is only meant for her to tie up any loose ends before she lets go of her freedom."

"But you didn't give her three months, only two," I said, my voice shaking, "and instead you made her hope she might be okay after all. That she didn't sign up for another hell."

Atalon shook his head and tsked. "She should've thought about it before she attempted to go on a nightly adventure with you," he said coolly. "A woman with her low status shouldn't have taken such a risk."

What a fucking snake. "Say I follow your logic, and she's now a . . . a blood slave," I said, still finding it hard to believe. "Then why the hell does she look like this after only a couple of days at the job?"

His face was sealed when he replied, "Blood slaves don't have long life spans, I'm afraid."

No.

No, no, no—

"Eventually, they run out of Lifeblood," he said, shrugging—shrugging!—as if he was simply talking about the weather. "Then they unfortunately meet their end."

I tried not to feel, tried to focus on what really mattered, and it was so hard, I felt myself dying inside. "How long?" I asked, grinding my teeth. "How long does she have?"

"Well," Atalon said, "the Gifteds seem to like her blood more than others, so I assume . . . one month? Perhaps two?"

This was beyond cruel. This was inhumane.

He shrugged now. "Either way, keep this quiet from *your friends*. I don't need them sticking their noses where they don't belong."

I heard the threat in his voice. I heard the disdain and condescension he had for my friends. How he saw them in reality.

How he saw *Isora*.

This was so much worse than anything else I'd encountered so far in the vampiric society. Throwing the weak vampires' lives away for the gain of those at the top.

It was no different, really, than human society. In both cases, those who had power used the powerless until they had nothing left to contribute.

Vampires were exactly like that. In some ways, we were even worse.

Just thinking about what was happening below the kitchen of the Atalon League, under all the Commons' noses, like what was happening in the Renaldi League, according to Eleanor's stories . . . it made me wish, not for the first time, that I hadn't been given the Imprint to begin with.

And also, it made me realize how lucky I'd been so far. Luckier than I'd thought.

While Isora had been anything but.

CHAPTER 19
AILEEN

When I returned to my room that night, I felt the awful powerlessness spreading over me, making me feel so weak and useless.

It was even worse, because Eleanor was waiting for me in the living room, excited for news—any news—about Isora.

And seeing her eyes sparkling so hopefully, innocently, blissfully ignorant of what Isora's slave status truly entailed, I was almost envious.

If only I could unsee what I saw.

And now, with Atalon's subtle threat ringing in my ears, I lied.

"Yes, Isora's great."

"Yeah, she met a few friends, and she's in charge of cleaning the gallery."

"Don't worry, I gave her your letter, and she read it and told me to send you her love."

"She's fine, Eleanor. I bet you'll be able to see her soon."

When she finally finished the inquisition, she went to her bedroom to catch a much-needed good night's sleep, worry-free.

And I went back to my room and had the sudden urge to trash it. To take all this useless, helpless anger out on something. Anything.

But before I could, there was a knock on the main door. And I had an idea who it was at this late hour.

I opened the door and stared at Ragnor. He was still wearing his suit, just like I was still in my supposedly formal attire. Before he could speak, I said, "Can we not do this right now?"

Ragnor's midnight blues locked mine in an unbreakable hold, and his face grew serious. "Something happened. Talk to me."

Talk to him? To another Lord who probably had his own bloodletting brothel beneath his League's kitchens? What a fucking joke. "I'd rather not," I said flatly. "So leave." I sucked in a breath before I added in a tight voice, "Please."

He gently turned me aside and walked into the suite, ignoring my words. After gritting my teeth, I said, "I can't do this right now, Ragnor. We can fight all you want tomorrow for all I care—"

"I'm leaving tomorrow morning," he said quietly, and I clamped my lips together. He turned to me with an inscrutable look. "I planned on staying a few more days, but an urgent matter arose, and I need to go back."

I tensed. "You don't need to explain yourself," I said, an ugly feeling crawling into my stomach. "It's not like we have a special relationship or anything."

His face darkened, but he took a deep breath and walked deeper into the suite. "Let's talk inside."

"I told you to leave."

"And I'm not leaving until you tell me what the hell happened in the few hours since I last saw you," he responded in a low growl.

I was exhausted. I was absolutely, utterly drained. Everything that happened today was so emotionally taxing, I didn't have any fight left in me anymore.

"Fine," I said wearily, leading the way into my bedroom. He closed the door after him, and I turned to face him. "Now what?"

"Talk to me," he repeated, taking a step too close.

I put up my hand, motioning for him to stop. "Nothing happened," I lied. It was easy now that I'd practiced on Eleanor. "My date with Atalon was a flop, thanks to someone, and now I'm tired."

A flop was an understatement. I would never, ever let that bastard touch me even with a fucking stick.

Though Isora becoming a blood slave wasn't the only reason. His words, his story about why he wanted to get back at Ragnor, were enough to turn off any sort of interest I might've had in him.

Ragnor's eyes narrowed. "Your lies don't work on me," he informed me flatly. "So if you really want me gone, just tell me what I want to hear, and I'll leave."

"Yeah?" I said, glowering at him. "Have it your way, then. Tell me, Ragnor, do you own blood slaves?"

If he was surprised at what I said, he didn't show it. "No," he replied curtly.

"Don't lie to me," I snarled, closing the gap between us of my own accord now.

"I'm not," he growled back, eyes not leaving mine. "I never owned blood slaves, and I never will."

"Oh really?" I laughed maniacally. "Then how are you getting the supplemental Lifeblood you Sacred and Gifted bastards require? Do you seduce them like you did me to gain access to their blood?"

Ragnor really tried to hide it, but I could see the anger flaring in his eyes. "By volunteers," he grated out. "I never forced or seduced anyone to give me, or the Gifteds, their blood. Never." He scoffed then. "And you didn't seem to hate it when I sucked your blood."

We locked gazes for a few loaded, silent moments before I turned around and walked to the adjoining washroom. I heard him come after me, but I didn't care. I felt suffocated. Angry. Caged to this existence I never asked for and was forced to live through anyway.

I took off the hair band and let my hair fall down. I shook off the dress and kicked away the heels. As I turned, I could see Ragnor's eyes flying back to my face. I almost laughed. "Are you seriously checking me out right now?"

His lips tightened. "I'm not a monk, Aileen."

I snorted, and an impulse made me want to push him further. Eyes on his face, I unclasped my bra and let it drop, my tits falling out, unrestrained. His eyes were drawn to their movement, and the anger in his eyes was suddenly sevenfold. "What are you doing?" he gritted out.

In my mind, logic screamed at me to stop, that this was Ragnor, the man who'd thrown me away after giving me the Imprint against my fucking will. But this, whatever this was, proved to be such a beautiful distraction from the despair eating me inside that I desperately clung on to this, everything else be fucking damned.

Slowly, I lowered my panties, and Ragnor's eyes followed their descent as if he couldn't help himself. When the panties were off, his breaths turned shallow, and his eyes were glowing neon blue with unhidden lust. A tent appeared in his trousers. "I thought you said you hated me," he said, voice like gravel.

Unabashed in my nakedness, I stepped toward him, watching him watching me with a feeling of euphoria so strong, my exhaustion became nonexistent. "I still hate you," I told him, my own voice husky as lust pooled in the pit of my stomach, anticipating what was to come. "I hate you so much I can't bear it."

His face contorted in what I would've thought was pain before he raised his eyes back to my face. "Then don't come any closer, Aileen," he said, voice so rough it was almost unintelligible. "I'm not that good of a man."

His words reminded me of Atalon's, but unlike then, Ragnor's words set me on fire. My nipples tightened, and his eyes sharpened at the sight. I felt the slick wetness dripping down my inner thighs. Seeing Ragnor struggling to hold in his lust, seeing him slowly losing every semblance of control, gave me a heady feeling unlike anything else.

For the first time in our turbulent relationship, I was in charge.

And I loved every moment of it.

I paused only an inch away from him, my eyes on his face. "I'm done talking," I told him, sucking in a breath as his hands went to my waist as if they had a mind of their own. "Now you have two choices."

He tore his eyes away from my body to look into mine. Desperate need flared in their brilliant pupils, making me gasp in unbidden excitement. "Choices?" he growled as his hands slid up my waist, as if itching to reach my swollen breasts.

"Yes," I said breathily, then bit my lip as his palms caressed the sides of my breasts. "First one is that you stay for the night."

He let out a shuddered breath. "And the second?" he murmured, pressing his front against mine as his hands were now on my back, stroking my shoulder blades and roaming down to my ass. I could feel his erection near my thigh, throbbing.

I sucked in a breath when he grabbed my ass cheeks so hard, his hands would definitely leave a print. "Second choice," I somehow said, almost mindless with need, "is you walk away."

"What kind of bullshit is that?" he growled again as he leaned his forehead against mine, eyes blazing as he nudged my thighs open, pressing his trousers-clad cock against my crotch. "Of course I choose option one."

Knowing that he was so mindless with lust for me that he wasn't able to think clearly made me feel even more euphorically giddy than before. Because the normal Ragnor would've known this couldn't be that easy. He would've known there was a catch.

I let him into my little catch. "There's a condition, though," I whispered against his mouth, pushing my crotch against his erection, causing him to thrust back. "If you choose option one, this will be the last night we'll ever spend together."

He froze.

"But if you take the second choice," I murmured, feeling so powerful, it was almost orgasmic all on its own. "If you walk away, I'll give you that one month."

He leaned his head back to stare at me, and suddenly, his face was a riddle. That made the sense of power I'd felt waver, so I thrust against his cock, and while he pushed me against him even harder, his face remained just as sealed, his eyes, back to their soulful midnight blue, utterly unreadable.

After a few silent moments, he finally spoke. "Which of these choices will make you happy?"

His question made me jolt and reel back, as if he'd just slapped me. Because that's what it felt like; one moment, I was on cloud nine, heady with power and control over the one man who never let go of his, and the next, he took all the air out of my sails, retaking that power and control as if I'd never had them in the first place.

I stepped away from him, eyes dropping to the floor, and hugged myself, my mind slowly coming back from its distracted haze and blasting me with a cold dose of reality.

I'd almost had sex with Ragnor.

After he'd thrown me away.

After what I'd just learned and seen about the dark side of the vampiric society he had forced me into.

After I'd seen Isora looking like a fucking corpse.

What the hell was I doing?

From the corner of my eye, I saw Ragnor moving to grab a towel. He then put that towel over my shoulders, helping me cover myself. "I'm going to leave," he said quietly, gently.

But I couldn't look at his face. Not after what had just happened.

"Aileen," he said softly, and his hand gently took my chin and raised my head, forcing my eyes back up. His face was cautious and serious, not a trace of lust left, but the need was still bright in his eyes. "You've obviously had a rough night, and I'm not going to take advantage of you."

"You almost did," I blurted out, blinked, and looked away, jaw locked.

He pulled at my chin, forcing me to face him again. His eyes showed more candidness than ever before. "Because I thought that's what you wanted," he said quietly. "But I know now that it's not."

He cupped my face fully with his palms and pressed his lips against my forehead, the act so gentle and true, affectionate and loving, that I had to close my eyes to keep the tears in. "Go to sleep," he murmured when he took his lips away, "and I will see you soon."

Before I could speak, he left. And despite it being what I wanted, I felt the loss of his presence, his touch, his warmth so vividly, I fell to the floor and wept.

CHAPTER 20
RAGNOR

The infirmary was dark when Ragnor stepped inside late at night. The nurse in charge, Marcello, was sleeping in his station, probably passed out in exhaustion. And the reason for said exhaustion was lying awake in the only occupied bed in the room.

Silently, Ragnor took a seat next to the patient. Never before had he visited the infirmary so frequently, and never because his most senior Lieutenant, Magnus, had come back from a mission so close to death, it was a miracle he survived.

Ragnor stared at his oldest League member and longtime friend, feeling as though he was living in a parallel universe of some sort. "How are you doing?" he asked quietly, knowing the question was redundant.

Magnus was the type of man who made everyone who saw him do a double take. Ragnor often heard women refer to him as the most beautiful man alive, and from a clinical point of view, Ragnor understood why. With golden hair and eyes, bronze skin, and a tall athletic form, he was often referred to as either Apollo, the god of sun and light, or Eros, the god of love and desire.

But right now, Magnus looked anything but a god. It was as if someone sucked the life out of him, with his body losing all its former glory and looking pale, thin, and frail. His cheeks were sunken, his eyes were bloodshot, and his lips had a faint blue tint to them that shouldn't have been there. Ugly spots covered the rest of his graying skin, and his hair, once as gold as the sun, had strands of wispy white within it.

This was why Lifeblood was so important to vampires. It wasn't just the essence that allowed vampires to be what they were, but it was also in charge of their health and vitality. Without Lifeblood, a vampire wouldn't just die but would slowly turn into ashes.

Ragnor never wished such a fate on anyone, which was why, as he'd told Aileen before, he would never have blood slaves. But the real mystery here was that Magnus wasn't a Common, who had only enough Lifeblood to maintain their vampirehood. He wasn't even a Gifted, who had double the Lifeblood of Commons.

The truth was, Magnus was Sacred. Perhaps the only Sacred who hadn't become a Lord.

And that meant he had an abundance of Lifeblood, so much so that he could go weeks, even months, without feeding from another vampire, like Ragnor himself.

Magnus had been away for only two weeks.

Therefore, him being depleted of Lifeblood shouldn't have been possible.

Unless he encountered the one being who could do this to him.

Magnus slowly turned his head toward Ragnor, his eyes so empty, it made Ragnor's rage rise. "The Jinn," his Lieutenant said weakly, confirming Ragnor's suspicions. "They . . . ambushed me."

Ragnor's hands clenched into fists. Last time he'd checked, there were only lesser Jinn in America. But Magnus seemed as though he'd encountered a greater Jinni.

But it made no sense. Certain conditions needed to be met in order for the greater Jinn to be able to manifest on earth. There was no way that these conditions could've been met. Ragnor would've known.

And yet here they were.

Letting out a rough breath, Ragnor leaned back. "How did you escape?" he asked, because in his current state, he couldn't have possibly done it alone.

Magnus confirmed his thoughts when, in a terribly frail voice, he replied, "Someone . . . helped. I don't . . ."

"You don't know who they were." Ragnor finished the sentence for him, and Magnus gave him a chillingly sad smile. Of course it would be some mysterious supposed Good Samaritan.

Seeing how tired his Lieutenant looked, Ragnor knew the rest of his questions should be answered at a different time. So, for now, he pulled back the sleeve of his coat and put his wrist to Magnus's mouth. "Drink," he ordered.

It seemed Magnus didn't have the strength to object, as he would've probably done under different circumstances, because he unsheathed his fangs and pressed his mouth against Ragnor's skin. Ragnor didn't even flinch when his Lieutenant's fangs cut his skin and he began to suck his blood.

Normally, Ragnor refrained from sharing his blood with other vampires. Even the newly Imprinted drank only human blood, while custom dictated the Imprinting Lord should give them the first sip. However, with Ragnor's blood being far more potent than a regular Lord's, he couldn't risk it. Thankfully, the newly Imprinted didn't need to drink from a Lord to gain vampirehood, since the initial Lifeblood transfer—the act of giving the Imprint—required an exchange of any sort of bodily fluids. The most traditional way was through blood exchange, but sex, or even a kiss, had always been far more popular than simply exchanging blood.

But with Magnus being Sacred, Ragnor didn't fear any repercussions. Especially in his current state, even a Gifted's blood wouldn't be enough to replenish this Sacred's Lifeblood.

For a few long minutes, Magnus simply drank. The more of Ragnor's blood he took in, the better his skin started to look, its sickly grayish tint slowly disappearing. The color returned to his cheeks as well, and the spots all over his body dissipated, as if they were never there to begin with. He was still thinner than he should have been and quite frail, too, but a week of daily feeding of Commons' blood, and he would be as good as new.

After ten minutes, Magnus retracted his fangs, and Ragnor withdrew his hand. "Better?" he asked.

"Yeah," Magnus said, voice stronger than before. "Much better."

"Good," Ragnor said, rising to his feet. "Rest now. I'll see you when I come back."

He was about to leave when Magnus suddenly said, "Who will you take with you to the gala, then?"

Ragnor couldn't help but smirk. "It's time I put your mentee to some good use."

Before he stopped for the day, Ragnor visited his town house aboveground.

In the living room, he found Eliza watching the TV, still wearing the attire from the evening before. Feeling his anger rise, he walked toward her and grabbed her arm, then pulled her up to her feet. "You have some explaining to do," he growled.

Unsurprised by his anger, Eliza shook off his hold and said in an even tone, "Did you really think I would let you handle the Child of Kahil on your own?"

His anger deepened. "Are you threatening me, Eliza?"

She scowled and glared at him. "I'm doing this for your sake, Ragnor," she barked out. "You're not rational when it comes to Aileen. So yes, I've been keeping an eye on her to evaluate how much danger she poses."

Before he could think it through, Ragnor wrapped his hands around Eliza's throat, his eyes glowing. "You should've never gone behind my back," he said quietly, voice low and terrible. Eliza winced when he tightened his hold on her neck. "You betrayed my trust, Wains."

She gave him a somewhat sad smile. "Think that if it makes you feel better," she said softly, "but, Ragnor, if I don't look out for you, then who will?"

He tensed. "I've been doing a fine job so far on my own."

"Famous last words," she said, daring to chuckle. "You can be mad at me. You can even tear my head off if you want—though we both know that won't be enough to kill me. But someone had to make sure you're not in over your head when it comes to this woman."

Furious, Ragnor threw Eliza on the ground and stepped back, glowering at her. "Stay away from Aileen," he snarled. "This is your last warning, Eliza."

She gave him an almost sympathetic look. "Hate me all you want, Rayne," she said gently, "but someone needs to do the job you're refusing to do—"

"She's *my* problem." He cut her off. "I will be the only one to deal with her. Not you, not Atalon, not anyone else but me."

She stared at him quietly for a few long moments before she sighed and looked away. "You have a month, Ragnor," she said quietly. "Find out what the fuck she is before then."

He bared his teeth. "You dare threaten me?"

"It's not a threat. It's a warning," she said matter-of-factly. "If you fail, I'll be forced to take drastic measures, whether you like it or not."

CHAPTER 21
AILEEN

With the gala event less than two weeks away, I should've been in full concentration mode. Not only was this the largest event of the Atalon League, but it was the most prestigious annual event in the art community. Everyone who was anyone in the art world would be there. Unfortunately, my concentration went out the window, with thoughts of Ragnor and Isora circling in my head.

Ragnor, invading my space and yet listening when I told him to back off to prove his sincerity.

Isora, whom I was helpless to help.

From memorizing every piece of art that was going to be exhibited to knowing the names and faces of all artists and compiling essays upon essays of notes and interpretations about each artwork, I'd tried everything in order to focus on my tasks, but my head and heart weren't in it. I was just going through the motions as my mind fled elsewhere.

Every night, despite managing to fall asleep due to the pure exhaustion of trying to do my job while fighting my turbulent thoughts, I experienced the worst nightmares I'd had in many years.

In some of the nightmares, I was dressed in those all-covering black clothes, with Isora sucking my blood, laughing at me, taunting me, and Eleanor, Oz, and Atalon right next to her, looking at me with disgust.

In other nightmares, Ragnor was walking away from me once he saw me surrounded by dead, tiny bodies.

But the worst nightmares were of that house by the river, with the staircases leading down to the basement. I dreamed that I was taking those steps one by one, hearing the familiar screams beckoning me, drawing me in. And when I finally reached the room, it was Isora dangling from the ceiling, her wrists and ankles shackled, begging me to save her as my father's arms wrapped around her from behind.

And those nightmares always ended with Isora's screams echoing in my head as I woke up, the smell of sickening smoke filling my nose.

To say the days passed peacefully would be a lie. Those nightmares haunted me during the days too. I might've been busy, but the nightmares lingered in the back of my mind, as if they were trying to remind me how bad of a person I was.

As if I didn't know that already.

A week after Ragnor left the Atalon League, I found myself walking to Atalon's office, a stack of papers in hand. I was running an errand for Zion, who'd become so busy with preparations for the gala, he barely had time to tutor me anymore. That meant he left all kinds of odd tasks to me, the most junior guide under his wing.

I hadn't seen Atalon since our visit to Isora, for which I'd been glad. I was in no shape or form to face him and the truths he'd revealed to me about how he was conducting certain affairs in his League—and between himself and Ragnor. To be honest, just thinking of him made my blood boil.

It wasn't just about what he did to Isora either. It was the fact that by dating me, he wanted to stick it to Ragnor.

When I arrived at his office, Atalon was on the phone. He motioned for me to enter, and I did, then closed the door behind me before I walked toward his desk. Once I put down the stack of papers, I sat and waited.

Atalon's eyes seemed questioning, but he didn't tell me to leave. Instead, he said into the phone, "Then see to it as soon as you can," before he hung up and turned to me. "What can I help you with, Aileen?"

His voice was so strictly business, it took me a moment to organize my thoughts. *No more being friendly, I see.* "I want to talk to you about something. It won't take long."

Atalon clicked on his computer keyboard, and the monitor blinked. He seemed to be checking something before he turned to me and nodded. "I have ten minutes until my next meeting."

If anyone else had said that, I wouldn't have thought twice about it. But Atalon's tone indicated that he was making a great deal of effort to give me these ten minutes. His eyes showed me such a lofty self-importance that it obviously had been some sort of an attempt at manipulation.

It almost made me smile. Almost. "Thank you so much for your graciousness," I drawled, not bothering to hide the mockery in my tone. That made Atalon's eyes narrow. "Anyway, first things first. I would like to know how you knew about Lord Rayne and me."

Atalon leaned back and looked at me, gaze calculating. He was done pretending with me that he was anything but a sociopath, it seemed. "I thought we're already over it." His lips stretched into a cold smile. "Does it even matter at this point?"

I folded my arms. "I'm here talking to you about it," I retorted curtly. "So obviously it matters."

He chuckled, and it was such a mechanical sound, it made me tense. "Fine, then," he said, smirking now. "I know how Rayne feels about you. I knew it since that time you came to visit my League during the field trip."

Oh. "That's it?"

He cocked his head. "Is that not enough of an answer for you?"

No, it's not, I wanted to say but decided to focus on another matter. "Then next question. What do I need to do for you to release Isora from her current job?"

I'd been sitting on this question ever since I visited Isora. It was true that I was powerless to help her as I was now, but there was still some hope. Atalon liked bargaining. Perhaps I could do something for him, and in return, he would let Isora go.

It was far fetched, but it was better than nothing.

Atalon's eyes flashed with interest. "That's quite the offer, Aileen," he said, his grin turning as sharp as a shark's teeth. "However, I'm not sure you're up for what I have in mind."

"Try me," I said boldly.

And when he answered, I realized just how boldly. "If Isora's removed from the feeding room, then it means we'll need a replacement." He chuckled now. "Ah, Aileen, you should see your face. Well, that's the only offer I can give you." He shrugged, his snakelike eyes gleaming sinisterly. "A life for a life."

It made sense when he put it so casually like that, but in truth, it was an evil deal. A devil's bargain. Curling my hands into fists, I grated out, "Isn't there anything else I can do?"

His grin widened, making him look almost monstrous. "I see your love for your friend only extends that far."

I jolted, feeling as though he'd physically hit me. "It doesn't have to be this way," I said quietly, trying to keep an even voice despite how shaken up inside I was. "I can be of assistance in thousands of different ways."

"Yes, you can." Atalon nodded. "But in the end, I'm the one who makes the rules, and what I say goes. This is my one and only offer." He paused. "Take it or leave it."

I rose to my feet and glared at him. "I thought you wanted us to join forces," I hissed.

"I did, yes," he said, his awful smile still intact. "And while I still do, the only way I want to do this is by you letting me have you. It's nonnegotiable."

Meaning I couldn't bargain Isora for this. He only wanted me to the extent of hurting Ragnor and nothing else. "You're despicable," I spat out.

"Be careful, Aileen," he said as I showed him my back and strode to the door. "I can easily decide that instead of an offer, it's an order."

I threw the door open and gave him one last glare before storming out, slamming the door shut behind me.

My nails were in tatters. I'd been chewing and nibbling on them for the past few hours as I tried to calm myself down.

Because in two days, the gala event would happen.

And I wasn't ready.

Not when Isora was still stuck in that room, with all those vampires feasting on her blood until she would have no Lifeblood left.

Not when Ragnor's absence had left such a large hole in my chest, a hole I was desperate to avoid, to deny, but left me feeling as if a lifeline I didn't know I needed had just disappeared.

But now the gala was almost here, and I felt so lost, I couldn't deal with it.

For the mere three years I'd had freedom, I'd learned how to keep myself busy and satisfied, to a certain extent. The worst problem I'd had back then was whether I could afford the yearly raise in rent. Other problems I solved by using my smarts and wits.

But just as it had been when Ragnor had given me the Imprint, my problems were out of my control.

I wasn't ranked high enough in the hierarchy to help Isora—unless I sold my soul to Atalon.

Even when it came to my relationship with Ragnor, I felt like any semblance of control I might've had disappeared. Because against my better judgment, against everything I'd promised myself, I could feel him pounding down the walls I put around my heart with far too strong a bludgeon.

There was nothing I could do about any of it, and the helplessness caused my anxiety to spike to new levels.

The night before the gala, I was pulled into the dream of the purple-skied field of wilted grass again.

With everything that had been happening with Isora, Ragnor, and Atalon, I hadn't had the chance to practice my time-stopping powers at all. In fact, it had been the last thing on my mind.

That, and the fact I'd met Eliza in real life and learned she was acquainted with Ragnor. His "friend," as she said herself.

Rising to my feet in the midst of the field, I looked around me, but to my surprise, I didn't find Eliza to be there. Instead, there was something like a torn notebook page resting on the wilted grass near me. Frowning, I picked it up and read.

> Aileen—
> I haven't been honest with you before, but I have my reasons. Just as you have your reasons not to reveal the nature of your powers to me.
>
> You must be angry with me for not telling you about my relationship with Ragnor Rayne. You may find my reason a bit lacking, but the truth is, I wanted to get to know you without involving anyone else. You are important to him, you know. Too important.
>
> Nevertheless, I won't be visiting you again. I think I gave you the basics and the direction to find out how

to control your powers from now on. Rest assured, I told none of it to Ragnor, or anyone else, for that matter. Your Sacred status is safe with me.

Next time we meet, I hope it won't be as enemies.

Take care,

E.

And just as abruptly as she appeared in my life, Eliza disappeared.

CHAPTER 22

AILEEN

A scene out of a movie spread out before me when I stepped into the Atalonian Hall.

All guests wore tuxes and evening gowns, appearing as glamorous as celebrities on the red carpet. Dangling lanterns fell from the ceiling in different lengths, like luminous raindrops. The Atalonian Philharmonic Orchestra sat at the back of the room, playing Grieg's *Peer Gynt*, conducted in a manner that helped it become background music rather than the main attraction. Which was just as well, considering what the main attraction was.

Paintings covered the walls and sat on easels throughout the room. Metal and marble sculptures were placed near the artwork in a complementary yet prominent way, what with the contrast of the checkered marble floor. Abstract video art played on the wall behind the orchestra, seemingly moving along with the bows of the strings section and the fingers of the wind players.

"Champagne, Miss Henderson?"

I tore my eyes away from the pretentious, awe-inspiring visual and looked at the waiter in full butler suit who held a round tray full of slender flutes. "Yes, thank you," I said, then gave him a nod of acknowledgment as he handed me a glass.

He gave me a respectful nod in return and left to offer champagne to the couple near me.

Pretending to enjoy the champagne, I walked deeper into the room, feeling out of place and out of sorts. Like most women in attendance, I was wearing an unnecessarily extravagant maxi dress made of silk and colored navy blue, which was skintight and had modest cleavage and a slit down the leg. The dress was paired with silver high heels that hurt my feet like a motherfucker. My hair was pulled into a tall ponytail, black as soot and as straight as an arrow. Heavy makeup made my eyes look as though I'd been sucker punched, and the dark-red tint of the lipstick somehow caused my olive skin to seem paler than usual.

I felt dressed up for a Halloween party rather than an exclusive VIP-only art-curation event.

Being surrounded by so many vampires, I had a hard time discerning who was an Atalonian—the name the Atalon League members adopted, as though the League was a country rather than, well, a League—and who wasn't.

Of course, there were not only vampires in attendance but humans too. But humans were far easier to recognize, especially after I'd seen many come and go during the Atalonian visitation hours. They seemed far less vital and more aged than vampires, even those who were supposedly in their twenties or thirties. It was as if I could smell their future graves.

"*Buonasera*, tesoro," a familiar voice whispered into my ear, making my muscles tense and the tiny hairs on my skin stand on end.

Stepping away, I turned to face Atalon. As always, he had a way of looking fresh and slick no matter the time of night, and his current appearance was no different. With his platinum hair pushed back and a dark-gray suit with a white button-down shirt underneath and a navy blue tie adorning his pale, tall, lean figure, in addition to a clean-shaven chiseled face with high cheekbones, he looked like a decadent movie star. He would've seemed like the epitome of classic perfection had it not been for his pitch-black eyes.

Those eyes were now gleaming in their usual calculated, cunning way as they scanned me from head to toe. "Exquisite," he murmured, his eyes lingering too long on my body before returning to my face.

There was no real interest in his gaze. He looked at me like one would at a dog he owned. And that made me feel as great as if I'd been hit by a wrecking ball. "Thank you, my Lord," I drawled, trying to hide my disgusted discomfort at both his gaze and words. "Now if you'll excuse me . . ."

Before he could stop me, I hurriedly walked away and searched for my boss.

I found Zion already working. He was quite in his element, too; he was talking to a group of humans about the painting behind him, explaining in expert detail the nuances of every brushstroke. I waited near the end of the group until Zion was done.

"Good evening," I told him before he could accompany the group to the next artwork. "When do I start?"

He checked the notes on his paper holder before looking back at me. "Your group is scheduled to commence in fifteen minutes," he said, then motioned toward the wineglass in my hand. "Make sure to get rid of it by then."

"Will do," I replied, and he left to rejoin his group for the next artwork.

Since I had some time until then, I downed the rest of my champagne and went to the square-shaped bar in the middle of the ballroom. I'd never been much of a drinker, but I had to admit I was a bit nervous. With everything going on, I'd barely had the time to mentally prepare myself. It was my first time working as a guide, and while I'd spent the last couple of weeks practicing for this moment after Zion exempted me from writing essays all day, I was still far too nervous for my own good. This gala was the most important event in the Atalon League. Fucking up wasn't an option, especially not now that I was on Atalon's radar for all the wrong reasons.

So, while I was far from a drinker, I felt that liquid courage was the way to go.

"A shot of whiskey, please," I told the bartender.

She nodded and looked behind my shoulder. "And for you, sire?"

I froze as I saw two hands resting on the bar on both sides of me, caging me against a hard chest I could feel at my back. "Same, and make it Macallan for both."

Barely noticing the bartender wandering off, I said quietly, "What are you doing?"

Ragnor's hot breath in my ear made my body involuntarily shudder. "Black hair suits you quite well, Aileen," he murmured, voice rough and sexy and . . .

Fuck. "Do you have to be so close?" I said in a taut voice, feeling my cheeks flush. *This is so not the time,* I thought desperately, trying to calm the sudden heat blooming in my crotch. *Remember what happened last time.*

Ragnor sighed and retracted his hands, moving to my side. I could feel the loss of his heat at my back, and a rush of confusing disappointment filled me, mixed with relief. "I can't help it," he said quietly. "You look ravishing, and I missed you."

My heart jolted, and slowly, I turned to look at him.

And immediately wished I didn't.

Wearing a black suit with a navy blue tie and with his hair pulled into a short ponytail at the back of his head and his face full of bristles, he looked so hot, the need to feel him up was almost unbearable. The heat in his midnight blue eyes as he looked made me want to drop my panties and spread wide for him to take me.

Sucking in a deep breath, I could smell his tasty cologne that made me want to lick his neck, and I forced myself to look away. "What a flirt," I said with a huff, trying to hide how his words truly made me feel, because I still refused to acknowledge his return to my life and his insistence on me giving him a chance.

"Only with you, Aileen," he said quietly. "No one else."

Thankfully, I didn't have to respond because the bartender returned with our drinks. Before he could say something else I didn't want to hear, I chugged the shot, welcoming the burn of the alcohol on my tongue, and I put the glass back on the bar. "I'm busy," I said, turning to leave. "Enjoy your evening."

He grabbed my wrist before I could even take a step, and I whipped my head toward him. The touch of his palm against the skin of my wrist shot a bolt of electricity straight to my loins, and I tensed. "Just a heads-up," he said, giving me a somewhat wicked look. "I'm part of your group."

Of course he fucking was. "Great," I gritted out.

He let me go and gave me a slow, sexy smirk that made me want to both punch him and kiss him. "I'll be in your care, then, Miss Guide."

Who the hell was this playful, flirty man, and where the hell had he hidden all this time?

In an effort to hide how much he got to me, I gave him a pointed scowl before I fled to the other end of the room, wishing the alcohol would take root until it was time for me to do my job.

My group consisted of vampires only. There was a reason for that, too: the vampires were here more as guests than curators, though they could buy artwork if they so wanted. The humans in attendance were the real deal; they were the ones who possessed the deep pockets and willingness to empty them.

Because I was a junior guide, I took the relatively risk-free group.

And that would've been fine if my group didn't consist of so many familiar faces. I wished the ground would split open and swallow me whole.

As he'd said he would be, Ragnor was there, accompanied by his plus-one—Cassidy Jones, my former best friend, and current Gifted vampire of the Rayne League. The last time I'd seen her was at the Auction, and I was caught off guard now by how different she looked, and not because she'd changed her general appearance; her charcoal hair was still as pretty as it always was, tied into a bun at the back of her head, and her feline-like green eyes and pale skin were just as lovely.

Yet her clothing and adornments had changed; she was wearing a suit—similar to the one Ragnor was wearing—only instead of combat boots, she wore moccasins. She barely had any makeup on, not even lipstick, and donned no jewelry either. Along with her stiff posture—again, what the hell?—that seemed far too militaristic to be natural, she could've passed as Ragnor's bodyguard or something, instead of companion.

She also gave me a nod of acknowledgment before returning her gaze forward, face sealed and eyes inscrutable.

Seeing her here without warning made me feel strange. Cassidy belonged to a life long gone. Even when I was a newbie in the Rayne League, we kept our distance from one another, as if we'd never been friends or even known each other. Back then, I'd been angry about it.

Now, though, I found that I didn't care about her or our past relationship whatsoever.

Because while Cassidy and I had been friends for three years, our friendship had never been a deep, true one. It was more of a friendship of convenience, really.

But with Isora, whom I'd known for about two months, I'd found a true friendship. A bond tighter and deeper than any I ever had with Cassidy.

So, for me, she was only somebody that I used to know, and nothing more.

The other members of my group bewildered me just as much. For starters, I had another Lord under my care—Lord Bowman, of the Bowman League in Albuquerque. He was the only Lord I'd met who was so presenceless and forgettable, he could've been invisible. With receding gray hair, pale skin, pale-blue eyes, and a white tux, he seemed almost like a ghost.

Another was a Lieutenant I recognized from the Renaldi League—Stefan. He was accompanied by another familiar face, Zoey, my former suitemate at the Rayne League.

She was thinner than the last time I saw her, her tall form far bonier than I remembered. Her sandy-brown hair had grown out of her bob cut and was now brushing her shoulders, with her fringes long gone. Her once heart-shaped face was now almost oval, as if it, too, had lost weight, and her long pointy nose seemed almost larger now because of that. As if to mimic her sad state, even her freckles, once so vivid and widespread, were smaller and paler now on her olive skin. She wore a ruby red dress that complemented Stefan's red tux, and the dress didn't seem to fit right, as if it was a few sizes too large.

Zoey didn't look at me as I said, "Hello, everyone. I'm Aileen Henderson, and I'll be your guide for tonight." She kept her head low, like she couldn't bear looking at me.

My chest tightened, and I silently promised that the moment I finished the tour, I would take her aside and ask her what the hell had happened to her.

I led the group toward the first exhibition—a seven-foot-tall sculpture of a chimera. "Demetria Holsten's sculpture is a captivating representation of a chimera, a legendary creature from Greek mythology," I said a bit too fast, hoping it didn't sound like I was spouting the facts I'd been drilling into my brain over the past two weeks, despite it being the case. "At its core, it has the head of a fierce and majestic lion, complete with a powerful, open-mouthed roar and a flowing mane that frames its face. The lion's eyes are intense and seem to pierce through you. Emerging from the lion's body is the midsection of a goat, with shaggy fur and a distinctively different character from the lion above. The goat's body is muscular, and it appears alert and aware, while its face carries a serene expression, a stark contrast to the lion's fierceness."

I could feel a certain gaze on my face, making my cheeks flame, but I ignored it and pointed with a bit of a shaking hand at the back part of the sculpture. "As you can see, a long sinuous serpent's tail extends from its rear, meticulously coiling itself around the body. The tail's curve is gracefully carved, ending with a sharp, pointed tip."

Bowman seemed to nod along, staring at the sculpture like it was an interesting mathematical problem. Stefan appeared bored, looking everywhere else with heavy lids. I realized then that his hand was holding Zoey's, not like a lover would, but like a jailer.

After clearing my throat, I continued, "The entire sculpture exudes a sense of dynamic tension as these different animal forms seamlessly merge and intertwine. It captures the chimera's mythical and otherworldly essence, giving it an air of mystery and awe." I fiddled with the wrinkles of my dress as I talked. "It's a compelling piece that evokes the wonder of Greek mythology and the blending of the real and the fantastical."

Proud that I remembered all the words, I instinctively turned to look at Ragnor.

His face was relaxed, and his eyes held a soft warmth within them as he stared at me, and it made me feel all sorts of ways. And when he mouthed, *You're doing great*, I felt my chest expanding as butterflies filled my stomach and my cheeks flushed with satisfaction.

How could he still have such an effect on me?

Tearing my eyes away from him, I found Cassidy staring at the sculpture, swallowing a yawn. Yeah, art was definitely not her thing, and even if she acted all bodyguard-like, it was good to see that she was still her.

I started to feel a little less nervous when we moved to the next artwork, a painting of the Triple Goddess. "Another Gifted of the League, Yoon Ji-Woo, has been studying the Wiccan traditions for his art and painted the Maiden, the Mother, and the Crone according to his findings . . ."

As the tour progressed, I noticed a few things. One, Stefan refused to let Zoey's hand go no matter what. Two, Cassidy kept her straight-backed militaristic pose for the entire time. Three, Bowman, the only one who spoke from time to time to ask me some questions regarding the monetary value of the pieces, seemed about as interested in the art itself as Cassidy. And four, Ragnor's eyes never left my face as he seemed to listen to my ramblings with rapt attention.

After forty long minutes, it was finally time for the last piece of art—and my favorite one, despite its artist. "Last but not least is the *Bird of the Nile* by Lord Orion Atalon," I said, motioning toward the heartbreakingly beautiful piece, and it seemed my thoughts and emotions about this piece came through my voice, because suddenly—in addition to Ragnor and Bowman—Stefan, Cassidy, and even Zoey came to attention, staring at the painting. "I don't believe words can describe this one," I said now, glad to have everyone's attention. Putting aside my feelings toward Atalon, I wholeheartedly believed his pieces deserved all the attention and respect in the world. "So instead, I'll let you have a look and feel the art for yourself."

Almost too fittingly, the orchestra began playing Barber's famous *Adagio for Strings*. Epic music for an epic artwork.

I looked at the painting along with the others, feeling myself fall into its magic once again. It made me wonder, not for the first time, what Atalon's actual magic was. He'd once said it was related to his artwork, but in what sort of way?

Whatever it was, the painting was magical enough in and of itself. So magical, in fact, that I could almost feel myself right inside it, in the Nile River in Egypt, watching the bird soaring above me not just as a silhouette but as a fully fleshed bird, with a pheasant's body, a long feathery tail, and large feathery wings, all of it painted bright red and orange, with a pair of brilliant yellow eyes looking right at me as the bird descended, its yellow gaze searing my skin, burning my bones, and setting my soul on fire—

I blinked. What the hell was that?

Then everything exploded.

CHAPTER 23
AILEEN

Fire was all I could see.

Smoke was all I could smell.

Ashes were all I could taste.

Heat was all I could feel.

Screams were all I could hear. Horrible screams that made me feel both hot and cold at the same time.

I found it hard to think, being engulfed by this terrible inferno. I didn't know who or what I was. I didn't even know my own name.

The fire and I were one.

Nothing corporeal existed in this infernal hell. Not a soul could enter without being scorched to oblivion. But the fire somehow became me, or I became the fire, and that protected me from the promised demise.

A wisp of a voice echoed in this fiery chamber, but I couldn't hear it beyond the screams and cruel cackling of flames. The voice flitted through the burning air again, louder but no less unintelligible.

When the voice came a third time, it was loud, strong, and clear.

WAKE.

Within one breath and the next, I was back. The infernal hell was sucked away, replaced by the Atalonian ballroom. I was back to myself, my body, and my name, my short amnesia gone now that I was separated from that fire.

I sucked in a deep breath, then another one and another one, until my rapid heartbeat quieted down and the perspiration sticking to my skin slowly dissipated. I pressed my hands down on my knees and saw red spots marring the hem of my dress. My nose was bleeding.

Embarrassed by the whole thing, I took one last deep breath and straightened to apologize to the guests, but the words died in my mouth.

Because what I saw was an entirely different scene than the one before the fire had taken me hostage.

In a span of what felt like a split second, the ballroom had transformed into a battlefield.

Creatures that looked like humans but could not possibly be humans raged around the hall. All of them were tall, far taller than six-five, with a pair of curved, pointed horns coming out of their temples and with hooves instead of feet. All of them were naked from head to toe, exposing skin in varying unnatural shades, from light blue and green to navy and emerald, and revealing their sex.

The creatures were actively attacking the vampires as the humans screamed and scrambled for the exit.

To my left, Stefan was facing a female horned creature with indigo skin who was attempting to grab Stefan's blond hair, but with his lean, nimble body, Stefan evaded her attempts, causing her large, humanlike eyes to bulge with rage.

What was especially odd was the fact Stefan had a deck of cards in his hands and was doing some sort of card trick while murmuring something I couldn't quite hear—but it seemed the creature heard, because she gave a chilling inhuman growl that made me freeze in place.

Then, using sleight of hand, Stefan made some cards disappear, pointed at the creature's face, and said loud enough for me to hear, "Let me show you where the cards are!"

The seven of hearts broke through the creature's eyeball from within, causing some sort of gold liquid to explode in the wound.

But I had no time to be shocked, because just then, another creature, this one seaweed green skinned, appeared from behind Stefan, about to catch him off guard. I was going to scream at him to look out when something white and fast crashed into the monster, pushing it against the wall, which cracked and began to crumble.

It took me a second to realize I'd just seen Lord Bowman in action.

Something flashed to my right, and suddenly Ragnor was in front of me, the sleeves of his shirt torn, the tie gone, and his hair freed from its ponytail. "Stop gawking," he barked at me and pulled me to my feet. Only then I realized I'd fallen down at one point. "Get the hell out of here—"

There was a sound so loud, it reverberated through the chaotic noises around the hall. As if he knew what was coming, Ragnor yelled, "Cover your ears!"

Automatically, I did, and so did Ragnor, but what came after was the eeriest thing I'd ever heard, accompanied by the scariest thing I'd ever seen.

Dust, debris, and shattered glass from the broken-in ceiling and the busted windows clouded the air as vampires and the monsters fought all over. Then a loud, almost deafening voice spread across the room, not singing any lyrics but humming a melody that made me shiver.

I also recognized that voice. I would recognize it anywhere.

Cassidy.

As Cassidy hummed in an unnaturally loud voice from somewhere in the hall, the vampires and the creatures slowly came to a stop, their eyes becoming empty and strange until they ceased to move.

It almost looked like time had stopped, I thought, and the moment I finished the thought, the song paused. The debris froze in the air. Ragnor was no longer breathing steadily before me.

I'd made time stop.

And it . . . doesn't hurt?

Slowly, hesitantly, I rose to my feet, letting my hands fall, and when I moved my head, a few strands of my hair fell over my shoulder.

Shaking, I raised the strands to my eyes. They were wavy and gold, not a trace of black remaining.

Then I lifted my eyes toward the *Bird of the Nile*, but when I saw the canvas, it felt like, along with time itself, my heart had stopped too.

The canvas was white.

Empty.

But the painting was just there, so how . . .

"My magic certainly works in mysterious ways, doesn't it?"

I whirled around to see Atalon walking toward me, the only one besides me moving in this scene frozen in time. My heart was suddenly beating again, and this time it was like a war drum, as if trying to warn me of something.

Because how could he move about when I had just stopped time for everyone and everything?

"How . . . ?" I blurted out.

But the question got lodged in my throat when I saw his face, and the expression there was the most terrifying thing I'd ever seen.

Atalon was smiling triumphantly. His eyes, a pair of black pits, were now glowing, but instead of a faint glow like most vampires', their glow was more like shadows cast on his face, giving him a fearsome, insane look I never wanted to see again.

It was the first time since I met him that I saw Atalon look absolutely elated, and the scary elation on his face was mirrored in his eyes.

He stopped a few inches away from me, his smile impossibly wide. "Aileen, Aileen, Aileen . . . I knew buying you would be worth my while."

Before I could react, or think, or do something, he backhanded me across the face so strongly, I couldn't even feel pain before darkness swallowed me whole.

CHAPTER 24

RAGNOR

One moment, she was there, right in front of him, close enough to kiss.

Then the next, Aileen Henderson was across the room, held in Atalon's arms as he carried her out of the ballroom, her golden hair veiling her face.

And only one thought passed through his head.

He had to save her.

He climbed to his feet and was about to run when a hand grabbed him. He was going to shake the hand away when he saw Cassidy, eyes wide with horror, staring at him pleadingly. "I can't make it stop, my Lord."

Then, as if all her strength left her, Cassidy fell to the ground, unconscious.

Fuck. Growling, Ragnor put Cassidy over his shoulder and began to run toward the exit, needing it to not be too late.

But three median Jinn suddenly surrounded him, eyeing him with drool dripping down their chins. They could sense his huge amount of Lifeblood, Ragnor knew, and that made them far too hungry for his liking.

Impatient, Ragnor didn't bother with discretion. He grabbed his own aura with his mind and shot it outward, expanding it in a split second until it engulfed all three Jinn. Then, like flipping a switch, he changed the tone of his aura from neutral to horror.

The Jinn's responding screams were bloodcurdling. So much so that the humans in attendance began running around aimlessly and fearfully, getting themselves killed.

Having no patience, Ragnor put Cassidy down and jumped from one Jinni to another, twisting their heads clean off their necks. It took all his physical strength to accomplish this feat, and by the time the beheaded Jinn's bodies fell to the ground, bleeding their corrupted golden ichor, he was utterly spent.

With what little strength he had left, Ragnor returned to Cassidy's unconscious form, draped her over his shoulder, and resumed his run to the exit. He'd nearly reached Aileen and Atalon when a Jinni slammed against the ceiling near the entrance doors, causing it to crumble to the floor and block the exit.

Ragnor's enraged roar echoed in the hall.

"My Lord . . ." Cassidy's voice was suddenly in his ear, weak but stable. "I . . . I think I overdid it this time . . ."

Ragnor changed routes and started running toward one of the shattered windows. "Logan's right outside," Ragnor said in haste, breathing heavily now that he was running out of strength. "Call him and have him get you."

He pushed through the open window and dropped down to the ground three floors below with a thud that normally wouldn't have made him shake in pain, but in his current state, he wasn't at his best.

Fighting the Jinn while they were actively using their ability to suck his Lifeblood at an exponential rate was taking its toll.

Ragnor placed Cassidy down on the grass of the museum's main courtyard and struggled to climb back up to the window. Out of breath and nearly depleted of physical energy, he barely managed to push himself through. Standing, he discovered vampire bodies scattered across the floor, with only a few left fighting the Jinn, Bowman and Renaldi's Lieutenant among those few.

He had to end this now. He was the only one who could.

Gritting his teeth, Ragnor leaned his worn-out body against a thankfully not-crumbled wall and tapped into his other power. The one unrelated to his Sacred magic. The one he'd been born with all those ages ago.

The one that could kill him.

Reaching for the ether, a call he hadn't made in so long that for a moment, he wondered if the power was still within him, he whispered, "Matareh." With immense relief and cruel delight, he watched as a crimson tether only he could see wrapped itself around each and every Jinni neck present and squeezed.

Thirty horned heads fell to the bloody floor, and for the first time in decades, Ragnor was so drained both mentally and physically that the long-forgotten oblivion threatened to come and stake its claim.

But Ragnor refused to give in to it. Leaning against the wall, he pushed himself upright and flung himself over the window. This time, he landed far from gracefully, and he felt his bones groan.

Just a bit more . . .

But his breathing was too heavy, and the pressure in his chest was too hard to bear. His legs were numb, and dark pinpricks appeared in his vision.

And so Ragnor's body had reached its limit.

CHAPTER 25

AILEEN

I woke up in a prison cell.

There was no other way to describe it, really. It was a dark room made of stone—the walls, floor, and ceiling—with slick metal bars and a little dangling lamp. Other than a sink, the room was completely empty. No furniture, no window, not even a sewer opening.

And no way to escape.

Without anything to do, I decided that at the very least, I should get comfortable. Grabbing the hem of my dress, I tore off a wide strip. Then I used the piece of torn cloth as a hair band and pulled my hair into a ponytail. Once I kicked off my heels, I felt much better.

Though not really.

Not after what had happened at the gala.

I had so many questions, starting with a few obvious ones: What were those monsters? Why did they attack us? How did the *Bird of the Nile* painting disappear? What had that infernal hell been? How did Atalon's time not stop while it had stopped for everyone else? Why did he knock me out and bring me here like a prisoner?

And what happened to Ragnor? To Cassidy? To everyone else? Were the humans all dead? What the hell was going on?

The sound of a door opening echoed in the stony dungeon, snapping my attention back to the present. I could hear footsteps coming from my right, and I watched unblinkingly until a disgustingly familiar man appeared.

With a dark-purple three-piece suit, a black shirt, a silver tie, and a shiny Rolex, Atalon could've passed for either a distinguished young CEO of an up-and-coming high-tech start-up or the head of a mob family. Considering his sinister smile, I was leaning toward the latter.

"I see you've made yourself comfortable," Atalon said as he came to a stop at the bars, hands in the pockets of his trousers. "I must say, incarceration suits you better than I would've expected."

Climbing to my feet, I glared at him. "I think it would suit you much more," I said in a thankfully steady voice.

He grinned and shook his head. "Well. Good to see you too. Where would you like me to start?"

I leaned against the wall and folded my arms. "I wasn't aware it was the villain's monologue time," I drawled, even though inside I wasn't as calm as I pretended to be. In fact, my entire body was shivering uncontrollably, and a suffocating feeling clogged my throat.

"It's going to be more of a dialogue, actually," Atalon said, chuckling in a way that sent chills down my spine.

Acting as sassy as I could to hide my true emotions, I asked, "Why did you hit me and put me behind bars when I did nothing?"

He shrugged. "It's more of a precaution, really. You see," he said, eyes brimming with that shadowy glow, "I couldn't risk bringing you back to the League without knowing what kind of magic you possess and if it's going to be a threat."

The triumphant glint in his eyes didn't match the words leaving his mouth. Atalon was lying. It reminded me of how my father looked when he was about to head to the basement after acquiring a new little bird. The only thing Atalon lacked was the absolute devotion my father had for his horrible task.

"Now that we established that, tell me, tesoro," he said, coming closer to the bars. "How come an insignificant little Common vampire not only managed to wrap the oldest Lord in the United States around her finger but also somehow, inexplicably and conveniently, became a Sacred after the Auction?"

I tensed and crossed my arms across my chest. As if I would answer that. It wasn't like I even could. I had no idea what was happening to me or how or even why. "How about you tell me how long you've known I have magic?"

His grin returned. "How about an exchange? A quid pro quo. Answer my question first; then I'll respond to yours."

"I know what *quid pro quo* means," I snapped, irritated by his condescendingly cheerful voice. Then, seeing as I was in no state to argue, I decided to reply with the truth. "I don't know. One day, I woke up, and I could use magic."

Something I couldn't quite read passed across his eyes, and I had the feeling he didn't buy my answer. But to my surprise, he moved right to answering my question. And that answer was far more shocking. "I've suspected that since the Auction, but tonight confirmed it beyond any doubt."

My heart boomed in my ears. "Is that why you bought me?"

Atalon smiled. "Indeed. Now tell me about your magic." He put his arms behind his back and began pacing. "In return, I'll tell you about mine."

Everything in me told me not to say anything, but what was the point? He already knew about my magic. He obviously knew its nature to a certain extent, considering the fact he'd managed to somehow negate the effect of my time stopping. So I gave him the truth. "I can stop time for a short period. That's all there is to it." I paused. "Now, tell me how you could move when I stopped time, as if it didn't affect you."

He smirked and, to my annoyance, ignored my question when he said, "There is no specific term for what my magic is, but I can describe it to you."

I glowered at him.

His face turned nostalgic. "At first, before I developed my Sacred magic, I was Gifted. Being an exceptionally talented painter in my human life, my talent transformed into a unique Gift that allowed me to not just master every art style but also imitate the styles of any artist I wanted down to the littlest detail."

He shoved his hands back in his pockets and resumed his pacing. "In the beginning, I'd made quite the business out of my Gift, under the name of my then Lord, Bowman." His voice took on a tone of fondness I didn't expect. "Selling copies of famous paintings while claiming them as the originals, so much so that even the greatest art experts couldn't notice any difference, was thrilling. A few hundred years into my vampirehood, however, my art style began taking an interesting turn." He paused again, his face filling with almost childlike joy. "It's as though my own talent was ready to be born after centuries of being dormant. And suddenly, my paintings weren't just copies. They were mine. And they were the best of all time."

He might have been speaking arrogantly about it, but I tended to agree. The quality of his paintings was out of this world. Coloring, techniques, the meticulous lines of his brush . . . Every painting he drew was a masterpiece.

"But there was a catch to this new talent of mine," he said, "and that catch was magic."

He stopped, closed his eyes, and moved his hands as though he was conducting an orchestra. "Every time I sit down to paint, my magic activates," he said with reverence that gave me the wrong kind of goose bumps. "The paintings are always pictures of either the past, present, or future of other people, and never mine." He opened his eyes to give me a smug look. "Humans call this kind of magic fortune-telling, only I'm able to enact it through my paintings."

Putting his hands in his pockets, he said, "Unfortunately, I never know whose fortune I'm telling. The paintings can show an image from the past, present, or future of someone in India for all I know. It's a very, very rare occasion for me to find out whose fortune I had once painted."

I remembered staring at the *Bird of the Nile* and feeling as though I was right there. The bird, a mere black silhouette in the painting, had become vivid, full of color, the longer I'd stared, until it felt like its yellow eyes were about to consume me. The memory made me shudder, an ominous feeling unfolding in the pit of my stomach.

"When you looked at the painting, it must have reacted to you, recognizing you as its owner," Atalon said now, eerie satisfaction in his voice, "and when you recognized it as yours, too, the painting disappeared, no longer needing to exist now that it found its owner."

His gaze locked mine now, and there was that gleeful triumph back to his shadowy, glowing eyes. "The moment you absorbed the painting, a bond manifested between the two of us. The painting let me know that it found its owner, you see. But it doesn't end there." His smile grew so sinister, it made me jolt. "The bond then showed me the painting's owner's entire past, right up to the present."

At first, his words didn't compute. I simply stared at him, as if still waiting for the punch line of some sick joke.

It was only when my knees hit the cold stone floor that I realized I was not only shaking uncontrollably but had lost all strength to keep myself standing.

Because he knew. Atalon's triumphant eyes told me that he knew.

"Now that you know what I'm capable of, I believe it's time that we start over," Atalon said, looking at me with a happy gleam in his eyes. "I know exactly when you received your magic. I know exactly what happened between you and Rayne. I know exactly what you did to that poor boy Logan. I know exactly what part you played in your father's crimes." He grinned. "So now it's time I tell you what I'm going to do with you."

Every word he said was like a kick to my gut. My mouth was dry. My breaths were shallow. My mind was numb. Everything seemed so surreal all of a sudden that I found it hard to concentrate on anything at all.

"There is someone out there who wants and needs you even more than I do," he said with a smile so happy and cold, all I could do was stare. "You see, the monsters who crashed the gala event are, in fact, the Jinn."

At this point, nothing could surprise me.

"I decided to strike a deal with the few who survived."

Or maybe I could still be surprised.

"They might be our natural enemy, but in this case, we have a common interest," Atalon said with so much satisfaction, my heart sank. "You see, the price they're willing to pay to rent you out for a few weeks is far too tempting to refuse, Natalia."

CHAPTER 26

RAGNOR

Ragnor paced in front of the large skyscraper in downtown Rochester, feeling as though someone had torn through his chest and squeezed.

"My Lord," Logan now said as he walked alongside him. "Maika called."

"And?" Ragnor prompted in a growl as he continued pacing, his strides quicker and wider.

Logan caught up with his pace. "She was told the Atalon League is under lockdown."

Under different circumstances, Ragnor would've understood. The Jinn had just destroyed the Atalonian Hall and the invaluable art collection that had been on display. That, and the fact a few vampires had gone missing from the event, some of them members of the Atalon League.

But these were not normal circumstances. Because Atalon hadn't simply put his League on lockdown—he refused Ragnor's requests to meet him.

Hardly anyone ever dared to say no to Ragnor.

And so Ragnor was on high alert. Something wasn't right within the Atalon League—not only the surprise attack of the Jinn. Atalon had abandoned his League members and guests to save not just his own ass—but unconscious Aileen's.

As if Aileen was worth more to him than anyone else.

But Ragnor had known Atalon for years. He knew the chances of Atalon falling for Aileen were slim, if only because he doubted Atalon was capable of such a deep emotion.

This mystery, added by Atalon's refusal to see Ragnor after such a massive attack, made Ragnor more than simply uneasy.

"Tell Maika to call them again," Ragnor now ordered Logan. "If that fails, we move to the next step."

"Yes, my Lord," Logan said at once and walked away, toward the Rayne League van waiting in the parking lot.

Once his Troop Commander was gone, Ragnor took out his phone and dialed a familiar number. After one ring, a tight voice answered. "How's Cassidy?"

"She's fine. Resting," Ragnor replied in a rush. "Magnus, I'm going off the radar for a while."

Magnus was quiet for a few moments before he asked, "What do you need me to do?"

"Take care of the League until I send word," Ragnor replied curtly.

Magnus let out a rough sigh. "Do I want to know what you're up to?"

Ragnor didn't want to go into detail. It was out of the question to tell Magnus that the moment he awoke at the van after the gala fiasco, his heart fell and he felt fear for the first time in centuries. Telling him this fear was for a woman, a Common who was no longer a Rayne League member, was beyond his capabilities at the moment.

He would explain everything to his oldest friend after he had Aileen back in the safety of his arms.

"Just text Logan that they can head back," Ragnor now said and hung up, feeling a sense of urgency. He glanced back at the van momentarily before he squared his shoulders and walked inside the skyscraper.

The lobby was empty, since it was close to dawn, and Ragnor's footsteps echoed off the marble walls. He'd reached the elevator when the sound of flapping wings resounded behind him.

Without turning around, Ragnor said, "Is the ether still uneasy around here?"

Luceras came to stand next to him as Ragnor pressed the elevator button. "Yes," the Malachi replied. "So you've encountered the Jinn, then."

"They attacked a hall full of vampires and humans," Ragnor explained quietly as the elevator doors opened. The two of them walked in, and Ragnor pressed the button for negative three—the lowest parking floor. "You must've heard about it by now."

Luceras's silence was answer enough.

They descended slowly, and once they reached the destination, Ragnor stepped out and turned to face the Malachi. "Is it stronger here?"

With a nod, Luceras looked around him before he began moving deep into the parking floor. Ragnor followed him, knowing Luceras was busy connecting with the ether to find exactly the point where the ether was making a fuss.

Stopping abruptly at a seemingly random spot—an empty parking space in the middle of the lot—Luceras turned to Ragnor and said, "If you go directly down a few floors from here, you'll find a few Jinn. I can't tell you exactly how many there are."

Ragnor stared at the patch of asphalt. Even though he could access the ether to a certain level, it was nowhere near close to the degree that the Malachi could. The Malachi were able to "bond" with the ether intimately enough to tell when it was unstable, while Ragnor could see the translucent thin dimension colored red as nothing but a tool to be used. He couldn't "bond" with the ether.

Though sometimes, he wished he still could.

"Thank you, Luceras." Ragnor glanced at the Malachi, who was now staring at him. "I'll take it from here."

“As you should, Deveran,” Luceras replied quietly. “Don’t forget; you owe me two favors now.”

Ragnor nodded gravely and watched as, without farewells, Luceras disappeared into thin air.

Staring at the asphalt again, Ragnor calculated how long it would take him to do what he planned. His Lifeblood levels were still low after his latest excursion and exposure to the Jinn, even after he drank from Logan, a Gifted. Waiting for his Lifeblood to return to normal by resting for a few days was out of the question.

So Ragnor sat down on the asphalt, closed his eyes, and did what he had to do.

CHAPTER 27
AILEEN

Hours after Atalon left, a new face appeared in the dungeon, belonging to a man I did not expect to see.

Oz entered the room, holding what seemed to be a large bundle of black clothes. He didn't say a word as he pressed some sort of button, making the bars retreat into the ceiling.

I knew why he didn't tell me something along the lines of *Don't try to escape*. In my current exhausted state, even sitting up took all my strength to manage. Running away? What a joke.

Surprisingly gently, Oz put the black bundle in his arms on the stone floor of my chamber before he stepped back out and returned the bars to their place. He looked at me, then at the black bundle before he motioned toward the latter and said, "Olive branch."

Then he was gone.

Confused, I turned to look at the black bundle and paused. Did it just . . . move?

An ominous feeling twisted in my stomach as I crawled toward the bundle and somehow managed to push some of it away. What I saw made me feel so sick that even if I had a five-star meal laid out in front of me, I wouldn't have been able to take a bite.

A bone stuck out between the black blankets. Or, at least, almost a bone. The skin that covered what seemed to have once been a person's arm was so thin, it was practically transparent.

Slowly, I pushed more of the black blankets until I found the vampire's face, and my heart sank. The cheeks were nonexistent. None of the skin on the face existed, really; it was thinner than the rest of the body, looking like I could cut it with a feather. The face bones jutted out, so sharp and visible as to be horrifying. The hair around the head was thin, too, and gray, devoid of all color.

My eyes told me it was a corpse. My mind said it was a friend clinging to what little life she had left to save.

My gut told me it was Isora. Sweet, sweet Isora who had been dealt a hand far worse than she deserved, not once, but twice. Just then her words came back to me: *From one hell to another.*

With a shaky hand, I reached out to her face and softly pushed back a few strands of hair. She jolted, almost like she'd received an electric shock but then stilled. Tears fell down on her cheek. My tears.

Because this . . . this was a nightmare.

Isora was my friend, and I . . .

I didn't save her.

My head rested against Isora's chest, listening to the slow cadence of her heart. That's what I'd been doing for hours: listening to her heartbeat to reassure myself she was still alive. Barely.

I had no idea what kind of "olive branch" Oz thought this would be. It wouldn't be long until Isora started crumbling to ash. So why bring her here? For me to say goodbye? For me to see evidence of what a failure I was? What a shitty friend I was? To prove to me that my influence with Atalon was done? That I was back to being a nobody like I'd been in the Rayne League?

Footsteps echoed through the chamber. Multiple footsteps, in fact.

Straightening, I stared as Atalon appeared, along with an entourage of about a dozen people I didn't recognize. Some of them looked normal, but there were three of them who were taller than basketball players, with horns and hooves.

The Jinn.

"Evening, Aileen," Atalon now said as he came to a stop before the bars. "Meet your new owners for the next few weeks."

A Jinni man walked forward, giving me a smile. He looked familiar. Maybe it was his unbound inky black curls or his startling violet-tinted silver eyes set in a ruggedly handsome face that sported a five-o'clock shadow. Wearing black cargo pants and a turtleneck shirt, he could've passed as one of those bad boys in the rom-coms I used to watch with Cassidy and Skye.

The only difference was that he couldn't possibly be human. In fact, as he walked toward the bars, his movements were languid and silent, a contrast to his ripped figure. I knew that even if I'd seen him on the street, I wouldn't have mistaken him for a human.

When his violet eyes landed on me, surprisingly kind, I jolted as a memory pierced my head.

A park in Las Vegas, being held at a scythe point by a hooded man, and a pair of unforgettable quicksilver eyes shining in the darkness . . .

Recognition spread through me, and I felt my face pale. This man was one of the three who had kidnapped me when I attempted to run away from the Renaldi League during the field trip with the Rayne League. His companions had been killed and beheaded by a monstrous-looking Ragnor at the time, and somehow, this one convinced my former Lord to let him get away.

And now he was here.

And by the warm look in his eyes, he recognized me too.

"Nice to finally meet you, Hemet," my past kidnapper said now. "I'm Wode."

I had no idea what *Hemet* meant, but something told me it couldn't be good.

Atalon pressed a button to raise the bars and turned to Wode. "As per our agreement, you'll take Aileen and the blood slave in exchange for the Tears of Euphorrey."

Wode's eyes didn't leave my face as he said, "Marcia, bring the box."

One of the seven-foot-tall Jinn stepped forward. She was stark naked, emerald green covering her large pierced breasts and hairy crotch, with long bright-red hair and a set of eyes with enlarged pupils. Curved horns, like those of a goat, sprouted out of her head, and horse-like hooves adorned her feet. She held a small velvet box in her wide palms as though it contained something fragile and got down on one knee next to Wode.

After taking the box, Wode handed it over to Atalon. "Be careful," he said, a warning in his voice as Atalon opened the box and stared at its contents, hidden from me, with cold yet greedy eyes. "The Tears are very fragile, and we expect you to return them in perfect condition."

"No worries," Atalon said dismissively, not taking his greedy eyes off the box.

There was something ominous about those Tears they were talking about. Why would Atalon exchange me and Isora for this thing? Isora was one thing—Atalon thought of her as disposable. But with me being Sacred, I thought he would've wanted to keep a leash on me. So these Tears of Euphorrey—or whatever they were called—had to be something worthy enough for Atalon to part with me for a while in exchange for owning them, even if just until I returned.

"Then I believe we're done here," Atalon said, motioning toward me and Isora. "They're all yours."

A noise from somewhere up above us shook the room, effectively cutting Atalon off. Wode glared at the ceiling while Marcia, the Jinni who'd brought the box, glowered at Atalon in suspicion. "What the hell is this?" she snarled, her feminine voice so normal, it was too much of a stark contrast to her grotesque looks.

Atalon seemed to be genuinely confused. "I don't—"

BOOM!

The stone ceiling suddenly broke in with such force, the ground quaked. I held on to Isora protectively, staring as Atalon backed away with wide eyes and the Jinni prepared for a fight.

When the debris settled, a man straightened, a luminous glow coating his skin. Cobalt blue eyes shone in his contorted face, and his fangs were unsheathed. His dark-brown hair rested on his shoulders in a haphazard mess, and his shirtless chest rippled with muscles. His barefoot long legs, covered by a pair of faded jeans, suddenly crouched, and in an instant, the man launched himself at the Jinni.

A fight broke out, so fast it was a blur—all I could do was simply stare, clutching Isora to me in fear. I tried to follow what was happening, but all I could see were heads flying into the air, following the horrible sounds of bones breaking and flesh being torn like paper. A pool of golden liquid, the Jinni's blood, covered the floor.

I glanced at Atalon, who stared at the scene in shock, the precious box forgotten in his hands.

Suddenly, Wode was in front of me, gold blood and a look of determination on his face. Before I could protest, he grabbed Isora and put her over his shoulder like a sack of potatoes, while with his other hand he pulled me quickly to my feet.

But before we could move, the luminous man came crashing into him. Wode let me go but somehow still got hold of Isora; then the luminous man was on me, his eyes glowing neon as he took in my state.

He didn't speak, however, as he lifted me in his arms and carried me princess-style, somehow enfolding my body in the same white glow as his, and, without a look back, jumped straight up into the hole he'd created in the ceiling.

There were screams and shouts from below as the luminous man moved so fast, it was as if he was flying upward rather than jumping from floor to floor. Quite belatedly, I realized he was taking me away, saving me, but—"Go back," I said, voice raspy. "We need to go back!"

Isora was still there.

I couldn't leave without her!

In less than a minute, the luminous man and I were suddenly outside the Atalon League compound and in a dimly lit underground parking lot. The man landed us on the floor next to a large hole in the ground and ran toward a sleek SUV. He quickly put me in the passenger seat, but before he could shut my door, I put my hand against it and looked at him, desperate and afraid to do what I assumed we were going to do next. "We need to get Isora," I pleaded. "She's my friend!"

The man paused, and suddenly he was no longer luminous, his eyes were no longer glowing ferociously, and his fangs returned to their normal size as he retracted them into his gums.

Midnight blues trained on me as Ragnor murmured something in a language I couldn't decipher, and against my will, my lashes were a heavy blanket across my eyes, and slumber pulled me under.

CHAPTER 28

AILEEN

I woke up in a small tacky room that looked as though it had been decorated in the fifties, with a floral tapestry, old pink sheets, and ugly pastel green curtains.

Trying to push the blankets off me, I could hardly lift my hands. My body was heavy—so heavy, in fact, that rolling onto my back took whatever energy I had left.

Footsteps grew closer, and I saw a gorgeous man with a far-too-small towel around his waist coming out of the bathroom.

And for a moment, nothing else mattered but Ragnor Rayne being in this small room, right before me, looking like a god.

I couldn't help but blatantly leer at his body like a pervert. Lickable, sun-kissed skin covered his tight pecs, leading to a sexy V barely hidden by the damned towel. Long powerful legs, taut with muscles, made me instinctually wet my lips. Raking my eyes up his body, I watched his biceps flexing as his corded arms used another towel to dry off his hair.

Despite the fact I couldn't move, my body seemed to be working just fine, if the slickness on my inner thighs was anything to go by.

When he turned his back to me and dropped his towel, revealing a muscular ass I wanted to bite, I wondered if he knew I was awake, considering he hadn't looked in my direction even once. Taking the opportunity to devour him with my eyes, I trailed my gaze from his butt to his back and up to his broad shoulders, where I could simply stare.

In the few times Ragnor and I had had sex, I'd never gotten a good look at his back. It wasn't that unusual, considering we were mostly fooling around in empty rooms and taking off only the clothes necessary to fuck. But even that one time we did have sex fully naked, I didn't get to explore his entire body.

So I never knew his back was full of scars.

Before I could study those scars, however, Ragnor pulled on a clean black tee that hid his spectacular body. When he put on a pair of jeans, I had to swallow my disappointment and come back to my senses.

What the hell was I doing, drooling over Ragnor Rayne like this? Did I have no pride?

"I see you're awake."

My breath got stuck in my throat as Ragnor faced me and sat down on the bed right next to me. "Here," he said, bringing his soap-smelling wrist to my mouth. "Drink."

I glanced at him, hoping my cheeks weren't red with lust when I said, "I'll be fine with human blood."

He gave me a somewhat wry smile. "You've lost a lot of Lifeblood, Aileen. Normal blood won't be enough to replenish it."

Having no desire to argue with him—my desires leaned in completely different directions at the moment—I attempted to raise my hands to grab his arm, but my hands fell.

Seeing that I could hardly move, Ragnor settled on the bed near me, and with his warm, big hand, he cupped the back of my head, lifting it to his wrist and pressing my lips against his skin.

Resisting the urge to lick his skin, I unsheathed my fangs and nudged them against his wrist. It was the first time, I realized, that I would be drinking from a living being, and a vampire at that. Swallowing hard at the sudden nervousness of the upcoming act, I tried to prick his skin and realized I couldn't.

Frowning, I tried again, but it was like his skin was too thick for my fangs to penetrate.

"Harder," Ragnor said in a rough voice. "My skin isn't easy to break, so you need to bite harder."

Following his words, I pretended Ragnor's wrist was juicy meat and forced my fangs to sink into his skin. Blood flowed into my mouth from the wound.

I jolted as I felt an electric shock coursing through my veins at the taste of his blood. Normally, human blood tasted like water. Some types were sweet and others a bit tart—still, some were bland, with hardly any discernible flavor at all, depending on the blood type, but Ragnor's blood tasted like nothing I'd experienced since he'd given me the Imprint.

Ragnor Rayne's blood tasted heavenly.

Like what I imagined ambrosia tasted like.

It had the pure sweetness of raw honey, the tartness of pomegranate, the bitterness of dark chocolate, and the salty flavor of the ocean.

I took a long, deep drink of his blood and shuddered. Nothing I'd eaten had ever tasted as good. It made me feel heady, almost drunk, the more blood I sucked.

At some point, I realized I was holding his arm on my own, not needing his help anymore, since my energy seemed to come back with every sip of his heavenly blood. I could feel the meat on my bones fattening, the vitality returning to my skin, and the exhaustion dissipating, making me feel more awake than ever before.

When Ragnor attempted to move his arm away from me, I moaned and followed his movement with my fangs, refusing to let him go, feeling so delirious from his deliciousness. But Ragnor didn't let me.

"Enough," he said quietly as he grabbed my hair and forced me to part with his wrist.

"No!" I said, suddenly enraged as I tried to launch at his wrist again.

But Ragnor was stronger, and he held me at bay as he pulled his wrist to his body. His midnight blue eyes lowered to mine. "It's enough," he said slowly, voice resolute but gentle.

I wanted to cry. I needed his blood. "Please . . . ," I said, pleading with him. "I need more . . . so much more . . ."

In one swift movement, he pushed me back onto the mattress and loomed over me, pinning my hands down with his. "Didn't you want to save your friend?" he said as he seemed to be studying me.

His words slowly sank into my consciousness, and I felt the fight within me die. My delirious need for Ragnor's blood abated as the memories of what had happened returned to me in full force.

Ragnor had saved me from being sold off to the Jinn.

But I didn't save Isora.

Shit.

I closed my eyes and took a deep breath before opening them again. "I'm fine now," I said softly, releasing my tense muscles.

Ragnor gazed at me with eyes gone neon. "Are you sure?" he asked, voice low. I realized then that I was still in my torn dress, showing far too much skin, while Ragnor, so sexy with his hair still wet from the shower, was right above me, his eyes taking me in from head to toe as if he couldn't get enough.

Sparks flew from where his hands held mine down to my loins, and I had to squeeze my thighs together as my breathing turned shallow. "Yes," I said in far too husky a voice.

He stared at me for a few more moments, and I could see the lust I felt mirrored in his eyes. But then he sucked in a deep breath and let me go, getting off the bed. "Take a shower," he said with a voice on the verge of growling.

With my Lifeblood replenished, I could finally shove the blankets off me and leave the bed. Without another word, I almost ran to the bathroom and shut the door behind me, then leaned against it in an effort to regain my composure.

Calm down, I told myself, trying to stop my heart from beating like crazy or my pussy from drenching my panties.

But Ragnor's naked body and delectable blood made me want to go back into the bedroom and jump his bones.

I squeezed my eyes shut. *Remember what he did to you, Aileen,* I scolded myself. *He threw you away, and even if he didn't, it's not the time for that. You need to save Isora!*

That last thought did it. My heart slowly returned to a normal pace while my thighs stopped squeezing with need. Agitated for a different reason now, I tore the dress off me and pulled off the makeshift hair band. Just before I entered the shower, I glanced at the mirror and froze.

My shaky hands rose to my hair. Right. The black dye was gone, replaced by my original golden locks. I remembered it had happened right after I had "assimilated" the *Bird of the Nile* painting—if what Atalon said about his powers was to be believed. But why? My hair had been rejecting the dye since the Auction and now had completely negated it in a single day. How? What the fuck was happening to me?

Whatever the reason was, I didn't have the luxury to worry about it now. Not when Isora was in the hands of the Jinn.

I wrapped myself in a towel and pulled the door open just enough for me to peek into the bedroom.

Ragnor lay on the bed with his eyes closed, his chest heaving softly. On the other side of the bed lay clean clothes about my size—jeans and a moss green V-neck tee. As quietly as I could so as not to wake him, I rounded the bed and, with my back to him, dropped the towel before I put on some new panties and a bra—where he got them and how he knew my size, I had no idea—and the clothes he'd prepared for me.

When I was fully dressed, I turned around, only to see Ragnor's midnight blue gaze on me.

Freezing, I stared at him. "I thought you were asleep."

He put his arms behind his head and gave me a languorous grin that made my thighs clench. "I figured it was only fair, since you peeped at me earlier too."

My cheeks blazed. And here I thought he hadn't noticed. Folding my arms, I looked away and said, "We need to talk."

Ragnor let out a heavy sigh. "We should order some food first."

"Speaking of which," I said when he grabbed the vintage cabled phone near the bed, "where are we?"

"An inn in Clyde, New York," he said absentmindedly as he pressed the numbered buttons. "Both of us needed rest."

When he finished dialing, he put the large phone to his ear, and once the receptionist answered, he said, "I would like to order two deluxe dinners to our room."

He gave them our room number, hung up, and patted a spot on the bed near him. "Come sit. The food's going to take a while."

I eyed the bed suspiciously before looking around the room. Aside from the bed, there was a wooden closet that had seen better days and a couple of ugly nightstands.

Since I didn't want to sit on the cold tiled floor, I settled on the bed as far away from him as I could. "First things first," I said, turning to face him, and I wished I hadn't. His eyes were staring at me with lust that I could feel down to my pussy. Swallowing hard, I averted my gaze, staring at a spot beyond his shoulder. "I need to save Isora."

He was quiet before he spoke. "Isora is your friend, right?"

I nodded jerkily and looked down. "She's a blood slave. When Oz put her in the prison cell with me, she was in a really bad state. The Jinn must've taken her already, and she won't be able to survive. She was barely alive when I saw her last." I clutched the blanket. I didn't want to imagine the unthinkable, without knowing how long it had been since Ragnor had rescued me from Atalon. For all I knew, Isora could already be dead.

I felt him shifting next to me, and when I glanced back at him, he'd sat up straight. "First, tell me about the deal Atalon made with the Jinn," he said, his face blank but his eyes a bright neon blue with anger.

Feeling angry myself, I said, "All I know is that Atalon was willing to lend me to the Jinn for a while, along with Isora, in exchange for something that's called the Tears of Euphorrey. And Isora would go with me, though I can't for the life of me figure out why he would offer to give Isora over too."

His face remained void of expression, but his eyes flared brighter. "Before then, did Atalon do or say anything?"

I know exactly when you received your magic. I know exactly what happened between you and Rayne. I know exactly what you did to that poor boy Logan. I know exactly what part you played in your father's crimes.

You see, the price they're willing to pay to rent you out for a few weeks is far too tempting to refuse, Natalia.

I flinched and looked away. "He said nothing."

Obviously, he didn't buy the lie. "Let me put it this way, then," he said quietly, and I tensed when he moved much closer to me. Ragnor took a few strands of my wet hair in his hand, eyes on me. "How long has he known you're Sacred?"

CHAPTER 29

AILEEN

Ragnor knew. Ragnor knew all this time. He fucking knew. And yet all he seemed to care about was when and what Atalon knew.

Still, I told him everything. My talks with Atalon. How Atalon seemed to want to get back at Ragnor and was using me to do so. By the time I finished talking, the food arrived.

We ate on the bed in silence. I glanced at Ragnor from time to time, but he seemed lost in thought. His eyes had yet to return to their midnight blue. It seemed his emotions were riding him hard.

Many questions ran through my head now that I'd finished telling him what Atalon said before—everything about his artistic powers and my time stopping. I wanted to ask him about it all and shake him until he gave me the answers I was looking for. I wanted to know how he had been flying and glowing. How he had managed to kill the Jinn. How he'd known where to find me.

But I had to bite my tongue and wait until dinner was over. It didn't feel like Ragnor was ready for another talk.

Once we finished, we cleaned up the trash, and then Ragnor said, "Let's go for a walk."

Since I was feeling stuffy in this room anyway, I was happy for the suggestion. Getting to spend time outside after being stuck in Atalon's dungeon was a gift, and I was going to have to remember to thank Ragnor for it later.

Ragnor took me to the village's park, which was illuminated by a few paper lanterns. We arrived at a river, and he led us to a bench on top of a hill with a splendid view of the village, the river, and the forests beyond.

The moment we sat, and without me even asking, Ragnor said, "I had first suspected you had some sort of power after the Auction."

Staring at the tranquil river, I felt anything but. "How?"

Stretching his arm across the back of the bench behind me, he said, "Before the performances, there was an essence of magic present."

I glanced at him as he stared ahead, a pensive look on his face as if he were actually remembering the Auction at that very moment. "It's not such an unusual case in a place where a significant number of supernatural creatures gather. Magical essence is bound to appear. But this time, it was different." He turned to look at me contemplatively. "This magic felt as if it was waiting for something or someone."

He turned his gaze to the river. "After you finished your performance, the magic was gone."

Despite how forthcoming Ragnor was, I couldn't shake the feeling of dread that settled in my chest. Getting answers to questions I'd had about myself since before the Auction from the man whom I'd tried my best to forget about felt anticlimactic and strange. Still, I hung on to his every word and turned my body in his direction.

"Magic is erratic, almost sentient, in a sense that it does things that don't always make sense." Ragnor grimaced. "That it left abruptly didn't seem odd to me, since magic behaves strangely sometimes. But when the Auction was over, I realized it disappeared only after you performed."

He returned his gaze to me. "After I give the Imprint to a newcomer, I taste their blood," he said. "It's to determine the levels of Lifeblood they have in their body, to know if they're Common or Gifted. Yours wasn't different from a Common's in the beginning, and it remained the same during the other times I drank from you. This was why, even after I realized that magic's strange behavior after your performance, I dismissed the thought of you being Sacred, though not only because of that. I mean, what are the odds of a Common becoming a Sacred after merely three months of vampirehood?"

"Zero," I answered, even though his question was rhetorical.

He nodded. "Since I didn't have conclusive proof, nor did I think it was plausible to begin with, I decided it wasn't worth thinking about." He paused. "Until the gala."

I locked his gaze with mine. "How did you know, then?"

He gave me an amused smile. "Your hair."

I blinked. "What?"

He chuckled, the sound low and sexy, and my heart flip-flopped against my will. "Magic requires its owner to be natural and without any body modifications," he said, his fingers brushing a few blonde strands from my face. "Piercings, hair dye, tattoos . . . Once the magic fully settles inside you, it won't allow you to have any of those."

And just like that, it made sense why my hair rejected the dye all the time. "So that means I can't dye my hair anymore," I murmured, bringing a few locks to my gaze, scowling.

Ragnor grabbed my chin and lifted my face to his. His eyes searched mine. "Why have you dyed your hair to begin with?"

I pushed his hand off gently, doing my best to deny the heat between us. "It doesn't matter now," I deflected. "If you don't mind, there are far more pressing matters than my hair at the moment."

He didn't speak for a few long seconds, and while I looked down at my hands, I could feel his stare boring holes in my head. Then he said, "All right. Let's talk business, then."

Glad he let it go, I returned my gaze to his. "I need to save Isora."

Ragnor gave me a nod. “I understand,” he said, face grim. “It’s partially my fault that she’s in danger now, so we’re going to do this together. Though it will have to be tomorrow; we still need more rest.”

I was relieved to hear him say that. Having Ragnor by my side was the best-case scenario. Despite all that had happened between us, I couldn’t save Isora alone. “Thank you.”

He cupped my cheek, his touch sending shivers cascading down my spine. “You don’t have to thank me, Aileen,” he said, face serious. “I’m here now. I’ll do anything you want me to.”

Heart an erratic drumbeat, I stared into his eyes and blurted out the exact opposite of how I was feeling right then: “Even if I tell you that what I want is for you to stay away from me?”

He gave me a humorless smile that made my chest tighten. “This is the one thing I can’t do,” he said quietly, his free arm wrapping itself around my waist and drawing me closer. “I need you, Aileen. I want you beyond reason.”

Pain filled me. “I don’t want to talk about this,” I whispered, not wanting to have this conversation but not yet ready to leave the warmth of his embrace. It wasn’t fair. Ragnor had betrayed me. He’d rejected me. He allowed me to be swallowed up by a monster. So no, I wasn’t going to make it easy on him to worm his way back into my life, even if he was going to help me save Isora. Not now, and perhaps never.

In one swift movement, Ragnor brought me onto his lap, enveloping me in his strong arms, his smell intoxicating. An involuntary shudder caused me to squirm against him as need burst to life in every part of me. “But I do, Aileen,” he said, sliding his hand from my cheek to cup the nape of my neck. “You need me to grovel? Need me repentant? I will grovel for the rest of my existence if necessary. I will apologize profusely every day if that’s what it takes to have one more chance.”

The pain of what he’d done pierced my heart, even more now that his own pain and desperation brightened his eyes. “You hurt me, Ragnor,” I found myself saying, anger and sadness bringing tears to my eyes. "I offered myself to you, laid myself bare for you, and you broke me to pieces."

His face contorted in agony. "I'm sorry, Aileen," he said raspingly as he pressed his lips against my cheek, catching a tear that fell with his mouth. "Back at the Auction, I had let my pride take over. I hesitated too much, even though I wanted to bid on you, wanted to buy you. But in the end, I was too slow to reach a decision because I was torn between what I should do and what I wanted to do."

Both his hands were on my cheeks now, and I found myself grabbing his shirt. "I begged you," I said, voice breaking. "I begged you to buy me. I never begged anyone like that in my life. And what did you do? How did the great Ragnor Rayne respond? You trampled all over me."

"I know," he said, growling as he pressed his forehead to mine. "I know, Aileen. I deserve your hatred and fury. If I was less of a selfish man, I wouldn't even dare ask for another chance. But I'm not that kind of man." He leaned back to look at me with cobalt eyes. "I'm jealous and competitive, and I refuse to leave you with the likes of Atalon, who only wants you to both spite me and to use your powers. I refuse to live with the regret of what could've been. I refuse to be away from you." His lips were inches away from mine. "Do you really feel like you can let us go without regrets?"

His words broke something inside me. His use of the word *us* both infuriated and healed me. Because Ragnor said everything I'd been feeling ever since he sold me. He was saying what I had wanted him to say since the Auction.

Behind my anger and disappointment that he'd taken so long to come to this conclusion and worry that if I took him back, he would hurt me again, there was this fear that I would never find someone like him or that I would never feel anything remotely close to how I felt with him. That I would never again be part of an *us*.

That's why I had been secretly relieved every time Ragnor came knocking on my door at the Atalon League.

That's why, deep down, I was relishing him chasing after me during his stay, feeling, for the first time, that someone was doing such a thing for me.

And when I gave him the ultimatum—have one last night with me or leave, and I'd give him a month to prove himself—he chose to leave, making me realize that he was serious about me, even if I refused to admit it.

At the gala, too, he tried to protect me from the Jinn's attack.

He came to save me from Atalon and the Jinn without hesitation.

He wanted to help me save Isora from the Jinn.

I would never be able to forget what he'd done at the Auction. It would always be a bitter memory, knowing that he'd thrown me away once.

But perhaps what mattered the most was what he would do going forward.

"One month," I said quietly just then, my lips against his. "After we rescue Isora, I'll give you that one month."

A victorious growl left him before Ragnor crashed his lips against mine.

CHAPTER 30

AILEEN

In less than five minutes, Ragnor and I were back at the inn. He dragged me up the stairs until we reached our room, and once we were inside, he slammed the door shut and ravaged my mouth.

Emotions exploded in my head. *Run away,* some inner voice told me, frightened beyond reason. *Run away now, before it's too late.*

But the desire I felt was far stronger than it had been back at the Rayne League, when I couldn't resist him, so I threw any and all caution to the fucking wind.

I wrapped my arms around him, allowing myself to enjoy the feel of his hard body against my softer one. A moan escaped my mouth, the heat between us growing with every passing second. I hung on to him tightly; it was almost like I was terrified he would come to his senses and leave me again, regret doing this, regret everything.

His hands were like fire on my waist as he picked me up and put me on the bed. My breath caught in my throat, anticipation raising goose bumps on my skin. Ragnor pushed my legs open, snuggled himself between them. Soon, his hands were everywhere, grabbing me fiercely and kissing and claiming me with his mouth, as though reading my mind, understanding what I needed.

He pulled back from my mouth and locked my hazel eyes with his neon-blue ones. "If we do this, Aileen, there's no going back," he warned me.

Lust fogged my brain. "How presumptuous," I said huskily, eyes hooded.

He unzipped my jeans. As if admiring a great work of art, he paused before hooking his fingers inside and pulling on the fabric, almost tearing the cloth in the process. With each movement getting us closer to being skin on skin, my body responded by pushing wetness from my pussy. As if he could smell my arousal, he dragged my jeans and panties down and away with a satisfied look on his face.

"Fucking beautiful," Ragnor said as his eyes lustfully roamed over my body. Seeing him look at me like that gave me chills. I wanted him on me.

Something sparked inside me just then, and I tugged at his clothes, needing to see his glorious body naked. Keeping his eyes on me, he helped me undress him, lifting his shirt over his head as I worked at the button and zipper on his pants. The sight of his chest made my mouth water, and I pulled back from his kiss to put lips on his skin.

As much as I had tried to deny my need for him, I'd been waiting for this for so long that I was utterly starving. I licked and nipped at his chest, my arms around his torso and my nails digging into his back. God, he tasted good. Even better than I remembered. Something about being with Ragnor now in this moment was different than it had been in the past.

He didn't let me be in charge for too long; he grabbed my wrists and put them on the mattress and locked my gaze with his. "Mine," he growled before tearing my shirt off and snapping my bra open, exposing every inch of my body to his unrelenting and greedy gaze. His hands returned to my wrists, and he lowered his mouth to my left nipple, sucking softly at first, nearly worshipping it. The more I moaned for him, the harder he sucked.

More, I thought, desire making me needy. *More, harder, more . . .*

As though he'd heard my prayers, Ragnor unsheathed his fangs and sank them into the flesh of my breast, causing me to gasp. It was like the sting of a needle full of the most euphoric drug, and the more I got, the more I wanted. He let go of my wrists and began kneading my neglected breast, making me writhe with pleasure under him, wanting more, wanting everything he had to give.

The feeling of his fangs on my nipple made my juices flow right out, dripping onto the sheets. My entire body jerked when he grabbed my nipple tightly between his fingers. It hurt in the best way when the pain gave way to pleasure so immense, I had to close my eyes to endure it.

He lifted his head from my breast suddenly, licking his lips as he stared down at me. I pressed my thighs together as a mini orgasm shook me at the sight of his gorgeous face looking at me as if I was a delicious meal he couldn't wait to ravish. I'd missed this, the way Ragnor knew my body and could get it to do exactly what he wanted. He fixed his neon-blue gaze on me and gave me a wicked smirk that made my pussy clench.

"Your eyes are glowing," he informed me just then as he lowered his lips to mine. "A beautiful red glow."

Before I could respond, his mouth was on mine again, fucking it with his tongue. That's how it felt, really; like he was consuming me, marking his territory, swallowing my moans down to his core. His fangs nipped at my swollen lower lip as his fingers toyed with my bruised nipples, coaxing pleasure from the pain.

Then, in one swift movement, he spread my legs wide and pushed them down. "Fuck!" I yelled as his mouth covered my pussy, his fangs grazed my clit, and his tongue gave my entrance long, deep strokes. My entire body shuddered, and I held on to his hair, writhing unabashedly under him. He held me immobile as he ravaged my pussy as if it was his last supper.

When he dug his fangs into my clit, drawing blood, everything inside me exploded and continued to explode as he sucked my blood straight from the bundle of nerves. I moaned and thrashed on the bed, trying to find solace from the unbearable pleasure, but he kept on torturing me with an endless chain of bliss after bliss, not stopping until I couldn't move a muscle.

The postorgasmic bliss was replaced with a desire to give it back to him just as good. When he left my trembling pussy and straightened, I pushed at his chest, and he raised his lustful gaze to mine, as though trying to understand why I was stopping him. I shot my hand to his already rigid cock. "I want it in my mouth," I told him, squeezing the base.

His muscles locked, and he gave me a strained grin as he got off me. I followed him, then knelt between his legs, right before his thick, massive, beautiful cock, and put it completely in my mouth.

The moan that escaped his mouth told me he liked it. He jerked, but I kept on sucking him, taking as much of him as I could until I almost choked on him. He tasted so good, I was tempted to simply swallow him whole. I massaged his balls, licking and sucking at the same time, and then I got the urge to give him the same wicked pleasure he'd given me. Taking my mouth off his cock, I stroked his length while taking his balls into my mouth, letting my fangs out, and using just the right amount of pressure to draw a little blood.

"Fuck, Aileen, that feels so good." He cursed, and I grinned, sucking the crimson drops straight from his balls.

Ragnor fisted my hair, forced my head up, and shoved his cock back to my mouth, fucking it. When I gagged a little on him, he moaned so deeply, I became lost in pleasing him. I stroked him, licked him, and almost bit him with how good he tasted.

When he was about to come, he took his hands from my hair, letting me know he didn't expect me to let him finish in my mouth. But I wanted his liquid inside me, wanted to swallow all of him just as he did me. So when I kept my mouth on his hard length and nodded, keeping my eyes on him, he shot his load down my throat, growling in the process. I swallowed every single drop as the warm, salty fluid coated my tongue. I massaged his balls while he ejaculated more and more. I lifted my mouth slightly so I could stroke his cock up and down until there was nothing left.

I raised my head, licked my lips, and gave him my own version of a wicked little smirk.

His eyes were impossibly bright as he stared at me with feral need. "On your hands and knees." He barked out the command.

My eyes dropped to his cock, and I was surprised to find him hard again so soon after I'd just sucked him off. "You're quick to recover."

"On your hands and knees," he repeated in a growl.

My heart jumped as lust took over me. Once I did as he said, he was behind me in a flash, his hands grabbing my hair, and he buried his cock balls deep inside me.

I moaned as he fucked me mercilessly, stroking in and out of me, his hand leaving my hair to play with my breasts, pinching my nipples hard enough to tear them off as he mounted me over and over.

He pulled me up until I was sitting on him with my back to his chest, and he plunged so hard inside me I saw stars, and his fingers played with my abused clit, drawing an unexpected orgasm out of me—and then another when he bit my neck and sucked my blood.

It made me realize how vanilla the sex we'd had before was. Perhaps he'd been holding back. I knew that I had been too.

But now, all inhibitions were completely gone.

I wanted to suck his delicious blood too. I needed to suck him. I turned around so I faced him and, without further ado, simply bit his neck as he grabbed my ass tightly, slapping the cheeks hard enough for me to groan in pain, and rammed into me with such ferocity and haste, I knew I was going to walk funny afterward.

He roughly pulled my head back using my hair and fastened his lips on mine, and we both growled into each other's mouths as he came inside me while my orgasm ripped through me, milking him, making him jerk inside me and causing another orgasm that made my back arch and his fangs bite into the side of my breast.

We were a gasping, sweaty mess, unable to move from our positions, with him still inside me, my arms still around him, his hands still on my ass, squeezing it, and I just let myself melt into this, into him, into the inexplicable force that made me want this man beyond any reason.

"Ragnor," I moaned into the darkness as Ragnor's front pressed tightly against my back, his arm around my waist, his fingers rubbing my clit leisurely.

His growl vibrated against me as I felt his hard cock pressing into my lower back while his fingers lowered from my clit to tease my entrance.

I wriggled my ass against him. "I need you," I murmured, needing his fingers inside. "I need more."

Denying me, he kept teasing me until wetness dripped down my thighs. With his other hand, he grabbed the nape of my neck and brought his lips to my ear, making me shudder. "No," he said roughly, his breath against my lobe.

Need burst inside me. "More," I argued insistently, trying to bring his fingers to where I wanted them.

He paused his movements, and I almost cried in frustration. "In bed, I'm in charge," he growled, squeezing my neck. "Unless I tell you otherwise."

I gasped, shocked at his audacity, when he suddenly plunged three fingers inside me, making my entire body tense up. "Ragnor!" I cried out when he fucked me with his fingers, ripping an orgasm out of me that made me spasm uncontrollably.

He didn't let me go, though. He kept fingering me, riding my orgasm, until I was an exhausted lump of flesh.

Slowly, he removed his fingers and put them to my mouth. "Open," he commanded in that growling voice of his.

Unable to resist, I opened my mouth, and he pushed his fingers inside, making me taste myself on him. I licked his fingers, and I felt his cock jerking against my back, rigid and ready to go.

He removed his hand from my mouth and put it under my thigh, pulling it up. "You've got a great pussy," he murmured into my ear as he nudged at said pussy with the tip of his cock. "The best fucking pussy."

In one swift move, he filled me to the brim, and I screamed.

With a bruising hold on my thigh, he fucked me from behind so fast and deep, I felt him reaching my womb. His other hand kept my head in place, his hold almost choking me.

"Beautiful," he said as my insides clenched, readying me for what was to come. "So beautiful you make me want to dirty you up."

I cried out as the orgasm split me in half.

He pushed me to my stomach with his hold on my neck and settled on top of me, still inside me. He drove powerfully in and out of me, slamming his hand against my ass over and over again before grabbing it and pulling my legs apart.

All I could do was lie there helplessly as he took me from behind, falling into an abundance of pleasure every time his hand crashed against my ass or his other hand squeezed my neck. When he released my neck suddenly, I was so disappointed, I moaned at the loss but then gasped when I felt that same hand coming down to my clit, rubbing it with enough force to draw another orgasm out of me.

But Ragnor wasn't done.

After flipping me to face him, he put my legs around his waist and grabbed my breasts as he drilled into me. I closed my eyes as I felt an insurmountable pleasure drugging me from inside, but then Ragnor paused. "Open your eyes," he murmured. "I want to see you."

Somehow, I managed to do as he said, and his eyes clasped mine in an unshakable hold. That's when he pushed into me, filling me up again, making me moan.

His lips were suddenly on my neck, his fangs digging into my skin. The pleasure was too much at that point, and I broke repeatedly, thrashing against him, needing him to both stop and continue.

But then he growled and pushed one last time into me, emptying his sacks inside. "Fuck, you feel so good," he hissed against my neck, licking the skin he'd bitten. "So fucking good, Aileen."

I put my arms around him, needing him to remain inside. "You're determined to break my pussy tonight," I murmured, and I licked the glistening skin of his shoulder.

He shuddered as he brought us to our sides, face to face, our arms around one another, his cock still buried inside me. His bright-blue eyes took me in. "We won't have much time for this starting tomorrow," he reminded me.

This was true. "You said we were going to rest, though." I bit his lip.

He smirked. "It's your fault."

Leaning back, I gave him a pointed look. "Who jumped who here?"

He slapped my ass, and I gasped. "Careful, Aileen," he said, grinning darkly as a flush of lust climbed to my cheeks. "Remember what I said before?"

"In bed, you're in charge," I repeated and gasped again when I felt him hardening inside me. "You haven't been this bossy before."

His eyes gave me an almost lewd look. "This is only the beginning," he said roughly before he drew out his cock and pushed back in.

Needless to say, neither of us truly rested that night.

CHAPTER 31
RAGNOR

Ragnor awoke to the sound of tapping on the window.

Immediately on alert, he pulled away from the beautiful woman lying in bed next to him and slid out of the covers. Aileen murmured something as she cuddled deeper into the duvet, and Ragnor's chest tightened at the sight.

Then the tapping on the window echoed again.

After quickly putting on some clothes, he strode to the window and pushed the curtains away. Outside he saw Luceras floating in the air, staring at him with profound jungle eyes.

Glancing back at Aileen, he motioned for the Malachi to wait and left the room. Once Ragnor was out of the inn, Luceras landed in the yard and approached him. "The number of Jinn congregating in Vermont has multiplied," he told Ragnor without preamble. "There also seems to be more vampires there as well, from what I could tell."

Ragnor grimaced. "My surveillance team is already on it," he said, referring to the intelligence department of his Troop. "I'm going to take care of it today."

Luceras's face remained as expressionless as ever, but his eyes seemed to flash. "The Seraphim have been uneasy as of late," he said, glancing at the window of Ragnor and Aileen's room. "It might have something to do with that woman."

The last thing Ragnor needed was either Luceras or the Seraphim to be aware of Aileen's ancestry—especially since Ragnor himself was not yet sure what it was, exactly. "She's a mere vampire," he now said evenly. "Hardly a threat."

This didn't seem to be enough to satisfy Luceras. "You know how well I'm bonded to the ether, Deveran," he now said, stepping toward Ragnor. "The same abnormal shifts in the ether I usually sense near the Jinn, I also sense now near this woman."

Ragnor froze. "I told you," he said, keeping his face schooled into neutrality despite his shock at this news, "she's only a vampire."

"That's not the only thing she is," Luceras argued, coming to a stop only a foot away. "The Seraphim are unaware of her existence at the moment, but I won't be able to hold them off for too long." He paused, giving Ragnor a meaningful stare, before he said, "Take care of the Jinn today, Deveran, so the Seraphim will be off both your and my backs."

Luceras raised his wings and took flight, turning invisible the higher he ascended.

Now that he was gone, Ragnor could let himself feel the bomb Luceras had just dropped exploding inside him.

The ether was a divine energy that existed everywhere on earth at once. Around humans, vampires, and other anthropomorphic races who were considered creatures of the earth, the ether was as tranquil as the ocean, since neither humans nor vampires were alien to this dimension.

Unlike humans and vampires, the Jinn were not created on earth; they were an abomination. Their presence in this realm was unnatural and disruptive to not just the ether but the ecosystem as a whole. This was why the ether always shifted oddly around the Jinn, acting as a warning to the Malachi that something was wrong.

Ragnor had never known any other creature who disrupted the ether in the same manner as the Jinn. That Luceras said he sensed the same kind of disruption near Aileen was another matter to be wary of where she was concerned.

It must have something to do with her being Sacred, Ragnor thought grimly despite the other nagging thought fighting its way into his stubborn brain. He hadn't been surprised to learn that she was Sacred, but that was supposed to be impossible for a newbie. And yet, it wasn't the only impossible thing Aileen Henderson had managed to achieve since he had given her the Imprint.

The utter improbability of everything that had happened since the night he'd seen her in the alleyway behind that dreadful excuse for a club weighed on him. Imprinting on her instead of killing her. Allowing himself to become involved with her. Luceras's warning. Eliza's insistence that she was not to be trusted. Even Atalon's interest in her. And now, the Jinn? What the hell did they want with her? What was it about Aileen Henderson that made everyone close to Ragnor want her? What made him want her?

Ragnor looked at the window and felt his chest tighten again, this time for different reasons than before. He had only managed to get her to give him another chance. Would he be able to convince her to tell him about the past she'd been desperately trying to hide?

He let out a sigh. There wasn't time for backstories and past lives. He had to prepare for the battle to come. Because saving Aileen's friend was only secondary to his eternal mission.

He would eliminate the Jinn from the face of the earth.

CHAPTER 32
AILEEN

Ragnor was quiet.

He was quiet once I woke up and found him tapping away on his phone.

He was quiet when we grabbed coffee and a few pastries to go.

He was quiet as he began to drive to some location in Vermont, as far as I could tell from the GPS on the dashboard screen.

I suspected his quietness had something to do with me, and I felt far too confused to try and break the silence between us. I mean, he'd been the one to practically beg me to take him back, and now he acted as if he wanted nothing to do with me? What was that all about?

The scariest thought, however, was that after our steamy encounter last night, he might've gotten what he truly wanted and stopped giving a shit about me.

Those thoughts were irrational, I logically knew. I mean, if he didn't want me anymore, then why did he take me with him?

But when it came to Ragnor, nothing about how I felt was ever rational.

As I watched landscapes outside passing by, sipping my coffee, I battled with whether I should talk. Ragnor didn't seem inclined to engage in any sort of conversation, considering he barely even told me good morning when I woke up. On the other hand, this silence was far too loaded to simply let it be.

Before I could make up my mind, Ragnor, to my surprise, decided to speak. "Let's talk about our plan."

Folding my arms, I kept my gaze on the window. "Fine."

Whether he noticed my tone, he didn't let on. "We're going to a place full of Jinn. Our only chance at getting your friend out safely is by going in and coming out as quickly as possible."

"Sure," I muttered.

"This is why," he went on, "we need to discuss the full extent of our abilities."

"Awesome."

He was quiet for a second before he said, "You're mad."

I scoffed. "I'm not mad."

"Don't play this game with me," he said, voice turning into a warning. "If you've got a problem, just say it."

Whipping my head toward him, I snapped, "It seems to me that you're the one with the problem, not me!"

He kept his eyes on the road, but I could see his jaw clench and his knuckles turn white. "And why, pray tell, do you think I have a problem?"

I gaped at him, incredulous. "You've been giving me the cold shoulder since earlier this morning!" I yelled, losing my temper. "You act like a one-night stand who can't seem to get rid of his fling!"

He suddenly pulled the car to the shoulder and slammed on the brakes before he turned to face me, eyes gone neon. "Do you really think I see you as a passing fancy?" he growled. "After everything we talked about? Really?"

"Look at how you're behaving, then!" I barked, motioning toward him with my hands. "Only a few hours after we decided to give us a chance, you're acting as if I'm contaminated!" To my horror, my voice shook, and I felt tears rising to my eyes. Looking away, I leaned back. "Forget it. If you don't get it, then—"

Ragnor grabbed my waist before I could finish and brought me to his lap so quickly, I didn't have the time to protest. His eyes, when they landed on mine, were full of remorse. "I didn't mean to make you feel this way," he said, wrapping his arms tightly around me.

I scowled at him, even as I grabbed the collar of his shirt and brought my face closer to his. "Why did you act so distant, if that's not it?" I asked, swallowing the tears. I wasn't a crier. Why had he made me cry two times in less than twenty-four hours?

He pulled me closer into a hug, resting his head against my shoulder. "I was simply going over the plans in my head," he murmured, and I felt his voice reverberating through his chest. "It's going to be dangerous, Aileen, and I don't want you to get hurt, so I was trying to come up with the best plan to avoid such an outcome." He paused, squeezing me tighter. "If it was up to me, I would've kept you out of this whole thing and done everything myself."

I hugged him tightly, melting against him. "I would've told you to shove it if you did," I said softly, caressing his hair, breathing him in, his soapy, masculine scent calming me down. "You should've shared your concerns with me, Ragnor. I wouldn't have misunderstood otherwise." I took in a deep breath. "I thought you got tired of me already."

He leaned back and cupped my face, eyes shining. "Never," he growled and planted his lips on mine.

Lightning bolts lit up my veins, and I moaned into his mouth, needing to be closer to him, to mold myself against him, to feel him everywhere.

He pulled back and gave me a regretful smile. "We don't have time," he said, pushing a few strands of hair away from my face. "But once this whole thing is over . . ."

I groaned in frustration, but I knew he was right. We'd already wasted precious minutes on this stupid argument. "Just promise me to communicate next time," I said, biting his lower lip. "Or I won't let you off the hook so easily."

His chuckles eased my fears. "I promise."

A few miles away from Montpelier, Vermont, Ragnor parked the car on a deserted cobblestone road. "The Jinni headquarters are ten miles ahead," he told me, "but if we get any closer, they'll be able to sense our presence."

"Is this where your powers come into play?" I asked as we got out of the car.

The entire drive was spent on Ragnor explaining his plan and us sharing information about our powers to make for better cooperation.

When he told me about his powers, I couldn't help but be fascinated. "I'm able to manipulate my aura in different ways," he'd said, "meaning that if I want to enhance my strength or hide my presence, for instance, I can make it happen with my aura."

"Is that what you did back in Rochester?" I was referring to the fact that he broke through so many levels with just his feet to get to the prison cell Atalon had locked me in.

He nodded. "That's not all, though," he added. "I can also stretch out my aura and engulf another person in it, almost like a reverse empath. I can then choose what my aura will do to them—either enhance their strength or hide their presence or perhaps even inject them with different emotions. I can amplify their existing emotions or remove them entirely. If you can imagine, all of that or even a little of it can be disorienting, even immobilizing."

"Emotions?" I repeated, something nagging at my memories at that word. "Like fear?"

"Exactly," he replied. "I can make others feel extreme horror after I envelop them with my aura, or perhaps even make them feel elated. It all depends on what I want to do."

A memory broke through in my mind, and I suddenly remembered two occasions when Ragnor was present that could fit this criteria. "A few months ago," I said, "when there was the case of Bloodlust in one of my classmates in the cafeteria. Is that the power you used?"

Ragnor gave me an almost sinister grin. "Correct."

I opened my mouth, about to mention another instance of him using his powers, most likely, but then closed it when I remembered he didn't know I'd been a witness to that event. It had happened in the Renaldi League, when Ragnor threatened Lord Renaldi and made him—and me, hiding at the time—experience such terror, I'd felt sick to my stomach.

And to think I was dating this terrifying man. I was pretty lucky.

Now, Ragnor wrapped his arm around my waist and tugged me close. His skin slowly turned translucent, as though he'd lowered the opacity of his visuals, and when I looked down at myself, I saw he'd used the same effect on me. "I have a question," I said as he lifted me into his arms.

"Ask away," he said as he entered the nearby forest.

"When you said you can make another person feel certain emotions," I said, "did you mean any emotion?"

He arched a brow. "Yes."

"Then," I said, grinning, "does that mean you can make another person feel as if they're having an orgasm?"

He paused, stared at me, and gave me a sly grin. "That could be fun, indeed," he murmured, squeezing me to him. "Now, was that your question?"

Belly flip-flopping and grin still intact, I nodded.

"Good," he said. "Then let's pick up the pace."

He sprinted forward so fast, everything around me was a blur. My heart quickened as I felt him growing faster and faster with every moment that passed, making me feel as if I was being sucked through time and space.

This was the capability of a vampire who grew into their true powers. Despite becoming Sacred, when it came to vampiric strength, I was still a noob. Abe, my former teacher, had said it could take vampires up to a year to be able to tap into our vampiric powers, such as better senses, supernatural speed, enhanced strength, and so on, but that we could do it even earlier if we did physical training.

I realized now that since I'd arrived at the Atalon League, I hadn't trained at all. I'd been too busy thinking about how to utilize my newfound magic that I'd completely put aside cultivating my physical assets.

I planned to remedy that once we finished our business here.

Not even five minutes later, the forest opened into a glade with a trimmed lawn in front of a huge villa sitting right next to a large lake. It looked like it could belong to some high-end conglomerate, seeing as it was all fancy, with a driveway and fountain in the middle of the pampered courtyard.

Ragnor put me down but kept me close to him as we walked around the villa, toward the lake. I saw him looking around and sniffing the air, as though he was searching for something. He glanced at me and nodded in confirmation.

The Jinn were indeed here.

Ragnor found a door at the back of the villa. It looked like a staff entrance. I grabbed the handle, with Ragnor at my back, and softly pushed. Thankfully, it was unlocked.

We cautiously peered inside and saw a hallway. Ragnor led the way, softly closing the door behind us. He pulled us against a wall covered in red tapestries, and I marveled at how the translucency of our bodies made it seem like we were part of the wall. We tiptoed along until we arrived at an open door. Ragnor motioned for me to wait, and he sneaked a peek around it.

I watched as he closed his eyes and sniffed the air before giving me an affirmative nod.

Footsteps echoed from the end of the corridor. Someone was coming.

Ragnor and I quickly entered the room—a kitchen—and Ragnor closed the door behind us. We both waited silently as we heard the footsteps grow closer. I held my breath until they passed us, heading to the exit.

Sighing, I turned to Ragnor, who pointed toward a trapdoor in the corner of the kitchen, right next to the butcher table. I stared at the table for a few moments, trying to discern the type of meat on top of it, since it smelled extremely foul, when Ragnor snapped his fingers, drawing my attention back to him.

He pulled open the trapdoor and motioned for me to follow as he began descending the narrow staircase.

The moment I took my first step, an image of a different staircase, in a different place, filled my mind. Ignoring the sudden thumping of my heart, I did my best to keep calm, stay focused, and follow Ragnor.

These were not the same stairs, after all.

This was not my father's house.

But then we arrived at a room that took all the wind out of my sails. My knees buckled, and my body sank to the floor alongside my heart.

And just like that, I saw another basement in front of my eyes. A basement I'd spent hours in, watching as little bodies dangled from the low ceiling while the lashes of a whip cut through their bare skin. A basement where dog cages full of dead bodies lined one of the walls. The stench in that basement—soot, blood, metal, and decay—was always mixed with the cologne my father used to wear, creating an unholy scent of fragrances that were never meant to exist together.

This basement was eerily similar, too much so. Instead of small bodies, large shapeless figures were shackled to the ceiling. Instead of dog cages, floor-to-ceiling metal bars separated us from living, breathing people behind them. Here, the stench was mostly of dust and dampness, as though no one had bothered cleaning the place in what seemed like ages.

"Aileen."

I heard my name being called. I also recognized the voice calling it. But all I could do was stare at the shackles. At the skin-and-bones vampires dangling from the ceiling, spots all over their bodies, their eyes half-open as though they were dead. These were vampires whose Lifeblood had been sucked out. So much Lifeblood they looked like Isora had the last time I'd seen her.

"Aileen!"

I blinked and realized Ragnor was in front of me, his hands on my shoulders, his eyes searching mine with deep worry. "Stay with me," he murmured, holding my gaze. "Whatever you're feeling, let it go. Your friends need you."

I sucked in a breath as his words slowly computed. "Friends?" I whispered, horrified.

He grimaced as he helped me back up to my feet and moved aside. Slowly, I tore my eyes away from him and looked at the people behind the bars.

There were six in total: four women and two men. Out of the women, I recognized two.

Isora dangled from the ceiling like a sack of bones, her blue eyes glassy and empty as they stared at nothing, her hair filthy and matted, her skin full of graying spots so much so there was little of its original tone left.

Next to her, there was another familiar face. A face I'd never thought I would see again.

Zoey.

My old suitemate.

The last time I'd seen her was at the gala event, which had been merely a few days ago yet felt like a lifetime. And somehow, it also seemed like a lifetime passed for her as well, since she was almost unrecognizable. While not shackled to the ceiling, she didn't look any better than Isora. She could barely sit straight, and I doubted she could even talk.

But I recognized her face, even as gaunt as it was. And I recognized her dark eyes, even though the defiant glint that usually burned within them was gone.

"We can't leave them here," I said, voice rising as panic stewed in my stomach. "Ragnor, we have to save all of them."

I could feel Ragnor's stare, but I couldn't take my eyes away from Isora and Zoey. *I have to save them,* I thought. *I have to save them, I have to save them, I have to save them.*

"We will." Ragnor's voice penetrated my hysterical thoughts. I heard him pacing through the basement until he found a button that lifted up the bars. None of the prisoners were able to move. Everyone seemed to be unconscious, despite having their eyes open.

Ragnor grabbed Zoey and put her over his shoulder before breaking the shackles holding Isora. He then took Isora as well and held her gently in his arms. "Leave the others," he told me. "I'll come to them after we get your friends to—"

A noise, followed by hard thumps, reverberated through the basement. Before Ragnor could complete his sentence, two large horned creatures with hooves and blue skin appeared.

Everyone froze, including the two Jinn, Ragnor, and me. At that moment, we were no longer translucent. Our presence now revealed, the Jinn looked straight at us, determination and consternation in their monstrous eyes.

A moment later a full-on battle erupted.

The Jinni closest to me kicked me, sending me flying into the wall so hard, I sucked in a pained breath as my ribs burned from the impact. The other Jinni went after Ragnor as he moved quickly to put my friends down so he could defend himself.

Likely dismissing me as any kind of threat, the Jinni who attacked me went after Ragnor. Before I could move to help, Ragnor shot me a glance and yelled "Do it!" as he began fighting back.

It was too much. Seeing Isora and Zoey in this state, the far-too-familiar feeling of the basement and all the horrible memories that came along with it, watching Ragnor fight the Jinni—I commanded time to stop.

And, as I wished, everything and everyone froze.

Not wasting a second, I did what Ragnor had done; I put Zoey on my back and Isora in my arms. Then, ignoring the pain in my ribs from the previous impact, I ran out of the room, up the stairs, through the kitchen, and back into the corridor.

Feeling blood trickling from my nostrils, I knew I had probably about two more seconds before I reached my limit. I managed to get us out of the villa before I had no choice but to mentally command time.

Resume!

As time moved again, I fell to my knees, out of breath and unable to go on. But I had to do something, to move somehow, to get my friends to safety before I returned to aid Ragnor.

But before I could figure out what needed to be done, someone hit my neck from behind in a swift chop, and all I could do was stare as a silver-eyed man moved in front of me, eyeing me with suspicion and catching me as I lost consciousness.

CHAPTER 33

AILEEN

I awoke with a start.

Drowsily, I pushed myself to sit up and looked around. I was lying in a king-size canopy bed in the middle of a room that could've belonged to a castle, it was so ornate and luxurious. Large windows to my left showed a familiar large courtyard bathed in faint sunlight, informing me it was sunset.

I was still in the Jinn's villa . . . but where was Ragnor?

I looked at the door, as if Ragnor would miraculously enter and explain everything. Unfortunately, it remained closed.

Once I was off the bed, I walked toward the door and pulled the knob. It was locked. Because of course it would be.

Grimacing from the pain in my rib cage, I went to the windows and looked for a way to open one of them. I was on the second floor, not too far from the ground. I could definitely make the jump.

But after minutes of checking, I found no way to force the windows open.

Great.

As I seriously considered attempting to kick the window out, the door opened behind me. I whipped around, steeling myself for a fight. A familiar man with inky black hair and a pair of silver eyes walked in.

Wode. The Jinni who'd kidnapped me in Vegas and the one who'd bargained with Atalon for me.

He came to a stop in front of me, and as he did, a chill crept up my spine. This man was obviously not on my side. How could he be, after what he'd done? Before he could talk, I decided to cut right to the chase before the exhaustion was too much. "What do you want?"

His lips twitched. "It's good to see you too," he replied, smiling. "Don't worry. I only want to talk."

A large *boom* shook the walls and the hinges. I widened my eyes. "What . . ."

Wode came to rest on the wall next to me. "That would be your boyfriend," he said, shrugging nonchalantly. "He's not very pleased that you've been taken."

I narrowed my eyes. "Just tell me what you want from me."

He chuckled. "Well, Aileen, one thing you can rest assured about: my intent is not to harm you in any sort of way."

"That's not enough of an answer," I said, folding my arms. "You struck a deal with Atalon to 'rent' me. And now you also intentionally antagonized another vampire Lord, a pretty stupid gesture since you know what Ragnor's capable of. That all means you want something from me."

He moved to sit down on a couch at the other end of the room. "Come sit with me," he said, tapping the empty space next to him.

I glared. "I'd rather stand."

Sighing, he gave me a kind smile I was certain was genuine. Even still, the gesture did little to ease my concern. "It's hard for you to stand, isn't it?" he said softly, nodding at the hand I had been holding against my bruised ribs.

"Don't worry about me. I heal quickly," I said, angry. "Can you stop talking in circles and get to the fucking point?"

Wode's smile disappeared and was replaced by a pensive expression. "How much do you know about us?"

"Enough to know you're my enemy. Or don't you remember kidnapping me in Las Vegas?" I responded through gritted teeth. What was the point of this question?

His chuckle was somewhat sad, and again, his emotion seemed sincere enough to confuse me. "No, Aileen. Vampires are our enemies," he said with an almost awestruck expression on his face.

I stilled. "I'm a vampire, though, and now that we are all clear about who the other is and where we both stand, can we please get on with whatever the hell it is you want to say?" I said, more confused than before.

He shook his head. "You don't know anything, it seems." He sighed before rising to his feet. "We don't have much time to talk, but let me just say one thing." He gave me a warm look. "We've been waiting for you, the last Child of Kahil."

As if on cue, the windows exploded.

Wode's body cradled mine as he lay on the ground with me squashed beneath him. Belatedly, it occurred to me he was protecting me from whatever had caused the glass to shatter.

From under Wode's body, I heard animalistic roars.

"Fuck," Wode barked, tightening his arms around me as the entire building shook as if hit by an enormous wrecking ball. "Hold on to me, Aileen!"

Shit. He really was trying to protect me. And last Child of Kahil? How the hell did he know about that?

The ceiling crumbled, and a large piece fell on top of him. I felt the pressure, but his body took the hit as his horns came more clearly into view the lower he curled around me. His eyes turned wild with what seemed to be rage. With a growl that was definitely not human, he pushed the large debris off his back, temporarily letting me go.

Heart beating loud in my ears, I didn't think twice about rolling away, choking on dust and dirt as I climbed to my feet. I would've started running had Wode not realized what I was doing and, with supernatural speed, grabbed me by my wrist, a questioning look in his eye. It was as if he had expected me to stay with him after his last statement.

"You're not going anywhere." He spoke in a low rumbling voice that made the hairs on the nape of my neck stand.

I didn't bother replying. Instead, I sharpened my mind and commanded time to stop.

It obliged; small debris, dust, and other particles froze midair. Wode didn't move or blink, locked in a state of rage. All sound ceased to exist. It was as though I'd stepped into a still picture. A paused movie.

Feeling the looming headache, I grabbed Wode's fingers and pried them from my wrist. Free of his hold, I turned around and ran quickly through the ruined hallways, to the exit.

I managed to stop time for about seven seconds, until the headache forced me to let time resume its course. And once it did, I was already descending the stairs to the lower floor.

Loud noises echoed around me, including shouts, screams, and bangs of unknown sources. But as I made my way, I didn't encounter anyone; in fact, it looked almost as if the hallways were completely empty. As I continued descending, I realized the fighting seemed to be happening at the ground level, getting closer as I approached.

I didn't stop to think, though, knowing that Wode was probably coming after me. So instead, I kept on running down, not even looking to see if he was behind me. My only goal was finding an exit so I could escape. I didn't know who was attacking this Jinni fort, and I didn't care; all I wanted was to find Isora and Zoey and get us out of here.

When I finally reached the ground floor and found the exit, I saw that the front doors were utterly broken, lying on their sides. However, a large unnatural boulder blocked the opening in the door's stead, effectively cutting off my escape route.

Footsteps thumped down the stairs from above. Wode. Running as fast as I could, wincing as my ribs squeezed with pain, I crossed the hall and was about to reach the other side when I caught sight of a Jinni fighting a familiar woman expertly wielding a dagger.

Cassidy, my former friend, the woman I'd thought would never lift a finger to kill even a cockroach, slashed bravely at a Jinni with her fangs out, eyes glowing green, tracksuit torn, and hair messy, and with not a drop of makeup on.

What was even more impossible was the fact that she managed to bring the male Jinni to his knees, roaring in pain as she sliced at his throat over and over again until his thick neck was cut and his head rolled off, sprouting golden blood that splashed all over Cassidy's face.

All I could do at that moment was stare at her, stunned at what I'd just seen.

She fought to catch her breath, when she suddenly jerked her head in my direction. Her eyes widened. "Aileen?"

I couldn't respond. I was still busy gaping at her.

She jumped off the Jinni's body and strode toward me. "Whatever you're doing, get out of here—"

BOOM!

The wall to our left exploded as a Jinni came flying through it, breaking it apart in the process. Both Cassidy and I were shoved back by the force.

My breathing turned shallow as I felt my ribs scream in pain. Gritting my teeth, I pulled up to my hands and knees and turned to look at Cassidy, which made my heart stop.

She lay next to me, blood dripping from a contusion on her head, eyes closed.

Fuck.

I grabbed her arm and put it around my neck, squinting through the smoke and debris to find a path that would lead us out of this damned place.

CHAPTER 34
RAGNOR

Anger was an emotion that, when managed poorly, got the better of its owner. It was an irrational reaction, a wild, volatile feeling that could take a person under.

Ragnor had successfully managed his anger for centuries. He'd turned anger into a frozen, obscure emotion he sometimes utilized to deal with his enemies. It had become a habit by now to treat anger as a means to an end and channel it properly so as to control it and avoid allowing it to control him.

But controlling his anger as of late had its limitations, especially when it came to his magic.

So Ragnor did what he very rarely allowed himself to do. He let his walls down, pulling his anger, fury, and rage free from their mental shackles and allowing them to consume him whole.

In the courtyard of the Jinni-infested villa, Ragnor pulled at the red elastic tether that was the ether and flung it at the large mansion. Like the sharpest of blades, the tether cut through the building as if it were only butter, wrecking its entrance and causing the fundamentals to destabilize.

After causing the tether to snap back into place, Ragnor turned around, eyes aglow, and stared at the people who came out of the woods.

The Rayne League Troop had arrived.

Once he'd killed the Jinn in the basement, Ragnor had finally called Magnus, his Lieutenant and the one responsible for the Troop, and told him it was time.

Unfortunately, when he finally got out of the villa in search of Aileen, he found only her friends. Aileen wouldn't have left them like that. Not after she'd seen what state they both were in.

That meant someone had taken her. AGAIN.

And he was going to take her back.

"Your only job is to kill them all," he said now, looking back at the villa. "There are a few vampire captives in the kitchen basement and two unconscious vampires in the backyard, near the lake. Take them to Rayne League. See that they get the care they need."

"Yes, my Lord," they all replied at once.

After giving them a curt nod, he said, "Go!" and watched as his people clashed with the Jinn streaming out of the building, some of which were morphing midrun into their gigantic, horned, monstrous forms.

But Ragnor couldn't afford to waste even a moment. He crashed into the building through a side window and let his nose lead him to his target.

The smell of smoke and embers, tantalizing and mysterious yet warm and passionate, filled his nose as he hunted it down. He ran through the hallways, letting his instincts and senses lead him rather than cool logic. This moment was not for thinking but for acting.

He came to a stop at the spacious entry hall, full of debris and dust from his ether attack. He tried to step forward, but his body locked unnaturally, as though he was a marionette and a puppeteer decided whether he moved.

"I had a feeling you'd come here, Lord Rayne." A melodious voice echoed in the room, followed by a man who came around a corner, a scythe in his right hand, and his left stretched forward, toward Ragnor. "But I'm afraid I can't let you go any farther."

Ragnor stared at the man, whose smell was vaguely familiar, though not his face. That mattered not, however; all Ragnor could see were the black horns in his head and the slit pupils in his irises. When Ragnor sniffed the air again, he noticed another layer of scent about the man: the scent of smoke and embers he was hunting, mixed with the shampoo she used that morning, sticking to his clothes and skin.

And Ragnor's rage multiplied.

But when he tried to move, he still couldn't. As though he knew that, the man smirked and made a sliding motion with his outstretched hand. Like a puppet, Ragnor's body followed the Jinni's order, and he fell down on the floor, his cheek pressed against the cold marble.

Belatedly, Ragnor realized he was dealing with not just a mere median Jinni but a greater Jinni.

The Jinni walked toward him. "Do you remember me?" he asked, cocking his head as though it was an innocent question. "We've met before. You killed a few friends of mine."

A distant image rose in Ragnor's mind: a forest park in Las Vegas. A hooded man with a scythe telling him to spare him and fleeing the premises. Then another image, a recent one from a prison cell.

And now he was familiar.

As though Ragnor could read his mind, the Jinni smiled. "I see that you do remember," he said, coming to a stop before Ragnor. He crouched near his face, grinning down at him. "Well, unfortunately for you, we're going to see this through this time."

If he couldn't move, then Ragnor could use other methods to get out of this man's control. On the outside, it looked like Ragnor was still aware and listening. But while Ragnor's eyes were open, his vision was not of the smirking greater Jinni but of a dark canvas with spots of lights in all colors.

Every light beckoned Ragnor, begging him to tap them, but Ragnor knew which of the lights he needed. He grabbed the crimson light, one of the darkest on the canvas, and imagined it expanding, as though he was zooming in, until all he could see was the crimson light.

He could hear the greater Jinni scream.

Blinking, he let the black canvas disappear and returned his vision to reality. But he held on to the crimson light in his mind still. He watched the Jinni on the floor, struggling against an invisible onslaught of pain.

Ragnor's Sacred ability, his aura manipulation, allowed him to inflict phantom pain on others, among different things. By inflicting this phantom pain on the Jinni, he made the creature lose his concentration and thus abandon his magical hold over Ragnor's body.

Jumping to his feet, Ragnor kept the phantom pain intact. He grabbed the man's head by his curly hair. "You touched her," he said now, voice a growl. "You touched my woman."

The Jinni shuddered and cried out as Ragnor upped the intensity of the pain. But he still heard Ragnor and managed to bite out, "Not your woman."

Ragnor's eyes cast a faint blue glow on the Jinni's horned face. "We'll see about that," he murmured before banging the creature's head against the floor.

The Jinni gasped but suddenly opened his eyes, glared at Ragnor, and let his jaw fall.

Ragnor did not expect what came out of his mouth.

A burst of blinding light exploded in the room, shoving Ragnor off the Jinni and pushing him back. Covering his eyes with his arms, Ragnor planted his feet on the ground, even though the light was almost like a storm, a hurricane trying to blow him away. Then the light thinned and became like a small meteor shower in the hall, except the light raindrops were as sharp as spears and were attempting to cut through Ragnor's body.

Unable to concentrate with his mind holding the beacon of phantom pain, he released the crimson light and used every bit of his athletic and acrobatic skills to jump out of the way of the spear-like light-filled raindrops, covering his feet with the white aura of enhancement.

When it was over, he found himself face to face with the Jinni, who was now back on his feet, breathing heavily. "You're a nasty bastard," he told Ragnor almost conversationally.

Not bothering to reply, Ragnor was about to tap into the black canvas again when a body came crashing through the front doors, ramming into the boulder blocking the entrance. The jet-black hair and turquoise eyes, along with the athletic build, told him the body belonged to Logan, one of Ragnor's formidable Troop Commanders.

Right after, another man stormed into the room, ice freezing the floor in his wake. When he saw the scythe-holding Jinni and Ragnor, however, he stopped. "What do we have here?" he asked, grinning.

Before anything else could happen, two other figures appeared from the opposite direction. And when Ragnor saw one of them, full of golden hair and pretty hazel eyes, her scent of smoke and embers crashing against him, he was suddenly filled with both relief and horror.

She looked at him and screamed, "Ragnor!" before another flash of blinding light blasted throughout the hall, shoving Ragnor back, farther and farther away from the woman who was his everything.

CHAPTER 35
AILEEN

The blinding light pushed Cassidy and me away from Ragnor and the Jinni like a tornado, and when it disappeared, we were in the front courtyard. Cassidy was still unconscious, but she seemed to be breathing.

Suddenly, the earth rumbled beneath us. I grabbed Cassidy, closed my eyes, and held on to her, protecting her once more.

Yet the earthquake did not cease; in fact, it only grew louder and stronger, making me hug my former friend tight enough to cut off her circulation. All around us, the villa crumbled as the earth seemed to curve inward, as if collapsing under the weight of all that was happening.

My ribs screamed, and I tried to breathe as I raised my head and forced myself to look at what the hell was happening.

In less than a minute, the villa was no more. Only a lump of painted stucco, crumbled concrete, and splintered wood was left.

Without warning, the earthquake came to a chilling and sudden stop.

And all I could think was *Ragnor was still inside!*

Shaking, I released Cassidy and sat up, assessing our situation. There was no doubt that this was magic. It scared the shit out of me that there was something, or rather someone, capable of doing such a thing.

But that didn't matter now. I had to get to Ragnor.

What about Cassidy, though?

Frantically, I looked around me until I spotted a tall, athletic man with jet-black hair and bright-turquoise eyes.

Logan.

My ex-boyfriend, and now a Gifted vampire of the Rayne League.

I grabbed Cassidy's hand and dragged her toward him. His eyes were open, and he seemed to be in pain, but at least he was awake and alive. "Logan," I said as I drew closer to him, and he turned to look at me, shocked.

"Aileen?" he said, frowning at first and then offering me a weak, confused, and relieved smile. "What . . ."

Ragnor had told me he would call backup from the Rayne League when we discussed our plan. But first Cassidy seemed surprised to see me, and now Logan. Why didn't he tell them I was here?

Pushing the unanswerable thoughts away, I said, "Please take care of Cassidy," before leaving the two of them and heading toward the rubble, my heart drumming in my ears.

But before I could reach the rubble, a large indigo-skinned Jinni's fist crashed against my side, sending me flying a few feet away as I gasped in agony. It felt like my ribs were broken apart.

The Jinni, a female, looked down at me, and her eyes widened. She seemed shocked and almost terrified, even. She crouched down near me, moving slowly and hesitantly, as she stretched her hand toward me.

Just then, a woman—a vampire, I realized—jumped on the Jinni's shoulders, grabbed her head, and twisted it so hard, the head disconnected from the body.

As the Jinni's body fell forward, beheaded and with gold liquid spilling out, the woman jumped back down to the ground and turned to me. She was quite the beauty, with smooth brown skin and dark, long frizzy hair and a pair of almond-shaped chestnut brown eyes. She was at least six feet tall and extremely muscular. She looked like a bionic woman, and the fact she just beheaded a Jinni with her bare hands seemed to only prove that.

"Aileen, right?" she said to me now, an unreadable expression on her face.

"Yes," I gritted out. Apparently, Ragnor did tell some of them I was here.

She sighed. "Good. Let's get you out of here, then."

She came as if to pick me up, but I shook my head. "Take care of them first," I said, pointing at where Logan and Cassidy were. Logan seemed to have fallen unconscious while I wasn't looking, blood trickling down from his head.

That didn't seem to be what she wanted to hear. "My orders are to take care of you first," she told me, arching a brow and folding her arms, as if to say she wasn't going to budge.

"I'll come with you obediently," I said quietly, "as long as you get them out of here first."

She studied my face before returning her gaze to the rubble. She gasped. "Logan?" she whispered, her eyes shocked and full of worry as she looked at the man.

Then, as if she heard something I didn't, she cocked her head, and her face suddenly cleared. Then I heard it too.

Something was coming.

Quickly, the woman's gaze returned to me, and she said, "Fine, but don't move an inch until I'm back."

As if I could do anything now. "You got it."

The woman rushed to pick up both Logan and Cassidy under her arms as though they were bed pillows. Then, as quick as lightning, she disappeared into the woods.

Just then, however, I saw three monstrous Jinn rush right after her, drool dripping down their chins. And I knew she wouldn't be coming back for a while.

That meant I had to fend for myself.

I tried to get up onto my feet, but my body refused. All I could do was crawl over the grass toward the rubble, needing to find Ragnor, to see if he was all right.

As I crawled, I could hear the sounds of battle all around me, but my sight was fixated on the far-too-still rubble. Determination was my only fuel as I dragged myself forward with agonizing broken ribs.

The earth rumbled, and I froze, listening as something seemed to be coming from underneath the rubble. The sound of the tremor rose and expanded, becoming deafening as it drew closer and closer, until an instinct told me to cover my head.

A moment later, an explosion came from within the rubble.

I planted myself on the grass, gritting my teeth as I felt wood and concrete flying at me from all directions. Pain coursed through my spine as some of the rubble crashed into me. When everything settled once more, I dared peek through my arms and watched, open mouthed, what was happening.

Ragnor floated, his entire body enveloped in a golden aura. His eyes were open wide, pupils and whites gone, only the neon blue remaining, glowing the brightest I'd ever seen them. His hand was wrapped around a person's neck. Wode's.

Wode appeared to be speaking, his lips moving despite being choked by Ragnor. The more he spoke, however, the tighter Ragnor's hold became.

Wode laughed just then. And a bright light, like the stormy blinding light from before, engulfed the two of them, hiding them from my sight.

"Ragnor!" I screamed, willing my body to move. Shakily, I managed to get up to my feet, battling the pain, and tried to step forward, toward the light, where Wode was attacking Ragnor.

"Aileen."

In a blink, Ragnor was in front of me, his eyes glowing, though no longer as unnaturally as before. His arms came around me, pulling me toward him in an embrace.

And just like that, all the fighting spirit left me, and the pain, the shock, the overwhelming relief caused me to go weak, and I fell deeper into Ragnor's arms.

He was alive.

We were alive.

That's all that mattered.

CHAPTER 36

AILEEN

The silence in the bus could be cut with a knife.

It was the same bus that had once transported the Rayne League newbies—and me among them—on the cross-country road trip to visit all other vampire Leagues. But unlike back then, the bus's interior had been changed from a normal everyday bus to something like a field emergency room.

Aside from the first two rows and the back row, the seats were rearranged into triage beds for the injured, all with the necessary equipment, such as IV drips, EKG machines, and the like. Two nurses went from one patient to the next, checking their stats and making sure they were recovering in the required speedy manner of vampires.

Among the patients was Logan, who'd lost so much blood and Lifeblood, what with the spots spread across his thinning skin, that he needed a special blood transfusion from none other than Magnus, one of Ragnor's Lieutenants. Magnus sat next to him, feeding him blood through a needle since he'd fallen unconscious.

Another patient was, surprisingly, a hawk. The hawk was attended to by one of the Rayne League vampires, who, more surprisingly, appeared to share his blood with the hawk. He seemed worried sick about the animal.

Isora and Zoey were on the bus as well. Both were receiving a direct blood transfusion from the dark-skinned woman who'd taken Logan and Cassidy before and whose name I learned was Neisha.

Meanwhile, I was sitting at the back of the bus, my ribs wrapped up and a cup of fresh blood in my hands. Ragnor sat next to me, and while he appeared expressionless, I had no doubt he was deep in thought, even as his eyes glowed neon blue.

Neither of us spoke. No one in the bus talked either. What would we say? It was as if there was an unofficial agreement to leave everything to silence in order to process all that had happened.

Still, my mind raced with burning questions, of course. But I was tired, exhausted even, and I couldn't bring myself to satisfy my curiosity.

And yet I couldn't rest. All I could do was look at the greenery outside as Abe, of all people, drove the bus toward Maine, to the Rayne League.

Hours passed as one landscape transformed into another. Eventually, I stared ahead, trying to wrap my head around how things had gotten this fucked up.

Despite my feelings about being sold in the Auction, I had only just started settling into life in the Atalon League. I'd already begun to accept that Ragnor and I were done, and I was preparing to become a museum guide assistant, poised to sell a lot of expensive art to quite a few rich assholes. I had found a friend in Isora and had even been friendly with more than just her. I was starting to accept my new League and was becoming accepted in return.

Then reality came crashing down on me.

Atalon wasn't the nice, forthcoming Lord he'd pretended to be.

Isora had become a blood slave and would've died in the Jinn's hands if Ragnor and I hadn't gotten her out.

Would I ever find a home?

Now, Wode's words and everything else that had happened since the gala event began to sink in. My father and I weren't the only ones who knew about the Children of Kahil. And worse than that, my father wasn't the only one willing to maim, destroy, or kill for the Morrow Gods.

A headache seized me right as a nearby voice took me out of my thoughts.

"I'm sorry."

My spine stiffened, and slowly, I turned toward Ragnor. He was looking ahead, at the injured and the nurses and the other vampires, but I knew his words were meant for me. "What for?"

For a few moments, Ragnor said nothing. Then he continued with "I'm sorry I didn't get the other captives out."

My heart jolted, and I clenched my hands into fists. Right. The villa had crumbled down, burying the vampire captives in the kitchen basement. But that wasn't Ragnor's fault. He'd done more than enough.

I let out a sigh and said, "Don't be," before I took his hands in mine. "All that matters is that you're safe, and so are the others."

The air was filled with things unsaid, but neither of us talked. All we could do was hold hands and wait.

It was early morning when we arrived at the warehouse that would lead to the Rayne League's underground compound. When I stood, Ragnor grabbed my wrist and said, "Wait."

Slowly, I sat back down and watched as Abe helped the nurses and the others take the patients out one by one. Only when the bus was empty did Ragnor rise to his feet and say, "Let's go."

I followed him out of the bus and into the familiar warehouse. Then, we took the stairs leading down to the elevator that would take us to the compound. We didn't speak as we boarded the elevator car, and we didn't speak as we exited it into the beautifully familiar entrance hall.

And just being here, in the hall, with its familiar marble floors and arched entry, made my shoulders sag in relief.

Ragnor led me to his suite at the end of the wing that held the Gifted residences. I'd been to Ragnor's suite only once before, but I remembered it vividly. It was large and spacious, with a private living room and a huge bedroom. There was even a little kitchenette adjoined to the room, along with a small dining table.

I went to sit at one of the plush sofas, groaning at the sudden comfort. Ragnor didn't join me, heading to the kitchenette instead. "Coffee?"

"Yes, black," I said, knowing I needed the extra caffeine to deal with what was to come. We had many things to discuss, after all. "Thanks."

Ragnor came back with our drinks and placed them on the coffee table before taking a seat on the sofa next to me. Despite our bodies being right next to each other's, I felt as if there was a gulf between us. A gulf that hadn't been there prior to our incident at the Jinni villa.

This time, I didn't want to jump to conclusions like before and assume the worst. So all I could do was swallow the concern and wait for him to speak.

We both sipped our coffees, and then, without further ado, Ragnor leveled his gaze on me and dropped the gauntlet. "I know you're an actual Child of Kahil."

Shock froze my body.

No.

He can't know.

"I have no idea what you're talking about," I said lightly, sipping my coffee, pretending his words didn't strike me like thousands of knives.

"There's no point lying, Aileen," he said quietly. "I know that you tried to summon the Morrow Gods back at the Auction. I thought you were simply a follower of the Children, but I know better now."

I forced out a laugh and put my coffee down before rising to my feet. "What the hell is this bullshit?" I said incredulously as I walked to the kitchenette, my hands shaking. This religion was a sham. I never believed in any of it, especially after seeing what my father did in the name of it.

And yet, Ragnor seemed to actually believe it. Why?

I stiffened as I heard him coming after me. "Thou shalt find pleasure in the agony of the feeble," he suddenly said, and I froze. "Thou shalt seal thy allegiance with a pact written in the blood of kin. Thou shalt be the harbinger of discord, for the Gods thrive in the turbulence of the suffering."

My hands landed on the kitchen island as I tried to bring my breathing back to normal. "Sounds like some zealous shit, these phrases," I said, voice on the verge of shrill.

"Aileen, please." He was right behind me, his rapid breathing and mine equally filling the audible space between us.

My heart stilled. I opened my mouth to speak, but my voice abandoned me.

He ran a hand up and then down my back now. "I won't judge you," he said quietly. "I want you no matter who or what you are. But I need to know." His arms enveloped me from behind, and instead of feeling warm, I felt cold all over. "Talk to me."

The first time my father was arrested, I was thirteen years old. At first, I was put in an orphanage, but two months later, Ella and Roger Kazar, Logan's parents, had taken me in as a foster child, with plans to adopt me down the line.

I'd heard many stories of kids suffering in the foster care system, landing themselves with the worst kinds of caretakers. But Ella and Roger weren't like that; they didn't need government money, what with Roger working in the oil industry and earning enough to last for a few generations. They voluntarily chose to be foster parents from the kindness of their hearts.

Even back then, I recognized them as good people. At thirteen, I already knew how to differentiate good from evil, and seeing how good they were to me didn't leave any room for questioning which side of the coin they belonged to.

But I was far too broken for them to fix, and a year into our life together, when they caught me cutting myself for a would-be tribute to the Morrow Gods, they did what any good, responsible foster parents would do.

They put me in therapy.

My therapist was called Dr. Jameson. He was a tall man with a large belly and white hair who looked like Santa Claus. He was all smiles and gentleness. The perfect therapist.

From the weekly meetings over the two years I spent in his clinic, I remembered only one session vividly. I was sixteen at the time, and as usual, he handed me a hot cocoa before he asked me, "How was your week?"

Being a typical teenager, I kept my answers short. "Fine."

He smiled. "Care to elaborate?"

"Nothing special happened," I said broodingly. "Got a D in calculus. Ella was enormously proud." Considering I'd been getting Fs for months before then.

Dr. Jameson didn't speak, simply prompting me with a look. He loved using the silent technique to make me talk, and it always worked; I hated sitting in his clinic with the oppressive silence surrounding me.

After letting out a sigh, I glared at him and said, "Fine. I had a nightmare."

He was quiet for a moment before he asked, "Was it the same one?"

I shook my head. "It was a memory. Or at least it started as one."

"Describe it for me," he requested gently.

Scowling, I looked away and folded my arms. "It's my first memory, from when I was like six," I responded, irritated. "Dad gave me a clean sheet of paper and a pencil and asked me to draw a scene from the book he was using to teach me."

Since I was homeschooled right up until his arrest, it was up to my father to give me a proper education. In his mind, he probably thought that he did just that. In reality, there was a reason I was getting Fs in most subjects left and right.

"Was the scene from that religious book?" Dr. Jameson asked quietly.

I nodded. "Yes. The Tefat," I said, grimacing. "Dad had me reading it front to back since the moment he taught me how to read, so I knew every chapter of this book by heart. I chose a scene from when the Morrow Gods visited Esheer, the Realm of Fire, to visit the infernal jail of Bennu, their ancestor spirit."

Dr. Jameson frowned. "You referred to Bennu as a bird a few months ago."

Shrugging, I explained, "Bennu is depicted in many ways throughout the Tefat. Sometimes it's a bird, other times it's a divine being titled the Creator, and there are times it even appears as shapeless flames. It depends which chapter you read and the context of the story." I gave him a smile. "Confusing, I know."

The good doctor smiled back. "So how did you draw the scene?"

"I painted the silhouettes of three grotesque men, as the Morrow Gods are often described in the Tefat," I replied, "and in the background I sketched some flames and straight vertical lines, like jail bars." I paused, recalling the nightmare, and pursed my lips. "But in the dream, the painting was a bit different."

Leaning back against the couch, I sipped my hot cocoa as I said, "In the real memory, I stopped at drawing the flames. In that nightmare, I continued the drawing, sketching a feathered bird behind the bars, with its wings wrapped around two metal poles. Then the bird's eyes flashed yellow, and I was suddenly set on fire."

Dr. Jameson was silent, watching me with an expression I couldn't quite read. Then he asked, "Did you wake up after that?"

I shook my head and shuddered. "I wish," I murmured. "Instead, as I became fire itself, the bird spoke to me."

He leaned forward. "What did it say?"

"That's the thing," I said, scowling. "I don't remember. All I do remember was staring at it, listening to its voice, and terror making me suffocate. That was when I woke up."

Dr. Jameson stared at me for a few long moments, seemingly lost in thought. I took the chance to drink my hot cocoa, which had already turned cold.

When he finally spoke again, his voice was contemplative. "How much do you believe in the Tefat?"

I looked pointedly at the chain cross necklace hanging around his neck. "Not as much as some do."

He smiled. "When was the last time you read the Tefat?"

Giving him an incredulous look, I snapped, "Are you really suggesting I reread that monstrosity?"

"All I'm saying is that sometimes, dreams, and even nightmares, are an insight to our true self," he replied quietly. "Perhaps, despite your denials, you're still a believer." He paused and gave me a kind look. "It doesn't have to be one way or the other, Aileen."

Anger erupted inside me so quickly, it almost gave me whiplash. "If you think my 'true self' is being a fanatic like Dad, then you're crazy," I snarled, slamming the hot cocoa mug on the coffee table so hard, it almost cracked. "You have no idea what being a devout Child of Kahil entails, Dr. Jameson." Thinking back to the atrocities my father committed, I hugged my knees to my chest.

"That's not what I was saying," he said so gently, it made tears rise to my eyes. "I simply meant that you must have internalized many of the things your father had taught you, and one of these things is the content of the Tefat. Perhaps this is why you're having nightmares—and this nightmare now too—and maybe the key to understanding these nightmares is learning where they come from."

I looked away from him, anger and pain clamping my mouth. I knew he didn't mean it that way, but I felt as if he just told me I was as much of a monster as Dad was.

And I didn't need to be told I was a monster. Not when I already knew that I was.

The session had ended not long after, and I remembered going back to the Kazars' and staring at the Tefat I hid in the back of my closet. Just the thought of touching it made me tremble in fear.

After that session, I did not mention the Tefat again.

"I can't," I said now, turning around to face the man who was pleading with me to talk. To tell him about the horrors of my past. To reveal the truth of what the Morrow Gods were and what I had been forced to do in their name.

There was a reason the Children of Kahil were no longer around. The reason why my father and I were the last descendants.

And while I wanted Ragnor with everything in me, I refused to speak of this. Because like my ancestors, some things should stay buried.

The main one being how much of a monster I was.

Because this was the truth. I was a monster of epic proportions, so much so that if Ragnor knew the extent of what I'd done, he would never, ever look at me the same again.

And the fear of seeing him reject me for my past was so overwhelming, I began to shiver. I could take him throwing me away because he didn't care much for me as a person. I could take him rejecting me because he put up walls around his heart.

But having him reject me on the basis of my monstrous acts was too much for me to bear. Even though I knew I deserved it.

He searched my eyes, his own dimming to their soothing midnight blue. Then, in a defeated voice, he said, "All right."

CHAPTER 37

AILEEN

That night, I could barely sleep.

With my ribs still healing, Ragnor and I didn't have sex. Instead, he simply cuddled me close and buried his head in my neck. Despite the tension in the air following our short argument, he fell asleep easily.

But I couldn't.

Not when I felt like I was ruining us before we even properly began.

So I stayed awake, listening to his soft breaths and sinking into his embrace, wishing I could erase my past and the irremovable stain of my bloodline.

When morning came, I gently pulled away from him. I thought he awoke when I did, but when I saw his heaving chest relax, I left the suite.

Walking through the hallways of the Rayne League made me feel nostalgic, a perfect distraction from the chaos in my head. When I arrived at the cafeteria, it almost felt like I was home.

But there was no place that could be my home. In my head, I would forever be a nomad. Yet the Rayne League, despite the bad memories it brought, felt like the only place I truly belonged. Perhaps because Ragnor stood at its head. Or because this was where everything started going astray, and thus this was the only place that could bring me back to the right path.

The cafeteria was mostly deserted but for a group of three kitchen workers wearing dirty aprons who were drinking coffee at one of the tables. When I saw who they were, I was suddenly swept away by emotions.

As I rushed toward them, they heard me coming and turned to look at me. Their eyes widened, and I found myself smiling from ear to ear, tears in my eyes, as I threw myself at one of them, the first person in the Rayne League who'd shown me kindness.

Jada. Along with CJ and Bowen. The dishwashing team.

I'd missed them so much.

"Aileen!" Jada screamed in happiness as she hugged me back. "What are you doing here?"

I leaned back from her and wiped my eyes. Damn, I had become such a crybaby in the past few days. "I missed you," I said, turning to look at CJ and Bowen, who gave me fond looks of welcome. "It's so good to see you again."

"The same goes for you," CJ said, his eyes trailing to my hair. "I see you've been through some changes."

I laughed tearily. "You have no idea."

"Sit," Jada commanded, pulling me to the chair next to her. "Bowen, bring coffee to our friend."

Bowen gave her a mock glare. "Are you ordering me around?" he drawled but then smiled and gave me a wink. "Kidding. You like it black with AB negative, right?"

"You remember," I said, warmth filling my chest.

"Of course I do." Bowen chuckled and rose from his seat. "Anything else? Lon's famous egg and bacon?"

My mouth watered. The Atalon League's food was great, but nothing compared to the Rayne League's chef's touch. "Yes, please."

Once I had my coffee and food, Jada said, "You've got to tell us everything! Last we heard, you were bought by Atalon."

I smirked. “You disappoint me, folks. I thought you were apt at collecting gossip.”

CJ snorted, rubbing his buzz cut. “Well, when it came to you, there seemed to be a severe lack of information.”

“Which is why you need to spill,” Bowen said, giving me a prompting smile. “Tell us everything. We’re dying for some news that isn’t about rapist noobs or Margarita’s incompetence.”

I jolted at his words and frowned. “Now I’m curious,” I said, thinking about Ragnor’s redheaded Lieutenant. “What’s going on here?”

The three exchanged glances before returning their gazes to me. “Do you know Tansy Contos?” Jada asked quietly.

The name stirred up a sense of nostalgia mixed with caution. Tansy had been a newcomer along with me and eventually was bought by Ragnor. She was an oddball, to say the least, always daydreaming and spouting nonsense.

She wasn’t strong, but she always made me put my guard up. She’d said some things back when we were suitemates that made me keep some distance between us.

“Yes,” I told Jada now. “She used to be my suitemate here.”

Jada gave me a somber look. “Several weeks ago, there was an incident.”

CJ cursed, and I snapped my eyes to him. He was glowering at his coffee mug. “Two noob men assaulted her,” he snarled, “and while our Lord took care of them, Contos has been hospitalized in the infirmary ever since.”

“They broke her.” Bowen shook his head, face both disgusted and angry. “Her mental state has been deteriorating rapidly. She has to be under surveillance at all times.”

My blood froze at their words. First, Zoey was a dead woman walking. Now Tansy was in a severe mental state. What was it about my former suitemates and misfortune?

“I’ll go visit her,” I said quietly, trying to process what they had just told me. What the hell had happened in the Rayne League in the past couple of months?

"You have to get the infirmary's permission," Jada told me softly, squeezing my hand. "I know the last time someone visited her, she had a meltdown."

I might not have been best friends with Tansy, but I couldn't help but pity her. She was already not quite there to begin with, and now this . . .

"Anyway," CJ said, giving me a pointed look. "It's your turn. What brings you here to our humble abode?"

This was a loaded question, especially since I didn't exactly know what I was doing there. Ragnor and I hadn't talked about my future in that sense. Officially, I was still part of the Atalon League, but there was no chance in hell I would go back there. Not after Atalon tried to "rent" me like some object to the Jinn.

But what would it mean for me, then? Would I become Leagueless?

And what about Isora? I refused to believe she would want to go back there. Yet what was the alternative?

"Hey." Jada's voice brought me out of my own head, and I turned to her. She gave me a worried look. "You don't have to talk if you don't want to."

The gnawing worries must've shown on my face. "Thanks," I said, smiling faintly. "Can you fill me in on some gossip, instead?"

Jada laughed, lifting the weight from my chest, if only temporarily. "But of course! Let's start with the latest news: Magnus, the Lieutenant, has been seeing the cute nurse who took care of him not too long ago . . ."

"Yo, Henderson."

The voice came from behind me and brought my gossip session with my dishwashing friends to an abrupt stop. I turned around and saw the dark-skinned bionic woman from the Jinni villa taking the empty seat in front of mine, laying down a tray filled to the brim with food, as though she was feeding an army. She seemed to ignore my friends, who were watching her with surprisingly awestruck expressions.

After clearing my throat, I said, "Hey" as she started gobbling up the food like a starved woman. Seeing her significant biceps flexing, I wondered if she was a bodybuilder.

I also wondered why she was sitting down with us—or, rather, with me.

Clearly thinking the same thing, Jada elbowed CJ and rose to her feet. "We'll talk to you later," she told me as Bowen followed suit. Jada turned her gaze to the bionic woman. "Have a pleasant morning, Commander."

The woman gave them a single nod, and before I could protest, the dishwashing group dispersed.

I returned my gaze to the woman, trying to understand what she wanted from me. Likely sensing my confusion, she raised her head and gave me a grin that was a tad too unhinged for my liking. "I'm Neisha," she told me, giving me a salute with a croissant. "Pleasure to make your acquaintance."

"Same, I guess?" I said, still not quite sure about her.

Grin still intact, she said, "Don't worry, Goldilocks. I'm simply here to accompany you later to see your friends. The Lord's orders."

"Oh," I murmured, my chest tightening. Ragnor seemed to know me too well. He knew I would want to visit Isora and Zoey, and so he arranged for a companion.

Though why I needed a companion when we were safe here was a mystery.

For a few minutes, we ate in silence. She seemed unabashed as she practically inhaled her omelet and slurped the thinly cut cucumbers like spaghetti. It was fascinating, I had to admit; I'd never seen anyone eat so much in such a short amount of time, and it made me curious.

She proved to be quite sharp, because she sensed that too. Chuckling, she said, "I started out as a Common, but my Gift is super-strength. Used to be a weight lifter in the past, you see." She motioned toward her tray. "Since my Gift consumes far more energy than most, I need to eat like a motherfucker to recharge."

I didn't think I'd ever encountered any Gifted who so willingly and openly disclosed the nature of their Gift. It was refreshing. "So you really are a bionic woman," I said. Something about her pretty face and deadly muscles made it impossible to tear my eyes away.

Shrugging, she leaned back, drinking her coffee. "Well, it's your turn," she said, giving me a wicked grin. "What's up with you and our Lord?"

Her question made me tense. "Nothing's up" was my immediate response.

She rolled her eyes so exaggeratedly, her eyeballs almost fell out of their sockets. "Don't bother lying," she said and pointed at me with a bacon-impaled fork. "Everyone knows something's going on between the two of you."

I folded my arms, jaw locked. "And what makes everyone so sure about it?"

Chortling, she stuffed her mouth with bacon. Once she swallowed, she gave me a somewhat sinister smile. "Three things. One, his erratic behavior in the past few months." She nibbled on a carrot before returning to me. "Two, the fact he joined the noobs' field trip twice, and in those two times you were involved in some sort of way." She sipped her coffee and shot me a knowing smirk. "And three, the fact you slept in his room."

As a private person, I didn't like any of that—especially since after our little chat yesterday, I wasn't sure where we stood anymore. I wasn't even sure we were still on for that one-month trial period.

"Also, there's another point," Neisha said, eyes flickering with amusement. "I heard you calling him by his name."

She was far too nosy. "You think you got me all figured out, don't you?"

She shook her head. "Not at all," she said candidly. "It's just that when it comes to such matters, I'm an expert. Though in your case, it doesn't take a genius to see that you and our Lord are utterly infatuated."

That was enough. "While your insight is . . . intriguing," I said, trying not to sound too irritated, "we're not close enough for me to talk to you about any of it."

She rose from her seat. "You're right," she said. "Then let's take you to those you are close to, shall we?"

I looked down at her tray. It was empty. Mine still had a piece of bacon left. But her words managed to erase any trace of hunger, so I stood up and said, "Lead the way."

CHAPTER 38

RAGNOR

The office was in utter disarray.

"My Lord!" Ragnor's head secretary, Dominic, jumped to his feet the moment Ragnor set foot inside the reception area of his office, watching as the other three secretaries were battling to answer the many incoming phone calls. "You have to take this!"

Dominic shoved a piece of paper into Ragnor's hands. Ragnor stared at it and saw it was an official-looking letter with the logo of the Atalon League at the top. Grimacing, Ragnor started reading.

> Dear Lord Ragnor Rayne,
> I am writing to bring to your immediate attention a matter of grave importance concerning the unauthorized possession of a member associated with my League, hereinafter referred to as the "League." It has come to my attention that you are currently in unapproved possession of the aforementioned League member.
>
> By this notice, I hereby demand that you promptly return the League member in question to me on or

before the date of February 28, failing which, legal action will be pursued against you in accordance with the relevant legal provisions.

You are hereby advised that your failure to comply with this demand and return the League member will result in legal action being initiated against you under the pertinent provisions outlined in Article 3.5 of the applicable regulations. It is presumed that you are cognizant of the implications and consequences associated with such legal action.

This notice is issued in an earnest effort to afford you an opportunity to rectify the situation amicably before resorting to formal legal proceedings. It is strongly advised that you promptly take the necessary steps to ensure compliance with this demand and prevent further legal action.

Your immediate attention to this matter is expected.

Sincerely,
Lord Orion Atalon

Ragnor had expected it, and yet the letter made him far too pissed to be able to think straight.

"Dominic," he said now, looking at his head secretary, whose worry was etched so deep in his face, he looked as though he'd aged ten years. "Please schedule a meeting for the Lieutenants and all Troop Commanders to take place in my office tonight. Once you do that, send the original email to my direct inbox and cc legal. I'll respond myself."

He paused, then said, "Also, schedule emergency calls with all North American Lords to be taken throughout the day. And, of course, cancel the upcoming Auction."

Dominic took a step back, eyes wide. After being his secretary for two centuries, Dominic knew what all this meant, and Ragnor knew he didn't like it. None of it. "My Lord," he whispered, "why?"

"Why else?" Ragnor replied, eyes flashing. "You know what this legal notice means, Dominic. You also know what Atalon is like. The true meaning behind this letter is clear."

Dominic's auburn hair fell over his shoulders as his head dropped. "But you can simply return that girl," he murmured. "There's no need to—"

"That woman is not going anywhere." Ragnor cut him off, warning in his voice. "Even if it means war."

Soon after, Ragnor abandoned the chaos in his office and left the underground, heading to the League-owned pub. The moment he stepped inside, Moses handed him his favorite Jägermeister wordlessly. Based on his grave expression, Ragnor knew he was aware of what was going on. When he wasn't bartending, Moses was part of his intelligence team, after all.

Holding the drink, Ragnor sat down at his usual table. Moments later, Eliza walked through the door and took the seat across from him, not bothering to order a drink. Moses, who'd already acquainted himself with her, knew what she liked, though, and brought her a gin and tonic shot.

It had been a while since Ragnor had seen Eliza. The last time they'd spoken hadn't been very cordial. In fact, after that conversation, Eliza had promptly left his town house, choosing to stay in a rental in the city instead.

But Eliza was the one who'd called him, and Ragnor knew she wouldn't have done so without good reason.

Now, Eliza turned her single eye to him, and instead of a greeting, she hissed, "What the hell were you thinking?"

"So you heard," he said, unsurprised. Eliza knew how to gather information almost as well as he did, though her methods were far more unconventional.

"Who didn't hear of you declaring war on Atalon?" she snapped quietly. "Are you seriously going to do this? I know you have . . . feelings . . . for Aileen Henderson, but that's—"

"It's beyond just my feelings for her, and you know it." Ragnor cut her off, anger in his voice. "Atalon has been biding his time to find a proper excuse to go against me. He acted all friendly and nice, but he was sharpening his claws behind the scenes. This is his opportunity to get back at me for all the alleged things I did to him."

Eliza scowled. "This is a fucking mess, Rayne," she whispered loudly. "You're going to war for a Child of Kahil. I can't support this."

Ragnor sipped his drink before he responded. "What you're worried about won't come to pass, Eliza."

Her eye glowered at him. "After centuries of peace, the Jinn are suddenly on the move," she said, voice tight. "A Child of Kahil has accidentally become a vampire and turned Sacred overnight. The Malachi have started meddling in earth's affairs. Don't you see what it boils down to?"

She was right. Ragnor knew that, but still—"A war between two vampiric factions should not lead to anything that would concern the Malachi. This is not the same as before."

Eliza slapped the table in fury. "If the Morrow Gods are resurrected, Ragnor, I swear to whatever divine being is up there, I will kill Aileen Henderson with my own hands. And then we'll see if that's something the Malachi will be concerned about."

Ragnor's hackles rose. "You won't touch a hair on her head, Eliza," he said quietly, eyes brightening to neon blue. "I won't let you. As for the Malachi, let me worry about that."

She closed her eye and let out a ragged breath. "I was born to do one thing only, Ragnor," she suddenly said. "Being on good terms with you is only a small part of it. But if I have to clash with you head-on to fulfill my goal, then I won't hesitate to do so." She opened her eye and gave him a deadly serious look. "The Children of Kahil aren't just your enemy but mine too. You may be blinded by love or lust or whatever this is, but I'm not. The existence of Aileen Henderson to begin with shouldn't have happened. Her being a vampire is the worst-case scenario. Her becoming Sacred isn't just a coincidence; it's an omen. A bad one. If the Morrow Gods are resurrected because of this war of yours, it won't just destroy the world. And if Esheer, the Realm of Fire, bursts open . . ." She sucked in a breath. "I implore you, Ragnor. Call this war off. Settle your dispute with Atalon some other way that doesn't include bloodshed. I do not want to make you an enemy."

Ragnor knew she spoke the truth. He'd known Eliza for a long time, after all. He knew she meant every word.

But calling this war off wasn't a possibility. As much as Atalon had been biding his time, so had Ragnor. He had as big of a grudge against Atalon as Atalon had with him. This had been a long time coming, with or without Aileen's involvement. And there was only one way to resolve a dispute between Leagues once and for all.

And that was the Hecatomb.

He thought of Aileen then. He could never send her back to Atalon even if he wanted to, and no matter what he did, Atalon wouldn't let it go. He would accuse him of tricking him again, like that one time many centuries ago. He would not listen to reason. In fact, Ragnor had a hunch that even if he sent Aileen back to Atalon, he would use her to wage a war on him anyway.

"I'm afraid there is no way around this, Eliza," he said quietly. "One way or another, Atalon and I were bound to go to war. It's not even about Aileen at this point but rather about the grudge he has against me."

Eliza deflated. "And you are so arrogant that you poked the bear. We could have avoided this for years more. You know how he is. He's a proud man. Maybe even just as arrogant as you. But you should have known better. I'm so mad at you, Ragnor," she said weakly. "Why did you give her the Imprint? Why couldn't you just kill her?"

Before he developed feelings for her, Ragnor had asked himself the same question. Back then, he didn't know the answer. He knew only that at that exact moment, he couldn't bring himself to snap her neck. He'd been under a trance, needing to give her the Imprint, to make her his.

And just like that, for the first time since he'd met Aileen Henderson, Ragnor came to a blinding realization of what she was to him. And that realization made him put down the whiskey glass and lean back, an unfathomable wonder blooming in his gut.

This can't be, he thought, dazed. *There is only ever one, and I found mine many ages ago.*

Ragnor couldn't speak. The epiphany stole all his words away.

Eliza stared at him, and as though she sensed something strange was going on, she suddenly sat straight, her eye widening. Before he could resist, she grabbed his hand, her own hand cold.

The eye patch covering her left eye was suddenly glowing. Ragnor couldn't bring himself to be mad that she was using her powers on him. In fact, it was almost satisfying to see her jerk her hand back, her breathing turning heavy and shivery. "No," she whispered, her eye impossibly wide.

All Ragnor could do was smile. It was a true, deep smile that came from the heart. Suddenly, he could no longer sit still. He had to find Aileen. He had to take her in his arms. He had to have her, the need so strong, it was almost debilitating.

Because Aileen Henderson was his Alara Morreh.

The one he never thought he would ever have again.

CHAPTER 39

AILEEN

As I sat between Zoey's and Isora's beds in the infirmary, watching their faces, pain spread through me. Neither had opened her eyes yet, but at least the graying spots on their skin were gone, and they seemed less bony than before, thanks to the blood infusions they were receiving nonstop.

And yet I couldn't help but think it was all my fault.

Logically, I knew their situation had nothing to do with me. Isora was bound to become a blood slave eventually, and I hadn't even seen Zoey since the Auction. But the guilt gnawing at me told me differently.

It told me that no matter who was near me, they would all end the same way the little birds did in my father's basement.

Glancing at Neisha, I saw she was talking with a nurse near the entrance, their backs to me. Turning my gaze to the other end of the room, where a bed was hidden with a curtain, I made a split-second decision.

As quietly as I could, I stood and gave my friends one last look before tiptoeing toward the curtained bed.

Earlier, when Neisha and I had arrived, I asked the nurse to see Tansy. She had refused without leaving room for argument. But I wasn't one to listen when told no.

After slipping through the curtains, I made sure to shut them before I turned to the bed.

Confused, all I could do was stare. The bed was empty. I put my hands down on the messy sheets. They were still warm.

"What are you doing?"

I whipped around to see the nurse glowering at me, Neisha right behind her. I was about to speak when the nurse's eyes went to the bed, and she paled. "Shit," she hissed and started running toward the exit.

"Wait!" I called and began running after her, Neisha following behind.

The nurse seemed to know where to go, because she took the staircases leading upward, to where the greenhouse was. She pulled the greenhouse door open so strongly, it almost got torn off its hinges.

Ribs aching, I kept on running after the nurse, deeper into the greenhouse, until we arrived at a staircase leading to a door. The nurse practically kicked that door, causing it to break, and when I followed her, cold, fresh air hit my lungs.

We were outside.

I had no idea there was an exit in the Rayne League other than the main one.

The outside was a plain of grass that seemed eerily familiar. If the sky above was purple instead of dark and the grass was wilted, it would've looked exactly like the field in my mind, where Eliza had visited me in my dreams.

The resemblance was far too uncanny, really, that for a moment all I could do was stop and stare, momentarily forgetting why I was even here.

That is, until the nurse screamed.

Snapping out of my ruminations, I ran toward the nurse and saw she had arrived at a cliff. And near the edge of the cliff stood a petite woman with knee-length strawberry blonde hair.

"Tansy?" I blurted out, shocked.

The woman turned around, her huge baby blue eyes staring right at me. They were as dreamy looking as they always were, as if her head was somewhere else, but there was hardness in them that hadn't been there before.

"Tansy." The nurse stretched out her hands, shaking as she took a careful step forward. "Everything is okay . . ."

Tansy's eyes left me in favor of the nurse, and the hardness in them increased, taking over the dreamy glassiness in them. I'd never seen her look this angry.

She didn't speak, though. All she did was turn back around and face the cliff's end.

"No," the nurse whispered, horror in her eyes. "Don't, Tansy . . . This won't help . . ."

The nurse's words made my heart freeze. If Tansy jumped, it probably wouldn't kill her—she was a vampire, after all, and unless she was decapitated or had her heart carved out, she wouldn't die.

"Then what will?" Tansy suddenly said, her voice so empty, it was like a slap to the face. "They told me nothing mattered. They said it was for the best."

The nurse was in tears. "There are no voices, Tansy," she said in a broken voice. "They're all in your head."

"Liar!" Tansy screamed and turned around, her eyes glowing. She snapped those eyes to me, and her face, which used to be all innocence and dreaminess, was now contorted in rage. "Tell them," she snarled like a wounded animal, "tell them that the Morrow Gods are real and that they want—no, need—me dead!"

I froze.

The nurse glanced at me. "She's suffering from schizophrenia," she whispered, agony in her eyes. "The voices in her head, these 'Gods,' they're merely a by-product of her mental illness—"

"No." I cut her off, cold sweat coating my skin as things began to make sense. "If I'm right, your diagnosis is incorrect."

My muscles tensed to a snapping point. I walked toward Tansy, not taking my eyes off her for a second. "The Morrow Gods have been dead for centuries," I told her in a quiet voice, calculating the pace of each step that I took so I wouldn't frighten her. "We can't bring them back. Everything you learned about them was a lie. Everything."

She shook her head, her hair flying around her. "They need me," she said tautly. "If they have me, the rite will be complete."

Memories flashed in my head, and I had to slowly breathe in and out, in fear of having a meltdown right there and then myself. Coming to a stop only a step away from her, I held her desperate gaze. "The Gods are dead," I repeated as softly as I could, my heartbeat like drums in my ears. "You are free . . ."

The words died on my lips as the anger was suddenly gone from her face, replaced by a smile so pure and delightful, the sudden contrast made me stagger back. "You can help me," she said in her familiar dreamlike voice. "You're his child, aren't you?"

I began to shake. I tried to speak, but my lips were dry. I tried to breathe, but I was suffocating.

And just like that, Tansy took a step back into the open air.

But she didn't fall.

As fast as lightning, Neisha bolted forward, grabbed Tansy's arm, and pulled her back. Tansy's eyes grew impossibly wider when Neisha chopped at her neck, causing her to lose consciousness.

Lifting her in her arms, Neisha glanced at the nurse. "Let's go, Leah," she said before turning her eyes to somewhere behind me. "She's all yours, my Lord."

I barely noticed when Neisha and the nurse, Leah, were gone with Tansy. Instead, I turned around to see Ragnor standing there, in the middle of the grassy field, like he did in that dream of mine so long ago.

His gaze, as midnight blue as the sky, landed on mine. "We need to talk," he said quietly. It wasn't a question.

He raised his hand toward me. With shaky legs, I approached him, took his hand, and succumbed to my fate.

My mind was in disarray when Ragnor and I arrived at his suite. My chest felt hollow, as if Tansy's words and actions had sucked out every little emotion I'd ever felt.

Everything began to make sense. Why Tansy was the way she was. Why she knew about the Morrow Gods. Why she was oddly fixated on me.

Ragnor led me to the couch in his suite's living room and gently helped me sit. He then walked to the kitchenette and started the coffee machine running.

I stared at his back, feeling like how I viewed my life as a vampire, or even life in general after I fled my hometown at eighteen, had just burst into flames right in my face.

I was foolish to think I would be able to atone for my sins by being there for Cassidy in the past, despite later realizing she did not want my help.

When I befriended Isora, I thought I could help her too. I thought I could save her from her cruel fate as a second-timer and then a blood slave sold off to the Jinn.

But what I seemed to have forgotten was that no matter what I did, the souls of those I'd helped kill, the lives I'd taken myself, would never allow me to find peace—and rightfully so. Nothing I did, no amount of saving innocents like Cassidy, Isora, or Zoey, would change what I had done. Nothing would make up for the lives I'd ruined.

Because I was a monster.

A mug of coffee appeared in my hands as Ragnor took a seat next to me. I felt his eyes on me, burning my cheek, but I felt such a sense of shame, of self-hatred, that I couldn't bring myself to look at him.

When he spoke, I squeezed my eyes shut as I felt my heart plummeting. "What happened out there, Aileen?"

That was a far more loaded question than it seemed on the surface, and I imagined he knew it. As loaded as him asking me about being a Child of Kahil. But there was a substantial difference between yesterday and today.

Yesterday, I believed the truth had to be forgotten. Hidden.

Today, I knew Ragnor had to know what kind of monster I truly was.

Because the truth was so horrible that any interest Ragnor had in winning me back would go up in flames.

He wouldn't be able to have any sort of feelings for me after he learned about my sins.

I sucked in a breath, closed my eyes, and let out a shuddering sigh. "My father's name, as you know, is Amir Zoheir-Henderson."

He froze, and I kept my eyes on the brown swirls of coffee in my mug. "My father was a very smart man. Some even called him a genius. He was top of his class both in his bachelor's and master's studies at Harvard, and eventually he went on to do his PhD at the University of Maine."

I sipped my coffee, holding the cup with shaky hands. "There are many holes in my father's stories regarding the past. All I know is that his paternal family have been devout believers in the Faith of the Morrow and called themselves the Children of Kahil for generations. My father was raised as a devotee, and he never abandoned his religious studies."

Pain and disgust filled my insides. "The Children of Kahil, like their name, are all descendants of the Kahil family, which supposedly existed sometime in the year three thousand BC. The Kahil family believed in divine beings called the Morrow Gods."

Ragnor said nothing. He was as still as stone, so much so that it was almost like he wasn't breathing.

"To explain what my childhood was like, you need to understand the Morrow faith," I said, and the first verse of the Tefat, the book of the believers, rose to the forefront of my mind. "'In the morrow that follows the dawn of the world, the Gods shall emerge as its masters, heralding a divine epoch.' This verse is what this stupid religion is all about."

I put my coffee mug down, still half-full. I wasn't thirsty. "The Children believed that once upon a time, way before the world as we know it, there were three Gods who commanded the universe," I said, thinking back on the Tefat chapters my father had forced me to memorize, anxiously thumping my foot on the floor. "Those Gods were given power from Bennu the Maker, their ancestral spirit. Then, according to the Tefat, the world shifted and changed, causing the Gods' demise. But their supposed descendants, the Children of Kahil, have one divine mission: bring them back to life."

This was so convoluted and terrible, I didn't want to continue speaking, but I forced myself to go on. Ragnor needed to know just what kind of monster I was. He needed to know what he was getting into. Twisting my hands together, I continued. "The methods the Children used to resurrect the Morrow Gods, according to the writings in the Tefat, require pagan rites of shedding innocent blood. At some point in the past—I don't know exactly how or when, but the Children of Kahil were hunted down and killed for their fanaticism," I said, bile in my throat as I shifted in my seat, anxiety rising inside me. "I don't know who hunted the Children of Kahil followers, but eventually, only one person remained, and that person was my great-great-great-grandfather, Anan Zoheir."

I glanced at Ragnor. He seemed to be lost in thought when he spoke. "Do you know if anyone else survived?"

His question caught me off guard, and I nibbled my lip before replying, "Well, according to my father, everyone else was killed." I looked away, hands clenched to fists on my lap. "Somehow, Anan survived and managed to continue the legacy of the Morrow faith, obscuring the traces of his bloodshed from those who wished him ill. For generations, the Zoheirs, my father's family, succeeded in hiding their existence as Children of Kahil. My father had also made me promise that I would never let anyone know about our existence. Of what we believe and what we practice. He'd said the world wouldn't understand."

A bitter, hysterical laugh burst out of me. Ragnor's hand grabbed mine and squeezed, offering comfort I couldn't quite feel at the moment. "Unfortunately, I broke that promise unintentionally, thanks to Atalon and his powers, so I guess it doesn't mean shit anymore." My laughter died down, and I closed my eyes, feeling him shifting closer to me. "In any case, my father took it upon himself to continue the legacy as he saw fit." I paused, feeling sick to my stomach, before I said, "The thing is, it was the perfect opportunity to give an outlet to his specific . . . tendencies."

The basement flashed in front of my eyes. The bodies and the screams. The smell of smoke and fire and burnt flesh. For a moment, my throat clogged, and I found it hard to breathe, let alone speak.

Ragnor's arm came around my waist as he pulled me toward him. "Tendencies?" he asked in a quiet voice.

Letting out a shuddering breath, I found it in me to continue as I rested my head against Ragnor's chest. "My father kidnapped young girls, tortured and raped them, then killed them brutally and burned their bodies. Every month, he took me to the river near our house to make the ritual to offer the sacrificial blood to the Gods."

I could feel his eyes boring holes in my head, but I refused to look at him. Not when what I was about to tell him would forever change how he saw me. "My first memory is of a girl as young as I was crying her heart out as my father loomed over her and . . ." I couldn't put it into words. It was far, far too revolting and agonizing. I remembered the look in her eyes vividly as I sat there, watching my father rape that girl mercilessly. I remembered the blood trickling to the floor from her crotch as my father gave me a look of exhilaration while I trembled in helplessness and fear. Because I knew what would happen if I tried to reach out and help the girl. I knew what would happen if I attempted to go against my father. I'd tried it before, when I was still naive enough to think my father wouldn't raise his arm against me. I'd almost succeeded, too, until my father caught up to me and gave me a beating I could never forget.

Ragnor's hand gently took hold of my chin, attempting to raise my face to meet his gaze, but I couldn't handle it. Shaking him off, I jumped to my feet and walked away, my back to him, unable to face him. "That's how I spent my childhood until I was thirteen. I witnessed all kinds of horrors happening in the name of the blasted Morrow Gods." I couldn't hide the disgust in my voice, hugging myself as I paced back and forth. "And you know something? I never did anything to help those girls." My heart jumped to my throat, beating hysterically. "I watched them all being molested and killed one by one and did absolutely nothing. Sometimes I even . . ." Tears welled in my eyes. "I wished they would just *die* so the screams would stop."

"Aileen . . ." Ragnor's soft, almost coaxing voice made me flinch.

Shaking my head as the whipping sounds of my awful past echoed in my ears. "I hit them over and over again," I whispered, "as 'preparation' for when my father would come and abuse them himself. It terrified the shit out of me to do it, but deep down, I knew that if I disobeyed his orders, I might end up as my father's next victim."

I was shaking all over now, but I had to keep on pacing, to be on the move, to hug myself, if I wanted to get through it. "I never tried to rebel. Never spoke out against him. I listened to everything he said, learned everything he'd taught me, and loved him despite seeing what he was doing in the name of his faith. But just as much as I loved him, I also feared him. I knew he could turn on me the moment I disobeyed him, and yet I wanted to have faith that he would never do to me what he did to those girls. That he loved me too. And so when he got arrested and went to jail, I promised myself to never, ever practice that faith again."

The sound of Ragnor rushing toward me put me on edge. "Aileen, look at me."

Goose bumps crawled all over my skin as I shivered. "There was one victim," I whispered, "only one victim who managed to escape, even after my father brutally assaulted her. I don't remember what she looked like. My father never told me the names of his victims either." I lowered my gaze to the floor as I thought of Tansy standing at the edge of the cliff, looking at me with those large blue eyes. "I think Tansy is that girl."

Words abandoned me just then. I couldn't speak of this anymore. There was so much else he didn't know, but I couldn't bring myself to disclose any more than this, because I felt so dirty, so monstrous, that I wished someone would just kill me.

Now, Ragnor knew the gist of my own crimes. I wasn't a simple bystander. Forcefully or not, I participated in those atrocities my father committed. Some of those girls' blood, as well as their miseries, was on my hands.

Before I could read, my father taught me to kill.

And the worst thing was, when life got harder, I still turned to the Morrow Gods and pleaded for their help. Like I did in the Auction.

After everything, after me claiming to be an atheist, not part of the Morrow faith, here I was, still holding on to a sliver of belief in spite of myself. Because if they weren't real, it meant all that pain and suffering was for nothing. That those girls died for nothing. That everything I'd gone through was . . . I couldn't bring myself to accept that so many of us suffered such horrendous things at the hands of my father and that the Morrow Gods didn't even exist.

If Tansy was indeed the one who escaped, then that meant not only that I was partially responsible for her obvious trauma, but she would remain as a constant reminder of my sins for eternity.

Which was just what I deserved.

Ragnor's combat boots appeared in my line of sight as he came to a stop before me. Wordlessly, he wrapped his arms around me and pulled me to him, softly embracing me.

I didn't deserve such softness. I didn't deserve anything, really. And yet I was a selfish, horrid person because I let his warmth engulf me as the dam broke and the tears fell one after another.

CHAPTER 40

AILEEN

I don't know how long it took for my tears to dry, but by the time I came back from that dark place, I realized Ragnor had moved us back to the couch, and he was holding me on his lap, cradling me close to his chest.

Ragnor let out a breath. For a moment, I tensed, fearing he would say something about what I'd just shared, like "It's not your fault" or other empty, meaningless words like that. But Ragnor didn't speak about my past. He didn't rightfully call me a monstrous bitch.

Instead, he said, "Eleven hundred years ago, I was given the Imprint."

I stilled.

He leaned his chin against my hair. "At first, I didn't have a League to belong to. I was Leagueless, a nomad with no place to call home. During that time, I did many things I'm not proud of." He played with my hair absentmindedly. "I tortured and killed those who posed a threat. I slit the throats of husbands in front of their wives, then took perverse pleasure in seducing those wives."

My stomach tightened; my breathing stopped.

"There's no excuse for the things I did," he continued quietly. "All I can say is that I was driven by madness. A madness caused by losing the ones I loved. That's what happens when you lose everything, and you know the one at fault was none other than you." His arms tightened around me. "I couldn't look myself in the mirror for many years. I felt like I needed to become even more of a piece of shit, feeling like I needed to justify my second chance at life in some sort of way," he said, and I could hear the pain in his voice. "It's not just that I was responsible for my past actions, from before I became a vampire. It was that I lost far more than I had ever bargained for."

I couldn't help but wonder what he had given up to become a vampire and whether it was worth it.

Cupping my cheek, he gently guided my face up, his eyes holding mine. "Your love for your father, despite everything he did and made you do, is not a sin," he told me softly. "Everything you did was because of your father. None of it was your idea. You didn't wake up one day and decide to commit those atrocities just because you wanted to. Your father used your love and fear to get you to comply with his perverse commands. He counted on your love—maybe even your fear—to keep you in line. He taught you a perverse sense of love and loyalty. The things your father taught you, Aileen, no child should ever have had to learn, especially not at the hand of a parent." He gave me a look full of so much sympathy, I felt weak in the knees. "Look at it this way. After he went to jail, you didn't continue with those crimes, did you? You said so yourself, that you promised to never do that again. This is all that matters."

He leaned his forehead against mine. "No one is entirely good or completely evil. This philosophy is false at its roots. Yes, you did those things. You inflicted harm on others. But at the end of the day, you chose not to do it anymore, once you were out of your father's mental clutches. That just means that despite what you think, you did and still do have a conscience."

Those words were more than what I would've expected from a man who had been emotionally unavailable since I'd known him.

And he was still here. Not running. Giving me the comfort I desperately needed. "I tried to save Cassidy," I blurted out in a mumble. "Back in the alley. I wanted to save her, to atone for what I did."

Leaning back, he gave me a sad smile that made me want to cry again. "I know," he said softly. "But you don't need to atone for anything anymore, Aileen. You need to forgive yourself. You need to move on."

Tears fell down my face, and he captured them with his fingers. "Thank you," he said, "for trusting me enough to tell me your story."

Hesitantly, I rested my hands against his chest, feeling his warm heartbeat. "Who did you lose?" I asked in a whisper.

He pursed his lips and softly grabbed my wrists. "I lost my family," he said quietly, looking down at my palms before he brought them to his lips. "I lost a friend." He put my hands on his cheek. "I lost a woman I loved. The only one I loved." Pausing, he raised his eyes to mine, and his shone a bright neon blue. "Until you."

The damned tears returned with a vengeance. His words both hurt and comforted me. To know he used to love someone in the past and that he lost her was far too painful. But at the same time . . . "How?" I said weakly, searching his gaze and finding only sincerity. "How can you love me after everything I just told you?"

"Because you're Aileen Henderson," he said, smiling almost defeatedly. "A woman who came into my life when I least expected it and made me fall for her." He brushed my tears away with his thumbs as he cupped my face again. "You were like a beacon of light in the middle of an endless, stagnant darkness. I wanted you since I gave you the Imprint. I wanted to feel you since the first time I pinned you to the ground and told you to yield. I needed you since you confronted me about my feelings." He paused, pressing his forehead to mine. "I love you, Aileen, and it took losing you to realize it."

My heart broke.

"No matter what you say or do, I would still want you. You want me to kill for you? I'd do it. Give me the word, and I will slit Atalon's throat right now for daring to do what he did to you," he said softly but convincingly, his breath against my lips. "Do you love me, Aileen?"

How could he even ask that question? "Of course I do," I whispered, then whimpered when he put his arms around me, his lips brushing against mine. "I love you so much, I don't believe I deserve you, Ragnor."

"The one who doesn't really deserve you is me," he murmured, "not after I sold you in the Auction. But I don't care about who deserves who." He brushed my hair back. "I'm too selfish to care about such nonsense."

Before I could argue the point, his lips pressed against mine. He cajoled me into opening up for him, and, unable to resist when it came to him, I did.

Our tongues crashed in a battle of need, and suddenly, nothing else mattered.

He pushed me to my back, still kissing me, before he suddenly pulled back and stared at me with eyes glowing brighter than before. "Your lips are mine," he said suddenly, brushing his thumb against my lower lip. "Your pussy is mine." His other hand trailed down my body to cup my crotch over the jeans, making me gasp. "Your entire fucking body, from the top of your golden curls to the tips of your little toes, is mine." He caressed the sides of my body, raising my shirt in the process. "Your mind is mine." He took off my shirt and unclasped my bra, then kissed down my naked chest. "Your past is mine." He pushed down my jeans and panties and spread my legs. "Your present is mine." He grabbed my breasts, causing me to cry out. "Your future is mine." He unzipped his own jeans and freed his beautiful cock. "You're mine."

He pushed inside me so hard, pain mixed with pleasure as I screamed, putting my arms around him, under his shirt, and digging my nails into his scarred back.

He pulled his cock out and shoved it in again, making my back arch. Grabbing my breasts again, he locked my gaze with his. "And I'm yours, Aileen," he said quietly, his voice a growl, as he flicked my nipples, making me dig my nails deeper into his skin. "All yours."

His words made my chest tighten along with my loins, and I pulled my hands from his back and cupped his face, bringing it closer to mine. "I'm not going to let you go," I said, gasping as he drew back and oh so slowly pushed back in, my tiny inner muscles squeezing him so tight, he groaned. "You gave yourself to me," I gasped as he buried himself inside me to the hilt. "You're mine now."

In response, he gave me a wicked grin, and then, pinning my thighs as far back as possible, he began to truly fuck me.

An orgasm tore through me, making me hold on to his shoulders for dear life. He drove in and out of me so fast and rough, I felt like he was splitting me in half. It was so good. When he let go of my thighs and grabbed my nipple with his teeth while pinching my clit at the same time, I broke again so suddenly, all I could do was cry out, "Fuck!"

He didn't let me go, though. He kept fucking me until I saw stars and broke apart again, squeezing him so tightly, he had no choice but to push deep inside me and fill me up with his cum with a deep growl.

He gently fell on top of me and gave me a wet, dirty kiss that made me tingle all over. "As if I can ever let you go," he murmured over my skin as his mouth trailed down my jaw to my neck, licking the sweat off my skin.

When I felt his fangs graze me, I grabbed his hair and pulled his head back. He gave me a very scary scowl, eyes shining in need. "I want your blood," he said, almost like a petulant child.

I found myself smiling, something I didn't think was possible after the heavy conversation we'd just had. "It's my turn," I said and rolled over him—something that I could do only because he let me, I knew. "You never let me drink from you."

"I let you drink before," he said, looking at me through hooded eyes filled with lust. I realized I was straddling him now, and when I followed his gaze to my pussy, I saw the cum leaking out, coating his hardening cock.

Flicking my eyes to his throat, I said, "Once is not enough," before I lowered my lips to his neck, unleashed my fangs, and dug in with all my might.

His cock jerked against my inner thigh when I sucked in his ambrosia-like blood. Moaning at the feel of his cock and his delicious flavor, I rubbed my entrance against his erection.

Grabbing my waist, Ragnor impaled me from below, and I groaned in absolute ecstasy into his neck. With a bruising hold on my butt, he started drilling into me so hard, his balls slapped against my skin.

When he slapped my ass, I groaned again, my loins tightening. As I wriggled my ass against his palm, he slapped the cheek over and over again, driving me so crazy, I couldn't handle it anymore.

Retracting my fangs from his skin, I straightened and put my hands on his chest, and, keeping my gaze on his, I rode him fast and hard, needing him to be as out of control as I felt.

His hands went to my breasts as I did, slapping the skin and toying with my nipples. My heartbeat was in my ears as I watched him sit up and put his mouth over my nipple like a starving man, unleashing his fangs to dig them into the sensitive skin of the areola. I screamed at the feeling of him sucking my blood directly from there as the release made me shudder all over, rendering me immobile as the waves of pleasure took me under.

Ragnor seized control immediately. Wrapping me in his arms, he rose to his feet and took us to the bed, where he practically threw me on the mattress and flipped me so I was on my stomach. He then grabbed my waist and brought me to the edge of the bed, where he stood and penetrated me from behind.

All I could do was hold on to the sheets as he fisted his hand in my hair and fucked me from behind, slapping my ass with his free hand before he traced his fingers over the tight, untouched skin of my orifice.

I gasped at the unfamiliar, strange sensation. He felt my sudden stillness and lowered himself so his lips were at my ear. "Feels good?" he asked as he softly pushed a finger inside the hole.

Tensing up, I didn't know what to think when he suddenly fucked me harder and faster than before while gently teasing my orifice with one finger.

When I shattered all over him, squeezing him tight enough for him to growl and shove one last time to empty himself inside me, I realized I liked it. I liked it a lot.

Unable to breathe properly after all these orgasms, and with my pussy feeling like it was run over, I lay there half on the bed, with my legs touching the floor, unable to move, I was so spent.

Chuckling at the sight of me, Ragnor took his cock out and spread my butt cheeks. "So beautiful," he murmured, and I jolted when he parted my pussy lips. I felt his cum dripping from inside to the floor. He growled in satisfaction.

Then he took the rest of his clothes off, got on the bed, and brought me to his arms, cuddling me close. I huddled closer, burying my head in his chest. "You know," I murmured against his skin, "you're still on probation."

He stilled. "Come again?"

I couldn't help but grin as I raised my head to look at his face. He stared at me with a hard gaze. "One month," I reminded him.

A furrow appeared between his brows. His previous look of satisfaction was completely gone, replaced by incredulous annoyance.

And despite everything that happened earlier, despite the intensity of our coupling, I somehow found it in me to chuckle. "If you thought you were done groveling, then you're in for a surprise."

He growled, and I was on my back suddenly, my wrist held by his hand above my head. "Not done groveling, you say," he murmured, staring down at me with a predatory look that made my inner thighs squeeze. "We'll see about it."

"What are we going to do now?"

My question lingered in the air between Ragnor and me after two more rounds of sex. We were now cuddled together under the blankets, with him still inside me. Neither of us pulled away, as if fearing for this moment to break.

But reality was waiting just outside the door, and I couldn't go on avoiding it. Neither could he.

"I mean, I'm still a member of the Atalon League," I said quietly, caressing Ragnor's glorious chest. "So is Isora. And Zoey is Renaldi's. Yet the three of us are here."

Ragnor squeezed me tighter to him. "I'm not giving you back," he answered matter-of-factly, almost coldly, even. But beyond that cold, there was a fiery resolution that sent shivers down my spine. "And if you say so, I won't be sending Isora or Zoey back either."

While a big part of me wanted to hug him in pure relief, I was far more concerned about other things. "But what about Atalon and Renaldi?" I asked, laying my hands on top of where his heart was. "Atalon won't let us go. He will fight you. And I have a feeling Renaldi will fight you, too, if you won't return Zoey."'

"Renaldi owes me," Ragnor replied mysteriously. "Getting him to release Zoey won't be an issue. As for Atalon . . ." His voice trailed off, and when I raised my eyes to his face, I saw it was grim. "He's already declared war earlier today."

My eyes widened. "What does it mean?"

"It means he sent an official letter," Ragnor said with a sinister grin. "Don't worry, though. I've been itching to wipe him off the face of the earth for a long time now. This just gives me a legal reason to do so."

He seemed far too smug about the situation that I didn't dare argue. But there was another thing I was curious about. "Atalon had told me a story about why he hates you so," I said, frowning. "Something about you defrauding him into selling a Gifted?"

Ragnor narrowed his eyes as he squeezed my buttocks. "Of course that's how he would see it," he murmured before sighing. "As I told you earlier, at first I didn't have a League to belong to. But some decades later, I received an offer of temporary membership with Bowman's League."

I scooted closer, watching him as he spoke.

"Bowman was in a certain war against another League and asked for my help. It was at his League that I met Atalon for the first time." Ragnor's face contorted angrily. "Atalon was a Gifted vampire back then and as much of a narcissistic, arrogant prick as he is now," he said, voice dripping with disgust. "He didn't like my presence in the Bowman League; he felt threatened by me, I believe. Until my arrival, he was the League's star, but then I came, and suddenly the spotlight was taken from him. That was his first grievance against me."

Why wasn't I surprised?

"During Bowman's war, I found out that the woman Atalon was courting at the time developed feelings for me," Ragnor continued, pursing his lips. "I refused her advances, but Atalon found out anyway and hated me for taking what he considered to be his. You can already see a theme here." He gave me a pointed look.

I shuddered in repulsion.

Smiling briefly at my reaction, he continued. "But most of his true grudge against me is regarding an opera singer he had his eye on," he said. "By then, both of us had already become Lords. I was courting that singer, who also wished to become a vampire, but before I could give her the Imprint, Atalon tried to one-up me by giving her the Imprint first." Ragnor grimaced. "That woman and I kept on meeting in secret. She told me she was Gifted and was terrified to tell Atalon about it. He scared her, you see. In the end, I struck a deal with him: a Gifted for a Common." He gave me a surprisingly boyish, lopsided smile. "I offered him a Gifted in exchange for the supposedly Common opera singer. He accepted. Later, he found out she was Gifted after all, and since then he never forgot that slight."

I couldn't help but roll my eyes. "You know, he forgot to mention that first part about him giving her the Imprint under your nose first."

"Sounds fitting." Ragnor chuckled before his face became serious again. "Atalon would've come after me anyway," he said, caressing my cheek. "You're simply the perfect excuse for this war, especially since he knows the price if he wins—a Sacred."

I leaned into his touch. "I can't believe you're going to war for me," I murmured, closing my eyes. "Especially after everything I told you."

He gave me a soft kiss, and I opened my eyes when he pulled away, giving me a reassuring look that made me feel all warm and fuzzy. "How about this?" he said. "Let's agree we're both monsters. Isn't it the perfect match, then?"

I couldn't help but smile in response. "You're far more sappy than I thought."

He gave me a warning look. "Call me sappy again, and see where it gets you."

"Naked in bed with you?" I arched a brow and made a show of looking under the blanket. "Been there, done that."

He growled softly. "Careful, Aileen," he murmured, pushing his knee between my legs.

I couldn't help but grin as I wrapped my arms around his neck. That night, Ragnor managed to ruin my pussy beyond repair.

CHAPTER 41
AILEEN

There were more nurses in the infirmary when we arrived the following morning. Most of those nurses stood near the curtained bed that most likely inhabited Tansy, but others were tending to Isora and Zoey.

Both of whom were awake.

Before Ragnor could stop me, I rushed toward their beds, relief washing over me. "Thank fuck."

Isora turned to look at me, far healthier than before, with her eyes burning bright again. "Aileen!" she called happily.

I hugged her, sagging against her. "I missed you," I said, my chest expanding. It was the first time I'd admitted that to anyone, but Isora wasn't just someone. In the brief period of time that I'd known her, she became a precious friend.

She hugged me back, laughing weakly. "I missed you too."

Pulling back from her, I scanned her face, so glad to see that vitality had returned to her cheeks. "You're doing all right?" I asked quietly, searching her eyes.

Smiling, she nodded. "I am," she said softly before looking behind me. "And I guess I need to thank you both for it."

I felt Ragnor coming to a stop next to me. "Don't thank me," he now said to my friend. "Thank Aileen. She's the one who insisted on saving you."

Isora's smile remained as she bowed her head to Ragnor. "But it wouldn't have happened without your help, my Lord. So please accept my thanks."

Ragnor's face was impassive, as it usually was in public, but I could see his eyes softening. "Then you're very much welcome."

"The same goes for me."

My eyes went to Zoey, who was sitting in the bed next to Isora's. She, too, seemed far better than before; even her freckles were back. "I would like to thank you for helping me," she said, her eyes meeting mine before she glanced at Ragnor. "I would also like to talk to you, my Lord, about my current situation."

Isora nodded, her smile disappearing. "Same goes for me, my Lord."

Ragnor grabbed a chair and sat down, looking at them. "You have three options," he said, causing Isora and Zoey to sit straight, determination etched in their faces. "You can choose to go back to your respective Leagues, you can choose to be Leagueless, or you can join my League."

Isora's and Zoey's eyes widened at exactly the same time—it was almost comical. "We can join the Rayne League?" Isora asked, disbelief in her voice. "What about Lord Atalon and Renaldi, then?"

"This is where the catch is," Ragnor said with a dark look. "Atalon has declared war against the Rayne League. If you join my League, know that you'll make an adversary of your former Lords."

Isora and Zoey exchanged wide-eyed looks before Zoey returned her gaze to Ragnor and said, "Pardon me, my Lord, but I couldn't give a flying fuck if Renaldi sees me as an enemy." A dark, ruthless expression appeared on Zoey's face that made me do a double take. "I would like to join the Rayne League. I believe I will be an asset not just in the war to come but after that too."

Isora's eyes shone with the same sentiment as she nodded. "I'll do whatever I can to earn my place here," she said resolutely. "A war against Atalon? Right up my alley."

Ragnor stared at the two determined women for a few silent moments before he turned his gaze to me. "Your friends are bloodthirsty," he informed me.

I gave him a grin. "Aren't these the best kind of friends?"

Even though his face remained as still as a sphinx's, his eyes sparkled in mirth before he returned his attention to Isora and Zoey. "Then welcome—and welcome back—to the Rayne League, Isora Elios and Zoey Rittman."

As if they planned it before, the two bowed as much as they could, being seated in bed, and said, "Thank you, my Lord."

Ragnor rose to his feet then. "Let's go," he told me, motioning toward the curtained bed.

Standing up as well, I gave Isora and Zoey a smile and said, "I'll talk to you later," before I left their beds and headed to the end of the large infirmary.

The first nurse who saw us was the one from yesterday—Leah. She strode toward Ragnor, her eyes narrowed. "She can't accept any visits, my Lord," she said, giving me a pointed, filthy look. "Not after yesterday."

Ragnor's jaw ticked. "Did she have another episode?"

Leah pursed her lips. "Yes," she said, eyes angry. "A few hours ago. She woke up screaming she was on fire. We needed to bind her to bed so she wouldn't hurt herself."

Terrible guilt crawled into my stomach.

"Is she awake now?" Ragnor asked, face grim.

Shaking her head, she turned to look at me. "Whatever you want with her can wait until she's awake and in her right mind. Seeing you might trigger her."

I had to agree with Leah on this one. I didn't want to cause more distress to Tansy than I already did in my stupid past. "Ragnor," I said quietly, tugging at Ragnor's hand. Leah's eyes broadened in shock. "Let's go."

Ragnor glanced at me and nodded before turning back to Leah. "Write me daily reports about her from now on."

"Will do," Leah said; then, with a pointed look at me, she said, "My Lord."

Ignoring her, I walked out of the infirmary with Ragnor, feeling all kinds of emotions. Relief that Isora and Zoey were all right. Remorse and shame when it came to Tansy's situation. Yet also smugness at the fact Ragnor was mine.

It seemed like forever since the last time I saw these purple skies over the wilted field of grass.

Groggily, I pulled myself up to my feet and looked around until I saw a figure drawing closer. Her sandy-colored hair was bound in a braid, and she was wearing different clothes than she was before; instead of casual pants and a tee, she wore a black, skinny, full-body suit along with knee-high boots. In her hands she held what seemed like a pole but with a blade on one end.

Eliza came to a stop before me, her open right eye glaring at me, which made me confused. "I thought you told me you won't come here anymore."

"Your boyfriend left me no choice," she said in a dark, lower voice lacking its usual light cynicism. "When you wake up, tell him his time is up."

Her words made me glare right back at her. "What the hell are you talking about?"

"Natalia Aileen Zoheir-Henderson, Child of Kahil," she suddenly said, making me freeze. "As a level-two threat to the Realm of the Living, you demonstrated powers that allude to you becoming a large-scale catastrophe; consider this a warning."

She took a step closer, raising her pole and aiming its bladed end toward me. "Under any circumstances, never again attempt to resurrect the Morrow Gods," she said coldly, her gaze not leaving my face. "Nor ever again visit Esheer or seek the Jinn. Failure to comply with these restrictions will lead to your demise."

"Wait," I said, mind racing. "What the hell are you talking about?"

"We've been waiting for you, the last Child of Kahil."

Wode had said that before, back at the Jinni villa. He'd told me that back then, as if he thought I'd know what he meant. As if everything I'd ever learned about the Children of Kahil, the Morrow Gods, and the stories in the Tefat weren't just part of some bullshit religion but were the actual truth.

Suddenly, she lowered her weapon, and her gaze softened, becoming sadder. "Please, Aileen," she said quietly, as though she'd suddenly returned to herself. "Ragnor won't be able to save you if you make me kill you."

A strong breeze suddenly blew over us, and only when it stopped did I see Eliza was gone, leaving me alone in the wilted field.

EPILOGUE

~1,100 Years Ago, Circa 920 AD
Sogn, Norway

The bonfire crackled as Ragnor placed a fresh new log within the flames. Welcoming the heat, he sat down on the small wooden chair and huddled next to the fire, not daring to take even one furry layer of his clothes off.

The fjords were no place for lone humans to live, and, not for the first time, Ragnor found himself filled with anger. As much as he tried, pride was a hard sin to atone for, and his pride didn't let him acknowledge the fact that he was a human now, and a human he would stay.

After grabbing the skinned gull he'd managed to hunt in the nearby forest earlier this morning, he impaled it on a thin branch and put it over the fire, then watched as the meat cooked. He then took some of the snow covering the ground, dropped it in the wooden cup he'd found in the little hut he now called home, and placed it over the fire as well. So far, he hadn't dared to venture too deep into the forest, so he had no idea where he could find a river, or a lake, or any sort of water dispensary. For now he settled for snow.

If his former folk could see him right now . . .

Gritting his teeth, he chugged the water in a swift motion before pulling the impaled meat to his mouth and biting it, the act so barbaric, the meat almost stuck in Ragnor's throat from shame.

Even though he'd eaten the entire bird, he was still hungry. The hunger wouldn't go away anytime soon, he knew. He was still wounded from his latest brawl with the local jarl—the event that had gotten him banished to these cold, snowy mountains—and without proper meals, he knew he wouldn't be able to both satisfy his hunger and heal well.

Ragnor knew his anger was a problem—or, rather, had been a problem throughout his entire existence. It's what led him down the path of humanity and what brought him so many misfortunes, Ragnor didn't know what he was even living for anymore. He was too volatile to be able to control himself and far too proud to even try.

Using the wooden staff he'd carved for himself the day before, Ragnor rose to his feet and limped to the hut's entrance door. After pushing it open, he stomped inside and fell on the straw-made mattress, too weak to keep himself seated.

He should rest, he knew, considering his aching bones and still-bleeding wounds.

But his fury did not allow for rest.

Growling, he covered his eyes with his arm and hoped that, at the very least, sleep would come and save him from his useless, meaningless existence.

Unfortunately, sleep didn't come. But something else did.

A knock on the door made Ragnor jolt, and he sat up too quickly. Grunting in pain, he forced himself out of the bed and limped toward the door, then flung it open. He didn't know what he should've expected, but a balding man with a small figure was not it.

Ragnor blinked and stared at the man who stood at the door wearing casual short clothes that did not go along with the snowy, stormy scenery behind him. Despite his skin seemingly being paper thin, the small man did not appear to feel the cold.

As Ragnor blatantly sized him up, the man gave him a smile. "I'm not your enemy," he said in Greek rather than Norse. "May I enter?"

He might've understood the words, but it had been far too long since he last spoke the language. Thus he said in Latin instead, "And you expect me to trust the word of a stranger?"

The man didn't budge. All he did was say three words in a language he should not have known, and Ragnor fell back, face tight, and let the man in.

Once inside, the man turned to him and said, "My name is Arphiase. I am an Ekimmu."

Ragnor knew of the Ekimmu. Ancient texts referred to them as the spirits of the dead who were unable to find peace in the Beyond. They were also said to be incorporeal, and yet Arphiase seemed to be a living, breathing being.

But that was beside the point. "How do you know Volancian?"

Arphiase gave him a smile that sent chills down Ragnor's spine. "That's a story for another time," he said, and from the way the Ekimmu spoke, Ragnor knew he wouldn't get the answer he was seeking.

So he asked instead, "Then what the hell do you want?"

Arphiase walked toward the small window in the back of the hut and leaned against it, seeming to welcome the chill from the glass. "I have a request from you, Ragnor Meha-Malachi."

Sitting down on a wooden chair, Ragnor felt his rage igniting. "That's not my name," he grated out. "Now tell me, what does a dead spirit want with the likes of me?"

The Ekimmu's dark eyes gleamed, though Ragnor couldn't decipher the emotion behind them. "That's a common misconception," Arphiase said, and while his smile remained intact, his face seemed taut. "And here I thought you know what I am."

"I've only heard of your kind before," Ragnor bit out. "Never met one of you."

"Ah." Arphiase nodded. "That makes sense now. Then let me tell you this; us Ekimmu are far from 'dead spirits.' In fact, any detail you probably know about my kind is false but for one." As he opened his mouth, Arphiase's fangs suddenly grew longer and sharper. "We do crave blood."

He retracted the fangs, and his face turned serious. "I don't know you, Ragnor," he said, "but I do know of you. I heard the stories. I followed the whispers. And from all the information I collected, I know one thing for sure." He paused, then said, almost pityingly, "Living as a mere mortal is a waste of your abilities."

Ragnor felt his blood boil. His quick-to-ignite anger was close to getting the better of him. "If you really know of me, then you must know I no longer have any of those abilities," he snapped, voice full of fury that was mostly directed at himself.

Because it was his own fault that this was his reality now. His, and no one else's.

"You're wrong," Arphiase said, shaking his head as he started walking toward Ragnor. "You lost your access to those abilities when you became a mere human. But you can regain them—if you listen to my request."

In spite of himself, Ragnor's interest piqued. He wasn't proud enough to turn away such an opportunity, even if he wasn't sure whether this man before him was friend or foe. "I'm listening."

And so Arphiase talked.

First, he told Ragnor of the true nature of the Ekimmu. He told him that the Ekimmu were a human subrace borne of a form of energy called Lifeblood. He told him the Ekimmu, while infertile, could change humans into Ekimmu, increasing their ranks, by giving them what the Ekimmu referred to as the Imprint—a certain essence only Ekimmu of great power could secrete from their inflated Lifeblood levels.

"I want you, Ragnor, to become an Ekimmu."

Ragnor stared at the man unblinkingly. "Why?"

Arphiase grimaced. "There are not many of us who are left around," he said quietly. "There have been certain . . . incidents that caused our ranks to dwindle throughout the ages. We have only a few dozen of us left in the entire world, and of them, only four, including me, are powerful enough to give the Imprint."

He was curious about those "incidents," but Ragnor didn't push. Instead, he said, "I'm not a normal human, though. How do you know if this Imprint would affect me?"

"There's only one way for us to know for sure," Arphiase replied, eyes locking with Ragnor's in an unshakable hold. "You see, in very rare cases, the Imprint can fail—and the human who was given the Imprint and didn't manage to adjust to the Imprint dies in those cases."

Ragnor tensed. "So you're saying that I can die."

"It's extremely rare, but yes, it's a possibility," he said matter-of-factly. "Especially as you said so yourself—you're not a normal human. I've never tried giving the Imprint to someone like you before, and I don't know of such cases in the past. This will be a first. An experiment, if you will."

"And what makes you think I would agree?" Ragnor asked, gritting his teeth and clenching his hands into fists. The Ekimmu was asking him to risk his life. Sure, his life wasn't much, but still . . .

As though he'd read his thoughts, Arphiase smiled, and that cunning gleam returned to his eyes. "If the Imprinting succeeds, I can guarantee you'll be able to access your abilities again in a few years. You will also become immortal, able to live until the end of time," he said quietly. "The alternative would be that you'll die as a mere human in this hut in the depths of some faraway fjord. And with how frequently you get yourself into brawls, you'll eventually die earlier than old age. So yes, you might risk death by being given the Imprint, but you also have a chance of a new life."

He paused, giving Ragnor a far-too-knowing look. "You might even be able to get back at those who wronged you. Those who took everything away from you."

Ragnor couldn't refute that even if he wanted to—and he didn't. Arphiase's request was more than tempting. It was as though everything Ragnor had dreamed of was being offered to him on a silver platter.

He could say no and remain in his current state.

Or he could say yes and risk dying a little earlier, but he would get a chance at the revenge he dreamed of.

The pros outweighed the cons. It was a once-in-a-lifetime offer. The most golden of opportunities.

Saying no wasn't even an option.

"I'll do it," he said resolutely.

Arphiase grinned. "I knew you'd come around," he said, satisfied. "Now, the second part of my request is this: if all goes according to plan and you are given the Imprint and rise anew as an Ekimmu, then I only wish for one thing in return."

In the many years to come, Ragnor would forget about this wish. He would roam the world as a Leagueless Ekimmu—or, using the modern term, *vampire*—and participate in both atrocities and good deeds, forgetting about the vampire Lord who'd given him this second chance at truly living.

Until Arphiase visited him one day, three hundred years later, and asked for his wish to come true.

So Ragnor used his immense power and magic to carve out Arphiase's heart and watch as his own Lord, his savior, finally found peace after thousands of years of misery.

And not for the first time, Ragnor wondered whether he would've been happy to end his own life as well. Whether he could really go on living without his Alara Morreh, the one who was always meant to be his, by his side.

That question had always remained in the back of his mind—until Ragnor pressed his lips against a woman hiding behind trash cans and, against his better judgment, gave her the Imprint.

A woman he now claimed as his.

His Alara Morreh.

AUTHOR'S NOTE

Many people are afraid of criticism, but I find it necessary. And without my readers' criticism, I doubt I'd be where I am today.

So for my readers, whether you liked or hated my books, adored or loathed my writing, understood or didn't understand my characters—I appreciate you all the same, and I can't wait for your thoughts on this book. Only with your help can I grow as a writer.

Thank you for picking up this book, and I'll see you in the next one!

ACKNOWLEDGMENTS

First and foremost, this book wouldn't exist without the amazing help of Georgia McBride and Jakob Straub, who helped me squeeze this book out during a long and excruciating labor. I will forever be in debt to your amazing minds. Thank you.

Second, I would like to thank Melissa Frain, whose editorial work on this book exceeded my expectations. The result is more than I could've asked for.

Third, many thanks to Montlake, who believed in me and this series and whose work has been impeccable.

Finally, I would like to thank everyone in my life who helped propel me to write this sequel and to write in general. Without you, I don't know where I would be. Mom—thank you for your continued guidance. Dad, or Yoni—I will never take lightly the faith you've put in me (and the same goes for little Bar and Sol). Gil—I already dedicated the first book to you, so I think you know how much I appreciate you. Nes, Matan, Ruth—what would I do without you?

Thank you, everyone, and I hope to have the opportunity to thank you some more in my future books!

INTRO TO BOOK 3: *Dance of the Phoenix*

In the Realm of Fire, the voice of Bennu resounded, saying, "For what purpose have you ventured unto Esheer, if not to unbind me from these chains?"

Three spectral men, concealed beneath cloaks of shimmering gold that veiled their countenances, responded, "We seek but your divine benediction, O Lord of Timeless Flames."

Bennu, peering through eyes enshrouded in billowing smoke, regarded them and declared, "You stand not as worthy recipients of my blessing. However, your progeny may yet be deemed fit. Depart henceforth, and bestow your Godly essence upon the Realm of the Living."

Then the men inquired, "And what recompense shall be ours?"

Bennu, unfurling his wings ablaze with fiery radiance, proclaimed, "That which dwells deepest within your yearning hearts: infernal dominion over the dwellers of the sky."

—Verses 18–23 in "O Promise Bound in Fire" from the Tefat

ABOUT THE AUTHOR

Photo © 2023 Monika Fitz

Sapir A. Englard is the author of the massive digital hit The Millennium Wolves. Published in 2019 on the Galatea app, the twelve-book series has amassed more than 125 million reads. The series is also available in French from Hugo Publishing. Englard's success has been documented in the *Boston Globe* and *Forbes*, as well as on TechCrunch and other websites. A graduate of Berklee College of Music, Sapir is a full-time writer and musician.